The Lockwoods

of

Clonakilty

The Lockwoods

of

Clonakilty

a novel

by

Mark Bois

www.PenmorePress.com

AUTHOR'S NOTE

This is a work of fiction. While the 1/27th Foot, the Inniskilling Regiment, is very real, the persons created in this novel are creations of the author.

This novel, unlike the first in the series, *Lieutenant and Mrs. Lockwood*, deals a bit less with the regiment, but the author should point out that he has once again inserted a very disreputable character into the ranks of the Inniskilling Regiment. That character is solely a product of the author's desire to tell a good story.

That being said, the settings and situations into which the characters are placed are as close to historical as the record allows. Modern Clonakilty is a charming place to visit, and a bustling town well removed from the sleepy Clonakilty of this story. On quiet mornings, though, one gets a sense of the quiet little town of two hundred years ago. So, too, we might believe that the kindness and liveliness of the modern residents reflects the spirit of the people who lived there in previous generations.

For those fortunate enough to visit Enniskillen, Northern Ireland, a trip to the regimental museum is a real pleasure. The records and exhibits make it a good place to learn about Irish soldiers in service to Great Britain. To learn about their families is more difficult; little honour, then as now, is paid to those who suffer at home. Perhaps this book will be some small compensation to those who wait, and care for the wounded who return to them.

Mark Bois

May 2015

Reviews

"Straddling the English and Irish worlds separated by class and culture, Lieutenant Lockwood lived a mixed bag of blessings and curses. A loving, loyal wife, an honorable but near fatal wound from Waterloo, money problems, family problems, a drug addiction and --oh, yes-- a syphilitic madman out for his blood."

Woody Carsky-Wilson, Major (retired), US Army

"A sweeping historical drama that follows the return of a seriously wounded Waterloo veteran to his family in an Ireland seething with rebellion. As the family struggles to heal his failing body they are threatened by a mysterious madman from his past who could destroy their way of life."

—Robert Burnham, Editor, *The Napoleon Series Website*

"Bois has accomplished a rare feat, in having written a sequel better than the first book. He demonstrates his attention to detail and meticulous research that we, the readers, have come to take for granted. He is a true storyteller, making you feel as if you are part of the story. You will devour this book faster than his first, and have you begging for a third. Bois proves he is here to stay."

Brad Luebbert, Colonel, US Army

Dedication

Arís, do mo bhean, mo chuisle, mo mhíle stòr.

Acknowledgements

I owe a great deal to great number of people: Michael James at Penmore Press, for his faith in me; the capable staffs of the Inniskilling Regimental Museum and the British National Archives, for their kind assistance and quite excellent tea; my friends with the Cincinnati Writers' Project, for their kindness, and for their pointed advice regarding the use of semi-colons; Brad Luebbert, Woody Carsky-Wilson, and Bob Burnham, my test readers and generous friends; Mark and Julie Wurster, my life-long friends and inspiration for much of what I know of friendship; my children, who taught me what love is. But in the end, I owe all of what I do, what I am, to Charmin Bois.

Chapter One

Lieutenant James Lockwood's wound was mortal. That, at least, was the opinion of the Assistant Surgeon who extracted the musket ball from the lieutenant's chest at Waterloo. It was the opinion, too, of the Belgian surgeon who briefly tended the lieutenant two days later, in a cow shed where Lockwood lay in agony with twenty other wounded and dying Allied officers. It was certainly the opinion of the surgeons at the Divisional Hospital in Brussels, and then of the Army Surgeons at Kilmainham Hospital in Dublin.

It was not, however, Lieutenant Lockwood's opinion. He had promised his wife that he would come home to her, and he had done so.

The baker, whose shop stood at the foot of Mill Street in Clonakilty, was not an especially kind man; that afternoon his mood was spoiled by the rising price of firewood. But he was fond of his daughter, so when she called to him from the front door of his shop he dusted the flour from his hands and joined her.

"Oh, Papa! Come and see the great chaise of the world! Four of God's own chestnuts, and the glorious carriage! Two post men, and a redcoat with his gun sitting on top! Oh, Papa, may I wave to the passengers, and them so high and proud?"

"Well, now, daughter, let a man see. Ah, well, now, of course you might wave, and I will join you, so. Do you not recognize dear Mrs. Lockwood from up the Scartagh Lane?"

"Oh, it is she! How beautiful she looks! Hello! Mrs. Lockwood, hello!"

A chaise and four was a rare sight in Clonakilty, and as it rattled up the street several other townspeople came out to see. Some waved; some chose not to.

"Papa," asked the baker's girl, "who was that big man sitting beside the beautiful Mrs. Lockwood? Him, with the whiskers and the paleness?"

"That, *a cuisle*, was Lieutenant Lockwood himself, home from the wars. Mrs. Lockwood has been gone this month and more, nursing him in the great soldiers' hospital in Dublin. And here they are, both home, joy. The Lieutenant is the father of your friend Joseph, and his brother and his sisters. It was he who was wounded at the great battle where the Saxon King's men threw down the army led by Bonaparte, the King of the World."

They were speaking in Irish, but Ireland was changing, and the girl typically spoke much more English than Irish. She thus needed to ask, "What does 'lieutenant' mean, please, Papa? Is Joseph's papa a nice man? And is it good to be 'wounded'?" She had hope in her voice. She liked happy endings, and her friend Joseph Lockwood had promised to kiss her some day.

The baker looked up at the sky and muttered, "Rain again." He then patted his daughter on the cheek with his floury hand and said, "A lieutenant is an officer, a great man in an army, *a grah*. And you'll know that while Joseph's mama is a fine Irish Catholic woman, an O'Brian, his papa is a Saxon, and while not a bad man to my knowing, a Saxon he remains."

Years before, the baker had served in the British army. Thus wise in such matters, he did not address his daughter's last question, but only muttered to himself as he returned to his work, "And wounding? The war might hurt a man inside as well as out, and not all are granted the healing."

As the chaise turned up Scartagh Lane, James Lockwood could see the roof of Fáibhile Cottage come into view. He coughed weakly, and asked with concern in his voice, "Shall they recognize me, do you think? It has been three years, after all."

Brigid Lockwood stroked his hair back into place and softly answered, "They would know you in an instant, in a crowd of a thousand."

He was in pain. The journey, two solid days in a poorly sprung carriage over potted roads, had in fact been exceptionally painful for him, but he was determined to greet his children upright and smiling. He could only maintain a sitting position a few minutes at a time, jolts of pain tormenting him, but at the thought of his children a smile came to his face of its own accord.

The chaise's course through Clonakilty brought no smile to the face of Private Diarmuid Doolan, the Lieutenant's soldier servant, who sat atop the box glaring down at the townspeople. Doolan had been a soldier for such a protracted period that he had come to view all civilians, no matter their nationality, with profound mistrust. Still, over the years Doolan had known and had come to love, in his own fashion, the Lockwood family. A soft, almost wistful, look crossed his face, a look that would have surprised any man in Six Company, First Battalion, 27th Regiment of Foot. When the chaise drew up in front of Fáibhile

Cottage, in many ways Diarmuid Doolan had come home as well.

Fáibhile means 'beech tree' in Irish, as the cottage stood in an ancient grove of lovely trees that had yet to fall to commercial axes. Fáibhile Cottage itself was rather a small house, especially as it was occupied by a family of seven, their housekeeper, and their very large black dog. The cottage sat on McCurtain's Hill, overlooking Clonakilty, Inchydoney Island, and the glittering sea beyond. Built of stone, it was not much different from the handful of prosperous farmers' houses that lay near Clonakilty, except that its slate roof marked it as the home of a gentleman.

For the past three years, the little cottage surrounded by its massive beech trees had been the stuff of dreams to James. But even his fondest dreams fell short of the swell of joy he felt when he saw his children, cheering, crying, waving, swarming through the garden and running to welcome him home. The youngest, three year-old Lucy, who had never met her father, contributed to the general tumult by loudly weeping into the shoulder of the family housekeeper, Mrs. Cashman. Mrs. Cashman hung back, though she too blinked back tears, speaking to Lucy in Irish, saying, "Will you not look, *a grah*, and see the fine black chaise, and the four shining horses? Look, now, it is your own Mama there in the chaise, and she has brought your Papa home!" While Lucy loved her Nana Kay, she brightened amazingly at the sight of her mother stepping from the chaise into the arms of her family.

The driver and his assistant busied themselves with unloading Mrs. Lockwood's trunk; hers was the only baggage, as the Lieutenant's trunk was still with his battalion, a world away, in France, perhaps even in Paris itself. With a foul look on his face, the driver's assistant looked up and down the narrow lane and, seeing it lined with beeches, hedges, and stone fences as far as the eye could see, growled, "Christ, Patrick, we'll have to go clear to Bandon before we can find a place to turn around." Then glancing over at the hugging, laughing, weeping Lockwood family, he muttered, "I wish they'd quit with their damned blubbering, so that we might get paid and be on our bloody way."

The driver looked over at the Lockwoods, smiled softly, and said, "Fuck you, Bob Touhy."

While her father's place in Irish society allowed Cissy Lockwood some freedoms, her gender, age, and religion often required her to keep her opinions to herself. Her older sister, Mary, was a renowned beauty, but Mary had few other interests beyond the men and boys who worshipped her. Thus Cissy had largely run the house while their mother had been away in Dublin; just that morning she had dealt in no uncertain terms with the saucy tradesman who repaired the leaking kitchen roof.

Cissy and her siblings had wept and laughed and gone quite awry at the sight of their parents' return, but it was Cissy who first recognized what needed to be done. Her parents were both exhausted, and her father was obviously in great pain.

To her brothers, she said, "Joseph, *a grah*, you will be running down to the Shannon Arms and tell Mr. Reidy that I shall need his people now, please. Richard, up to Mr. O'Leary's, now, and we shall need himself and his sons, and I will hear nothing about cows that need tending. That man and his cows...."

She then shooed Mary back into the house with, "Dear, might you bring out the sandwiches you made with such care? And the tea?" When Mary hesitated, looking a bit cross with her younger sister, Cissy added, "It might give you a chance to dry your eyes, and perhaps get your hair back in place." At that, real concern flashed onto Mary's face, and she quickly headed back into the house.

Cissy then smiled and nodded to Mrs. Cashman, who strode up to the chaise, gave Mrs. Lockwood a kiss, and slid the now smiling Lucy into her mother's welcoming arms. Mrs. Cashman then made her curtsy to the Lieutenant, and said, "I welcome you home, sir."

"Thank you, Mrs. Cashman. By God, it is good to see you."

"And you, sir."

James's eyes locked onto Lucy, but the little girl would not return his tenuous smile.

"Lucy," Brigid said softly, "this is your Papa." Lucy, however, flinched at the enormity of that statement, and began to wail into her mother's shoulder.

Seeing her father's obvious confusion, Cissy hurriedly said, "If I might suggest, Papa, that you and Mama stay in the chaise a few minutes more, as the rain is coming as sure as," she nearly said "death," but the angels whispered in her ear, and she smoothly said, "Christmas. I shall have six strong men here in a trice, to help us get things settled. And who is this, now?"

Diarmuid Doolan slowly climbed down from atop the box. At Kilmainham Doolan had heard rumours of the troubles that were flaring up again; those rumours, combined with his naturally suspicious nature, had prompted him to ride atop the box with his musket loaded for every foot of the two hundred miles from Dublin. He had been convinced that Whiteboys, Peep o' Day Boys, or unaffiliated hooligans would assault the chaise at every turn. He thus did not look or feel his best, though even his best would not typically allow him to enter a decent home by the front door.

It had been long years since Doolan had last seen Cissy Lockwood. He thus only put a knuckle to his forehead and hoarsely said, "Private Doolan, ma'am."

Cissy smiled at him, the smile of girl grown a woman, and said, "Don't you dare 'ma'am' me, Diarmuid Doolan."

Doolan smiled timidly and offered his hand, but Cissy walked up to him, kissed his cheek and said, "Welcome home, old friend."

Doolan blushed like a maiden, and muttered in Irish, "What a great lady you have become, sure, Cissy Lockwood."

"No lady me, you fine talker. Now, before we get you a bite and a bed, might you be going back to the old stable and bringing out that great door that lies there, so that the Lieutenant might be carried up to his bed?"

Cissy turned to the post boys and, still in Irish, said, "Postilion, at the crest of the hill you shall find the entrance to *gortcolmán*, the dove's own field, where you might unhitch your team and get them turned. I shall have six good men here in a handful of time, and it is they who will help you turn the carriage itself. Until then, I have beer and a bite for you, if you will step around to the kitchen door."

No one was surprised that it was Cissy who organized things. Politely but efficiently directed by that capable young lady, the two post boys, braced by beer and stew, joined the O'Leary men and the men from the Shannon Arms, and James Lockwood was carried upstairs strapped to the door with only moderate damage to the walls.

The stress of the journey, the emotion of his return, and a large dose of the alcoholic tincture of laudanum ensured that James was asleep the instant he reached his bed. He slept for nearly fourteen hours. When he woke he was surreptitiously treated to Mrs. Cashman's specialty, a cup of whiskey-laced coffee (James thought that it would better be termed coffee-laced whiskey). "A sure cure, Lieutenant *a grah*, but as Mrs.

Lockwood is asleep in Mary's bed after sitting at your bedside all night, she need not be told about it, at all, at all."

"It is so quiet," whispered James.

"The Missus has sent the children to stay with their Aunt Anne for a day or two, so that you might be settled like a Christian. They are dears, but they make noise that would put a *bean sídhe* to shame." James looked puzzled, so Mrs. Cashman added, "A *bean sídhe,* sir, a 'banshee' in the English, a womanly spirit who will wail and keen in the darkness when a human is soon to die." As she carried her tray out, she muttered, "And if one shows herself around here, won't I kick her arse for her, won't I just."

James could not contain his astonishment at being in his own bed; he had dreamt of it for so long that even the smallest details were enchanting. Mrs. Cashman had scrubbed the room past even her exacting standards, though there was not much that she could do with Sergeant, the old family dog, who napped by the door. The worn, dirty patch on the rug betrayed the frequency with which Sergeant had slept there while his master had spent three years abroad. Sergeant, who shared his master's capacity for vivid dreams, twitched his paws and whined in some unknowable canine fantasy. It was just as well that the dog slept indoors now, as he was grey around the muzzle, his life clock spinning fast, unfairly fast; James watched him sleep, the dog a mirror.

While James had surprised the doctors with his slow but continuous recovery, they had warned the Lockwoods in no uncertain terms that the balance of James's life was likely to be short, possibly very short indeed. But James had defied them thus far, and was determined to continue to do so.

James winced as he lifted a spoonful of soup to his mouth.

Brigid, who sat anxiously at his side, said, "Oh, my dear, will you not let me help?"

James frowned at the soup as if it were a recalcitrant recruit, and said, "Thank you, no, love. I shall master this, or it shall master me." He was a powerfully built man, accustomed to having his body do what he willed. To be unable to complete even basic tasks was exceedingly frustrating; and, as he was also a proud man, such disability was growing increasingly embarrassing. A jolt of pain nearly made him drop the spoon but he forged on, his face growing red, then pale. Twenty minutes later the bowl was empty, and James lay panting but victorious.

Brigid rearranged the quilts and said, "I was thinking of allowing the children home tomorrow; they are so longing to see you again. But do you think you are strong enough to have them about?"

James buried his face into the cool side of his pillow, an unspeakable luxury, and said sleepily, "Of course they must come home. They, and you, my love, are the only reason I reached home. My God, but this is wonderful."

The next day came, and the children clumped upstairs to stand shyly at their father's bedside. They had been scolded into silence. The raucous excitement of their father's return was tempered. They stood warned of the severity of his wound, and for his need for rest and quiet, and were thus subdued, silent, and respectful.

The seven Lockwoods were packed into the bedroom at the top of the stairs, Mrs. Cashman and Diarmuid Doolan standing at the door, all suddenly and painfully conscious of the gaps between them, of the lives lived in a quiet Irish town, and the lives of men who had seen years of war across Europe and America. The shyness and awkwardness, anticipated by James but painful nonetheless, was broken by Sergeant, who shouldered his way through that forest of legs, lunged up, and with his front paws on his master's bed he barked with fierce joy.

In the ensuing days James made it a point to ask each of the children to come sit with him for a few minutes every day to slowly become reacquainted. Mary and Cissy, who had been much older than the boys when their father had gone to war, quickly fell back into their old roles, comfortable and cherished. Months before, on a winter afternoon when she tearfully realized that she could no longer remember the details of her father's face, Cissy had begun a watercolor of a soldier of the Inniskilling Regiment. She was at last able to present the painting to her father, to universal praise.

The boys, Joseph and Richard, took longer to grow comfortable in speaking with their father, only really coming to life when he expressed his interest in the fort that they had built in the woods, with promises to inspect the works at the first opportunity. Stories of Portuguese, Spanish, and French castles followed, the boys listening entranced. As a *father*, he told them of the great medieval castles he had seen, with details of their towers, keeps and dungeons. As *Lieutenant* Lockwood, however, he remained silent. He would share no details of sieges, of Badajoz in the hellish darkness, of trenches, revetments, and the nightmare quality of violent death in narrow rock-strewn breaches, or of Waterloo and the shattered bodies of thousands.

Brigid had long worried over how the delicate Lucy would react to the appearance of her father, the father whom she had never met. She was quite correct in her apprehensions, as the little girl would tearfully, frantically, cling to her mother's skirts at the sight of the very large man with the whiskers and the deep voice. Only after two weeks did an afternoon come, a shy, peeking afternoon, when Lucy Lockwood went exploring on her own and discovered, amazed, that her Papa kept a small bag of sweets under his pillow, sweets that he would slyly share with her, silent and secretive, the only sounds being confidential whispers and the occasional thump of Sergeant's tail on the floor. Lucy would have been distressed if she had seen her Mama, who stood stock-still at the top of the stairs with her hands to her face, blinking back tears as she intently listened to her husband and her little girl ruin their dinner.

James soon grew strong enough to attempt the stairs unaided, though not unnoticed; the satisfaction of this feat, down and up by God, being somewhat dampened by seven voices that had begged him not to be so reckless, certainly he must have help. The stairs conquered, though with rather more pain than he had bargained for, but conquered nonetheless, he was tucked back into bed with only moderate clucking, and left alone with his newspaper. He was feeling so strong, so much like his old self, that he decided to take advantage and read three full pages of the paper before he swallowed his physic and settled in for his nap. So long as he kept his elbows close to his sides he could hold the paper upright with only moderate discomfort.

He had read the whole of the first page and was just beginning the second when he jumped as if he had been slapped. He forced himself to read the whole column again, slowly, rationally.

Cork Mercury, *20 March, 1816*
At the assizes of Sligo, Thomas and John Fenton, Esqrs. were tried before Justice Fletcher, for the murder of John Hillis, Esq. who was shot in a duel by the former; they were acquitted.

The Lockwoods of Clonakilty

At the assizes of Tralee, which ended on Saturday, Rowan Cashell, Esq, was tried for the murder of Henry Arthur O'Conner, Esq. and acquitted.

James was not acquainted with either the Brothers Fenton or Mr. Cashell, nor was he surprised by their acquittals, as dueling in Ireland was so common as to merit only the most casual review by the magistrates, and by the papers. James was, however, fixed upon the next article on the page, as he was all too well acquainted with its subject.

Captain Charles Barr of the 1st Battalion, 27th Regiment, has been found guilty of taking away a bay mare belonging to a British regiment, after the battle of Waterloo, and afterwards effacing the regimental mark on her side, and offering the mare for sale in Paris. And also of a second charge, which bore that he had given no satisfactory account of his opening the baggage of several officers of said regiment. Of a third charge, of appropriating their contents to his own use, he was found not guilty. In consequence of the first and second charge being satisfactorily proved, the Court sentenced him to be dismissed his Majesty's service. The Prince regent has confirmed the sentence of the Court; but in consideration of several circumstances, has mitigated the punishment to Captain Barr's retiring on half-pay.

James lay awake, considering, his dose lying ignored. "Christ," he thought, stunned, "I would have given a year of my life to have been there, to have seen that." With pagan superstition he quickly retracted the thought. If he had been raised a Catholic he would have crossed himself, but lacking that particular implement of faith he could only tell himself, "I didn't say it out loud, so it doesn't count."

He was still thinking of the implications of Barr's fall when Brigid came up to check on him, and he offered her the paper with a significant look. He took a quiet joy in studying her face; as expected, the tip of her tongue still found its way to the corner of her mouth, slowly being replaced by a growing look of complete delight. He was reminded yet again of how he loved her.

"Oh, they have gotten him at last!" said Brigid. "They didn't need your charges at all! Oh, what a pity that he was found wholly guilty of just two of the charges... he was certainly guilty of all three, the *coirpeach*... though having been charged with such offenses must surely paint him as a complete scoundrel, does it not? But will he be destroyed by this? He must be scorned by every officer in the army, by all society, for what he is, for how he has threatened us, his black soul to the devil."

"Still," said James, "it may be that his friends or his family had enough influence to have the sentence reduced to half-pay." He had to halt a moment to catch his breath, then went on, "But it is more likely that being a wounded Waterloo man is the only mitigating factor. Perhaps the reviewed sentence will be better for us." He was learning that after speaking even a short sentence, he would need several breaths before speaking another. "If he was completely destitute he might be driven to some act of desperation, and drag us down with him."

Now Brigid noticed how he struggled to speak more than a few words at a time. James took a halting breath and went on, "As it is, he can live on his half pay, all two shillings four pence a day, may he choke on it."

Brigid watched him lying weak and pale, and in a brief, selfish moment she asked herself in Irish, "When might I come to lie with him?" But she quickly scolded herself and only said,

"If his family worked to have his sentence reduced, might they help him now that he is out of the service?"

James coughed a bit, then said tiredly, "The word in the mess was that his father and older brother were decent enough, and had turned their backs on him long ago." A pause. "Not rich men, not by any means, but respectable. I doubt they will ever want anything more to do with Charles Barr. May God grant that he just disappears."

Brigid tore the article from the paper and went to press it between the pages of her bible. Her husband, though, had time to mull over the options open to a dishonoured, impoverished Charles Barr. The Lockwoods had long before sealed a pact with Barr: they would not reveal to anyone the fact that Barr had contracted syphilis while in the company of common Dublin whores, and Barr would not betray certain details of the Lockwoods' marriage. James was soon haunted by thoughts of what Charles Barr might choose to do with his days, loose upon the world.

Chapter Two

James measured his return to health by tracking the distances he could walk before he had to sit and gasp for air. A month after his mastery of the steps, he made a trip to the kitchen; two months later, that feat was surpassed by visits to the garden. Two months more saw Lieutenant Lockwood standing out on Scartagh lane, that triumph eventually followed by the monumental victory of walking to town and back. In those two years he pleased his family, and surprised his doctors, by recovering most of his strength, and much of his breath.

He did, however, still sleep a great deal, and continued with mild doses of laudanum to ease the pain that never completely faded. Brigid waited for an afternoon on which the children were out of the house, and James was both well rested and clear-headed, to join him in the drawing room with an anguished look on her face.

James did not look up, as he was engrossed with a newly arrived letter. "Here, my dear, is some good news," he said in a delighted voice. "I believe that I have mentioned Captain Dumon of the French army?" When Brigid sat beside him on the settee and did not respond he went on, "He is the fellow that hosted me at the Palais in Ghent when we stood guard for old fat Louis. Just imagine, that fool is king of France again. At any rate, as Dumon had the good sense to declare himself a Royalist, he has done well since we hustled Bonaparte off to St. Helena. He has retired as colonel, and is coming to Ireland with his son to attend to business and do the grand tour. And he wishes to come visit us! What fun that shall be—but come, my dear, what is amiss?" He had finally looked up to see her face, ashen, as she sat bolt upright with a letter of her own, but this one crushed in her hands.

"Charles Barr has written to me again."

James was in an instant rage. "Has he, the dog? My God, the insolence!"

In the voice she used to calm him, she quietly said, "It has been two years since the last letter; before Waterloo. I had hoped that his being dismissed the service would put an end to it, but it appears not. He grows more horrible." With tears in her eyes and in her voice she said, "James, I hesitate to have you read this, but I shall keep nothing from you; we have always faced him together. But pray, *mo stor*, do not grow angry, do not allow Barr even that small victory."

James nodded, opened both his hands to show his calm, and Brigid finally handed him the letter.

O'Brian,

If you are fool enough to still be with Lockwood, you may tell him that I know him for a coward and a fool. Upon reflection, though, I wonder if he is already dead? I have friends at Kilmainham who say that he is quite doomed; only a matter of time before he drops, and then where will you be, my little Irish slut?

James leapt to his feet, both hands grasping the letter, roaring, "My God, that devil! How dare he address you in such a fashion!"

James strode toward the fire, but Brigid held up a hand, and insisted, "You must read it all, James. You must!"

And so James Lockwood paced the floor of Faibhile Cottage, and read.

I am in London these days, though I may go across to Paris once the Season is over. While the ladies of London have their charms, Frenchwomen are so much more liberal in the application of their affections. In my studies, I have found some Irishwomen quite as passionate as the French. I wonder, how you would be?

I shall know you some day. On your terms, or mine.

I was so close, those eighteen years ago, and yet you slipped away from me. Brigid O'Brian, the last unanswered question.

Leave Lockwood. He can be no kind of a husband for a woman like you. Can he bed you properly, a weak, wheezing, shell of a man? How you must yearn for me.

Come to Paris; I shall keep you like a pet. My own.

Until then...
C.B.

Aghast, James let the letter slip from his fingers. As it dropped to the floor he said, "I shall find him, and finally put an end to this. I cannot ask you to bear such abuse."

Brigid had been sitting very still, eyes to the floor, but then she looked up at her husband with fierce determination and said, "I have borne it, and I shall bear it yet. We have had this discussion a thousand times; even if you should fight him, kill him, he would still expose us."

James ran a hand through his hair and said, "I am so very sorry, my dear."

Brigid softly shook her head, and forced an amused tone into her voice. "And to think I once allowed that man to call on me. Enough of him. Come, my love, let us go upstairs, and put Charles Barr to shame."

One misty afternoon of his second spring at home, James walked to town for an appointment at Dr. Kelly's office on Shannon Square. Kelly had been the military surgeon who had tended him in Brussels, and who had transferred with his patients to Kilmainham. Only weeks after James's return home, the Lockwoods had been delighted to hear that Dr. Kelly had resigned his post to take over his uncle's practice in Clonakilty.

James Lockwood was not an inherently deceptive man, but before his appointment with Kelly he took a few deliberate minutes to sit on a bench in the neatly manicured little park in the center of Shannon Square. Dr. Kelly, however, long used to the irrational ways of humanity, was not deceived. After he examined James he said, "Even after the very moderate exertion of your walk down the hill to see me, you wheeze like a set of Connacht pipes. I would pay a guinea to hear your breath after you walk back up the hill. But I confess that I remain pleased, I will not use the word amazed, with your progress. And so, James, I must ask, are you still determined to return to your battalion?"

"I am."

"How does Mrs. Lockwood feel about this determination to return to active service?"

"She is a soldier's wife, and she knows that I have been at home longer than a serving soldier can honourably ask. Still, she has always wanted me at home, even before this damnedable wound. As pleasant as this has been, it is time, I think. She knows how important my captaincy is to me. To us."

"Very well, then. I cannot in good conscience suggest that you not go; in fact, Gibraltar weather may serve you. But I will remind you that over these past two years you have contracted several bronchial infections that nearly killed you. You will be escaping these grey, wet Irish winters, but you must remember that in your weakened state any fever can turn very serious, and pneumonia would certainly do you in."

James pulled his shirt on, and as his face reappeared it bore a wry smile. "I shall remember, John."

"I am serious, James. It is amazing that you have recovered your strength, your breath, to this level. But in all honesty, I suspect this is the height of your recovery, your zenith. While I cannot definitively say, you might find yourself in decline at any time. You alone can decide how best to spend your days."

With a sigh Kelly turned away to scribble his notes, while James tied his cravat, his face in a dense frown. Still facing away, Kelly said, "I know you still have friends in the battalion, who might aid in your return. A reliable servant will also be critical to your well-being. Pray, what happened to that wizened, unpleasant fellow who saw you home from Waterloo?"

"You mean old Doolan. I had to turn him away, back to the battalion, just a few weeks after I got home. We could not afford two servants; Doolan was understanding, saying it was all the same to him, though he had to go back and carry a musket." James's voice wavered a bit as he added, "When he rejoined, one of the new officers asked him to act as his servant, but Doolan declined, saying that he'd rather wait for me to return."

James then rubbed the side of his nose and said, "Now, if I may, please, John, ask you a rather obscure question? I cannot explain what prompts me to ask such a thing, but how long might a man live with syphilis?"

Kelly bobbed his head in surprise and said, "Syphilis? Well. The initial symptoms, lesions and such, may manifest just weeks after the... encounter. Ugly, but not fatal. No, the more severe symptoms present over time, from three to twenty years or so. The symptoms are as erratic as the timing; papules and gummas for some poor devils, dementia and madness for others. The severity may wax and wane, but in the end death is inevitable. As to the root of your question... how long? If pressed, I would offer between four and twenty years."

"Thank you, John, that was most... helpful. I have recently heard from a fellow who... "

There followed an awkward silence, as Kelly sat at his desk and leafed through unnecessary papers. As James put his coat on, he tentatively said, "One last thing, please, John. I am not sure that a medical man's interest runs into such areas, but for the past weeks I have had the same dream almost every night."

Kelly laced his fingers across his belly and gave James a half-smile. "You are full of interesting questions today, James."

Absently fussing with his coat, James went on, "In the dream, you see, I relive a few minutes from Waterloo. It is quite amazing, correct in every detail. I go back to the battle, the minutes just before I was hit myself, when a ball came and took off both the legs of a man who was standing beside me, a Private Kelly. A fountain of blood, of course, very unpleasant. I knelt and stayed with him for a moment. He grabbed hold of me as he lay dying, and in a fierce voice, I recall it vividly, he said, 'You'll remember me, won't you, sir? I have no family, none at all. I am Liam Kelly, born in the village of Enniscorthy, in the barony of Westwood, in the parish of Omarah, in the county Clare, on the first day of January, 1785.' And a moment later he died, both hands still clutching the front of my coat."

Kelly sat at his desk, his eyes closed, slowly rubbing his forehead. He muttered, "A Kelly, was he? Distant kin to me then, another soul adrift."

James stood at the door, his eyes and voice unfocused. "It is odd, you know; he was one of the draftees from our second battalion, so I scarcely knew him. Yet I think of him more often than I care to admit."

James put his hat on, and with one hand on the doorknob he said softly, "All those books and articles about the battle, and never will you see a word about Liam Kelly. To the world, he is an insignificant little fellow whose sole achievement was to die in tangled agony atop that God damned ridge. And yet his memory clings to me like a wet shirt."

Kelly sat alone in his office for long minutes after Lockwood left, until he opened a desk drawer and pulled out his diary. On the page titled May 16, 1817, he wrote, "Liam Kelly of Enniscorthy, County Clare, died at Waterloo, 18 June, 1815. Remember him."

Brigid made it a practice to watch the editions of the *London Gazette*, though it was not until 21 June, 1817, that she gleefully purchased one. It was an *Extraordinary Gazette*, the first *Extraordinary* issued since the announcement of the Waterloo victory two years before, to announce the release of the long delayed, shamefully delayed, Waterloo Prize Money.

She carried the *Gazette* home with great excitement, 'greed' not being a term that could be applied to a woman who was attempting to support a household of eight souls on a lieutenant's four shillings eight pence a day. With some ceremony the children were called into the drawing room where their father said, "Some good news, my dear family, as we

Waterloo veterans are to receive our Prize Money. As we look through the awards, pray notice why it so important that I am determined to return to the regiment and gain my captaincy. The benefits are so much greater once an officer is made captain." Reading from the table of payments, he said, "We have here a case in point: even the most senior lieutenants will be granted only the same monies as the freshest ensign. All subalterns, that is, ensigns and lieutenants, are classed together, and will be granted £34 14s. 9d. for their service, while the captains will be given £90 7s. 4d."

There was a general howl of disbelief, and Cissy said, "Oh, that is so unfair, Papa! You are one of the most senior lieutenants! And you were wounded! And you commanded a company! You should certainly be given the same reward as the captains!"

"That, my children, is how much of the world works, and you will please realize that as quickly as you are able. Do not expect fairness. If you want to see true injustice, look at the monies to be given to the fellows who did most of the fighting and dying: the poor rankers. Here, I shall read you the full list:

Corporals, drummers, privates £2 11s. 4.d
Sergeants £19 4s. 4d.
Subalterns £34 14s. 9d.
Captains £90 7s. 4d.
Colonels, majors £433 2s. 5d.
Generals £1,275 10s. 10d.
The Duke of Wellington £61,000

Can you imagine such a fortune? Sixty-one thousand pounds!"

The family exploded in unbridled passionate cries of indignation, sympathy, fantasy, or greed, according to their various temperaments, but James only smiled, as he had been a soldier long enough to be accustomed to such inequities. He flipped forward a few pages to look over the names of his brother officers, thinking of how they might spend their long-delayed prize money, when he suddenly cried out, "Quinn, Ives, Morris! And Becker! These fellows were taking their leisure at sea during the battle, and yet are to receive the same prize as we Waterloo men! I have never heard of such a thing."

The *Gazette* announced that the award was made to every man who had fought in the Campaign of 1815, up to and including the comparatively bloodless capture of Paris. James made a count, and of the seven men of the 1/27th paid £433, only one, John Archibald, served at Waterloo. Six men were paid at the captains' rate; only three, Captains Pratt, Towne, and Barr, were at Waterloo, all casualties. James thought of Pratt, who had been carried past James's company with much of his skull missing. Deliberately pushing that memory aside, he took some satisfaction in thinking of Barr's wounds: a bit of French shell in his hand, a mysterious pistol ball in his leg, the loss of his career, and of his honour.

On one of the rare dry days of that summer, the three Lockwood girls were lying on the grass in their front garden, looking up at the clouds.

"That one, I think," said Mary, pointing at one cloud with a giggle, "looks much like Stanley Robinson, don't you think? He is so handsome."

Cissy made a quick frown and said, "It most certainly does not. You seem to be seeing Stanley Robinson everywhere, dear." But then with a laugh she pointed out another cloud to Lucy, and cried, "Oh, look, *a grah,* that one looks so like Delores!"

Delores was the Guernsey that routinely grazed along the hedge that bordered the rear of Fáibhile Cottage, and Lucy quickly recognized the bovine shape far above. Seeing her father stroll into the yard, Lucy leapt up and called, "Oh, Papa, you must come and see Delores up in the sky!"

James put his hands on his hips, made a silly face, and said, "Oh, you girls are making game of me. I am reasonably sure that cows do not fly." Lucy laughed delightedly, and led him out into the yard. James lay down, squeezing between Mary and Cissy, not very gracefully, perhaps, and he had to make a conscious effort not to grunt or wince as he did so. Lucy, who had just turned four and had grown very affectionate with her father, pointed out the cloud in question, then lay by her father and gently played with his hair. The girls were delighted to have him there, so relaxed and in such good humour, but still Mary asked, "Father, should you be lying on the hard ground? Perhaps you should restrict yourself to your bed?"

"Miss Lockwood, I have lain on the hard ground many a night, and pray believe me when I say that this patch of ground is considerably drier, softer, and warmer than most." He turned his head to kiss Lucy, and grasping the older girls' hands he added, "And never have I had such lovely companions."

Cissy giggled and said, "That is a weak compliment, Father. I should think that you would find anyone's company more pleasant than that of a hundred dirty smelly old soldiers." As if to prove Cissy's contention, Sergeant waddled over and flopped down next to Lucy, his nose nearly in James's ear. While Sergeant was loyal and essentially good-natured, his merits did not extend to regular bathing, and James was indeed reminded of Six Company.

There was a pause until Lucy innocently asked, "Papa, do you miss the army?"

James swallowed his first response, instead giving it some thought, until he answered, "Yes, dear heart, I suppose that I do." A moment passed until he added, "It is an odd notion, but I feel as if I owe it to someone, that I return to my men. I feel them waiting for me." The four of them then lay in silence, each digesting that confession in their own way, as the clouds and the day floated by slowly, but relentlessly.

Mary and Cissy were very close, but they were not above a degree of competition. While they had their suitors, they did not squabble over any of the local young men. Mary's fascination with the opposite gender had once led to a brush with one very knowing, and very ill-natured, young man named George Boffut, a brush which had frightened, but educated, both girls. Boffut's removal from their lives was complete; while an anonymous musket ball had deformed his features to a hideous state, it was the revelation of his rape of two village girls that had removed him from society and made necessary his retreat to a remote Welsh tower.

Thus wiser in the perils of courtship, the girls' sense of competition was most evident when they shared a mirror. Their mother would growl at them if this grew too obvious; nevertheless nudging and dramatic rolling of the eyes were not unknown. They were energetically primping in the front hall mirror before walking down to call on the Blackwells when Cissy said to Mary, "I do wish, *a grah*, that you would not wear that bonnet when we go calling; the lace is horribly frayed."

"Thank you, Brigit," replied her sister, who used Cissy's given name whenever she wished to deliver a barb, "but I believe that my lace is quite fine, though I might suggest that you not leave so much of your hair across your forehead. It is *outré*."

"At the last dance Michael McCarthy said my hair was enchanting, so you may...."

Their father came up behind them, straightened his cravat in the mirror, and, as he was an involved parent, gave them each a moderate swat on the bottom. "I believe that I shall walk as far as town with you, if for no other reason than to prevent you two from doing each other serious injury."

"Oh, Papa, we were just teasing." They each gave him a kiss on the cheek. "But yes, we would love for you to come walk with us. It is good to see you feeling so well."

James walked over to the banister and called up the stairs, "*A cuisle*, I am going to take our two elder daughters into town and sell them to the tinkers; would you care to join me?"

In a surprised, happy voice Brigid called down, "The tinkers, is it? Give me two minutes, and I am your man."

While they waited, James and the grinning girls strolled into the garden. Mary took advantage of their father's good humour and placed a pink rose behind his ear. James, who needed more than a pink rose to challenge his masculinity, left it there, and when Brigid joined them he coyly turned his head to look off into the distance.

"Oh, my dear, you are quite lovely," Brigid said with beaming admiration. The girls were delighted with their father's appearance, but especially by the playful banter between their parents, an essential element of the early years of their marriage and now all too rare an event. The four of them walked down Scartagh Lane comfortable in each other's company, particularly as James, more than Brigid, spoke to the girls as if they were adults, and capable of intelligent conversation.

At the Western Road the girls headed off to visit the Blackwells, though only after Brigid had noticed they had been staring at clouds again, and carefully brushed the grass from the backs of their dresses. As they watched the girls walk down the hill Brigid said, "I am so glad that I looked them over before they reached the Blackwells. They are dear people, but grass on the back of a young lady's dress might be misconstrued."

"Oh," said James, honestly taken aback, "I would never have thought of such a thing."

"That, my dear, is why you married me," Brigid said with a smile. "I am wise in the ways of the world." With a playful tilt to her head she asked, "Would the Lieutenant perhaps care to take the long way home? A wee walk would do us both a world of good."

James pointed to the western skies and their very convincing threat of rain, but Brigid persisted, "Oh, it shall be hours and hours before it rains. I was raised here, you may recall, sir, and we native Irish have an uncanny knowledge of the weather." With that she plucked the rose from behind her husband's ear and stuck it behind her own.

James wagged a knowing finger at his beautiful wife and said, "Very well, my dear. You seem to be exceptionally wise today, far above the plodding ways of a common soldier. But I wager that we shall get half way through our walk, far beyond the Pale, and the skies will open. You, young lady, will be drenched to the skin." Patting the haversack thrown over his shoulder, he continued, "I, forever the pragmatic soldier, have brought my oilskin cloak."

With a sympathetic look that barely constrained a giggle, Brigid said, "I am so sorry if I have terrorized you with the possibility of getting damp, dear. I would have thought that a soldier was used to some risk, some mild hardship if things don't go exactly his way. But I shall not question you, sir, as a wife's duty is to suffer in silence. If I must, I shall walk alone, and risk the consequences." She gave him a playful slap on the arm, laughing as she pranced out into the road, leading the way into the hills above town.

Lieutenant Lockwood had English blood in his veins, but his skill at predicting the rain proved superior to that of his Irish wife. They were more than two miles from home when a gentle sprinkle of rain became a torrent reminiscent of the weather that James had seen during his march to Waterloo. He did not mention that analogy to his wife, contenting himself with holding her hand as they ran to the shelter of a massive beech that stood alone along the isolated path. The tree shielded them from the worst of the storm, while the sharp roar of the rain cut them off from the rest of the world as completely as a thousand miles of ocean. James threw on his cloak and stood with his back against the smooth grey trunk, and with a laugh he opened his arms wide and brought Brigid in. Together they looked out at the driving rain, huddled under the cloak as the rain pounded around their island, their private refuge. It was perfect, so much like the idealized memories of their youth. For that little while, at least, they shared a deep intimacy, an intimacy that was in many ways the core of their lives, a love that defined what they were as people.

Chapter Three

As deeply as James cared for his family, he did yearn to occasionally have the house to himself. He would admit that having been shot in the chest had temporarily restricted his ability to fend for himself, but he was finding his family's incessant attention somewhat confining. His frustration made for some tension in the house. When weeks passed with Mrs. Cashman steadfastly refusing to prepare anything but cold gruel and warm milk for his breakfast, he was eventually goaded to burst out in a tone familiar to his company, "Hell and death, woman! I'll have eggs and sausage this morning, or there shall be a flogging by noon! Is there no notion of discipline in this house?"

It was, then, of some relief to all concerned when a shining summer morning came and the carriage from the Shannon Arms arrived to carry Brigid, Mrs. Cashman, and the children to an outing at the ancient stone ring of Drombeg. James, who was looking forward to his time alone and who had eaten enough of his meals out of doors to exorcise any desire to picnic, waved them down McCurtain's Hill and spent his morning contentedly napping.

He eventually stirred long enough to make a small luncheon. Then treating himself to three fingers of Mr. Jameson's whiskey, he turned to a slim book that Tom Mainwaring had given him, a collection of comic advice for army officers. Tom, too, was slowly recovering from a wound suffered at Waterloo; they had been very close friends for many years, and James smiled as he recalled some of the foolish jokes they had shared. Flipping through the book, James laughed aloud at several passages, and when he came across the advice for army surgeons he grinned and marked a paragraph to share with Dr. Kelly.

When a soldier receives a wound on a leg or an arm, immediately fix the tourniquet, though there may be the fairest prospect of preserving the limb. This will save you a world of trouble, and your patient a vast deal of pain. You will besides do him a most essential benefit, in sending him to enjoy the repose of Chelsea hospital, instead of being dragged from one place to another, at the perpetual risk of having his brains knocked out. Partial evil is universal good, and the sacrifice of a limb may eventually be the preservation of all the rest of the carcass.

James was displeased when his reading was interrupted by a persistent knocking.

"A parcel for you, sir, if you please."

He was puzzled by the long, slender box carried by the drayman, but the label did indeed read "Lieutenant J. Lockwood, Faibhile Cottage, Clonakilty, Ireland." He signed the freight bills, handed over a few coins, and said, "Pray, sir, accept this for your trouble."

The drayman smiled, tipped his cap, and said, "Thankee, sir. Faith, it is always a pleasure to deal with a real gentleman."

James was not immune to the pleasure of an unexpected gift, and as the dray cart rattled away he once again studied the label, in an unfamiliar hand and with no return address. He found the box's lid securely tacked down, so he carried the box back to the empty stables and searched for the small crowbar he recalled seeing amongst the dust. With a moderate sense of accomplishment he came upon the crowbar, and prying up the lid he found the box stuffed with wood shavings. When he groped into the box his hands fell upon cold metal, and he muttered softly, "Oh, my God."

In the dusty half-light of the empty stables his shaking hands pulled his sword from the box.

He had been given the sword ten years before, when he gained his lieutenancy. It had been an unexpected gift then as well, when the sword had been delivered to his billet in a tiny Spanish village. His father had forbade him any but the most basic support, but it was his mother, his quiet, timid mother, who sent him the elegant blade. It had long meant the world to him, but he had last seen the sword on June 18, 1815, when the Inniskilling Regiment stood and was torn to pieces above the Charleroi Road at Waterloo. It had been thrown aside when he was wounded late in the day, and he had given up all hope of ever seeing it again.

It was a 1796 pattern blade, not the standard Arsenal product but the finest work from Brunn, Prosser, and Salter of London, a long straight blade with a deadly point, a true gentleman's weapon. He would admit the balance was poor; in a standard fencer's grip the point was far too heavy, and the narrow pommel easily slipped from sweating fingers. But any officer worth his salt knew to break his wrist to the left, so that the blade's weight came through the butt and into the base of the hand. Further, a horizontal blade would pass more easily between a man's ribs. Lieutenant Lockwood had experience in such matters.

He stood completely still for a long while, slowly turning over the blade, the beautifully blued steel now filthy and rusty. The elegant sword knot was missing, and the brass and leather of the sheath was still stained brown with his blood.

He set the sword aside when he saw a letter amongst the shavings. He broke it open, and was stunned to recognize Charles Barr's hand.

> *Lockwood,*
>
> *In passing through Brussels on my <u>grand tour</u> of Europe I came across this worthless blade of yours lying neglected in a filthy little shop. I thought that I recognized it, having seen it so often <u>rusted into its scabbard</u> at your side, and my memory proved correct when I saw your name engraved on the guard.*
>
> *It is a sad little sword, but surely even you must have felt some shame when you threw it down at Waterloo and fled to the rear, crying out your ridiculous little wound? You have always been the most miserable <u>coward</u>, Lockwood; it is a wonder that the army has not yet found you out, and dismissed you the service.*
>
> *Perhaps you will have the good sense to die before any further disgrace taints O'Brian. I wish her to be at least respectable when I take her for my own.*
>
> *I send this sword to you <u>not</u> as a gift—I would sooner send you a bullet—but only as a reminder of what a low coward you are, and of what I shall do to you some day. I am not sure when I shall get around to it, but sooner rather than later, I think.*
>
> C.B.

James sat heavily on an old cobbler's bench. He ran a hand through his hair and muttered, "Christ."

The solidity of the old sword connected him to the memories of the battle, of the friends he had lost, and of the men of his company, who had stayed with him even as they were killed and maimed at his side. It also brought into sharp focus the haunting threat of Charles Barr, a lingering shadow no matter how bright the lights in his life.

He read the letter a second time and in a burst of rage he hissed, "That poxed son of a bitch!" He angrily wadded up the letter and was about to throw it in to a corner, but then, remembering the vow he had made to Brigid, smoothed the letter and carefully folded it into a pocket. They would share everything.

James sat for a long while, absently rubbing his fingertips together, until he quickly stood, put on an old apron that hung on a nail, and set to work. He spent hours cleaning, polishing, and putting a razor's edge to the blade. He then spent the rest of his afternoon furiously practicing his sword drill, his shirt soaked with sweat, his wound a relentless, red-hot stitch of pain in his chest, as he prepared himself for the day he was sure would come.

Summer came, but the four of them had quilts across their laps as the chaise trundled further up into the low, green hills. They were just a few miles from Leamaneh Castle, one of the great country houses of the County Clare, and part of the Lockwood holdings for the past hundred years.

James frowned and said, "I spent several summers here; the last when I was twelve or so. It was a cold, grey, inconvenient, unhappy place then, and I cannot imagine it is any more comfortable now."

Brigid looked out her window and said in a wistful voice, "It is a lonely corner of the world, sure. Here in the west the old gods still walk, I think." She cleared her face and asked in a more natural tone, "How often does your father open the house?"

"Not more than once a year, I think, and then just for the shooting. They shall blast away at anything that moves."

Turning to Mary and Cissy, James waved a finger at the grassy hillsides and went on, "Girls, all this country is part of the estate, but it is not worth much, now that they have pulled down every tree bigger than your thumb. Much of it is too steep and too rocky to plow, though the grazing can be good. But the majority of the estate lands lie north of here, up in the Burren, all rock, ancient tombs, and heartache."

Mary, who was not happy about having to ride in her grandfather's third-best carriage for two days and one hundred forty miles facing backwards, glanced out the window and then returned to her nap. Cissy, however, looked intently about her.

The chaise clattered past a handful of deserted cabins, their roofs pulled down, the walls still black from their burning. A few ragged people poked through the ruins, retreating at the approach of the chaise. Brigid reached out her hand, as if to soothe the scene of desolation, and said, "Oh, those poor people."

Cissy said in a low voice, "It looks as if Grandfather Lockwood is no kinder a landlord than the rest of the Ascendency." James caught a hint of both anger and disgust in her tone. It did not surprise him. He was proud of her, of her great heart and her good head. While he was pleased to hear her speak her mind, he was also worried that she might someday go too far. Her mother's O'Brian blood ran hot, but like it or not, she was a Lockwood, and of a class apart. James leaned over to look at the burned cabins through Brigid's window. "Actually, it is Mr. Gruffydd, land steward of this estate, who orders the evictions. He has been here forever; a nasty old Welshman who lost an arm in my father's battalion on the Plains of Abraham. But, yes, my father would not blink an eye at evicting every soul who owned him ha'penny. My brother will doubtless continue the tradition when his day comes."

James reached over and put his hand atop his wife's, but he turned his face toward his own window. After a long pause he said, "It is shameful, I know. They wring every penny out of their tenants, and invest nothing back into their holdings. I tell myself that I only draw a pittance every month from the family, that I am not to blame, but I do benefit from the sufferings of these people."

Brigid tore her eyes away from the ragged peasants to study the gloves in her lap. In a breaking voice she said, "Oh, yes, my dear, shameful. Shameful, that a woman who is as Irish and Catholic as those poor souls is carried past them in luxury, for three days of high living and foolish chatter with the very family that has driven them from their homes. I was a fool to come here; you should have come alone." They were silent for long minutes, swaying and lurching as the chaise bounced up into the hills, until James said, "We need more of the family money if I am ever to purchase a captaincy, if ever we are ever to buy our own home, and to get the children into good schools. But by God, I shall I not crawl. None of us shall crawl."

They crossed a small stone bridge and a cluster of houses, and James said, "This is Corrofin. We are nearly there. Girls, that is Lough Atedaun to the right, and you shall soon see Inchiquin Lough to the left." He then opened his window, leaned out, and called, "Johnson, pull over and let us take a look at Leamaneh when it comes in sight, if you please."

There followed the usual rituals found at the end of a long journey, as shoes were slipped on, quilts were folded, sleep was wiped from eyes, and the four suddenly reinvigorated passengers prepared for a return to bipedal life. Mary, in particular, made every effort to restore her appearance by pursing her lips, pinching her cheeks, and straightening her bonnet in the window's reflection.

The coachman halted his team on the crest of a low hill, and the Lockwoods stiffly dismounted to see Leamaneh Castle, tall and grey, standing on the crest of the opposite hill.

"Oh, Papa," cried Mary, "how romantic!"

With some amazement Brigid said, "It is massive, sure, but grim as the grave."

Cissy said nothing, but her look was disapproving.

James crossed his arms and stared at the old place for a moment, then said, "More a large house than a castle, though it does look imposing, does it not? But it is not as grand as it may appear; the house is much like my father. Tall, wide, but not terribly deep." Pointing to the right side of the house, he said, "The east side is a medieval tower; you can tell it is old, as there are no true windows, just arrow slits. It was built by some Irishman around the year 1500 or so." He grinned at Mary and added, "It has a spiral stone staircase that leads to dank little rooms far up in the tower. Romantic, *a grah*, but amazingly uncomfortable."

Then pointing to the left, he went on, "The main part of the mansion was built about 1640. Those were violent days, so the place is built like a fortress, stone mullions and walls eighteen inches thick. Of course that means cold, musty little rooms, except the great hall, which can come off well." They could see people coming out the front door, so with a resigned smile he said to Brigid, "It looks as if we have been spotted; too late to flee. Shall we face our demons, my dear?"

Chapter Four

The rumpled Lockwoods of Clonakilty made their bows and curtsies, and were greeted in return by a scant nod from James's aging father. It had been five years since James had last seen his father, John Lockwood Sr., a tall, fierce figure in his son's mind. James now noted, and was ashamed to find himself pleased by, his father's rapid decline to a bent old man.

More formal greetings followed under the grey skies and the grey façade: James's older brother John, tall, thin, vaguely pleasant but not overly bright, and his wife, Elizabeth, whose nature mirrored her husband's; James's sister Mary, a beauty if one cared for sharp, angular features, and her husband Zeresh Muir, a fat, angry man of great wealth and little charm; lastly the steward, the gnarled Gruffydd, in plain, dark clothes, with an appraising eye and an empty sleeve pinned to the front of his coat like a badge of honour.

Twelve servants stood in a line to one side with their eyes to the ground. Flicking a hand toward them, old Lockwood said, "We have brought a few of our maids and valets, though we have none to spare for you or your women. And of course we brought Hannity, as there is not one Irishwoman west of Naas who can cook anything but mud. These others we have hired from the inns in Kilfenora and Lisdoonvarna. What a scruffy lot."

James studied the line of servants and said, "Father, I do not see Mr. McLaughlin."Old Lockwood growled and said, "I dismissed the scoundrel last week, as soon as we arrived. There was dust in the upper chambers that would scandalize a brothel. If he is too old to traverse the stairs, then he may seek employment elsewhere and no longer take advantage of my good nature."

James frowned and offered, "Father, McLaughlin has been caretaker here since I was a boy. Certainly...."

Old Lockwood irritably waved him off, saying, "I shall hear none of your nonsense." But the old man softened a bit when he added, "Though that is what your mother would have said, once."

Quietly, James asked, "How is Mother, Father?"

"The same. She may have recognized me, I think, when I went to see her before we left. I mentioned that we were going to see you here, but she did not flicker at your name."

James nodded as pain and memory flashed on his face, but his father had lied to him. His mother was far gone, never a rational word coming from her mouth, but when she had heard her husband mention James's name she had smiled for an instant. Old Lockwood took it as a deliberate insult, that she should ignore her husband's presence but be delighted at the mention of her son's name.

The rest of the party stood within earshot, awkwardly quiet.

Gruffydd was lurking at the edge of the family; in the uncomfortable pause he stepped forward and said in a sharp voice, "You were quite right to drive off that villain McLaughlin, sir. There can be no notions of kindness when dealing with these recalcitrant Irish."

There were grumbles of agreement from John and Muir, so, warming to the occasion, Gruffydd went on in a fervent tone, "This house is a case in point. Its builder was an O'Brian and a rebel, and righteously slain by Cromwell's avenging army. His widow, the famous Red Mary, only managed to keep a roof over her head by bedding and wedding the first Cromwellian officer that would have her. That is a man's way to handle the Irish: the sword or the bed."

There were some grins and soft laughter, and with a wry, acid, unapologetic smile Mary Muir nodded toward her sister in-law and said, "Mr. Gruffydd, it may interest you to know that Mrs. James Lockwood was born an O'Brian."

Gruffydd shot her a look and said nothing until he caught James's angry glare; then Gruffydd finally offered, "Beg pardon, ma'am," meaning nothing of the sort.

Brigid smiled graciously and replied, "Not at all, Mr. Gruffydd. The house was indeed built by Toirdelbhach Donn MacTadhg Ó Brian," the ancient name sparkled coming off her tongue, "King of Thomond, back when the world was young. I do, however, hesitate to claim any kinship to Red Mary, especially as she was born a Mahon. In my family she is called Maire Rua, and, as I recall, she is alleged to have murdered, what, twenty-five husbands in various fashions?"

James laughed, and in a voice that carried both playful and serious notes, he said, "A warning from history, I think, not to toy with an Irishwoman."

Brigid, Mary, and Cissy Lockwood all stood a bit straighter. Their eyes flashed, and as the party walked into the house the servants kept their eyes down, but their ears had caught every word.

At dawn next morning there was great activity as the gentlemen gathered to go shooting. James's brother and brother in-law, braced by pulls from flasks of brandy, climbed aboard a carriage while the servants loaded a jaunting car with baskets of food, numerous bottles, and the Lockwood collection of fowling pieces and hunting rifles.

The gentlemen and their manservants were dressed for the hunt, all except James Lockwood, who stood by the great door of Leamaneh Castle being scolded by his father.

"It is damned churlish of you not to come shooting, James. I went to great expense, you know, to have you and your women brought up here. You might show some small degree of God damned gratitude by doing as I ask, at least once in your life."

James replied formally, with no hint of anger, "I am sorry to disappoint, Father, but I am not overly fond of shooting these days."

"Damn your whims, sir! I have hired two dozen of the local peasants to beat up game for us, at great expense, sir! And when did you grow so discerning? I know for a fact that you once hunted with the best of them; you had a real gift, then! I recall an eight-point buck that you brought down on Lord Howard's estate when you were no more than a boy! And now you find it repulsive to knock over a rabbit or two?"

James merely nodded and replied, "Not repulsive, sir, please. In fact I wish great success to the party. But my profession has given me intimate experience with killing, Father. While I shall never hesitate to do what my duty requires of me, I find myself grown averse to shedding blood... recreationally."

The old man sniffed in fury and stalked back to the carriage where John and Muir sat watching, the old man calling to them in an angry, derisive voice, "My gentle son! The soldier who does not care for the sound of gunfire and who is not fond of killing! A damned poor choice of profession, if you ask me!" Then as the coachman helped him up into the carriage the old man muttered, "And they say he did so well at Waterloo. Stuff and nonsense. He confounds me at every turn... marries that tart... won't come shooting...."

James heard none of that, as he had gone back upstairs toward his room. He had to stop and catch his breath at the top of the steep staircase; he found that he lost his breath more easily than even a few months before, though he would not tell anyone so. In the cool, dark room he took off his clothes, slipped back into bed with his warm, pink, sleepy wife, and slept most of the morning away, with never a nightmare.

A large walled garden stood to the west of Leamaneh. The walls were steadily crumbling, the rusty gates swung loose in their hinges, and the garden itself was no longer well-tended, but still its flowers bloomed with a wild intensity that summer. One evening Brigid slipped into the garden to fill a wicker basket with flowers. She was doing so hurriedly, and was just preparing to leave by the rear gate when Mary Muir and Elizabeth Lockwood strolled arm in arm through the front.

The three traded the requisite curtsies and nods, and Mrs. Muir said to Brigid, "Mrs. Lockwood, that is a prodigious collection, though the mix is... might I say, undisciplined? I trust you do not intend to place them in the house?"

Brigid was annoyed to have been caught in the garden, as she had intended to carry out her errand unnoticed. But she would not be shamed, and with a polite edge to her voice she replied, "Thank you, Mrs. Muir, but I had a notion to honour some graves that lay nearby."

Mrs. Muir gave her sister in-law a condescending smile and said, "Surely you are mistaken, Mrs. Lockwood. To my certain knowledge there is no church within miles of Leamaneh."

"No church, surely," said Brigid, "but it is a *cillin* that lies in the fields just beyond that ruined old tower, east of the house."

With a dismissive roll of her eyes Mrs. Muir said, "Really, Mrs. Lockwood."

Brigid explained, "A *cillin*, Mrs. Muir, is unconsecrated ground where unbaptized children are laid to rest. A tenet, an unfortunate tenet, of the Catholic faith decrees that babies who die before baptism are not to be granted heaven, and may not be buried in holy ground. We of the faith who do not care for such a harsh and painful philosophy care for the *cillini* as best we can."

"You question your own church, madam?"

"I have my faith, but I have a heart and a head as well, madam."

Mrs. Muir was nonplussed for a moment, then with a mix of derision and anger she scoffed, "And such a thing lies on the grounds of Leamaneh? I am astonished! Such superstitious nonsense! The graves of babies!" She turned to Elizabeth Lockwood and said, "Have you ever heard such madness, my dear sister?"

Until that point Elizabeth had added nothing to the conversation. She ignored Mrs. Muir's question and instead asked Brigid, "Pray, Mrs. Lockwood, might I join you? Those poor, dear, children." She then separated herself from the astonished Mrs. Muir and quickly gathered a handful of flowers.

Mrs. Muir turned and stalked back toward the house, clearly angry, though for once Elizabeth Lockwood did not seem overly concerned with her opinion. Instead she walked out the rear gate beside Brigid and confidentially said, "I must say, Mrs. Lockwood, I find your determination to honour these poor babies entirely honourable."

Brigid was surprised and pleased; she had never heard her sister in-law offer an opinion regarding much of anything, as Elizabeth had never been anything but distantly polite with her. Elizabeth rarely spoke, and typically receded into the background of her husband.

"That is most kind, Mrs. Lockwood," replied Brigid. "I am so pleased to have you join me."

They walked together in silence for some time, through the waning light into the fields east of the house. Suddenly Elizabeth burst out, "I have lost four babies, you know. Four! My fondest wish is to be a mother, and I shall never, ever, hold my own baby!" She wept as she walked, and Brigid gently reached across to take her hand.

"I am so sorry, my dear, I did not know."

"Mr. Lockwood does not wish it to be widely known. So you may understand if I grow upset at the thought of babies going untended in any manner. But why would the babies be buried here, so far from the villages?"

"The priests turn the families away, so the *cillini* are often in such places, a safe, secret place. Perhaps it is a place of some significance, some magic, from back when the world was young. Some of the stones in this *cillin* look as if they have been there a very long time, though sadly one of the little graves looks quite new."

The two women walked across the field, the grass green and trimmed by sheep. They passed the low, grass-covered ruins of two ancient ring forts, fairy forts, the country people called them. Elizabeth wiped some tears away and said, "My, Mrs. Lockwood, I do not believe that any of the family has ever walked these fields. How ever did you find yourself so far from the house?"

Brigid had taken to long morning walks to escape the tension inside Leamaneh, but she was hesitant to explain herself to Elizabeth, so she only said, "Oh, since I was a child I have always enjoyed exploring such places."

They then came upon the *cillin*, and perhaps it was a coincidence that the sun broke suddenly through the clouds, and golden light painted them there. The cemetery lay atop a low mound in the corner of a green pasture, framed by a tangled hedge and a cluster of holly trees, ancient and evergreen.

"It is a lovely place, after all," said Elizabeth.

They set to work. Elizabeth, who was not the most demonstrative of women, was very active in brushing leaves from the stones and neatly arranging the flowers. She bent closely over one stone and said, "Mrs. Lockwood, this stone has such an odd symbol carved into it. It is very faint, but you might just make it out."

Brigid joined her and said appreciatively, "Oh, my, yes, well done! Those are Ogham letters, the writing of the ancient Irish."

Brigid could rarely display any skill that could possibly rival her sisters-in-law, as they were both well schooled in music, stitchery, literature, and every other skill required of a lady of the day. But here she shone, and with a degree of pride she went on, "My grandfather could read the Ogham very well, and he taught me a bit. Those lines are *gort, ruis, and ailm*, or ivy, elder, and fir. Those are the 'g', 'r', and 'a' sounds. '*Gra*' in Irish, Mrs. Lockwood, means 'love'."

"Love," whispered Elizabeth wistfully, as she brushed the tips of her fingers across the old stone.

They tended the *cillin* as best they could and, after offering simple prayers over the tiny graves, they walked back towards Leamaneh in the dusk. Elizabeth softly took Brigid's arm and meekly said, "Pray, Mrs. Lockwood, might I in the future address you by your Christian name?"

Brigid gave her a soft smile and answered, "I should like that of all things. We shall be Elizabeth and Brigid to each other, as sisters ought."

"Elizabeth and Brigid. I shall enjoy that very much, sister."

In truth, the Great Hall of Leamaneh Castle was not an especially large room, nor an especially grand one, but on the last evening at Leamaneh a roaring fire in the massive fireplace and dozens of flickering candles gave it an air of magnificence.

The Clonakilty Lockwoods had survived three days of the Malahide Lockwoods, three days of icy conversation, exquisite courtesy, and the occasional barb. The formal dinner on that last evening, with all the local gentry invited, was to be the pinnacle of the family's visit to Leamaneh. The entire party would leave the next morning, and most of the baggage was already in the coach house. The Lockwoods of Clonakilty were especially anxious to return home; Brigid was an affectionate mother and was eager to have her boys and her little Lucy back under her wing.

That night James wore his best uniform and his gleaming sword; that tall mass of scarlet, buff, and gold posed a stark contrast to his bent father, his willowy brother, and his portly brother-in-law.

Mary and Cissy each wore a gown they had worn only once before (a fiasco in which Mary had sampled the punch and had very nearly been groped by the drunk young man of evil intention). While the cost of their gowns was a pittance in comparison to the fortunes spent on the elegant Dublin, London, and even Parisian fashions worn by the other ladies, the girls' natural beauty and shining innocence made their father smile broadly and whisper, "They glitter like a handful of diamonds."

Brigid wore a dress she had borrowed from Mrs. Butler, the wife of the Church of Ireland minister in Clonakilty. Mrs. Butler was a striking woman who did not deign to dress like a minister's dowdy wife, so Brigid stood at her husband's side in a dark blue silk that complimented her chestnut hair and perfect complexion. It was cut in a manner that Brigid considered daring, but she was prepared to do battle with James's family in any way she could, modesty be damned.

Most of the other guests were local landowners, some of whom agreed with old Lockwood's land policies, some of whom pointedly did not. As the guests arrived and introductions were made, there was a moderate degree of the tension and awkwardness typical at the start of such events. The Clonakilty Lockwoods did, however, sense potential allies in a young militia officer and his shy, even younger, wife who had come up from Lisdoonvarna for the evening. After only a few minutes of conversation with Ensign and Mrs. Keane it was determined that both Brigid and the impossibly sweet Mrs. Keane had O'Leary blood in common, and they immediately broke into the time-honoured Irish tradition of determining how they were related.

The long, elegant dining table was laid with the massive Lockwood silver, and each place setting bore an elegantly written place card. The Lockwood patriarch, a thorough-going member of the Ascendancy, was mad for status, so long hours by him and his daughter had determined a precise seating arrangement, one largely based on the power of one's family and one's position within that family.

Just before the diners were called to table, however, James snuck over to review the seating and found that his wife and daughters were scattered amongst the older, more conservative guests. He cheerfully rearranged the middle of the table to put this wife and daughters together, near the Keanes, and when the diners were called to table old Lockwood watched with a scowl as his plans were thrown to the wind.

Conversation was at first restrained in both tone and topic, but as the courses and the wine came in successive waves the volume of the party rose accordingly. Several animated discussions broke out regarding leases, evictions, tenant rights, and the incendiary topic of Catholic Emancipation. No one in that room would have the least sympathy for rebellion, but some were in favour of conciliation with the Catholic majority and of a peaceful sharing of power. They were in turn viewed with derision by most of the party, who viewed their right to rule as God-given and absolute.

Despite her earlier misgivings, Brigid was having a delightful evening with the Keanes on one hand and an interesting barrister from Ennistimon on the other. It was odd, however, when a footman leaned over her as he poured her a glass of wine and whispered, "*Tá tú aon rud a eagla, bean caoin.*" You have nothing to fear, gentlewoman. She looked after him, but he moved smoothly on to serve Mrs. Keane. Brigid sat puzzled for a moment and nearly rose to speak to him, but she knew it would be exceedingly improper, and she was then pulled back into the whirl of conversation as Mrs. Keane asked her opinion of the Union.

Eventually a pause came, in which old Lockwood waved a fork at his younger son and loudly said, "James, you were so tardy in coming to the house, you may not have heard that I arrived here in time for the summer quarterly session. I felt compelled, compelled, I say, to travel down to Limerick with our faithful Gruffydd..." in turn pointing his fork at the gnarled Welshman, who blushed with pleasure, "...to bear witness against a pack of rebellious devils from my own estates who were grumbling republican heresy. Thomas Paine, forsooth." Most of the diners turned to listen, as old Lockwood continued, "You see, for these past months I have been corresponding with Lord Matthews."

When James raised his fingers from the table and raised his eyebrows, his father bellowed, "The magistrate, man, the magistrate! Good Lord. At any rate, we are determined to do a complete house-cleaning. Matthews has arrested every scoundrel on which he has anything resembling evidence, and I have agreed to toss out every other scoundrel who has so much as whispered treason. Good Gruffydd has kept me up to date on the various miscreant factions in his monthly reports. We have seen a round dozen transported this session, and we are in the process of evicting another thirty or so. Such a house-cleaning! The peasants shall be silent and docile, or by God—"

Mrs. Keane surprised everyone by calling out, "My God, sir, what have you done! What of those poor families!" and the table exploded in a cacophony of raucous debate. The vehement conversation mellowed only when the footmen appeared with the venison, though several of the diners continued to glare at one another.

Dinner proceeded, but when a naïve young man at one end of the table asked about the Rebellion of 1798 several people turned to listen, sensing blood in the water. A rather drunk gentleman who had been openly eying Cissy offered, "I was only a boy at the time, you know, but I rode with my father in the Ennis Cavalry and helped hound the rebels in Sligo. What slaughter! The formed troops..." He reached over to pat Cissy's hand. Cissy withdrew her hand and discreetly rolled her eyes as the man continued, "...those are the foot soldiers, my dear, with their muskets and cannon. Well, those muskets and cannon mowed down the rebels, those fools and their pikes, after which we gallant horsemen galloped in to cut down the survivors.

Pikes, for God's sake! Children with sharp sticks. As long as we keep guns out of the hands of the peasants, we shall rule this island as God intended!"

With a look of disgust Ensign Keane turned away from the drunkard and said, "I beg your pardon, please, Lieutenant Lockwood, but I understand that you were involved in the suppression of the Rebellion?"

More people dropped their conversation to listen. James nodded and said, "I was, sir, when I was an ensign, about your age. Nowadays people laugh about the rebels and their pikes, but I can tell you that the rebels showed amazing levels of courage, charging formed troops, and in many cases closing with them. There were instances when yeomanry and militia, even with their muskets and cannon, were overwhelmed by men with nothing more than pikes, pitchforks, and scythes. Our victories were often narrowly won, and then only with regular troops. I would not care to face such men again."

"Particularly if there was shooting involved," said his brother John *sotto voce* from behind his wine glass, drawing a titter from his friends.

Keane, intrigued, asked, "Pray, Lieutenant, where were you engaged with the rebels?"

James waved his hand and said dismissively, "I was with the Westmeaths down in Cork, a mere skirmish."

Brigid flared and said boldly, "My husband is being modest. He was at the Battle of Shannonvale, a key action that held Munster for the King. He was in the worst of the fighting, played a key role in the victory, and was mentioned in dispatches by Lord Cornwallis himself."

The Keanes flushed in admiration, a few smiling diners uttered their congratulations, and some of the gentleman raised a glass and said, "A glass of wine with you, sir."

Old man Lockwood, annoyed, said, "Yes, yes, we all did our part." He then got an unpleasant look on his face, and looking around the table he burst out, "What the deuce? Why is the dessert wine not brought in?"

He harshly rang the bell, but no one came.

"Damned people... incompetent fools.... John, you are better at thrashing the servants than young James. Pray go to the kitchens and remind them of their duties. I shall dismiss the lot of 'em, and they may go whistle for their wages, the blackguards."

In a moment John returned with a puzzled look on his face. "I say, Father, the servants have all gone. There is not a soul back there, and they have left the back door wide open."

For an instant the entire table sat puzzled, until James leapt to his feet and in a booming voice ordered, "John, get back to the kitchen and bolt that door! I shall bolt the front; Keane, the tower door. Quickly, now!"

From the head of the table the elder Lockwood shrilly raged, "James, you will not order people about in my house! By God, the nerve, sir! The nerve!"

But then a sudden fusillade of shots was fired from the low wall in front of the house. One musket ball shattered a pane of glass and buried itself in a wall. A second struck Gruffydd, who fell face first onto the table in a spray of blood. An instant later a third ball struck old man Lockwood in the arm as the party dissolved into screams and mad panic.

Chapter Five

One older woman, a Mrs. Blair, drenched in Gruffydd's blood, stood ashen and wide-eyed, frozen in horror until her husband pulled her violently under the table. As he ran to secure the doors James threw a candelabra to the floor and called down the table, "Stay down, and get those damned lights out!" Mrs. Keane kept her wits and extinguished the candelabra at one end of the table, and Cissy leapt from her chair to dash out the candles that lined the serving tables.

The candles were extinguished, but the fireplace at the end of the room roared on. As James returned, he passed the windows in a half-crouch and calmly urged, "Quiet now, quiet!" Most of the screaming and yelling subsided as James moved to the head of the table. He found Brigid at his father's side, looking frightened but resolutely tending to the old man's shattered arm.

James was wracked by a sudden fit of coughing, but shaking it off he went to peer out the windows. There was only a half moon, but he could make out twenty or more shadowy figures lining the crumbling bawn.

A voice boomed from the wall. "Send out Gruffydd and old man Lockwood, and no one else need be hurt!"

James leaned toward one of the broken panes and called out, "They are both dead!"

Shouts of joy came from the darkness, but the strong voice called again, "Bring them out then, and show us!"

James had been around Irish soldiers for most of his adult life, and had picked up an expression appropriate to the occasion. "*Téigh trasna ort féin!*" he yelled in a defiant voice, drawing a chorus of insults and several more wild shots in response. In the half-light of the fireplace those near James could see a wild gleam in his eyes.

Mary clung to Cissy and hysterically cried, "Mr. Gruffydd… is dead! Right in front of me! Who are those men? Who would do such things?"

Cissy gave her sister a quick, hard shake and harshly said, "Do you not see? It looks as if Grandfather's tenants have had enough." Seeing some sense return to Mary's face Cissy went on, "But do not worry, Father will see us through. Now, to work. He desires the ladies to retire upstairs. You will help Mama with Grandfather, and I shall gather the others."

Cissy quickly went to Mrs. Blair, who sat on the floor by her chair, nearly comatose. Cissy wet the corner of a napkin, gently wiped Gruffydd's spattered blood from the woman's face, and said, "That was very unpleasant, I know, ma'am. Shall we get you upstairs and find you a clean gown? Yes, come along, now." She urged the women along, at one point having to say, "Mrs. Macy, while I feel it prudent of you to stay low, I do not believe that you need crawl." Several of the women tearfully embraced their husbands and sons before going upstairs.

Brigid stopped Cissy at the bottom of the stairs and said quietly in Irish, "By God, this is terrible, terrible."

Cissy hissed, "Sure, the old man's madness may have killed us all."

Brigid was startled by the venom in Cissy's voice, and paused to look at her daughter for a moment before putting a hand on Cissy's arm and gently saying, "We shall put our faith in God, and your father. See the ladies settled upstairs as well as you can, *a grah*. I shall stay near your father for a bit."

James gathered the men near the massive front door and looked them over; Keane and a tough looking man named Thorn were steady, but the rest of them looked as if they might break at any moment. Muir was so far gone as to spout, "I believe that I shall retire upstairs and place myself at the side of my dear father in law, to tend his wound and defend him to the last extreme against these vile peasants."

In a calm voice James replied, "Muir, there are only eight men left to defend the house, and we must entrust my father's care to the ladies." Muir continued to edge toward the stairs until Keane put a hand on his shoulder and steered him back to the group. James gave Keane a subtle nod, then addressed the frightened men. "Gentlemen, when we bolted the doors in their faces, it seems as if we ruined their plans. They are doubtless now deciding whether or no to try the house. I believe we have a few minutes to gather ourselves. Those people outside are not professionals, but I saw at least twenty of them, and I wager there are as many again in the stable yard. Still, the odds are even, as this house was built to be defended, even if they are better armed than we."

James's brother barked an odd laugh and said with a note of panic in his voice, "James! You are much mistaken! We have my coachman's blunderbuss, and the two pistols I always keep in my valise. And eight, no, ten, fowling pieces, and three rifles. A mountain of shot, and a twenty pound keg of the finest powder. We might rival your company in firepower, little brother."

James shook his head in disbelief and said, "Do you not realize, John, that those weapons were with the luggage, out in the coach house? They now belong to those fellows outside. Likely those were the weapons that were just fired at us."

John went pale as the truth of their situation went home, but James went on in a more reassuring tone, "Not to worry, John. At least ten shots were fired in that volley, but only two went home. A couple of those fellows know their business, but no more, I think."

John remained pale, and most of the others looked very grim. Businesslike, James went on, "Ensign Keane and I have our swords, and we have those pikes that hang on the wall in the tower. Does father still keep that gun cabinet up in his room?"

It took John a moment to shakily reply, "We keep no firearms, powder, or shot in the house, as father was sure that the servants would steal them. No, we brought all our arms with us from Dublin."

James looked each of the frightened men in the eye and said, "Not an ideal situation, but I have seen much worse, gentlemen." Getting a few tenuous nods in reply, he went on, "Now, to work. Ensign Keane, there is a stout door into the kitchen, and three small windows at the rear of the house. Take two men and post yourself there, please. You will find those pikes in the tower useful."

There was no fear in Keane's slender young face, only fierce excitement. If James had his way he would have taken time to counsel the youngster, but there was no time. He could only nod as the boy tapped the shoulders of an aging landowner and his son, and trotted off in search of weapons.

Even in the weak light from the distant fireplace James could see Muir's hands shaking. "Muir, I wonder if you might post yourself at the tower door, please? It would take an elephant to get through that great old thing, but do sing out if you hear anything, won't you?"

Muir did not stir. James gave him a quick grin and said, "You know, I remember now, there is a murder hole above that door; John and I used it to dump cold water on Mary back in our misspent youth. I wonder, Muir, if you would go over to see if it is still there?"

Muir said nothing, but being given a mundane task prompted a more human expression to cross his face. He nodded nervously and moved off, carrying a candle back into the gloomy rooms at the far end of the house. James then turned to the rest of his command: John, Thorn and the ashen drunkard, the aging Blair. In a commanding voice James said, "Gentlemen, we four shall defend the front of the house. May I ask, please, that you pull these curtains down, and break all that glass out? And you will knock all the broken glass out into the garden, please; if any of those fellows outside are barefoot they might soon regret it."

James looked outside. All was quiet. He then remembered the old rapier that hung above the massive fireplace. He gave his pale brother a grin and said, "John, do you recall your lessons from the *salle d'armes*?" Striding over to the fireplace James found the sword tarnished and dusty, but as he pulled it down he thought it looked well made. He ran a thumb across its edge and muttered, "Dull as a vicar." He waved it about, then tested its strength by thrusting its point into the stonework. With a grim smile he said, "Well, here's a surprise; what a fine old blade this is. No pike for you, brother." Brigid appeared from the shadows at the base of the stairs and ran to the back of the house, returning with a damp towel and the kitchen's whetstone. James smiled and said, "You are a true treasure, my love." He sat on the floor by the fire, and after a few minutes of work he could make out the name "Tomas Aiala" etched into the blade. He tested the now-gleaming edge, tossed the sword to John, and said, "It is not Tower of London work, but it shall do." Brigid stood watching from the shadows, and despite the knot of fear in her chest she watched her husband jump to his feet like an agile boy. John made a few mock thrusts and parries, and James said in a satisfied tone, "Three swordsmen, now. We may just make a fight of it yet."

A tense half-hour passed; there were times James could hear shouted commands outside, and some arguing in response. James moved from room to room, giving direction and encouragement as the men posted at the doors and windows of Leamaneh settled into a grim determination. Their lives, and those of their wives, mothers, and daughters upstairs were at stake, and they had come to realize what was expected of them.

They waited, every man on edge. Thorn drank steadily with a fierce look on his face. When Blair could no longer stand the tension he blurted out, "What are they waiting for? Why do they not come?"

James came to stand with John by a front window, and peering into the darkness John said, "Can it be? It looks as if the mob has shot its courage, and gone home."

"Oh, they are still there, brother," said James, not unkindly. "Look how those shadows by the gate shift. See? There.... yes, they are still out there." In a low, instructional tone, he went on, "And they are no mob. They cover every side of the house, and are well posted to take advantage of available cover. They have some organization, and a leader who knows his business. But, still, they are not soldiers. They do not blindly follow orders, and some, perhaps most, of them will be hesitant to kill. It takes time and training to teach a man to kill without flinching. If they make an attempt on the house we must pick out the ones who look most willing, and put them down. That should make the others, the decent men, falter. We are done for, else."

In the low light of the fire Thorn said, "Lieutenant Lockwood, my family has lived here for generations, and I am certain to know some of those men outside. Hunger and evictions have rendered them desperate. I was thinking that if I might address them, to convince them that this is madness—"

Flames suddenly blazed beyond the bawn, and a number of men carrying torches and pikes dashed toward the front windows. In a cool voice James said, "Stand to, gentlemen." He kept to the edge of his window, but he saw John and the others needlessly exposing themselves.

It all happened very quickly. James called to the others, to have them keep down. But at a shouted command from the darkness the attackers in the garden dropped to the ground, their torches lighting the whole front of the house. A well-directed volley was fired from the wall at the exposed defenders. For an instant James had a cool, professional thought, "That was neatly done." Much of the fire went wild, but Thorn fell, clutching his bleeding face.

Discipline dissolved. John threw himself to the floor and froze; Blair dropped his pike and ran to help Thorn. Muir ran from the tower calling, "We are lost!" and bolted up the stairs, crashing into a number of women who were half-way down, a frantic handful who had broken past Brigid and were screaming for their husbands and sons.

Thorn staggered to his feet, blood streaming from his wound, and took up his pike. James grabbed John and Blair, throwing them back to their posts, but then the two men who had been posted to the back of the house with Keane came running into the hall, clearly terrified, calling to the women on the stairs that they were not hurt.

James pointed at them in fury and screamed in a voice that brought blood to his throat, "You men! Back to your posts!" But then a huge crash came from the back of the house, followed by two shots, and a roar of triumph from a dozen voices.

James ran toward the back of the house, roaring "To me!" but no one followed. Flickering torch light came from the kitchen doors, illuminating Ensign Keane, bleeding from a shoulder wound, falling back, his sword flashing, as a pack of cheering men poured into the hallway after him.

Before James could reach them, a huge man with a naval cutlass skillfully parried a lunge from Keane and his riposte caught Keane off balance. In an instant James noted that the man was missing most of his teeth and his tattooed arms were knotted with muscle, and in the next instant the rebel thrust the cutlass deep into Keane's stomach. As Keane collapsed gasping to the stone floor, the giant raised his cutlass and brutally swung it down, nearly taking the boy's head off.

James was on him an instant later, burying his long blade in the rebel's throat. The hall was filled with spraying blood, flickering light, and cries of effort and pain in a brutal, close quarters fight as the pack of men drove down on James. He fell back slowly, deliberately conceding ground, using the length of his arm and of his blade to advantage, the pikes of the rebels darting out at him from the mass of humanity.

For a moment James found his brother beside him, but when a pike grazed his arm John screamed in pain, dropped his sword, and fled up the stairs. James noted it, but in a cold, unemotional manner. The same pikeman now lunged at him. James deflected the point with a snap of his wrist, and his riposte thrust his point deep into the man's chest. A pistol shot flashed from the mass of rebels, the ball plowing a groove in James's scalp. He staggered, and a pike thrust caught him in the thigh. He nearly fell, and the encouraged rebels surged forward in fury. But then two pistol shots came from above. As the two leading rebels dropped to the floor James looked up to see Brigid and Cissy on the stairs, holding smoking pistols with determined fear in their eyes.

In a desperate rage James rose and threw himself roaring onto the rebels, blindly thrusting into the wall of men. They fell back, leaving their leaders dead and wounded on the floor. James lunged over and over, driving the rebels back. But then he tripped over Keane's body and a swinging arm brought a pistol butt down on his head. As the darkness folded around him he saw Thorn and the others running to his aid with pikes leveled.

Chapter Six

Dr. Kelly poked James's leg and muttered, "You heal like a young dog."

James grimaced and said, "I model myself after young dogs at every opportunity."

Kelly sniffed and unceremoniously examined James's head, his strong fingers probing the wounds. "The grazing pistol ball and this blow to the head caused no lasting damage, though I am sure they gave you the urge to lie down and have a good bleed. You must have looked rather a sight."

"Yes, when I regained my wits Brigid and the girls were rather upset. But a Dr. Hurt—a delightful name for a surgeon, don't you think?—came up from Lisdoonvarna to tend the wounded, and I was ready to travel in no time."

"I have read the accounts in the paper, but pray, what was the final butcher's bill?"

"In the house four of us were hurt, and good Ensign Keane was killed. A fine young officer; his wife, the sweetest child, is quite shattered." James paused for a long moment and rubbed the side of his head. "Outside, four dead and five badly wounded. The yeomen who rode down from Galway found those five the next day. It turned ugly as quickly as you'd think.

The magistrate gave the wounded men a cursory look, and they were all five strung up without ceremony. Their families were turned out and their cabins were burned, and when the dead were identified their families were driven out as well. As we were leaving, the yeomen were kicking down every door on the estate, searching for weapons and brutalizing the people, looking for anyone else who was there that night. There never was a better method for breeding more rebels. I can't tell you how glad we were to get out of that God damned place."

Kelly began to pack up his case and said, "Well-bred gentlemen do not idly take the Lord's name in vain."

"The Lord can come down here and discuss it whenever He pleases. I have a few other questions for Him, as well. What a fellow."

Kelly gave him a fleeting half grin and said, "I shall sadly report to Mrs. Lockwood that you are returned to your normal senses."

"And I am fit to return to my battalion?

"Another month or so, I think, will see your leg and head sufficiently healed for sea travel." As he snapped his case closed Kelly added, "But your breathing is growing worse, is it not?"

"A bit, I think."

"More than a bit, James. Your colour is poor, and while these new wounds heal well I detect a pronounced weakness in you. All this dashing about in Clare was not good for you. And yet you are determined to return to active service?" Kelly looked steadily at James, but he did not flinch. Kelly gave a quick, significant nod, and went down the creaking stairs of Fáibhile Cottage to report to Brigid and Mrs. Cashman.

As he passed the kitchen door he found the five children drawn up there, all of whom had remarkably similar looks of concern on their faces. As a scientific man he briefly wondered if it was a physical inheritance or something as common as growing up together that gave them such similarity. He had long considered them children of the generic sort, and he had little use for children. But he reconsidered the older girls, and saw the elder becoming a beautiful young woman. The second, he had no memory for names, a slender girl, lacked her sister's overt beauty but she had a spark about her that a perceptive young man might find intriguing, perhaps enchanting.

Pushing aside his reflections, he gave them a gruff nod of confirmation, upon which all five took up similar looks of relief and proceeded upstairs bearing soup, tea, biscuits, the as-yet unfinished *Pride and Prejudice*, and Lucy's gift, a shining piece of quartz she had found in Mr. O'Leary's pasture.

Brigid came upstairs and sat by her husband's bedside. She had earlier been rather cross with him, when James had spoken in eager terms of his return to his battalion.

In a conciliatory tone she said, "*Mo cuisle*, what with all the excitement of our return home, I have quite ignored the mail until this morning. These two arrived for you while we were at Leamaneh, and this third one came this morning. I do hope they carry good news."

She gave him a quick kiss, and with a sly smile she reached across and took up his book. James held up a finger in protest, but Brigid said, "Oh, pooh, sir. You have your letters, and might spare your book for a few minutes. I am so fond of Lizzie." She frowned her comical frown and said, "No woman should emulate Mrs. Bennet—she is such a ninny—but I wonder if I have done enough to see my daughters married?"

She crawled into bed beside her warm husband, and as she returned to Chapter Three James opened the first of his letters. With her so close by, he made a conscious effort to breathe as quietly as possible.

Gibraltar 14 February 1818

James,

A quick note, as most of us are off to the King's Arms to bid Blakeley adieu. I assume that he has already written to inform you, but he has inherited a few coins upon his Uncle's recent demise and is selling out to return to the life of a country gentleman. He should have no trouble finding an eligible wife; a retired lieutenant and grizzled veteran of the Waterloo Campaign, bearing a wound of honour, all by the age of <u>twenty</u>. Such a puppy; one can only shake one's head. He speaks of you often, in the most affectionate terms. You will forgive me a brief moment of sober reflection to note that you did much in shaping that boy into quite a likeable young fellow.

Lastly, I am in receipt of your letter of 30th June, and am exceptionally pleased to hear that you are returning to us. I trust that Brigid and the children are not unhappy in losing you once again to your profession; doubtless they are content, consigned to the life of a soldier's family in a quiet Irish town. Pray give them all my dearest love.

I remain Your Most Devoted Friend,
Thomas Mainwaring

James grinned, fondly remembering Tom and the rest of his friends. He turned to Brigid, intent on conveying Tom's regards from Gibraltar, but when he saw her engrossed in her reading he thought better of it, and so tore into the second cover.

The Lockwoods of Clonakilty

My Dearest Friend and Comrade, Lieutenant James Lockwood,

My pen takes delight in your name, James, mon ami! Time being what she is, we have yet to fulfill our vows to visit one another after the final overthrow of the evil tyrant Bonaparte.

But Fate is suddenly kind! I am called to London by my family's man of business. With the coming of Peace our wine is now very popular amongst the English! Business prospers!

For me to travel to London without making a visit to your home in Ireland would be a most pitiable shame. Thus, I trust it not inconvenient to call upon you in Clonakilty in early October. I hope then to have the honour of making the acquaintance of your dear, dear, family, and to allow me the pleasure of introducing to them my son, Guillaume, who shall accompany me in my travels.

I shall bring a cask of my Terrasses du Larzac; I shall beg you to tell me of Waterloo! Such glory, mon frère, such glory!

To our Immortal Friendship and Imperishable Honour,
Jean Alexandre Dumon
Colonel in the Service of His Most Catholic Majesty,
retired

James laughed aloud, but then coughed painfully. Brigid turned to him, looking anxious, but James only laughed again and said, "Dear old Dumon is coming to visit!"

"Dumon? I don't recall you having mentioned...."

"Come, my dear. My royalist friend, the French captain who befriended me while the battalion was in Ghent, just before Waterloo? You remember, certainly, the fellow who sold me Mémoire. Such a charming horse; I hope that stuffy little Guards officer is treating her well."

"Oh, of course. I am still so sorry that you had to sell dear Mémoire. But will your friend arrive before you leave? Perhaps you shall be forced to delay your departure?"

She asked with such hope that James said, "Perhaps, my dear, perhaps." He turned back to the letter and added, "He is bringing his son. Perhaps he and our boys shall be friends."

James read the letter aloud, then Tom's as well. Brigid smiled with only a hint of sadness and said, "Tom is such a good friend to you. If I must lose you for a while, I am glad that I lose you to him." They were silent together for a time, each with their own thoughts, until Brigid opened her book, and James reached for his third letter.

My Dear Lieutenant James Lockwood,

I am directed by your father, John Lockwood, Sr., to increase the allocation due you monthly from the Lockwood family estates to £25.0.0.

Pursuant to this increase, your father requests, in the greatest confidence, only that you are not overly conversant regarding some of the incidents manifest at the family holdings in Clare during the recent rebel activity, in particular the actions of certain family members, which might cause discomfiture to the family, were they discussed at length, in the light of public scrutiny.

Lastly, I may mention that your father has decided not to repair the damages done to Leamaneh during the attack and subsequent vandalism. He will not visit again.

I remain your Humble Servant,
George Bettany

Beaming, James handed the letter to Brigid and said, "An extra ten pounds a month! All because that old fool was afraid I would blather on about Leamaneh. Still, that and my pay should see us through nicely. Tomorrow morning I shall march you down to Mrs. Daugherty's shop and we shall buy that pretty jacket you tried on last week. Three letters, all three such good news! A great day indeed."

Brigid scanned the letter and quietly said, "And so the great old house will fall into ruin, and the ghost of Maire Rua shall wander its halls undisturbed. God please, poor Keane's spirit shall not be trapped there with her. I shall pray a Rosary for him at St. Brigid's, sure." Brigid crossed herself and leaned over to kiss her husband's cheek. She would not tell him of the fourth letter that the Postman had carried. She had recognized the hand, and decided that James had been through enough. Late that night she pulled the fourth letter from her bag and slipped into the drawing room, where she pulled the loose board from the back of the bookcase and slid the unopened letter into the narrow little space that held dozens of other letters from Captain Charles Barr.

Cissy crossed herself and said through the wicker screen of the confessional. "Bless me, Father, for I have sinned. It has been two weeks since my last confession."

"Tell me of your sins, child."

She paused a breath before saying with a tone of sudden realization, "I have killed a man."

Father McGlynn said in an officious tone, "My child, your mother has come to me to confess of the same sin. The attack on Leamaneh is the talk of the country; there is no sin in protecting those you love. Say ten Acts of Contrition to help you recognize sin in daily actions, words and omissions." The Father was silent for a moment, but then in a much quieter voice he said in Irish, "But there are those who say that someone who defends the house of the most despised landlord in the West is no friend to the poor, and thus no friend to those who wish to overthrow their oppressors."

Cissy flared and replied in Irish, "Those who would say such thing are fools. It is a true friend of the oppressed I am, but no friend am I of those who murder in the dark. Who could condone such madness?"

The priest whispered harshly, "Sure, it was wrong they were, but they were driven to it, driven, they had no choice! And word has come down from Clare that your mother had been warned of the action, and two pistols left for your protection!"

In a voice that would have surprised anyone in her family, Cissy hissed, "Father, I will hear no word spoken against my mother!" Settling into a strong steady tone she continued, "As much as she loves the people, she shall always be loyal to my father before all else. And you call it an 'action', do you, neat and tidy, when it was blood and horror in the darkness! We used those pistols, sure, and we used them to save my father's life, and likely our own, in my grandfather's house! Is this what you would have me join, Father, men with murder, not justice, in their hearts? I will have no part of this...."

"Yes, yes," the priest said, frustrated. "It was done badly, I concede to you. But you see, then, why it is that I wish you join the organization? The violence can run wild if there is no organization, no leadership, no plan. It is the organization we need; the United men are long broken, while the Defenders and White Boys are scattered bands with great heart and little head. But we are rebuilding, Cissy. With God's help and those of noble heart, those such as yourself, we shall build an organization which shall at last drive the English away and give hope to the poor. Do not doubt, Cissy Lockwood, that the day is coming when you shall be forced to declare your true loyalty."

Cissy held her tongue. McGlynn sat up straight, straightened his cassock, and, reverting to English and his officious tone he said, "Beware the sin of pride. Your sins are forgiven. Go in peace."

The carriage clattered up to Fáibhile Cottage, and before it came to a full stop Colonel Jean Alexandre Dumon bounded from its door. The Lockwoods were drawn up in the garden with a military precision which James found appropriate, but which the other members of the household found tiresome. Not standing upon ceremony, Dumon strode up to James, heartily embraced him, and kissed him on both cheeks.

"My dear, dear, comrade," said Dumon with tears in his eyes.

"My God, Jean. It is so good to see you again. Welcome, old friend."

Propriety reasserted itself as James introduced his family with the necessary bows and curtsies, and Dumon introduced his son. Whereas the elder Dumon was balding, tall and heavy, his son was a slender young man of about twenty years, moderate height, a fair complexion, a winning smile, and masses of dark, wavy hair. James could see that Mary and Cissy were immediately charmed by the young Guillaume Louis Antoine Dumon; even Lucy looked at the boy with something like rapture. James was thus prepared to dislike the young man, perhaps even dislike him very much.

Guillaume Dumon, however, was such a soft-spoken, modest young fellow that James soon found him as likable as his gregarious father. The Lockwoods and Dumons blended perfectly, spending that week, and then a second, seeing the sights and delighting in one another's company. The Dumons soon learned the secret of visiting Ireland without going mad, in that they took advantage of the good days, did not mind a bit of drizzle, and were wholly content in spending rainy days indoors with good friends, long naps, hearty food, and excellent refreshment.

One result of those days together was an obvious and growing bond between Guillaume and Mary. While no one forced the matter, both families certainly allowed it, and the young couple was soon missing from the rest of the party whenever the weather allowed a walk into town or into the fields above.

The Dumons delayed their departure as long as possible, but the day arrived. That morning the Lockwoods left home early to breakfast with Jean and Guillaume at the Shannon Arms. The boys staged foot races down McCurtain's Hill with Lucy, races which Lucy won on a consistent basis, outcomes sufficiently unlikely to prompt Lucy to cry, "Oh, Joseph and Richard, you are not trying! I shall spank your bottoms like a Kerry *bodhrán* if you do not try your hardest! It is not fun to win if you do not try!"

The teary-eyed Mary walked on her father's arm, James offering, "Things shall work out, one day, I am sure, my dear." It was not especially sage advice, but it was his best, and Mary took some comfort in her father's assurances.

Cissy walked with her mother. After some opening small talk, Brigid finally found the moment to ask, "Cissy, I trust I do not ask you to break a confidence, but do you think that Mary and Guillaume have… come to an understanding?"

Cissy did not hesitate to share. "They are very near, I think, Mama. Guillaume desires to become a partner in his father's endeavors before he marries, though he may speak to Papa before they leave us. Just think! Mary might be married, and living in the south of France. It makes me very happy, and very sad."

The lengthy breakfast led to lengthy conversation, so it was just as well the carriage to carry the Dumons to Dublin was tardy. The children wandered off to look in shop windows, while Mary and Guillaume left for a walk as their fathers traded a significant look.

The eventual arrival of the carriage recalled everyone to their duty. The young couple returned to the inn arm in arm, looking profoundly happy, and Guillaume formally requested a few minutes of Lieutenant Lockwood's time. Mary and Cissy sat together by the fire tearfully whispering in excited voices, while Brigid took Jean's arm as they strolled out onto Western Road.

"I think, Monsieur Colonel," Brigid said wistfully, "that we may receive some very welcome news. It shall be most welcome, especially as James leaves us as well, all too soon."

"Indeed, Madame Lockwood, indeed. And Madame Dumon, my Pauline, will be most pleased as well, I assure you, as she is a woman of great heart." Jean smiled down at Brigid and added, "I have never possessed a sister, and I look very much forward to seeing you as such." But then he grew more serious. "I worry, though, about my dear brother James. He is so thin, now, I think? And his colour quite concerns me. *Oui*, my dear Brigid—I honour myself by using your Christian name, see what a *coquin* I am—I am anxious with our friend. Gibraltar—it is charming, I think, how James calls it "Gib"—is not France, but by sea it is not really so far from Marseilles, is it? And our wine sells well there, and business being it she is, I shall call there when I can. It shall be such an enjoyment—I shall act as your agent and report his progress. You need not worry, *chérie*. He shall have friends there, and so shall you."

Chapter Seven

Another day, like every other day in God's own universe, relentlessly approached. Lieutenant Lockwood was to leave for Gibraltar.

The family was determined to make a brave face of it, while Mrs. Cashman outdid herself preparing a suitable farewell dinner. The best that Clonakilty could offer, filtered by what the Lockwood budget could afford, was supplemented by the gift of a fine salmon from the Cashman family, venison from the Butlers, and a plump goose from the Shannon Arms. In the kitchen Mrs. Cashman was seconded by Mrs. Keefe, on loan from the Butlers, and Liam O'Flynn from the Shannon Arms who served as a resplendent, if chatty, footman.

The dining room of Fáibhile Cottage was small and inconvenient, but when illuminated by an extravagant number of candles it took on the air of a great hall. As dinner wound down, James tapped his glass with a spoon and announced from his seat, "I must beg everyone's pardon, but I need to address a few issues. Please understand that this is difficult for me, but I have talked this through with your Mother, and I, we, have decided that I need to discuss certain matters with you children before I return to my regiment."

The family went silent, as did the voices in the kitchen. "My father," said James, "never discussed his life with his children and, looking back, I think that was a serious error. Your Uncle John, your Aunt Mary and I grew up... oh, how can I say it... lost, I suppose... no knowledge of how the world could be... should be... and we all grew up so different from one another, as you have perhaps discerned on your own."

Brigid and the children were all very quiet, perhaps too quiet for James's comfort, as he now felt the full glare of their expectant faces. "Well. Two topics, I think. The first is my return to my regiment. Please know I am leaving you only because I must." The pressure of openly addressing an issue that lay so close to his soul was even more difficult than he had imagined, and for a moment his lungs nearly closed up. He took a sip of wine; his first impulse was to drink it all quickly, but he was determined not to be drunk.

"I must return to the regiment if I am ever to gain my captaincy. As the girls and I discussed the other day, I do miss my friends in the battalion, but beyond I feel I owe my men a great deal, a debt I have yet to repay. I have examined my motivations at some length, and believe I can honestly say I am not driven by vanity or ambition." A pause, as the next words would burn in his throat. "But it is only with a captain's pay that I can hope to support my family, you dear people. I cannot continue to rely on my father's whims to support us indefinitely. My father, my brother, my sister, and I all essentially differ on many subjects, the most important of which," his throat began to close, which made him angry, and he could not look up at Brigid's tear-filled eyes, still he forced himself to go on, "is the choice to be happy in one's life, and not always be bound by the whims of society. I may be on a fool's errand, but if I could get that captaincy I can perhaps be free not just of my reliance on my father's money, but of his, of all of their, hints and suggestions and interference in my life. Our lives."

James was nearly angry, determined as not to make a fool of himself in front of his wife and children. But their whole-hearted support buoyed him, as Brigid and the girls wept with smiles on their faces (a condition that James always had had trouble understanding, until that day) and the boys alternated between somber maturity and the blinking faces of boys who loved their father.

Embarrassed, James tossed down the rest of his wine without thinking, but did not pour another. "Well. That was... difficult, and I thank you all for your... very kind support. Now, let us forge ahead. Yes, quite. Topic the second. Again, a very difficult topic for your father to address, but I feel I must do so before I leave." He wished now he had refilled his glass, as he twirled the empty glass in his hands.

"Particularly as you boys, you young gentlemen," he added with pride in his voice, a pride that made the boys swell, "are considering a career in the army, I need to explain some of the details of my past service. The Anglican faith does not hold to confession *per se*, but it would be of some relief, I think, if I might unburden myself regarding an incident from the Rebellion. I have never considered myself a bad man, though I don't feel I can claim to have been an especially good one." His family drew breath as if to argue, but James held up a hand and said, "Now, now, recall, please, that I have the floor."

James coughed a bit, but his colour was so good that Brigid gave him a proud, open, if nervous smile. He continued, "You all know of the fighting up at Shannonvale in the '98. It was no battle, really, just a short, vicious little skirmish." He rubbed his temple said, "My first real fight, when I was all of eighteen years old. I must confess I first killed men there, never anything to be proud of. At Shannonvale one of the men I killed was your mother's cousin."

The shocked faces of his children told James they understood the impact of his confession. "I did not single him out, of course. In that confused knot of pushing, swinging men there he was; he lunged at me, the poor little fool, a brave, clumsy stroke. I parried, and my riposte killed him. Jesus." He found that Brigid was holding his hand. "So you might understand why your mother's family is so very distant from us. Your Aunt Anne has a great heart, but you know now why most of your mother's family will have little to do with us. It is not simply because of my birth and faith, but because Fergal O'Brian was killed at Shannonvale, and I was the man who killed him."

James sat up straight, cleared his voice, and in a stronger tone said, "You all know that my family is unhappy with me, for how I have managed my life, especially in that I broke some etched-in-stone rule and married for love, outside their notions of class and birth and faith. And you now know why your mother's family is so distant. Those are the burdens this family carries; so much separates us from the rest of the world. As I leave, I urge you to cling to one other. You cannot rely on much else."

The Café Marengo was the least elegant café in Boulogne, but the wine was cheap and none of the staff was of a particularly inquisitive nature. It was there that Captain Charles Barr, half pay, 24th Foot, sat with remarkable ease, sipping his coffee. The ease with which Barr drank his coffee was remarkable in that, just hours before, he had killed a woman in an alley behind the Rue du Havre.

While he was typically brutal with whores, he had only killed once before, the Dublin girl who had given him syphilis on Montgomery Street some twenty years earlier. Doubtless he had since killed many others, indirectly. If he thought about it at all, he took a subtle pleasure in passing on the tortures of syphilis.

He used whores at every opportunity. He despised them, but he required them. It was only if they insulted him that would he hurt them. He could bear their drunken laughter, the coarseness of their character, the crudeness of their touch, but he would bear no slander of his honour. He considered himself first and foremost a gentleman.

Barr's French was excellent; the Boulogne whore had thought him a Frenchman. He used her in a gloomy alley, and when he finished he had pushed her away and thrown a single franc at her feet. She screamed that what she had done for him was worth a Louis D'or on the Grande Rue, that he was a bastard. Cursing him, she followed him from the alley into the dimly lit street. In the flickering lamp light he saw her face clearly for the first time and staggered, his white with shock.

She was the very image of Brigid O'Brian Lockwood.

She may have lacked O'Brian's flawless complexion, but the shape of her face, the flashing eyes, the rolls of chestnut hair, even the manner in which she carried herself made his heart soar. Barr said nothing, but he handed her every coin in his purse, and shakily giving her his arm he gently led her back into their alley.

In the alley he found a spot where a narrow beam of light from the street eased the darkness, and there he studied her, tenderly kissed her, and gently holding her he croaked protestations of love. The whore had been pleased by the money but began to struggle as he held her, confused by his switch to English and his increasingly irrational tone. Soon she began to struggle wildly, and still he held her, in an increasingly fierce grip. She clawed his face; she was a woman who had walked the streets of Boulogne for some years and was no easy prey, but he was a man who had abused women for most of his adult life. The syphilis had taken some of his strength, but his madness gave him an intensity of purpose that rendered him immune to her struggles.

He back-handed her across the alley, then grinning madly he began to systematically beat her. When she lay unconscious and bleeding in the filthy alley he tried to take her again, but was unable. So he instead cut her throat, her blood spraying into his face as he lay atop her.

He stayed and held her for a dreamy, immeasurable time, until the first streaks of dawn lit the sky above. He stirred and staggered uncaring toward his hotel, his face a mask of dried blood and madness. His luck held again and he passed no one in the street.

He rested, washed, and slowly recovered. The café was his morning routine and he kept to it, though his mind was spinning at a fantastic rate, charged with new life and vitality. He sat and gleefully reconsidered his affairs. He did not much care for Boulogne, but it was convenient to his purposes. Here his five shillings a day saw him through with moderate comfort. Paris had far too many British officers, on duty or on holiday. In Boulogne he could be Major Barr and no one contradicted him. Most importantly, no one there was acquainted with the fact that he had been court martialed and dismissed the service.

He found his reinstatement to the half-pay list of the 24th Foot comical; the army had taken pity on him, a wounded veteran of Waterloo. He had not bothered to explain to the army surgeons that the wound to his thigh was not delivered by a Frenchman, but by that pretentious little bastard Blakeley in an impromptu duel well behind the lines. It was Blakeley who had found him going through Lockwood's trunk as the battle raged, stealing what little money the fool had and looking for anything incriminating.

Barr took another sip of his coffee and mused. After he had seen to Lockwood and O'Brian and their miserable whelps he might just turn his attention to Ensign Blakeley.

Beyond his half-pay Barr had little contact with the army. He did, however, receive the occasional letter from Ensign Slattery, the least capable officer in the Inniskilling regiment and one who still fawningly sought Barr's favor. Slattery had recently shared the news that Lockwood was returning to the battalion in Gibraltar. Barr toyed with that information at some length; he was steadily saving some money, and he debated using it to travel to Gibraltar to murder Lockwood, or perhaps to Ireland to do what he pleased with O'Brian. Dear God, what he might do to O'Brian. He reveled in the time he had, and the wondrous options open to him.

In a remote wood far from the nearest road, John Cashman quietly stood with his eyes closed, waiting for a chaffinch to sing. Minutes went by before the little bird flittered into a tree near him, and the instant she began to sing John whirled around and threw a doubled-edged knife, burying the blade into the trunk chosen by the bird.

He walked over and examined his aim; he was an inch or two wide of center, but the height was good. If a man had been his target he would have had a knife in his heart, thrown from thirty feet away. John freed the blade, closed his eyes, and waited for the bird to mark his next target.

No one opposed to government dared carry a musket, pike, or sword in daylight, but any man might carry a knife. Few men could handle one like Catherine Cashman's eldest son. Time passed, the bird sang, and the knife found its mark. As John recovered his blade, he heard someone approaching, noisily crashing through the undergrowth. He listened for a bit, and when he was sure that his visitor was alone he stepped out from behind a tree and called, *"Cia sud thall?"* Who goes there?

An annoyed, breathless voice called back, *"Mise Tadhg."* I am Teague.

The two men approached each other. John returned his knife to his belt and said in Irish, "McGlynn, you should never leave the town. Sure you sound like Donn Cuailnge himself crashing through the woods."

The priest leaned against a tree to catch his breath and said, "It is you yourself choosing these mad places to meet, John Cashman. And you must address me as Father McGlynn, my son, talk we of rebellion or no."

John scoffed and answered, "My only father died an honest fisherman's death years ago, and I have no other, Michael McGlynn. And you might keep in mind that your Pope would excommunicate you in a heartbeat if he knew of you leading your flock to rebellion, even if against the Heretic King."

"Well, yes, there is that, sure," McGlynn said as he sat on a fallen tree. "I have a funeral this afternoon, so we had best tend to business. The Committee has identified Gerald Monyhan as a traitor, and his name is placed upon the Death List."

"Just that simple, eh? You write his name, and he dies. It must be heady stuff, to have such power. I wonder it doesn't drive you mad."

"God guides my hand. And you would not be so glib, my good son, if Monyhan knew your name, and you saw him keeping company with militiamen, and fresh shillings in his pocket. We'll be needing to make an example, so his death will be as public as possible. One of our people in town will tend to him, though if he flees—he has family in Wexford—we may have need of your special talents."

"I joined to help decent poor folk, not to hunt frightened fools."

"You will do as you are told," McGlynn said grimly. "Depending upon the extent of his treason, Monyhan's family may need suffer as well. That is yet to be decided."

They dealt with several other topics, primarily targets that John and his band of Whiteboys might strike. There was no love between the rough rebel and the polished priest, and when their business was finished McGlynn curtly nodded and started to walk off. His steps disturbed a rabbit; when the creature hopped into their clearing John flicked his knife, and in an instant the screaming rabbit was pinned to the ground. With a shocked look on his face McGlynn watched the rabbit struggle, vainly kicking the air.

John strode over and efficiently finished the rabbit. "Meat for supper tonight." As he stuffed the rabbit into his haversack he went on, "It is unpleasant, blood and death, is it not? Keep it in mind, priest. This, a thousand fold, is it what may come of your plans."

McGlynn glared at John and said, "You are a dangerous man, John Cashman. Ah, now, I remember one other matter to discuss. Earlier we were speaking of family. If you have a message for your mother you may safely pass it through the younger of the Lockwood girls, the dark-haired one, Cissy, she is called."

"That wee slip of a girl?" John asked in genuine surprise.

With a small smile of satisfaction the priest said, "Yes, I am working to bring her into the fold. In fact, I think a message or two may be a good test of our new bonds. One day she may prove a valuable asset." Then with a leer the priest added, "You know, the girl, then? You have an interest in her, perhaps?"

"Ach, priest, am I not old enough to be her father? But my own mother loves those people, and that girl in particular, I think."

Half to himself McGlynn went on, "A most valuable asset indeed: impeccable credentials, daughter to an army officer, the granddaughter to a pillar of the Ascendancy, with a most laudable love for the poor. Though I'll need to bring her along slowly, slowly. What she might be some day...."

With a hard look on his face John quietly said, "You and I have chosen our paths, priest. God knows if Ireland shall ever be free, but I wager that neither you nor I shall ever see heaven. But if you have put a noose around that girl's neck you deserve all the fires of hell."

Chapter Eight

Captain Barr strolled the streets of the Quartier Saint-Germain-l'Auxerrois in a new uniform coat, scarlet trimmed with the blue-green facings and silver lace required by the 24th Foot. British officers were common on the streets of Paris, though few wore a uniform of such quality. He had spent every penny remaining to him to have the scarlet coat tailored to perfection, as his new-found profession required an exacting appearance.

His appointment with the Countess of Bessborough was for two that afternoon, and he was prompt to the minute. He was shown up to the spectacular drawing room by an exquisitely formal English butler, where an exquisitely formal maid presented Captain Charles Barr of the 24th Foot to the Countess and her companion, the aged Lady Chelmsford. The Countess was once a renowned beauty, though age and unhappiness had rendered her plain. Lady Chelmsford was ancient, proper, and largely absent.

Barr made his leg, consciously holding it for just a beat longer than courtesy required.

"Will you take tea, Captain Barr?"

"Thank you, no, Your Ladyship, I am determined not to detain you for more than a moment."

"That is just as well, I suppose, as my daughter and her... friend... are to call, and we have some personal matters to address. But do sit, pray."

"You are most kind, Your Ladyship. I would be remiss in not taking the opportunity to thank you in deigning to receive me, Your Ladyship. I am certain that a person of your standing and reputation attracts a great number of admirers no matter how far afield you might travel."

"*Noblesse oblige*, my dear sir, *noblesse oblige*," she said with a wave, but Barr could see that he had flattered her. With the faintest blush in her worn complexion she went on, "Your letter, Captain, captured the attention, I do not exaggerate in saying the sympathies, of both Lady Chelmsford and myself."

Barr smiled and replied, "I confess to find your interest thrilling, Your Ladyship, wholly thrilling."

"You have just recently come to Paris, I think, Captain? I do not recall having seen you in attendance at any of the routs or balls."

"Oh, how I love balls," said Lady Chelmsford, suddenly coming to life.

Barr's face went blank for a beat, but he smoothly went on, "You are most discerning, Your Ladyship. I have just arrived from the coast, intent upon my mission." Barr opted not to mention the beautiful whore he had murdered in Boulogne, or the awkwardly persistent magistrate investigating her death.

"Pray, Captain, do share the details of your honourable cause."

Barr took a deep breath and said, "Pray know, dear ladies, my interests lie only in the welfare of a brother officer and his family. This fellow officer and I were both badly wounded at Waterloo...."

"Waterloo!" cried the countess. "My son, Frederick Ponsonby, was wounded there! I cannot believe that one man could take such abuse, and yet he lives!"

"Noble Ponsonby! He fell not far from where I fell; we have never met, but our wounds mark us brothers!" Barr loathed Ponsonby; another glory-hungry fool who was shot and stabbed a dozen times or more in a mad charge. Barr's wound was in fact nothing more than a cut on the back of his hand from a bit of French shell, a cut which he waved to Major Archibald as an excuse to hastily leave the field. While the Inniskilling were fighting for their lives atop the Mt. St. Jean ridge, Barr had strolled to the rear, wrapped his handkerchief around his hand and wandered off to loot the battalion baggage.

Barr shook his head sadly and said, "Whereas the God of Battles has allowed, in His divine mercy, men such as your son and myself to recover, He has left my noble friend to linger in anguish. My dear brother officer clings to life only by the narrowest of margins, no longer capable of serving King and Country."

"How terribly tragic," muttered the countess with tears in her eyes. But with some concern she went on, "But are you yourself quite recovered, Captain? You seem, perhaps, unwell?"

Barr averted his eyes and with a breaking voice he said, "My sufferings are nothing in comparison to his. He lies bedridden, tended day and night by his devoted family!"

"Oh my," said Lady Chelmsford, who had come to the surface, "he is a man of family, then?"

"A wife and five children, My Lady, a more worthy band I have never seen! A noble family, they would sooner die in anonymity than be the subject of pity, let alone of charity, but my brother officer, their beloved husband and father, is likely to pass to his heavenly reward at any moment, and that honourable family shall be cast penniless onto the streets, adrift and bereft!"

The ladies gasped and clutched their hands, and Barr took a moment to manfully compose himself. "I confess to having exhausted my modest resources in their support, and mortgaged what little property I have, property on which I had banked the security of my own retirement. But my efforts are a handful of sand against the tide of their debt! I am thus determined to raise a subscription for their support. I trust you will understand my decision to keep the recipients of the subscription wholly anonymous; their honour shall remain inviolate." Barr reached into his coat and produced a handful of elegantly written letters. "Pray allow me to offer up these testimonials from a few of those who have already contributed; Generals Lambert and Hill have been most generous." Barr was very familiar with the contents of the letters, as he had written them himself the night before in a dank, filthy attic on the Rue St. Avoye.

"There is no need, no need, my dear Captain!" cried the countess. "We are quite moved by your kindness, and your honourable conduct! Pray, how might we assist this noble family? How I honour them!"

The ladies were most obliging, and they were good enough to write letters of introduction so that Captain Barr might call upon other generous English ladies who were wintering in Paris.

That very afternoon Barr bespoke a suite for a month at Le Meurice on Rue Saint Honore. He dined well every night, and soon acquainted himself with the numerous and experienced Parisian whores. Yet for all their experience, they did not suspect such a stylish, wealthy British officer would carry such a virulent syphilis.

And every night Barr mused on Lockwood and O'Brian, and how he would someday deal with them. He had found the Boulogne whore's murder surprisingly memorable, indeed pleasurable, and now his fantasies grew wholly dark.

17 June, 1818
My Dearest Brigid,

I am arrived in Gibraltar. My journey began badly, as I was forced to wait for days at Gosport for a Gib-bound transport. A peace-time army is so very different from the days when the military's needs came first, at every turn. The voyage south was long but not unpleasant, as the weather was nearly always fine, even if the winds were not always co-operative.

It is such a pleasure to see Tom and the others again, though of course so many of my old friends were lost at Waterloo, or have been promoted out, or retired. Colonel Nelson is much aged, but his reception was most gratifying, and he hosts a welcome dinner for me tonight. More tomorrow.

I put pen to paper here in my new lodgings; such a rat's den you cannot imagine. There are five battalions packed onto this miserable rock, so all of the prime berths are taken. There are no officers' quarters left, so I have taken up residence in a tiny hovel close to the parade ground. The housing allowance is only six dollars a month, so Tom and I are going snacks. Like old times; he is such a good friend to me.

My company is up at Windmill Barracks, and I am pleased that perhaps a quarter of them are my old Waterloo men. Doolan is aged but attentive, as pleased to see me as he is capable. He desires me to forward his very best regards to all there, and to beg that plenty of dung be heaped upon the potato patch before the next planting.

It is so warm and dry here that I am certain to live to be a hundred, preserved like some shriveled bog man. Our surgeon is named Pitcock, a very capable fellow who is mixing me up some thunderous good physic.

Per usum, I enclose notes for the children, in hopes that this letter arrives before the four oldsters leave for school. I know how hard their leaving must be for you, my dear heart, but we must be excited for them as they move ahead with their lives. I think we will both be forced to concede it is good of my father to pay their tuition. The girls will thrive at Malahide (they are certainly wise enough to take my sister and that fool Muir with a grain of salt) and I can only hope that Mary can put aside thoughts of the Dumon boy and be as serious about her studies as Cissy.

I confess that I am very proud to see the boys follow my example and study at Barron House. Surrey is sadly a long way off, but at least you shall have Lucy for company, and Mrs. Cashman.

Off to drill.
With great love,
James

July 11, 1818
Dearest James,

I write this letter under duress, as Lucy is in the background begging, "Please, may I go, Mama, oh please!"

The Lockwoods of Clonakilty

I have received a letter from your brother John (I confess that when I saw it I had unkind thoughts for the man, a sin for which God may forgive me) reporting that he has become acquainted with Mr. Fitter (I hope that you remember him, the older man who owns the Linen concern in town) and that Mr. Fitter has convinced him that in today's world young ladies merit a superior education.

Fitter's daughter Caroline leaves for this Richmond Academy it is near London in a few weeks in company with Hannah Butler and your brother thinks that Lucy should go as well he offers to pay for everything (you know how all in John's world revolves around money) and Caroline and Hannah have told Lucy about it as if all was decided.

Somehow I feel very managed and yet I cannot help but be thrilled at her opportunity I can reconcile myself with having the older children away at school, but for your brother to want to send Lucy away at such a young age she is only six makes me feel as if your family wants me completely separated from my children as if they do not trust me to raise the next generation of the Lockwood line I was already so very lonely without you, then Joseph and Richard left, and Mary and Cissy are to leave very soon, and if Lucy should go as well I do not know what I would do with my days.

Do write as soon as you can with your opinion as Fitter will escort Caroline and Hannah to England in time for the Fall term and Lucy would travel with them how I would worry.

With all my love,
Brigid

Joseph, Richard, and Lucy left for school in England, and Brigid's heart nearly broke in the parting. Mary and Cissy were to leave her in just a few days more. For all her life Brigid had disliked being alone, and she privately dreaded the thought of her house empty and cheerless.

Brigid and her sister shopped together every Friday afternoon; though, as neither woman had much money to spend, their visits to the shops were largely ceremonial. Their wandering eventually led them to Mr. McAuliffe's book shop, where Brigid leafed through the latest *Gazette*. "Oh," she said to Anne, "look at this, *a grah*."

Gazette, *10 August, 1818*

27th Foot: Brevet Lieutenant-Colonel John Archibald to be Major, by purchase, vice Sparrow, who retires. Dated 30th July 1818.

Lieutenant Richard Elliott to be Captain of a Company, by purchase, vice Archibald. Dated 30th July 1818.

"I am sorry, *piteog*," said Anne with a frown, "it's not a word of this that I understand, with its purchasing and vice. Is this good news, or bad?"

"Oh, good, I suppose, but news at any rate. Dear old Archibald and Elliott are to be promoted. They are both deserving fellows, though I wonder where they got the money to buy their steps. James is one spot closer to his captaincy, as Elliott is only twenty-nine days senior to him. But it looks as if purchase is the only path to promotion. Short of another war, when the next spot opens James shall need nine hundred fifty pounds we do not possess."

"Nine hundred fifty pounds!" cried Anne. "A fortune of money!"

"Yes, indeed. He will be passed over, the junior men moving past him, and it shall break his heart." She placed the *Gazette* back on the counter and left a hand on it for a long moment.

They wandered then, chatting with a few friends in the street, until they came upon the Post Office, where the Post Master said, "Ah, Mrs. Lockwood! A letter for you, please, from Gibraltar itself!"

Her heart raced for a moment, but she was disappointed and a bit puzzled to see it was from Colonel Dumon.

Gibraltar

My dearest friend, Mrs. Lockwood,

As I vowed, a quick note, as my business has brought me to Gibraltar. I am with grief to report that our beloved James is taken ill. His friends have no trust in me, and will not confide in me, an inquisitive Frenchman, as old wounds are slow to heal.

James was taking large doses of medicine. I fear it is laudanum, and he was thus perhaps not quite himself but I was honestly wounded that he would spend little time with me, despite—

Brigid and Anne heard a voice in the street call, "Here they come!" The sisters hurried to the shop door to see a crowd gathering, lining the Western Road as a company of the Westmeath Militia slowly passed. Several of the redcoats were roughly bandaged, and a cart following the slow-moving company carried several badly wounded militiamen. Their officer waved the cart toward Shannon Square, and Dr. Kelly's offices. Last in the column came a second cart, loaded with dead men, soldiers and civilians thrown in together. The militiamen were battered and silent, their heads down, as they headed toward their barracks on the far side of town.

Anonymous whispered voices followed them, passing news up the street. "The soldiers ambushed a party of Whiteboys last night out near the wilds of Knockawaddra."

"Some say that it was Charlie Moy who sold them to the redcoats."

"Traitors will be the end of this land."

"It looks as if they made a fight of it. A pity it is, such blood. How many were lost?"

"I heard four soldiers and nine Whiteboys are dead. Eight soldiers wounded."

"No prisoners, I suppose?"

"Prisoners? Not with four of their own lying dead. The soldiers killed all that they could lay hands on."

"I saw Bob Clerkin himself lying dead in the cart; and Cormac McCarthy says that the soldiers mean to throw our dead into the crab pit."

"Bastards, they are, to do such things. Go, Colleen, run and beg Father McGlynn to come and speak to the soldiers. Surely even the Saxons would not treat the dead in such a shameful fashion."

Brigid and Anne were standing with Mr. McAuliffe at the door to his shop when his young son ran up and said excitedly, "Have you heard, Papa? It was John Cashman who fought his way out of the ambush, soldiers' blood on his blade, and it was he alone who escaped into the darkness."

"A Cashman, do you say?" asked Brigid, trying to control her voice.

"Aye, Catherine's boy," said Mr. McAuliffe softly, but with steel in his voice, "who has come back to fight for the justice that he could not find in the '98. No secrets to be kept now, ma'am. Every red coat in Munster will be turned out to seek our John."

Brigid did not pause to consider McAuliffe's connection to the Whiteboys, only squeezing her sister's hand before she bolted back up the road toward home.

In the front garden Brigid clutched her bonnet in both hands and said in Irish, "Catherine, sure I knew you had friends who might be resisting the English, but your own son!"

Mrs. Cashman nodded grimly and said, "I'll be packing my chest and will gone by evening, ma'am."

"Oh for God's sake, woman, stop with such foolishness. Together we face this, but what can we tell the soldiers when they come? They have the name of John Cashman, and they will hear your name soon enough. I shall go to speak to Colonel Simon... yes... that would be best... I shall tell him, and you must say the same, that you did not know John had returned to Munster, and you have not heard his name for these many years."

Mrs. Cashman replied with tears behind her determined eyes, "I thank you, Missus, but I shall tell you in all truth—"

"Tell me no more, Catherine! What I tell to Simon I shall believe to be the truth. We shall get through this, but we must act quickly."

With that Brigid embraced Mrs. Cashman, kissed her cheek, and hurriedly strode down the hill toward town. Mrs. Cashman ran into the house in search of Cissy, and begged her to leave that minute to go to speak to Father McGlynn, but Cissy would not go, and neither would she allow Mrs. Cashman to go. Cissy forced them to adhere to routine. The Lockwoods typically went to confession on Wednesdays and Saturdays, and she would not allow anyone see her blindly bolt into town to speak to the priest. Cissy had only made a few hesitant steps into Father McGlynn's organization, but she knew that government had spies everywhere.

When Saturday came Cissy asked the distraught Mrs. Cashman to remain at home, instead walking to St. Brigid's alone, perhaps more quickly than usual, her heart in her throat.

Her tenuous connection to rebellion left her little to confess, so she quickly practiced the rite and passed on to urgent whispers in Irish. "More blood, Father! My mother brought home news of the fighting, and Mrs. Cashman's own son amongst them."

"Traitors are everywhere, Cissy, everywhere!" whispered the priest. "Our men fought like lions, though surrounded and outnumbered in the darkness. But now many of those brave souls stand before God, holy in their martyrdom. Those who betrayed them shall be found out, fear you not, and sent before the same God for judgment and damnation!"

With emotion breaking her voice Cissy said, "Catherine Cashman begs for news of John Cashman, her own son."

"You should not know that man's name. He is in a different group, and anonymity is our best defense against the traitors. But as his return to Munster and his allegiance to the cause are spoken of in the very street, you may tell Mrs. Cashman that her John is well, not a scratch on him, and he is safely away. Even I do not know where he hides, safe from the King's own dogs."

"I am to leave for school in a few days, Father, and I do not know where to turn. I have read Rousseau and Paine, I have my faith in my heart, I understand the plight of the people, but I cannot bear to see this blood spilled to achieve nothing."

Cissy could hear Father McGlynn shift closer to the screen, and in a conspiratorial whisper he said, "That is how you can best assist the cause, can you see, Cissy ni Brian *a grah*? You must use your position to grow closer to those in power, and find out what they know of us, what terrors they plan to inflict, and we shall confound them at every turn!"

Aghast, Cissy replied, "You would have me play the spy, Father? I am an honourable woman! You would have me betray the trust of those who have me into their homes? Is that what your cause and your God would require of me?"

"You dare say 'your God', young woman!" Behind the screen of the confessional Cissy could see the priest gesticulating wildly as he hissed, "There is only one true God, one true church, and there is no room for doubt or the affectations of heretics! God's will steers this movement, and God's will alone!"

Cissy could control her tears, but not her anger. "God, is it, Father!" she said in a voice no longer conscious of conspiracy. "A God of murder and treachery!" She burst from the confessional to see old women staring at her from the pews, dark eyes under dark shawls. Cissy left her shawl around her shoulders, and did not allow herself to run. Her hands were shaking, but by the time she reached the rear of the church they had grown steady. She had always been of a decisive nature, and she made a decision then. She let her rosary beads slip from her fingers and watched them drop to the cold slate floor. She then strode to the doors and out into the street with controlled steps and dry eyes.

Chapter Nine

Cissy found conflicting emotions disconcerting. She did her best to resolve them, in her head if not in her heart, and she found long walks granted her the solitude to ponder her options. She now used much of her free time at Malahide to explore the paths above the Irish Sea.

She was quietly thrilled to be attending such a prestigious school, though she was disappointed that the curriculum concentrated more on etiquette and decorum than on literature and history. On the other hand, her heart broke to think of her mother and Mrs. Cashman alone in Fáibhile Cottage. She was glad to be far from Father McGlynn, though a restive desire to help the countless poor constantly nagged her soul.

She was afraid that her old life would not be waiting for her when she returned, even if she returned that very day. Her world was quickly changing, and she was unsure what to make of it.

Cissy and Mary had been at Malahides School for nearly two months. There were few Catholics there, and to be a Catholic with no friends at school, a limited wardrobe, and unpolished country manners might have made their lives a burden to them. Any ridicule of the Lockwood girls was, however, soon squashed by the appearance of their Aunt Mary and Uncle Muir. Those two icons of the Ascendency had come to the school for a brief, uncomfortable visit, and in their own icy fashion they had marked the two Clonakilty girls with the invisible but potent sign of aristocratic favour.

Their family connections aside, Cissy was very pretty, Mary was beautiful, and they were both friendly, personable young souls. As acceptable members of society the girls made a few friends, and in fact Mary soon bordered on popularity when she secretly shared, with a frequency that annoyed her sister, her story of unrequited love with her handsome, dashing young French aristocrat, and the likelihood of him sweeping her away to the impossibly romantic hills above Marseilles.

Cissy grew disappointed with her sister, jealous being too strong a term, so while the other girls gossiped away their extensive free time, Cissy walked.

She routinely passed through a thick copse of trees on her way down to the beach paths. She was musing over the conjugation of French verbs when a man suddenly stepped out from the trees and said, "*Dia agus Mhaire duit, a Inion ni Lockwood, a grah.*" God and Mary be with you, dear Miss Lockwood.

She was startled, but not frightened. The man was much older than she, and though he did not have a handsome or especially kind face, he had an honest one.

"God, Mary, and Patrick be with you, sir," she said, still in the Irish. "Pray, do I know you?"

"No, Miss, though we both love the same woman. I am called John Cashman." John could see doubt and caution flash in her face, so he gave her a hint of a smile and added, "My mother sends me. She says 'Sergeant, Elizabeth Bennet, and *mo cuisle*'."

Her dog, her favourite character from her favourite book, and Mrs. Cashman's pet name for Cissy. Her doubt left her and she anxiously asked, "Is all well at home still? Do you bear ill news, John Cashman?"

"Your mother and mine are well, Miss, if lonely, and worried."

Cissy relaxed a bit and said, "Thanks be to God." With a small smile of her own she went on, "You will know, sir, that I am not in the habit of speaking to strange men in lonely woodlands, especially when those men are fugitive's from the King's justice."

John nodded and said, "And it is a good thing you are not, young gentlewoman." He looked at her with some understanding and said, "You and the priest have parted brass rags, I think?"

"It was a fool I was to listen to that manipulating dog of a man."

John grinned and said, "Clever girl, you, with your sharp tongue, and wiser now."

Cissy's curiosity flared and she asked, "Pray, now, John Cashman, what brings you to travel the long miles from home to Dublin to speak to me?"

"Yes, we must tend to business. You will forgive me, Miss, as I so seldom speak to one who knows my true name and my life as it once was. I keep from Cork most of my days, as the redcoats and their slaves know I am returned. My dear mother sends me to warn you of a man called Charles Barr."

Cissy was puzzled and said, "I know of no one called Barr... save the man in my father's own regiment?"

"It is he, sure. There are letters that set your dear mother to weeping with the fear and the anger; and as my mother does not read she has quietly passed a few to me, and I tell you now, young gentlewoman, the man is mad, and capable of great evil. You must be on your guard."

Cissy was amazed. "Why would anyone ever...."

Laughter and the sound of young voices came from further up the wooded path. John urgently said, "We do not know why, but it remains, notwithstanding. I must away."

John stepped into the trees, then quickly turned and emphatically pointed at Cissy. "Captain Charles Barr. I know no more than this: he would kill you all if given the Devil's own chance."

John disappeared, and as a handful of girls from school came down the path Cissy quickly resolved not to tell Mary, but her potent fury was irrevocably turned against this man named Barr.

Brigid expected Colonel Simon and perhaps another officer or two, but the better part of a troop of the Camolin Yeomanry Cavalry reined up in front of Fáibhile Cottage.

Brigid and Mrs. Cashman stood in the door together; while Brigid had long before learned to steel her nerves in the face of authority, Mrs. Cashman's hands betrayed her terror. In Ireland the yeomanry served as the private army of the aristocracy, and the Camolins were notorious across Munster.

A few years earlier Colonel Simon had subtly tested Mrs. Lockwood's attachment to her husband, but since that frustrating experience he had noticeably aged, and he now dismounted his bay mare with difficulty. Simon entered the front garden with a Captain White in his wake, a tall, harsh young officer. Greetings and introductions were made as Mrs. Cashman stood ignored, until the young officer turned to her and asked with a sneer, "This is the mother of the murderous traitor, then?"

"This woman has been in the employ of this family for nine years, sir, a good, loyal, and honest woman, and I would thank you to address her as such."

White turned to confront Brigid, but she did not blanch at his anger. Simon gathered his energy and waved White back. He questioned Mrs. Cashman in a firm but respectful voice. "You are Catherine Cashman?"

"I am, your honour."

"And you are the mother of John Cashman, a fugitive rebel and murderer?"

Mrs. Cashman almost said something in quick response, but she calmed herself and said softly, "Yes, your honour."

"When is the last instance in which you saw your son?"

"The night before Shannonvale in 1798, your honour. I begged him never to go, but he was seduced to his ruin by Tadg An Asna O'Donovan."

"And so you swear by God?"

Brigid thought she saw a twinkle in Mrs. Cashman's eye as the old lady said, "So I swear, by God, your honour."

Later, Mrs. Cashman went down into town to go to confession and attend mass. Brigid retired to her bedroom to closely read once again the letters she had received earlier in the week.

Gibraltar 29 July, 1819
Dear Brigid,

I am sorry for not writing more often, but I am so bored that I really have nothing to communicate. I have fallen ill several times, confined to my bed for days at a time; all behind me, dear, as I now feel quite well. It is unfair of me, I know, to ask you and the children to write at every opportunity, as I so rarely respond, but I beg you to continue, as your letters are my only source of cheer. Another year gone by without you. My fondest possession, perhaps my only true possession, is this bundle of letters from you dear people.

I have grown snappish, and only Pitcock's potion, a soothing mix, keeps me going. Last week when I was feeling particularly blue I am afraid that I handled Tom very rough when he suggested that we move quarters down into town. He is right in thinking them more convenient to what little diversion Gib has to offer, but living in town, close by the King's bastion, would mean shagging up this damned hill to our drill grounds by Windmill Barracks several times a day. That would be quite beyond me, and I told him that I was surprised to hear him so inconsiderate of my health. I suppose that I phrased it rather unkindly, and he took offence, and we exchanged the first truly cross words that I can ever recall. He has always been a sensitive cove, and he lashed out amazingly. We have spoken little since then. While I may not have been overly kind in my replies to him, he was the one who proposed the move to town, and I do not think that I have anything to apologize for. Honestly, my dear, I beg your opinion: am I wrong in this? I do not know what I would do without him.

James

A few days after her letter from James, another cover had come from Gibraltar, with two letters enclosed.

1 August, 1819
My Dear Mrs. Lockwood,

I am your honourable husband's commanding officer. I am issuing this correspondence in concert with another officer under my command, Lieutenant Thomas Mainwaring, to recommend that Lieutenant James Lockwood return home.

You will please understand that I am the most ardent and consistent admirer of your husband's honour, bravery, and dedication to King, Country, and this Regiment.

It is, however, my considered opinion that Lieutenant Lockwood should return home as soon as medically feasible, and transfer his commission to a Royal Veteran's Battalion. That posting shall guarantee his pay as a serving lieutenant, and, more importantly, preserve his honour and standing in the service.

I remain, madam, your most willing,
humble, and obedient servant,
Lt. Colonel Lemuel Nelson
First Batt., 27th Regt. Of Foot

Brigid's hands were shaking as she opened the next letter.

29 July, 1819
My Dear Mrs. Lockwood,

I write to you without the knowledge or approval of your husband. He and I grow sadly estranged, but for the sake of all that we have meant to one another I must then beg your pardon, and silently, his, if I offend in communicating so frankly.

I must tell you that he is drinking more than the people who love him desire, and he is so very melancholy. The medicos give him laudanum, and while it perhaps makes his life bearable it changes his demeanor, very much to the worse. I have begged him to seek other medical advice, to get him away from this fool Pitcock, but he refuses me in this, as in so much else.

Many of our Waterloo friends are no longer with the battalion, and while he is so very fond of them, it has broken his heart to see them purchase and be promoted ahead of him. What little time he has away from his bed is spent in dreadful boredom (it is so very dull here) as he waits for the men ahead of him to fade away. But if no new war comes that time will be very extended, and (I beg you to forgive my frankness) I wonder if he has the time to spare. He grows weaker every day, and the fevers are coming more often, and stay longer. I force myself to tell you, I once again beg your forgiveness, but the sound of his breath is so strained, so shallow, as to make one weep.

No captaincy is worth the suffering he endures here.

Colonels Nelson and Pritchard have used their influence to garner him a posting to a Veteran's Battalion, where he might stay at home and draw his full pay indefinitely. It is a handsome compliment, but he has refused it, and in doing so he may ruin his chances.

For God's sake have him come home.

Your most devoted and humble servant,
and I flatter myself, friend,
Thomas Mainwaring

Upon receipt of this letter, Brigid paced her drawing room, blind with indecision. She could not, would not, risk dishonouring her husband, herself or her family; she could think of no one to whom she might turn for advice. At last she sat and wrote Dr. Kelly to beg his opinion; but as he was in Paris for lectures at the Sorbonne, she would wait for weeks for a reply.

Those weeks dragged past, with no word from James. She wrote and threw aside countless letters, some begging him to come home, some trying to cheer him, hoping she might find just the right words, words which would help to heal him.

Finally, one October day, as the first sharps edge of winter cold came whistling in from the sea, a letter came. Not from Gibraltar, but from Paris: at last, word from Dr. Kelly.

13 October, 1819
My Dear Mrs. Lockwood,

I am in receipt of you letter of the 22ⁿᵈ ultimo. It grieves me to hear of James's declining health, and I am in full agreement that he should return to Clonakilty as soon as possible.

To your private ear I confess a lack of confidence in the Surgeon currently posted to the 1/27ᵗʰ, as his sole resort is laudanum in ghastly dosage. Upon James's return home I beg you to have Dr. Hickman see him as soon as possible. Dr. Hickman is a capable young man, but again I beg your discretion when I admit that he was not my first choice to tend my practice while I am away. He does well enough in extracting a tooth or setting a break, but he is of limited familiarity with higher notions of medicine. Still, I trust he shall aid in weaning James away from his laudanum, and I shall write Hickman to suggest he bleed James only as necessary.

My course of study here in Paris will conclude in four months, and it is my intention to cancel my planned consultation with Dr. Wurster in Berlin in order to return to Clonakilty as quickly as possible.

Your devoted friend,
John Kelly M.D.

Chapter Ten

James lay gasping for breath in his bed in Fáibhile Cottage, trying to reconcile himself with his defeat, his soul-crushing defeat. In his hand he held the pen with which he had signed his resignation from the First Battalion, 27th Regiment of Foot, and his acceptance of a lieutenancy in the 3rd Royal Veteran Battalion.

He had entered the service an ensign, and in twenty-one years of service he had advanced precisely one step in rank. He would linger as an invalid and die a lieutenant, leaving his wife and children a mere lieutenant's pension. He was embarrassed, ashamed of doing so little, and being judged a failure by all he would leave behind.

James's greatest regret was not putting an end to Charles Barr. Before James left Gib he had received a letter from Barr in Paris, full of taunt, insults, and threats. James looked back on his dealings with Barr and saw opportunities where he should have called Barr out, consequences be damned. But he had not done so; James came to the conclusion that he had been a fool and a coward, and now his family was at risk.

He sought refuge in laudanum.

Downstairs Brigid sat alone, absently twisting the wedding ring on her finger, thinking of the long siege to come. She doubted her strength, and was so very afraid.

In a sordid London pub Charles Barr sat composing another letter to James Lockwood. He leered drunkenly and muttered, "I trust that you are suffering the tortures of the damned, Lockwood. But do die soon, won't you? I do so want to get my hands on that slut O'Brian." He roared with laughter and called for more rum.

Six Company, First Battalion, 27th Regiment of Foot spent every Tuesday morning drilling on the hot, dusty parade ground at the foot of the Rock of Gibraltar. When the Inniskillings had first arrived at Gibraltar, Private Diarmuid Doolan had marveled at the massive tower of rock, but it was now as familiar as the endless wheels, pivots, and obliques Six Company executed in its shadow.

When the company had been marched back to their barracks and dismissed, Sergeant Major Morrison sought out Doolan, jerked a thumb over his shoulder, and said, "Doolan, Handsome Tommy is looking for your sorry arse."

Doolan strolled over to the headquarters building in search of Lieutenant Thomas Mainwaring, where he found that gentleman seated at a desk, aswim in his company's rosters and accounts. Before he interrupted the lieutenant, Doolan studied Mainwaring's face with something like affection. Mainwaring had been so handsome, once. But at Waterloo a French musket ball had passed through his cheeks and shattered his mouth. Doolan absently stroked the thick scar where his own left thumb had been shot away. He had suffered the wound as he had helped carry Lieutenant Lockwood, shot in the arm and the chest, to the rear.

Doolan stepped in front of the lieutenant's desk, made his salute, and said, "I suppose it's time, now, is it, sir?"

Lieutenant Mainwaring looked up, nodded solemnly, and said, "With Lieutenant Lockwood's departure there is no longer any reason to delay the inevitable, Doolan. Your papers are come through, and you are hereby considered 'no longer fit for service' and will be discharged in three months' time."

Doolan nodded resolutely and said, "And about fucking time, too, me being such a creeping old relic." Mainwaring frowned at Doolan, but Doolan went on unfazed, "And it's you giving me the news, is it sir, and not Cubigg?"

"Lieutenant Lockwood, on his departure, requested that I look after you. Captain Cubigg was good enough to allow me to see to your discharge. And mind you, Doolan, whether we care for it or not, Captain Cubigg now commands Six Company." Mainwaring dusted the front of his jacket, averted his eyes, and continued, "Despite our regard for Lieutenant Lockwood, we must move on. He is gone, and his good ways with him."

Doolan nodded and said, "Yes, sir, and with all due respect to Captain Dubigg, even if he has no experience in war, having to buy his rank," then clearing his throat he said *sotto voce*, "the fat little eejit—"

Mainwaring held up a finger and said, "Doolan, any other officer in the British army would have you up on charges and see that you get a dozen for speaking like that."

Doolan grinned a bit and said, "But you just aren't another officer, are you, now, sir? And neither was dear Lieutenant Lockwood. Cubigg is an agreeable fellow, but a greater fool I've never seen. All nonsense aside now, I'll say that you, Lockwood, and a few of your kind are the best of this battalion's officers, and me and a few dozen other Irish gravel-pounders are the last of this battalion's heart and soul. It's glad I am to leave now, rather than see the 1/27th melt into some bored, drunken, red-backed garrison battalion commanded by fools and martinets."

The lieutenant gave a small grudging bow to the grizzled old private. After a moment Mainwaring said, "I shall ask the adjutant to submit a Request for Pension. Major Archibald, I am sure, will join me in ensuring you a 'good conduct' rate, which is no small miracle, Private, so that you might draw a pension. I believe that Waterloo privates are typically granted a shilling a day. You have, what, twenty-one years of service?

"Every minute of that, thankee, sir, nearly every minute with our dear old Lockwood. I've carried an Inniskilling musket since 1799... the last century."

"Plus the extra year of service for being a Waterloo man."

"Waterloo men we are, sir. By God, but we held them there sir, didn't we, we held them." Doolan frowned and continued, "Being a Waterloo man once had these new lads looking at us with... what is the word, now, sir? Awe. Yes, sir, awe, it was, once. But now to be a Waterloo man means you're a doddering old relic, and I shall not take that from any man, sir, in thought or word, especially these new pups they're bringing in by the bucket. I shall draw my pension and move on."

"I understand; in just the five years since the battle there are only three officers here who served at Waterloo. In fact, I will soon go on extended leave myself, back home to Leicestershire to be married."

Doolan smiled and said, "*Mo cheol tu, a* Lieutenant Thomas Mainwaring, *a grah.* May God bless you both, and pave your path with Munster roses."

Mainwaring again nodded his thanks and asked, "So, wherever will you go, Doolan? You were from Cavan, once, were you not? Have you any family left in Ireland?"

"Family?" Doolan scoffed gently. "Family, is it, now? Faith, not a soul left above ground." But he slowly nodded his head as if he had come to a decision and added, "But there are a few good folk I may call on after a while, in the south they are, the green south."

James had been at home a month when Brigid helped him out to the chair that was his post on dry, warm days. Zeresh and Mary Muir were visiting; neither offered to give him an arm, rightly sensing that James, no matter how weak and gasping, would have refused it. Leamaneh had only confirmed his opinions: he did not much care for his sister, and he casually loathed her husband. The Muirs had brought Mary (James once again regretted naming his first daughter after his sister) and Cissy home for a visit, so Brigid and James made at least an effort to be welcoming. Brigid had wanted the boys and Lucy to come home to see their father as well, but James convinced her that their travel would be too long and expensive. More than that, to be the object of so much pity was beyond him.

Out in the garden, Muir pounded Sergeant's flanks harder than the otherwise patient dog cared for, and Brigid feared that Sergeant might remove an Ascendency finger or two.

"Quite a powerful animal, Lockwood," said Muir in an over-loud voice. "Yes, quite."

James only nodded and looked out toward the sea. Muir caught his wife's eye, and Brigid saw them both roll their eyes in disdain. Muir went on in a knowing tone, "Of course, such a heavy brute is not fit for a fox hunt. I was out with Johnstone's pack, oh, perhaps two weeks ago. Well-trained dogs, a capable leader, and a dozen well-mounted men who were serious about their hunt. A bracing pastime, though Mrs. Muir reminds me that you are not much for hunting, Lockwood. It is a manly pursuit, quite beyond you now, I suppose."

James nodded, and Brigid winced. She very nearly mentioned Leamaneh, where their roles had been very clearly defined, but she held her tongue. She would hold her tongue for her family, but how she loathed those people.

"Yes, a strong dog," continued Muir, as James made no sign of joining in the conversation, "and decent lines, if one can overlook that over-muscled stance, though he might just do for fowl, even if his head is rather large, and his mouth looks none too soft. Tell, me, Lockwood, do you hunt him?"

James looked fondly at the old dog, and said in a surprisingly strong voice, "Oh, yes, we have had him out several times, but he just stands there and makes no sport of it at all. I have never had the heart to shoot him."

Muir was nonplussed for a moment, until his wife said acidly, "Muir, I believe that my brother is being droll." Muir went red and stalked back into the house.

James had a coughing fit and turned away. Brigid watched his face, searching for the twinkle that typically sparked his eye when he made one of his jokes, but it was not there.

James was restricted to his bed most of the time, thin, pale, and ill-tempered. Sergeant bore much of the brunt of his ill humour, as it took some time for the old dog to adjust to his irritable master's return. Sergeant took to barking at shadows to prove his worth, and unfortunately those shadows were most evident late at night. When their parents weren't about, the girls laughingly referred to the dog by his new name: Sergeant-the-God-damned-dog.

Cissy was up early the second morning of their week at home, and took the opportunity to speak to her mother alone. "Mama, why is Papa so very cross? Is he angry with Aunt and Uncle Muir? Or have we done something to displease him?"

With several bottles laid out before her on the dining room table, Brigid was preparing her husband's morning dose. As she carefully poured the ingredients, she strained to smile and said,

"Oh, my dear, you must never think that your father is unhappy with you; you children are the joy of the world to him."

With a fleeting frown she added, "And certainly he may learn to love Sergeant again, if he will ever quit his foolishness."

With a deeper frown, she measured out fifty drops of laudanum and firmly corked the bottle.

"While you may understand that he is not over-pleased in the company of your Aunt and Uncle, the primary cause of his bad humour is this *nimh damanta*, this damned poison," tapping the bottle of laudanum. Brigid rarely swore, especially in conversation with her children, but she made no apology.

"Dr. Hickman and I are in league to steadily cut back of the laudanum in each dose, and add a bit more brandy, until the joyous day when he has just a touch of the laudanum in his glass, and I shall have James Lockwood home, not," she did not use Hickman's term, 'a mere opium eater', instead saying, "some ill-mannered old bear."

In a very adult voice Cissy said, "Mama, surely you know your plan may clear his mind, but it will not help his breathing. I too have spoken to Dr. Hickman, and he said that—"

Brigid would hear no more; she topped off the glass and hurried out. Cissy raised a hand to soothe her, but she was across the room, and too far away.

The morning that the tearful girls joined their impatient Aunt and Uncle in the chaise to return to Malahide, Cissy pressed a novel into her father's hands, although he was not typically fond of such books. "It is called *Pride and Prejudice*, Papa. Oh, do please read it! Mary and I laughed so, seeing so much of Mr. Bennet in you. Not the weak parts, just the humourous parts...oh, do please read it, Papa."

Brigid wept at the girl's departure. James was pleased to be shed of the Muirs, and in a way he did not care to explore he was relieved to see the girls go as well.

After the chaise had gone, Brigid tucked James into his garden chair and he broke the novel open with resolve. He was hesitant to attempt it, but the range of diversions open to a gentleman of his health was narrow.

To his surprise he was captured by the first few paragraphs, and was soon enveloped in a rare sense of wellbeing. The weather could not be considered perfect, but as he was fairly cocooned in blankets he was comfortable, and while it was cloudy there was no scent of rain. "This is not so bad," he mused to himself. "A mere lieutenant, come home to die, but still, a dying lieutenant with a glass of Madeira, a new book that looks to be interesting, and a tolerable day. I should hope for nothing more." Such a bold statement certainly tempted fate, and a gap in the otherwise complete clouds allowed a shaft of afternoon sunlight to brighten his corner of Ireland. He did not look up, but he did think to himself, "I stand corrected." Then after a moment he thought, "I really must try not to be such a sullen old bull." The sunlight lasted only a few moments, but it made him think of the joys that he might find in his life, if he would calm himself enough to sense them. "I have some time. Not much, certainly, but perhaps enough."

Christmas came, and the Lockwoods threw financial caution to the wind and had all their children travel home. It was such joy to be together once again, and they all took delight in the approach of Christmas Day, though Brigid and the children forced themselves to wait until mid-December to erect the Nativity scene James had sent from France in 1814. The full array of animals and *dramatis personæ* took their carefully posed wooden posts, and on Christmas Eve the youngest of the family, the elfin Lucy, was tasked with reverently placing Christ in his manger. Shortly thereafter, however, she ran into the kitchen and cried, "Mama! Sergeant has taken baby Jesus!"

There followed general mayhem, pursuit, and exclamation, while Mrs. Cashman threw her apron over her head, crossed herself, and fell into a long string of Hail Marys, knowing they were all surely going to burn at the instigation of that galloping apostate of hell.

Sensing that her delicate frame did not qualify her for close combat with Satan's imp, Lucy ran to the bottom of the stairs and called up to her father with a degree of panic in her voice, "Papa! Sergeant has Jesus in his mouth!"

James, who now had only enough laudanum in his system to instill a moderate element of glee, still smiled madly and thought, "A Christmas miracle indeed... speaking in tongues, as it were... and God knows he has tongue and to spare... though that is certainly not an orthodox aspect of either the Anglican or Catholic rites... perhaps our Sergeant has become a raving Methodist."

Sergeant broke free from his pursuers, thundered upstairs, and, with nails clicking on the hard wood floor he trotted into James's room. The big old dog stood there wagging his thick tail, holding the somewhat slobbered but wholly content Christ child at a cocky angle in his capable jaws. James saw wild delight in those brown canine eyes, until Brigid and the children tackled Sergeant and recovered their Jesus. They were all sufficiently soaked in Christian truth to view the kidnapping of the Christ as a great sacrilege, while James lay in his bed wheezing laughter until tears rolled down his cheeks.

"Laugh away, James Lockwood," said Brigid, looking beautiful in high colour and honest, righteous anger, "but I'll not see the miracle of our salvation disparaged in this house by man or beast." The strength of her Irish accent coloured her voice, and James fiercely loved her. Turning from her grinning husband, she addressed her grinning dog, holding up the Messiah and saying, "Sergeant Lockwood, if there is one tooth mark on baby Jesus—one!—I shall see you sleeping outside, cold rain or no; and as God is my witness I shall give the scraps from the Christmas roast to Twinkles McCarthy!"

This only increased James's mirth; but Sergeant, recognizing the name of the odious little bitch from down the road, assumed a posture of mournful regret.

Turning to her children, who all shared their mother's abhorrence of even a hint of disrespect to the high veneration due Christmas, Brigid said, "Please take Sergeant downstairs and have him make peace with Mrs. Cashman, if ever she can find room in her heart to forgive him." All five of the children took an iron grip on Sergeant's collar, and in a knot of humanity they walked him down the stairs, the shamed, vilified, and wholly downcast dog brought before the most Catholic Catherine Cashman for judgment.

Brigid scowled at her husband, and seeing that he was not to be swayed from his pagan mirth she gave him only a frustrated "humph" as she turned to join her children in the reclamation of what little soul Sergeant could field.

James coughed and wheezed for a bit as he drifted back toward sleep, his heart light and happy for the first time in a very long while. He listened to the wall clock steadily ticking time away, but it was soon drowned out by the sounds drifting up to him, the laughing voices of those he loved.

Chapter Eleven

James's fever returned, and Brigid found the tall, thin, nervous Dr. Hickman to be of little use in battling it. But Hickman was committed to weaning the lieutenant from laudanum, and he and Brigid implemented a deliberate course of restriction. James had a difficult withdrawal, and there were occasions when consciousness was agony, as he gasped for breath and his mind called for air, but his body was unable to provide it, a terrifying experience as he surfaced from his drifting dreams. One morning, however, he awoke completely calm and lucid. He knew not to move or to grow excited, as his body would fail him and ruin this near-perfect moment.

Someone else was in the room, asleep. He could not tell who it was, but the steady breathing from the chair was soothing. The window was open; the cool air was gentle on his face, and by its smell he knew rain was coming. He was pleased to hear birds singing; had they always made such a cheery racket? But the little birds were soon silenced by the harsh, strident caws of a crow. James could picture the finches cowering, fearful and nervous, and he wished he could retrieve his old fowling piece and show that crow the door. The crow held sway until he flew off to bully some other neighborhood, though when the little birds resumed their singing they seemed to lack the unrestrained glee they had shown before.

James wondered if he had been too hard on his children. He could remember sometimes having been harsh with them, particularly the boys, when they were little things. Certainly their innocent joy had been worth preserving; had he stepped on them, shaping them into what he expected them to be? Had he committed the unpardonable sin of having behaved like his father? He drifted back to sleep with that disconcerting thought in mind, though a short while later the soft breathing beside him stirred and Cissy, who despite her womanhood was still capable of a child's freedoms, walked softly to her father's side, straightened the blankets, stroked his hair, and gently kissed him.

Spring had come. The roses were just beginning to bloom, and Brigid Lockwood stepped into the garden to welcome her guests. "He is asleep in his chair," she said. "When you see him you must not be shocked by his appearance. He is terribly thin, and his breathing is... distressing. Pray do not be offended if he does not speak much."

Tom and Julia Mainwaring looked happy, nervous, and concerned, then suddenly alarmed when they saw their dog lift his leg over one of the sprouting roses bushes. They hoped Mrs. Lockwood would not notice.

"James was so looking forward to your visit," Brigid continued, "that he ignored his morning dose, determined to be of a clear mind. But getting him down the stairs was such a trial he had to swallow a glass." She was relaxed and comfortable in speaking to Tom, but turning to Julia she was more stiffly formal. "I do apologize, Mrs. Mainwaring, for such an unconventional, inconvenient greeting; the garden is no place to congratulate a new bride."

"Not at all, Mrs. Lockwood; you are most kind, and your roses are lovely. I do hope that you do not mind us bringing our dog; before I met Tom, Milo was the only male in my life, and he pines so when we are separated."

Brigid could not think of anything charming to say, so she offered only a flat, "Not at all," that sounded much more daunting than she intended.

Both Brigid and Julia knew there was an unspoken expectation that, in light of their husbands' deep friendship, they should become fast friends as well. Both the ladies felt awkwardly nervous under the weight of that assumption, and Tom was disappointed to see them eye each other with a degree of wariness. He was taken aback to realize he had no method at hand that would make them care for one another.

Their conversation was polite but strained, and all involved were relieved when Mrs. Cashman came out to announce that the Lieutenant was prepared for company. After the genuine joy of their reunion and the introduction of the new Mrs. Mainwaring, the session in the drawing room was little more comfortable than the session in the garden. James could say very little, Tom was nervous and awkward, while the ladies remained cool, polite, and unsure of how not to be so. In a clever gambit, however, Julia Mainwaring offered, "I had quite forgotten, Mrs. Lockwood, that we picked up a small gift for you in Dublin on our way down. I confess to an undying love of Belgian chocolates, and we thought that you might enjoy them as well."

Brigid was prepared to accept any opportunity to bond with Julia Mainwaring, and an offer of chocolate went straight to her heart. She and Julia broke into the chocolates, the word 'pounce' perhaps being too strong a term, without waiting for their husbands.

With a laugh, Tom asked, "I trust that you are enjoying your chocolates, Mrs. Lockwood?"

With laughter in her eyes, in a husky half-whisper Brigid said, "I love these more than anything else in all the world."

James made a face of playful anguish. Discreetly licking a bit of chocolate from her finger, Brigid looked at him with an unapologetic look and said, "We shall still be friends."

Julia dissolved in a long, loud, unladylike, wholly human laugh that made Brigid love her. Tom offered James his arm and helped him outside, the gentlemen beaten from the field.

The two old dogs followed them out. Sergeant made it a point to stay close to his master, as he mistrusted the Mainwarings' golden Milo. There remained a degree of ill-will between the dogs until they realized a shared loathing of gulls, coming to that happy agreement in a frenzy of barking and aged trots.

It took some time for James to catch his breath after even that short walk. Tom sat beside him, sharing a companionable silence as they watched the old dogs play. The two soldiers had fallen into their past ways with unconscious ease and great satisfaction.

After the long silence Tom said softly, "You know, in all my life I have never had a better friend than you, James." They both stared off toward the distant sea as James placed a shaking hand atop Tom's. Tom finally said, "I am pleased that Brigid and Julia seem to be getting on. They are both bright, clever girls; I believe that you and I agree in our preference for women of some intellect.'"

Sergeant and Milo tumbled about the garden, both soldiers grinning at their antics. Tom continued, "Foolish women are of course more easily steered; 'manipulated' is an unpleasant term. Still, for all their malleability, ninnies can be tiresome, and are often a burden, even an embarrassment, in company."

James nodded and absently smiled as he watched the dogs finally collapse into a panting pile.

"I am reminded," Tom went on easily, "of a dinner we attended recently; Julia's father is a chronic entertainer. There was a woman there, a young, amazingly attractive creature, the target of all of the young men of the area, who insisted that she would take a coach and four to Paris, and that anyone who was so hopelessly old-fashioned as to go by sea was to be pitied. Can you imagine being married to such a person?"

James smiled again, remembering some of the women once pursued by Tom; he could recall none who were prized for their wit, though he could recall some with other, more tangible, charms.

Tom had known that James would not speak much, but the reality of that disconcerting truth now pained him. He began to chat at length to compensate, and while their silence had been so comfortable, the more he spoke the more they fell away from that unthinking comfort.

When Tom paused for a moment James held up a finger and whispered, "After I am gone, Barr"—gasping breaths—"poses a problem."

Tom turned to face James and said, "If Brigid hears one word from him, she must contact me immediately."

"Brigid knows him," more breaths, "but we have never told the children. He may try—something."

Tom turned in his seat to look out to the distant hills. After a moment he said, "You know, I have been out four times, and have been in numerous battles and skirmishes and such, and yet it is odd that I have never directly killed anyone. Unusual, is it not? I wonder if Barr shall be my first."

More time passed. It might have been a comfortable pause if either man knew what might need to be done, but it was not. Charles Barr had long been James's mortal enemy, but he now had a second. Time stalked James Lockwood, and Tom was desperate to stay its course. He searched his mind for a topic to discuss, anything to get his mind from the notion that James was slipping away. He came out with, "Brigid mentioned that Dr. Kelly is due back from Paris at any time, and she has great hopes for his insight into your health. She speaks most highly of him, and after this time studying in Paris he must be the best-educated physician outside Dublin."

James sniffed in amusement, but said nothing.

There came another silence, until Tom offered, "*The Times* says that Bonaparte is dying; it is nice to know we have outlasted that fellow."

James tilted his head and gave a quick nod of affirmation.

Tom wracked his mind for more. "Oh, do you recall Mrs. M'Mullen?"

James shook his head, but with an interested look on his face.

"You are grown ancient and forgetful, brother," and fearing that he had struck too close to the truth Tom quickly went on, "She was the wife of Private M'Mullen at Waterloo; I forget his Christian name. My company; worthless fellow. Oh, certainly you recall her; I let her ride my horse for a while during the march across Belgium, as she was so large with child."

James grunted and nodded with a small smile.

"Yes, that was her; an unremarkable person, but she had her moment of fame. At the close of the battle, some time after you and I had made our dramatic exits from the field, our dear Mrs. M'Mullen came up from the baggage looking for her husband. She found him unhurt—he always was a lucky devil—whereupon she celebrated the moment by depositing a baby girl onto the Waterloo grass. They named her something suitably Irish, I suppose, but a writer from *The Times* heard about it, and wrote it up in that sensational fashion of theirs. Before long the Duke of York took note. He gave them a small provision, more money than they would normally see in a lifetime, and arranged for M'Mullen to be discharged. The happy couple was so pleased that they changed the baby's name to Frederica Waterloo McMullen. I joke not."

James whispered, "Frederica," and wheezed a laugh, weakly trying to participate.

Tom meant to stop at that, but in his anxiety he went on. "It ended badly, of course. *The Times* trumpeted the news when it was happy, but only later did I hear the rest of the story from Archibald. M'Mullen planned to use his fortune to open a public house in Fermanagh when his discharge came through. But the baby died at the camp outside Paris, and he took to drink and abusing his wife, blaming her, as men often do. So she left him and took up with some dragoon, and he threw away his fortune on drink and grief. They found him dead in a gutter some weeks later." He instantly regretted his wandering story, hoping that James would not take it the wrong way.

In an other-worldly voice, James whispered, "So much... ends badly."

The chaise waited impatiently, far into the evening, as the Mainwarings and Lockwoods sat together, inseparable in the drawing room of Fáibhile Cottage. James was exhausted, and was soon asleep in his chair. After some whispered goodbyes, Brigid led the Mainwarings out to the carriage.

"It was so good of you both to come," Brigid said, her eyes wet in the quivering light of the chaise's lanterns. They all maintained their composure, kind and supportive, with promises to see each other again, come the summer.

Julia embraced Brigid; Tom, who had been standing stiffly at her side, suddenly muttered, "This... this might very well be...." and hurriedly strode back into the cottage. Brigid saw him kneel by James's chair for a moment, holding his hand as James stirred. Neither of the ladies could hear what they said to one another, only watching as Tom embraced his old friend and gently kissed his forehead. With that, Tom bolted back outside, his face wet with tears. He held Brigid for a moment, a strong, whole embrace, then joined Julia and the carriage rattled away. Brigid felt an enormous love for the Mainwarings. Her eyes were wet, but she did not weep. She slowly returned to her husband's side, wiped away his tears, and held his hand as he slept.

The Mainwarings had not traveled more than a few miles before Julia asked if they might stop at the next inn for a bit. Collecting his thoughts, Tom forced a smile, lowered his window, and called up to the driver, "Postillion, the next decent inn, please!"

At the Golden Prince in Bandon, Julia went upstairs and Tom walked into the tap room. There were just a few other men scattered across the room as Tom stepped up the bar and said, "A pint of your best, please."

As he pulled the pint the barman nodded toward Tom's uniform and said "The 27th, if I do not mistake, sir?"

Tom took a long drink of the ale, then said, "You are correct, sir. I assume you were a soldier, once?"

"Corporal O'Malley, 12th Light Dragoons, until Salamanca, and I lost a foot," said the barman, tapping his leg.

Tom gave him a small salute and said, "Then pray pull yourself a pint with my respects, Corporal."

As he did so O'Malley said, "My thanks, sir. It is always a pleasure serving a fellow soldier. Though I must say, sir, you are a great deal more the gentleman than the last officer what came through."

Tom was in no mood for banter, so he asked only, "A difficult character, I assume?"

"A right bastard, sir, if you will excuse the expression. Last week, a captain of the 24th Foot. I was obliged to drive him from the house."

Tom's face went taut and he quickly demanded, "His name, man! What was his name?"

Startled, O'Malley said, "I... I don't recall sir. Terrible thin, pale, seemed rather sickly?"

Tom was ashen. "Barr? Was his name Barr?"

"Well, aye, sir, that was his name, aye."

"Sweet Christ. Where is he now, man? Where!"

O'Malley nervously licked his lips and said, "I don't want trouble, now, sir, none at all."

Tom reached across the bar, grabbed O'Malley's collar and hissed, "Is he still here, man?"

Sensing trouble, the other patrons of the pub quickly fled. Freed of their presence O'Malley said with a nervous smile, "I take it this Barr is no friend of yours, sir?"

Tom nodded tensely, and O'Malley went on, anxious to please, "After I drove him out, in the street itself he made as to have his way with one of the local girls. Gentleman or no, no man dare try that in Bandon. He was taken up by some of the lads, and they beat him something awful."

Tom smiled grimly and said, "God bless them, too. Tell me they killed him."

O'Malley gave another flash of a smile and said, "Ah, nothing as bad as that, sir, please. But they did throw him onto the mail coach to Dublin bruised from head to toe. They told him if he ever came back they'd do him in. I hope that news pleases you, sir?"

Tom released O'Malley, placed two guineas on the bar, and said, "When those men next come to your house, pray give them every drink they can hold."

When Julia Mainwaring came downstairs she was surprised by the ferocity on her husband's face. Tom gave her an intense look and said, "My dear, would you mind if we stopped in Dublin before going home?"

Chapter Twelve

Brigid sat by James's bedside, reading his copy of *Pride and Prejudice*. She was deep into the story, so much so that she jumped when James whispered, "You are an exceptionally lovely woman."

Brigid gave him a soft, tired, smile and said, "And you, my dear, are an exceptionally handsome man."

They held hands for a few moments until James gasped, "When I am—" she heard the anguish in his voice, "—Barr will come."

"James, I will not hear you say such things. Dr. Kelly will come, and you shall be well, and Barr—" She could only hang her head; she would contest with her last breath that James would recover, but she could not deny that Barr would come.

Exhausted, James was drifting off again when Brigid whispered, "Barr can cause me no greater pain, but what might he do to the children? Whatever can I tell them?"

In a half-conscious whisper, James said, "Tell them evil still walks."

In a shaky tone Hickman pronounced the situation grave, but Brigid would not relent. "We shall wait for Dr. Kelly no longer. We must take James to Bath. Everyone knows those waters have restorative, even miraculous, properties." Hickman was disappointed, but not surprised, to see a degree of wildness, of irrational denial, begin to build in her eyes.

"Mrs. Lockwood, if I may, a man in the Lieutenant's condition is not to be shipped across the Irish Sea, and one might suggest there is no sense in spending a small fortune—"

"We will not discuss the cost of what needs to be done, please, sir. What say you to Mallow? Mallow, of course. No sea journey would be required, only a brief carriage ride, and I have often heard Mallow's waters are the equal to Bath or Spa itself. Mallow, certainly, will do him a world of good. The children are all returned to school, and we could travel tomorrow if we so desire."

"Mrs. Lockwood, you must prepare yourself for what may well be the inevitable outcome of these recurrent fevers—"

But Brigid shot past Hickman with blind energy, calling for Mrs. Cashman.

The plans for Mallow had been made, and they might have left Clonakilty a week before if only James had been up to it. The fever spiked, and he was nearly comatose. Brigid had little sleep; she spent endless hours sitting at his bedside, silently urging him to breathe. She was dozing in her chair, just past dawn on a Tuesday morning, when she was jolted awake by the sound of a carriage roaring up the lane, and she reached the window to see the coachman pulling his lathered team to a halt in front of Fáibhile Cottage. In disbelief she watched Dr. Kelly and another man tumble from the carriage, each clutching a medical bag.

She ran down the stairs and reached the door even before they could knock, and flinging open the door she breathlessly embraced Kelly. "My dear doctor! You are most welcome!"

"Yes, yes, yes, thank you, my dear Brigid, that is a most gratifying welcome," he said absently as he and his companion hurried inside. Absently waving toward the short, stocky, unshaven man who followed him up the stairs, Kelly made a nod toward courtesy with, "Oh, Mrs. Lockwood, pray allow me to present my associate, Dr. Julian Veilleux of the Sorbonne. Dr. Veilleux, Madame Lockwood."

Dr. Veilleux, who smelled strongly of brandy, grunted something that might have been a greeting, and without further ceremony they stomped into the Lockwood bedroom. In an excited voice Brigid began to say, "Doctor, James has—" but Veilleux unceremoniously hushed her, and Kelly drew a long flared brass tube from his bag.

Brigid had never seen such a thing. Kelly held the narrow end to his ear and then placed the wide end at various places on James's softly rising chest. Veilleux took a turn doing the same, as they muttered to one another in Latin. Brigid, who despite her faith possessed a familiarity with Latin roughly equal to her familiarity with Hindi, still took enormous comfort in their presence and from what she hoped were satisfied tones in their conversation.

After a few minutes some decision was reached, and the two men began to take off their coats and roll up their sleeves.

Kelly said, "Brigid, Dr. Veilleux studied under the esteemed Dr. Larrey. He has made the study of empyema his life work, and, as I hoped, our friend James presents the most gratifying example. We shall operate immediately."

Brigid, wide-eyed, said, "Christ and His nails, Doctor! What, here, now?"

Displeased, Kelly replied, "Well, of course, woman. Have we not traveled like furies across land and sea to do so? Now, go and fetch a large bowl—"

Veilleux waved a finger, shook his head, and eyeing James's chest said, "*Forte situlae.*"

"—very well, then, a bucket, please, *a grah.*" As he shooed Brigid out the door Kelly added, "And would there be a Christian cup of tea in the house? I have not had a decent cup of tea in months. I famish."

Kelly and Veilleux sat on the stone wall in front of the cottage smoking cigars with an air of accomplishment. Latin is not a language typically associated with a state of relaxation, but Veilleux exhaled a lungful of smoke and smoothly said in that tongue, "That, colleague, was certainly the most satisfying drainage of a pernicious empyema of my experience."

"I am so pleased, Dr. Veilleux. My affection for the patient and his wife aside, I found the operation of exceptional interest. But I am afraid that decorum will require us to both shift our clothes at the first opportunity." Wiping at his sleeve, then eying Veilleux's shirt, Kelly frowned and added, "I do not envy the laundress who is faced with these spattered effluvia."

Veilleux huffed and said, "The uneducated might find such a spray of blood and pus to be distasteful—"

"The faint of heart might deem it even horrifying."

"—but for a man of discernment, a student of the natural world, such an explosive drainage is a validation, nay, a vindication, of many theories regarding fever, infection, and evil humours. But in honour of your hypothetical laundress, I shall admit that the effect to our clothing, not to mention the Lockwoods' carpet and walls, is to be... regretted."

Kelly waved his cigar, tilted his head to Veilleux, and said, "Still, I offer my heartiest congratulations on your success, dear colleague, as well as my sincere thanks. Further, I intend to follow your example of vinegar as a proof against suppuration.

Now, as to post-operative care. I believe your regimen requires the drain to remain in place no longer than twenty-four hours?"

Wiping his filthy hands on his filthy apron, Veilleux replied, "Yes, and not one moment longer; the pus, the minimal, laudable pus, to be expected by that point should run clear. Might I be so bold as to mention that my inner man lies ravenous? I wonder if Mrs. Lockwood might be persuaded to leave her husband long enough to prepare an omelet. Though an Englishwoman can scarcely be expected to cook anything remotely edible."

"Mrs. Lockwood is Irish."

Veilleux sniffed and said, "Then I shall not allow my hopes to wander beyond beer, whiskey, and potatoes. Now, as to bandages, they should be as air tight as possible, changed three times daily."

Dr. Kelly was so relieved, so pleased with James's immediate positive response to the surgery, that he responded only to Dr. Veilleux's professional comments, saying, "I shall inform Mrs. Lockwood that even such a successful surgery will require weeks to see final scarring and healing, in light of such a lengthy and chronic period of infection."

Veilleux took a long last pull at his cigar, and, flipping its butt into Brigid's roses, he said, "And such a chronic infection is certain to have permanently affected his lungs. He shall no longer be the most active of men. But, barring catastrophe, Mrs. Lockwood shall have her husband's company for some years yet. Further, I believe I shall prescribe the regular application of tobacco smoke, to stimulate the airways. Being a man of a generous nature, I shall leave a number of my own cigars to initiate the habit."

Chapter Thirteen

Agnes ni Geraghty shuffled up Dame Street, both arms holding the *London Gazette* close to her wizened chest. She was taking no chances, no indeed, lest any stray raindrop hit Captain Barr's own *Gazette*. He was most particular. No *Belfast Gazette,* or *Edinburgh*, but the *London* itself, and God help her if it wasn't perfect as the Christ child. Once, early on, when the Captain had first come to the Horse, she had handed him a *Gazette* that had a bit of mud on it, and hadn't he given her a broad-handed slap that had knocked her across the room, oh my yes. There was a man who knew how to hit a woman. Agnes had long experience with men who could hit a woman, from her father to that day. She had learned early on that subservient anonymity was her only refuge, and she had lived all her life tiny, silent, and alone.

She was an old woman now, old before her time, a maid at the Black Horse, and she counted herself lucky to have the job. Bent and rheumatic, she was invisible on the street, limping back with the Captain's *Gazette*, price sevenpence, which was sold only in the finer parts of the city, down near the River Liffey. Her route back to the Horse took her south on Patrick Street, past St. Patrick's Cathedral and the God who had yet to demonstrate any particular interest in Agnes ni Geraghty. With just one lingering glance back toward hope, she turned a corner and was back on the Coombe, the heart of St. Luke's parish, the poorest parish in all Dublin.

It was in a shabby room on the upper floor of the Black Horse that Captain Charles Barr resided. He had recovered from his beating, but his syphilis had flared. Alone in the filthy attic he had sunk into a twitching madness that even his most determined enemies might have found sufficient. His mind was nearly unhinged, its only anchors being an immutable hatred of James Lockwood and an equally passionate irrational fury of love, lust, and loathing for Brigid O'Brian. Only hatred and a manic thirst for vengeance gave him reason to draw breath.

It required all of Barr's half-pay for the landlady, the grasping, penny-pinching landlady, to put up with the Captain's endless stream of abuse. Only once a day would the aged Agnes be sent up with a tray of food, a pail for his soil, and the latest newspapers. Agnes told the landlady that the Captain was most particular about the newspapers, always anxious to see the pages that dealt with marriages, births, and deaths, oh, especially the deaths.

Agnes made her way up the dark, creaking stairs that seemed to get steeper with every passing day. The tray was heavy, and the empty pail slapped against her sore leg.

She set the pail down on the landing and tapped at the door. "Your tray, please, sir, and the *London Gazette*."

"Come in then, damn you," came the croaking response.

The room was gloomy; only a few muted streaks of dusty light snuck through the shutters, shutters that had not been opened since Barr came there. The bedding had not been changed in weeks, and the room's smell was sickening.

Agnes had long before established a quick routine, but Barr swore foully until she hurriedly handed him the *Gazette*. On that particular July day, Agnes heard something she had never expected to hear in that room: Barr laughed. The *Gazette* carried the announcement he had long awaited.

> London Gazette
> *War-Office— 2 June, 1820*
> *27th Foot: Ensign Llewellin Nelson to be Lieutenant, without purchase, vice Lockwood, appointed to the royal veteran battalion.*

Barr sat grinning for some time, and Agnes watching him, fascinated; it was like watching a serpent coil.

"You, bring me some wine," Barr hissed. "Good French wine, none of your God damned bog water. And pen and ink; paper, too. Watermarked paper. And hurry, damn you." His claw-like hand scrabbled into a drawer at his bedside, and he threw a handful of money at her. "That is more than enough. I have been saving for this day." As Agnes gathered the coins and hurried from the room, Barr went on quietly, "He must be inches from the grave for him to finally take a posting to the Veterans. That bastard is dying, and I have work to do."

In a dank basement office of Dublin Castle a junior clerk was the first to receive the letter from Captain Charles Barr of the 24th Foot. The letter lay in a tray for a few days until the clerk noticed that it was addressed to Lord Kerr, Lord Lieutenant of Ireland, and he flipped the letter into the appropriate box.

The letter was then forwarded to a senior clerk, who performed the same functions as the junior, whereupon it was forwarded to the Lord Lieutenant's most junior assistant, who finally broke its seal, and finding its contents intriguing he forwarded it directly to his superior. That superior, in turn, served society by making his check mark on the bottom right of the letter, after which the letter was forwarded to Henry Graham, Senior Secretary to the Lord Lieutenant, who would determine whether the letter was worthy of consideration by Lord Kerr himself. Graham was a cousin to the Lord Lieutenant, an experienced diplomat and a bitter little man who thought himself deserving of a better post than that of his fat cousin's secretary.

Graham saw a small mountain of paperwork every day, but he was instantly pleased with this letter from Captain Barr. Graham may have been unhappy with his post, but he had long before found playing the outraged patriot was a sure path to promotion. He thus kept a special red folder to hold the files which he believed his cousin would find most interesting. Graham read Barr's letter through three times, and then with a contented air he slid it into the red folder.

Graham carried the red folder into Kerr's office every Monday morning, when Kerr was well rested and ready to fulfill his notions as to what constituted service to king and country. Kerr was a heavy, unimaginative man. Powerful factions had smoothed his path to the rank of Lord Lieutenant of Ireland, as Kerr possessed the requisite wealth and pedigree; but while he was no fool, his powers of decision were remarkably inconsistent. At the sight of the red folder he rose like a shark in bloody water.

"Ah, the red folder," said Kerr. "Very good. What have you for me today, Graham?"

"Two issues for your attention, My Lord. The first involves a popish priest named McDevitt and a man named Berkley, both of Mayo, who physically interfered in the legal eviction of a number of tenants who had defaulted on their rents."

Kerr looked over the file, asking without looking up, "I assume this Berkley is also a papist?"

"No, my Lord, it seems that Mr. Berkley is a Protestant, evidently a gentleman."

"What! A Protestant gentleman ignoring his God-given birthright to side with some damned priest! We will put an end to that, Graham, must we not? Oh, yes, indeed. We shall preserve the peace at all costs. How found the court?"

"Both were found guilty of interfering with a court officer in the conduct of his duties. Both to stand in the stocks for twelve hours."

"A slap on the wrist! That is a very mild punishment, is it not, Graham?" said Kerr.

"I quite agree, My Lord. The Mayo magistrate did, however, note some irregularities in the evictions; Lord Michaels is most anxious to enclose the land in question. And there are of course the rumours of crop failures, potatoes rotting in the fields and so on. We have a letter from some of our own churchmen, including Bishop Stock of Killala, regarding fears of starvation and pleas for relief."

Kerr sniffed and said, "Stock did well enough in '98, but he has developed a very unorthodox regard the papists. Starvation? He certainly exaggerates. Simply a matter of slothful peasants who prefer charity to hard work."

"I am certain you are correct, my Lord. Returning to the case, the court transcripts clearly state that both McDevitt and Berkley used their sticks to effect: the bailiffs were quite battered. Further, there is suspicion that the magistrate ruled in fear of the local ruffians, as the presence of the militia is very thin there, and evidently many of our militiamen are in sympathy with the evicted tenants."

"There is no question of death, I suppose? Am I empowered to declare a death sentence in such matters?"

"The statutes do not currently allow that punishment, my Lord, though we might perhaps find grounds for additional charges. Then again, the Catholic bishops do so often pose a problem in the execution of priests."

"Damn all bishops. Except ours, of course. No matter the obstacles, we cannot allow wayward Protestants to ally themselves with disruptive Catholic elements. We learned that in '98. Certainly. Both these meddling fools will be immediately charged with sedition, and upon conviction, and they shall be found guilty, will they not, Graham? I shall see them sentenced to transportation. Let us see how well these two get along in Botany Bay. In the meantime I will order the Kilrush Yeomanry to Mayo. They are to be relied upon to achieve results. A man of my position need not burden himself about how the peace is restored, only that it is restored, and quickly. What next?"

"A most disturbing letter from a Captain Charles Barr, My Lord, who makes some most serious accusations against a Lieutenant and Mrs. James Lockwood."

"The Lockwoods of Malahide?"

"That is the family, my Lord; he is their second son. I have made some discreet inquiries regarding Captain Barr. He is a Waterloo veteran, wounded there, though of no family. He served with the 27th, the Inniskillings, along with Lieutenant Lockwood. Captain Barr contends that Lieutenant and Mrs. Lockwood intend to defraud the pension system."

"That is quite bad, is it not, Graham?"

"Oh, yes, My Lord, a most serious crime, if proven. It seems that Lieutenant Lockwood is indeed near death, and in his final days is conspiring with his wife to perpetrate a deliberate crime against government."

Kerr frowned deeply and said, "This is most unfortunate. So, does this Barr tell us how the Lockwoods intend to execute this fraud?"

"The Captain is quite frank in his allegations, the most serious of which challenges Lockwood's eligibility for any pension at all. As you are of course aware, My Lord, the death must be due to a wound suffered in the King's service. Captain Barr alleges that Lockwood's wound was suffered during a sordid affair whilst in the company of a Belgian courtesan."

Kerr, who frequented more brothels than any man in Dublin, huffed and muttered, "Whoring, was he?"

"Barr also contends, My Lord, that the Lockwoods intend to claim five children, children who or may or not exist."

"Oh, indeed? Fraudulently inflating the claim... most disreputable," said Kerr.

"Then, there are serious questions regarding the legitimacy of some of the five children listed by the applicant."

"The woman is a trollop and a liar, then?"

"Further, my Lord, Captain Barr has offered testimony challenging the legality of the marriage. Lockwood was of course a Protestant, but he found it necessary to marry a Catholic, an O'Brian, at that. It seems that Captain Barr was witness to the marriage, in the year of the rebellion itself, and is willing to swear an oath that the marriage was conducted by a Catholic priest, and at the bride's insistence no Protestant clergyman was present."

"By God!" shouted Kerr, now fully enraged. "A deliberate felony, a flagrant public flaunting of the law. Such a criminal action, in the same year as the Croppie rising, is tantamount to treason! Am I wrong in this, Graham?"

"Oh, no, I quite agree, My Lord. Perhaps you would care to review Captain Barr's correspondence personally."

Kerr quickly scanned Barr's letter, his jowls growing redder by the moment, finally exploding, "That seals it! This blasphemous fool Lockwood takes up with a papist wench who takes him for every penny he has, producing papist whelps which may or may not be his own, and when he finally has the good sense to die to escape his disgrace, she attempts to bilk government of more money by claiming fraudulent children, so that she can continue to suck at the teat of established authority. I won't have it! Handle this, Graham, or as God as my witness I shall send to have the local magistrate strip her, tie her to a wagon wheel, and flog her in the town square!"

Graham, who was inordinately prone to lascivious thoughts, had heard that the papist wench in question was quite a lovely piece, and very nearly offered to carry out Kerr's suggestion. But as he still lacked the actual Application for Pension from the widow, Graham contented himself by spending that afternoon writing several letters, often with a satisfied grin on his face.

Agnes made a special trip up the stairs to the Captain's room. She was, in fact, thrilled to do so, as she bore a letter from Dublin Castle itself. Agnes ni Geraghty, delivering a copper-plate wax-sealed missive straight from Satan's throne, would wonders never cease.

Even through his horribly disfigured features, Barr's satisfaction was soon evident.

> *Dublin Castle 4 July, 1820*
> *My Dear Captain Barr,*
>
> *You have no doubt received the official notice from our mutually esteemed Lord Lieutenant, informing you that your letter regarding possible improprieties in the pending Lockwood pension application has been received and its contents noted.*
>
> *You will please give me the pleasure of conveying my personal thanks for your timely information, and the admiration I have for its source, a man conscious of the delicate condition of Irish society, the rule of law,*

and the absolute need to keep the Papist masses subject to legitimate authority, both legal and moral.

You will please allow me, my Dear Sir, to give you my personal assurance that every possible measure will be taken to ensure that justice is done in the instance of the Lockwood pension, as abuse of the pension system is crime enough, but crimes against the natural order, the fabric of society, are so unconscionable as to merit the most severe punishment.

Lastly, your letters mention that you are not in the best of health. Doubtless you are suffering from the effects of the wounds suffered in your valiant defense of King and Country. With trembling hand allow me to salute you, my Dear Sir, and wish you a speedy recovery. Rest well, knowing that men who fancy themselves your equal in passionate loyalty to King and the Protestant Ascendancy stand guard over Ireland.

I remain, Sir, your most humble servant,
Henry Graham

Agnes hurried out of the Captain's room. If she had remained she would have heard the second bit of laughter that Barr would utter at the Black Horse.

"Wounded in action, oh my yes," he cackled softly. "Wounded twenty-five years ago by that poxed whore on Montgomery Street. But I served her out, didn't I? Twenty-five years; that son of a bitch Lockwood should be in his grave any day now, and by God I shall ruin that whore O'Brian. Her God damned pups too. My honour redeemed." Still muttering to himself he stiffly rose from his bed and opened the largest of his three fine trunks.

He dressed in his best uniform, standing ramrod straight in the King's scarlet, growing strong and fierce, a predatory gleam in his eyes. From deep in the trunk he pried open a hidden compartment and pulled out a large purse stuffed with shining guineas, the bounty of his frauds amongst the aristocracy. With a sneering grin he muttered, "Duty calls."

Lieutenant Thomas Mainwaring was adjusting with only moderate difficulty to a life of afternoon tea, gentle conversation, and lace tablecloths. In the drawing room of their Belfast home he and the lovely new Mrs. Mainwaring were going through their morning post. Julia flipped a letter closed and told her husband, "McSweeny reports no sign of him in either Cork town or Clonakilty."

Tom looked up from his letter and said, "Our man in Dublin has no news either. Evidently Charles Barr has dropped completely from the face of the earth. Perhaps that beating in Bandon drove him out of Ireland."

Julia pursed her lips and asked, "And we are to expect no help from Horse Guards?"

"No. They say the regimental agent for the 24th Foot has every right to withhold information regarding Barr's whereabouts. He is forwarding Barr's half pay, but he will not tell us where, no matter how I plead." In a grim tone Tom added, "Perhaps I shall travel to Charing Cross, find this Mr. Chedwick, and beat it out of him."

"My dear, please."

Tom recovered himself and said, "I beg your pardon, my dear. Too long a soldier." He forced a smile onto his face and went on, "For now, though, let us put all thoughts of Charles Barr aside and tend to our packing. Our wedding trip at last! How I long to show you Paris."

When the school's trap carried the girls the short distance to the Muirs' house, that elegant, imposing, frigid edifice, four servants were instantly there to assist the two young ladies. The Muirs' servants were typically formal and silent, but as one of their footmen handed the girls down he very quietly murmured in Irish, "On behalf of the staff, may I bid you good welcome, young gentlewomen." He had said it so softly, scarcely moving his lips, and it was so out of character for any hint of humanity to flicker in that house that both girls were briefly startled out of their nervousness. Mary began to turn to speak to the footman, but he turned away quickly, returning to his business. Cissy took her elbow and steered Mary toward the door, only murmuring to the footman, also in Irish, "That is most kind; you will please give the staff our thanks, and they so kind." As they walked up the many broad steps to the front door, Mary looked at Cissy with a puzzled look, and Cissy whispered, "Don't you see, dear, if Aunt or Uncle saw the servants speaking with us they would be out on the road in a heartbeat. And in Irish! It must be hell to be in service here."

The stiffly formal butler received them and, after a moderate but meaningful wait, he then showed them into their Aunt's sitting room. It was her private room, but it lacked any feminine touch of colour or warmth, wholly formal and cold. Their Aunt stood tall and intimidating in the center of the room, the central element of a choreographed reception. The girls each made their perfectly formal curtsy, and their Aunt returned it, but carefully, precisely less deeply than her nieces.

There was an awkward silence for a moment, a moment in which their Aunt reveled, until she said, "I had the pleasure of seeing you girls last weekend. Does your schoolwork not keep you occupied, or have you perhaps gone through your allowances already?"

"We beg pardon for the intrusion, Aunt," said Cissy, nervous but determined, "but we are in receipt of a letter from our mother, who tells us that our father is much recovered, and she wishes that we might return home to share in their joy."

"Certainly not," scoffed their aunt, "you shall not abandon your studies every time your mother imagines some miraculous recovery. As you girls learn more of the world, you shall find that there are women who crave attention and who will do anything to get it. While I do not wish to overtly denigrate your mother, or to ignore the enormous loss that she shall suffer in the death of my dear, dear brother, I feel that you are old enough to face the fact that your mother is likely one of those deliberately self-serving women."

Mary was silent, her head down, her cheeks red, while Cissy said in a controlled voice, "I am grieved, Aunt, to hear that you do not hold our mother in the same regard in which we do. I assure you that your unfortunate impression is groundless. Her letter is most encouraging. Our mother speaks of a surgery, a quite innovative surgery, performed by an eminent French surgeon, in company with our own Dr. Kelly."

Cissy handed across the letter, and after briefly scanning it her Aunt handed it back disdainfully, saying, "Dr. Kelly? My Muir often says that an Irish physician is like a black trained to speak English: merely an animal doing tricks. I might also suggest that this Dr. Kelly allowed my poor brother to sink to such a dangerous level, which is scant recommendation for any physician, and I am shocked that you would value the opinion of a man who fails his profession in such obvious fashion."

The three women still stood in the gilded room; there was no offer for the young Lockwoods to sit. Cissy and her Aunt faced each other, Mary off to one side, her cheeks glowing but with her head now raised, yet still it was the younger sister who spoke. "Our family has the utmost faith in Dr. Kelly, Aunt, and it was he who arranged for this French surgeon to save our father."

Aunt Muir waved her hand dismissively. "As you wish. But to return to the purpose of your call, which I must say has been delivered in a most surprising, confrontational, and unpleasant manner. I am adamant: neither of you shall go anywhere but back to school, where you are to devote yourselves to your studies, which I trust will include increased coursework in the courtesy required of a lady when calling upon her most devoted family members."

Before Cissy could reply, Mary finally spoke, with a high, sharp edge to her voice, the words bursting out. "I am sorry to find you so resolute, Aunt, but my sister and I are equally resolute. While you and Uncle Muir would not allow us to return home when our father was so very ill, we are determined not to be managed in such a fashion again. We shall travel to Clonakilty as soon as arrangements can be made. We both thank you for your concern for our welfare, but at the risk of sounding unkind I will tell you that the welfare of our family, our immediate family, is our prime concern. The unfailing regard in which we hold one another is the foundation of our family, even if it is a quality quite unknown in your own. Good day."

The two girls executed a simultaneous about-face that would not have been out of place at Horse Guards, walking out arm in arm, perhaps shaking a bit, while their aunt, beyond livid, followed them out into the marble hall, calling up the stairs, "Muir! Muir!" then to the girls' backs, "You two young ladies will not take one more step until you have spoken with your Uncle Muir!" then to the butler, "Freely, you will not open that door!"

Mary and Cissy reached the door, where the butler could only look at them with a pained expression. "Oh, have some backbone, man," said Cissy, and she opened the door herself.

Mrs. Barbara Orr brought afternoon tea into the Headmaster's office. She politely poured him a cup, though she would have preferred to pour it into his lap. She had worked for the previous Headmaster for several years, and she had come to love that kind old gentleman, but he had died that past spring. Now this trim, neat, self-important, condescending Ebenezer Dempster had inherited Barron House Academy, and Mrs. Orr was unhappy with the abrupt changes being instituted. Two of the teachers, who had no other means but their meager pay, had been dismissed without notice; but worse, far worse, was this new Headmaster's insistence upon having even the youngest boys beaten for minor infractions of the rules.

Dempster's chair was low and soft, making him ridiculous behind his massive desk. He did not look at Mrs. Orr, and certainly did not thank her for the tea, instead keeping his nose in his correspondence, only saying, "Mrs. Orr, it seems as if the Masters Lockwood are to return home until next term. You will please see to their trunks."

"I do hope that there is no ill news concerning their father, sir? Both boys are terribly concerned for this health."

"No, it seems as if Lieutenant Lockwood is quite recovered. But be he upright or no, the Lockwoods owe two semesters' tuition, and will I see a penny of it? I very much doubt it, no matter how strongly I press the issue. I can thank my father for allowing the Irish into this establishment. Bog-trotting Papists, with no discipline, no notion of honour, to allow debt to accumulate in this fashion. I ought to hold their trunks in compensation. I shall certainly bring suit."

Barron House Academy was a very large old house, once an exclusive residence but now well past its prime. No one was precisely sure how old the place actually was, but a plaque in the great hall from 1591 gave some indication.

Mrs. Orr was the Lady of the School, a tall, elegant woman, who supervised the household staff and the care and feeding of the nearly two hundred boys. She was well known throughout the school, indeed throughout Mitcham, as a woman with a heart of gold, but nonetheless a woman who was not to be trifled with, up to and including any ill-considered questions regarding the whereabouts of Mr. Orr. In this particular instance her patience was being very severely tested by this new Headmaster, who droned on, still speaking as if he were addressing the cat, "I shall have them out by the end of the day. Behind on their tuition, and now I shall be forced to bear the cost of their travel home, depending on their parents' tenuous promise to compensate me at a later date. Their parents. There is money in the Lockwood name, and how they managed not to garner their share raises questions, quite pressing questions, in my mind, regarding their capability, perhaps even their morality. And they write a very poor letter, addressing me as "Mister" when they very well know that I am Headmaster here, a title of great distinction, though these Irish bumpkins do not evidently deem it so."

Mrs. Orr found Master Aidan Dunn where she had left him shortly before, standing by a table in the dining hall. He had been caned that morning for his evidently mistaken belief that Tir na nÒg lay somewhat west of the Blasketts, or to their south, as the place could shift by magic, do you see, no matter what Mr. Lloyd might say. Aiden was one of the youngest boys in the school, and Mrs. Orr had tried to recover him with a surreptitious glass of milk and a slice of strawberry tart. Mr.

Dempster's canings were serious affairs, but still, strawberry tart is a powerful stimulant, and Mrs. Orr saw that his sniffling had ceased. "Aidan, dear," she said, (when in private, she called all the boys by their Christian names, to their delight), "please run up and ask the Lockwood brothers, if it is quite convenient, if they might join me in the parlour in five minutes."

But even strawberry tart failed to brace young Dunn for such a reckless venture, the boy piping, "But ma'am, they are oldsters! I was told that if I were to set foot in the oldster hall I should be impaled, and my eyes popped out of my head for the cats to play with!"

"Oh, now...."

"And my home burned to the ground, the sorrow and woe!" he added. "My family driven out into the hedges, the cows should go dry, and the fields of Ballykissane sown with salt!"

"And they certainly would be," soothed Mrs. Orr, "if you were so foolish as to go there unbidden, as the oldsters are very terrible. But you will keep this card in your hand," giving him a bright red card, "and those gentlemen will know that you are on an errand from me."

Thus Aidan Dunn passed into Elder Hall of Barron House, the scarlet card held up before him like a holy relic, before which even the hulking Butcher Hook quailed. Master Dunn found the brothers Lockwood together in William's room, where they spent most of their free time together. Young Dunn delivered his message in stammering awe, as the Lockwoods were the heroes of all the younger boys.

Doing his best to sound casual but failing, Richard asked in Irish, "Did Mrs. Orr say why she wished to see us?"

Joseph gave his brother's a few sharp slaps on the leg, such gestures being a common mark of reassurance among young men of that age, and said, "No matter. Please to tell Mrs. Orr *a grah*, that it will be the pleasure of the world for us to see her in five minutes' time."

As Aidan retreated Joseph called after him, "And for your own mother's sake, bear high that card of red, and pass like one of Saint Eogan's faithful through the enemy host, at Lettach it was." Then in English, harshly calling down the hall, "Fletcher, as you value your teeth, you'll not be saying one word to that wee gentlemen, will you, now?"

Mrs. Orr had a great fondness for the Lockwood boys, as her soft heart always went out to the boys who were at a disadvantage. Indeed, when they first arrived at Barron House some years before she had worried over them a great deal, as two polite, soft-spoken Irish boys were certainly a target for the older boys, and Barron House was never short of bullies. To be Irish was bad enough, but being Catholic, and from a family that was so obviously lacking in funds, made Joseph and Richard the butt of every possible cruelty. It was only after four months of such hazing that their Irish had surfaced, and in a blind, savage, fist-swinging rage the two brothers fought four of the school's worst tyrants to a bloody standstill. Thereafter their stock rose amazingly, and Mrs. Orr had watched the brothers blossom.

While it did not appear that the brothers would grow to be as tall as their father, they were clever enough to inherit a moderate degree of their mother's elegance of face and form. Scarcely a year apart, they each had their mother's chestnut hair and blue eyes, their father's unique mix of reticence, charm, and occasional fury, and they were, in fact, so similar in appearance that they were often confused one for the other, except that Joseph was left-handed, and Richard right.

Handsome young men can be insufferable, but while the brothers Lockwood were handsome creatures, the both of them, they were fortunate in not to seeing themselves so, indeed they would have been wholly embarrassed if anyone had ever thought to say such a thing. Such handsomeness would normally have rendered them very eligible to the young ladies of Mitcham, (young ladies of that area being notorious in their appetites), if only the Lockwood boys had not been quite so Catholic, and not nearly so Irish. Still, the two young men, for they were indeed growing into that confusing, promising state, were returning to Clonakilty not quite so pure as Father McGlynn might have wished. There were some young ladies in Surrey who were so unpopular and poor, or so popular and rich, that they could dare risk overlooking the boys' glaring deficiencies in favour of gentle manners and those sparkling blue eyes.

When the two brothers joined Mrs. Orr in the faded parlour of Barron House Academy she quickly dispelled their anxious faces, holding aloft the letter from home and brightly saying, "Happy news, boys. You father is recovering quickly, and your parents desire that you return home as soon as you may, and the seven of you shall spend the summer together in Clonakilty."

Lucy Lockwood sat contentedly in a sunny classroom at Richmond Academy, where Miss Christine Paige was teaching Lucy and ten other girls to embroider, a requisite skill for those desirous of the status of gentlewoman. It was her favourite class, as she was stitching an image of Fáibhile Cottage, its massive beeches, and her achingly distant family.

She was a small girl, not terribly strong, and quiet. She was not overly popular at the school, but she had become close friends with Priyia Bellamy, the half-Indian daughter of a retired Company official.

When the Headmistress came and sternly called Lucy out to the hall, both she and Priyia blanched, as Priyia had received word of her mother's death in just such a fashion. Miss Paige, who was aware of the precarious health of Miss Lockwood's father and so looked concerned as well, led Lucy out into the hall. Miss Paige was gone only for a few minutes, however, and when she returned she did so with a smile, bringing a smile of relief to the good-hearted Miss Bellamy.

"Girls," said Miss Paige, "Miss Lockwood has been called home to see her father, who is recovering from the wound he suffered at Waterloo. We shall all wish her joy. Now who can tell me what armies fought at Waterloo, and the outcome of—"

Before she could finish her question, however, Caroline Fitter and Hannah Butler both urgently raised their hands and begged, "Oh, please, please, Miss Paige, might we go home as well? Oh, *please*? Lucy must certainly not travel alone!"

Several other girls suddenly got tears in their eyes and begged to go home as well, please, as it wasn't fair that only Lucy got to go home. Miss Paige came from a military family, and she employed a considerable measure of that heritage in her teaching. She thus applied a mix of firmness, rational thought, and an elusive but discernable element of kindness, in quieting her class. She informed Miss Fitter and Miss Butler that Miss Lockwood required no escort to Clonakilty, as her brothers (at the mention of the Lockwood brothers both Miss Fitter and Miss Butler got stars in their eyes) were to travel to Richmond by the mail coach, and they were then to travel together back to Ireland, and home, the word *home* carrying as great a meaning to the young ladies of Richmond Academy as it did to anyone in the world.

Chapter Fourteen

Joseph Lockwood took his brother's riposte square in the chest and dramatically dropped to the ground. His father, who sat on the garden wall nearby, said, "My son, if you do not learn Guard Two, and elevate your point like a Christian, one day such a thrust might well put you in a real grave."

Lucy, who sat beside her father on the garden wall, had laughed when Joseph fell, but when he did not rise she ran to him with open concern. James said firmly, "Joseph, get up, please. Do not frighten your sister."

Joseph raised his head just in time for his little sister to give him a scowl and a surreptitious kick. As he rose and dusted himself off Joseph asked, "Father, may we not use real swords now? It would be so much more interesting if we used real swords."

Richard joined in with, "Yes, Father, learning with sticks is humiliating. If Scabs Butler rides by and sees us dueling with sticks we will never hear the end of it."

James motioned Joseph back to his place opposite Richard and said, "Master Butler may have a charming nickname, his own horse, and a shining new épée, but he is the son of a minister. While Reverend Butler is a renowned Hebrew scholar and a fine man, to my certain knowledge he is no hand with a blade. You two young gentlemen have the advantage of being trained by your devoted father, a King's officer of many years' standing. An officer, incidentally, who does not believe in training with buttons on the point of one's sword. Buttons have been known to fly off during a sharp exchange, and, before you know it, a training session turns tragic. I have seen it happen, and until I am certain you know what you are doing you shall battle with nothing more lethal than sticks. Now: Draw swords. Slope swords. Engage. Point in Quarte... nails up, Joseph... engage... point in Tierce... engage."

Brigid came out to the garden to watch, and when James finally allowed the boys a few minutes rest she told them, "Remember, please, that I agreed that you might ask your father to teach you just the basics. He is still recovering his strength, and besides, you shall never need to fight anyone. I will not have you going about challenging renowned duelists over imagined slights. My sons are nice boys."

"Yes, Mama," they both chimed.

James nodded and added, "Well said, my love."

After Brigid returned to the house James drew a deep breath, winced, and called his sons back into position with deadly seriousness. "Now. The *High Seconde* is coming into fashion these days, especially amongst the dandies. You will please ignore it. It requires a great deal of effort to hold the guard up by one's shoulder, and if some fool attempts it against you, you shall eventually have him. Pay attention; this may save your life one day."

James was in his chair flipping through a small book as Brigid passed by, and looking up he said, "My dear, do you recall me mentioning Ensign Thomas Smith?"

He is that boy who is such good friends with Ensign Digby, is he not? The fledgling poet? You mentioned him in one of your letters from Ghent. And then he was wounded at Waterloo?"

"Yes, a musket ball in the leg, but he recovered in time to rejoin the army outside Paris. At any rate, Smith has had his book of poetry published, and young Digby has forwarded a copy with the kindest endorsement; you might read it later, as it is frankly embarrassing to read aloud. He has also enclosed the most clever letter, full of humourous anecdotes. He tells me, for example, that in Paris the French call the men of our regiment *'les Goddamms'* due to their habit of using that phrase on every occasion." James laughed, his typical huge, roaring laugh, which always brought a wry smile to Brigid's face.

"And so, sir, I might assume his poetry is equally amusing?"

"Oh, goodness, no, the poetry is of an entirely different nature. All deadly serious, romance and battle and such."

Brigid was standing at the bottom of the steps with her arms full of sheets, and as she spoke with her husband, Joseph, Richard, and Lucy tried to slip past. She frowned at them, pointed back upstairs, and said, "You three know very well that it is laundry day. So you will march right back up those steps, gather your things, and bring them straight down. You shall then help Mrs. Cashman spread them outside to dry." The children, downcast, clumped back upstairs and Brigid backed through the kitchen door, where Mrs. Cashman was brewing on a massive scale.

A few moments later, Mary and Cissy came downstairs loaded with laundry. They were intent on passing through to the kitchen until their father held up his new book and said, "Ladies, I have here an opportunity for you to display the benefit of your elegant education."

The girls looked intrigued, so their father continued, "I am in receipt of a book of poetry, written by a young fellow named Ensign Smith, a gift from one of my friends in the service, Ensign Digby. . Pray, give me your opinion of this verse, from a piece about Waterloo." In a deep voice he considered appropriate to the topic, James rumbled,

"The sanguine hills for many a rood,
With dead, or dying forms, were strew'd
All ghastly pale, or blood imbrued,
That never the eye the like beheld!
For them, their Country's tears shall swell,
Their Country annals proudly tell
The battles where they fought and fell,
The foes their study valour quell'd—

"I ask you, honestly, now, is that not the equal of Milton and Chaucer and that lot? In all fairness, is this lad not a major talent?"

Mary, more familiar than her sister with the art of disarming gentlemen, managed a smile and said, "That is quite grand, yes. Thank you, Papa."

Cissy raised her eyebrows and hesitantly said, "Yes... quite. Tell us, Papa, does the entire poem carry on in that same... style?"

"Oh, goodness, yes. Until the end, at any rate, where he turns quite poignant, and dwells on urchin's cheeks and widow's anguish and such. Thunderous good stuff. Shall I read you more?"

"Oh, Papa," said Mary brightly, "we were just helping with the laundry, then we are off to meet Helen Blackwell... perhaps we might borrow your book this evening, and read to one another as we prepare for bed?"

Cissy tentatively asked, "Though perhaps bedtime might require a different verse from that gentleman? Perhaps one not quite so... stirring?"

"As you wish," said James, returning to the book. "Yes, you may prefer page sixteen, and this piece called 'Elegy on the Surrender of Valencia.' Capital."

Left alone again, James read on. He had expected just such a reception of Smith's verse, but the poems struck a chord deep within him. When the poem spoke of the dead and wounded, ghastly pale, James saw them clearly, and he read the poem again and again, tenuously exploring his own memories and the deeply felt emotions they loosed.

The gentleman's appearance was so unusual that several people stopped to watch him trundle down Astna Street. People in Clonakilty had a rather narrow definition of normal behavior and appearance, though they were polite enough not to point out, in public at least, anyone who did not fall within those narrow limits.

In this instance it was not that the gentleman was dressed badly, as his fine suit of clothes marked him as a wealthy man. What drew such attention was the distinctive nature of his person, as his belly was of amazing prominence, reaching from his chin to very near his knees, while the rear of his body was of such a diminutive nature that passers-by feared that he would tumble over forward. The baker's girl watched him from the window of her father's shop, and being a sympathetic child she feared the fat man might come to grief when he turned right to walk up the steep slope of McCurtain's Hill Road.

If the gentlemen's appearance was noticed in town, his call at Fáibhile Cottage was even equally unconventional. Brigid happened to glance out a window to see the fat man sitting on the stone wall outside their front garden, gasping for breath and mopping his sweating face with a handkerchief. In a hurried half-whisper she called Cissy to join her, and they watched from the corners of the curtains until the man had faded from such a remarkable shade of red, to open the door and tentatively ask if they might be assistance to the gentleman?

The man slowly took his feet, and stuffing away his kerchief he muttered, "I had no concept of a Christian home standing at the top of such a precipice."

The gentleman made an effort recover himself, proffered a card, and began again. "Good afternoon. My name, ladies, is Jeffries. I am an attorney with offices in Dublin, and my services are on retainer to the firm of Dumon Père et Fils, of Marseilles."

Cissy gasped, her hand flew to mouth, and she whispered, "Guillaume?"

"Yes, Miss, that is the younger gentleman's name. I have a matter to discuss, if you ladies might grant me five minutes of your time. I have pressing business to return to in Dublin, and I have hope of catching the next mail coach back to Dublin, and so would appreciate a degree of alacrity in dealing with the matter."

Cissy hurried upstairs to call Mary while Brigid showed the lawyer into the drawing room. She was clever enough to steer Jeffries away from the settee, which looked unlikely to bear his weight, instead offering James's chair, as she had left her husband sleeping upstairs.

Brigid said, "May we offer, you, perhaps, Mr. Jeffries, a cup of—" but Jeffries, all business, drew a few sheets of paper from his elegant leather valise and said, "I carry two letters, please, one for Miss Mary Lockwood, and another for Lieutenant and Mrs. Lockwood...."

"My husband has just taken his dose, Mr. Jeffries, but I may just go to fetch him...."

"Pray, madam, do not disturb him." As Cissy and a pale, wide-eyed Mary came down the stairs to stand behind their mother on the settee he continued, "My business will, I pray, take only a moment. To wit: an express dispatch from Messrs. Dumon has reached me, in which they announce that Messr. Guillaume Dumon is made partner in his father's business."

Jeffries paused to pull his watch from a vest pocket and said, "I must fly. You will pardon the lack of formality and sentiment, ladies, but it is the wish of the younger Messr. Dumon that both the elder Lockwood daughters might sail to Marseilles on the next suitable vessel, whereupon Miss Mary Lockwood—" he looked at the two young ladies with a question on his face, whereupon Mary, amazed, hesitantly, softly, raised her hand, "—yes, you, Miss Mary Lockwood, might wed Messr. Guillaume Dumon, and you, Miss Brigit Lockwood, shall share their home."

Brigid sat stunned; both Cissy and Mary stood stock-still with round eyes and astounded expressions until they both spoke at the same instant, waving their hands and saying with varying degrees of conviction, "I could not possibly—"

Jeffries, who had perhaps been an attorney for too long, was not a gentleman overly receptive to any ideas that were not completely in line with his own. "Ladies, my instructions are quite specific. I intend to begin my return journey to Dublin, the long, torturous return journey, on the next mail coach, and I have no time for coyness, no matter how well delivered."

Mary's hands began to shake, the welling tears flowed, and she turned to her sister. "Could it be? Am I to be married? My dear Guillaume! Oh, whatever shall I do, Cissy? Would you come, Cissy, *a grah*, will you come? I cannot go without you!"

Mary soon dissolved into frantic, joyful tears, retreating to her room to read the tender letter from Guillaume. Brigid hurried upstairs just behind her, crying as well, saying only, "I must wake your father...." Cissy gathered herself and, with as much calm as her eighteen years allowed her, politely showed Mr. Jeffries out, and as he pointed his bulk downhill she took a few selfish moments to ponder what all this might mean to her.

James knew something was amiss. He had been a husband and the father of daughters for many years, and had grown at least moderately sensitive to the manifest signs: constrained conversation, blinking eyes, and the tense expressions of women who were in some manner upset.

And while he knew something was amiss he was not overly eager to learn the cause, as he was not a man who relished emotional turmoil. At some level he would have preferred to remain ignorant. While he loved his wife and daughters, and would do anything to assist and protect them, he frankly preferred to be called in on only the major events.

In the early years of his marriage and of his fatherhood he had at times been sadly misled. There had been, for instance, an occasion where he had feared the world was coming to an early end, only to discover that the distress was sparked by a dead kitten in the road. He had, in fact, in that instance been unwise enough to say it was "only" a dead kitten in the road, and he had been savaged in no uncertain terms.

So, when James Lockwood woke from his nap and found his wife, his daughters, and his housekeeper speaking in fast, moist, emphatic whispers in the drawing room, and then when Cissy and Mrs. Cashman hurried past him with averted eyes and waving handkerchiefs, he was entitled to grimace and tell himself, "Oh, I'm for it now."

Brigid sat close beside Mary on the settee, while Mary steadily cried and Brigid studied the floor, all the while balling a kerchief and trying to control the delicate muscles of her face, though largely failing. The teary Mrs. Cashman hurried back in from the kitchen under the pretense of tea, but she left the clattering service on the sideboard (James did not dare go over to pour a cup, let alone draw his biscuit ration) to sit beside Mary as well.

"Has someone died?" James asked, in tone he considered to be considerate.

"Why, of course not, sir!" cried Brigid.

"Oh, fie, sir, how could you say such a thing!" added Mrs. Cashman.

This upbraiding was followed by another bout of communal crying, which brought Cissy hurrying in from the kitchen with chocolate to comfort her sister, though only after giving her father an angry, emphatic, and wholly undeserved glare.

There followed a general scattering of commentary from which James gleaned, "Great fat barrister... no soul, that man, at all!... a gentleman who will not take time for tea is no gentleman at all... such a hurry... given no time to craft a considered response...."

James then guessed, "I hope, then, the news is good?"

Brigid stared at him in some surprise and said, "Well, of course it is good news, James! Indeed, joyful news! Is Mary not to be married?"

"To young..." the angels whispered in his ear at the last instant and provided the name "... Guillaume?"

"Well, certainly, Guillaume, has she not been weeping her eyes out with love for that boy?"

"I am sorry, I had thought that... well... I had thought such news would... be... well..." finding himself ignored, he trailed off to a barely audible, "... better received...."

At that moment the boys and Sergeant came through the front door in their typically loud, crashing manner. Sergeant, that great heart, instantly perceived the mood in the room and went over to lie across Mary's feet in a warm, if confining, show of affection. The boys, being decent young men but no fools, quickly determined the cause of the tears, called "Give you joy, Mary," and beat a thunderous retreat upstairs, earning a jealous grimace from their father.

A boy from the Shannon Arms came to the front door with a message. After rewarding him with tuppence and an apple, Brigid carried the note upstairs to James and said, "A note from town, my dear: 'Lieutenant and Captain the Honorable Edward Granville requests the honour of calling on Lieutenant and Mrs. Lockwood at One O'clock this afternon.' He misspelled afternoon, the poor man, but I told the boy to offer our respects and to say that one o'clock was perfectly convenient."

James looked at the elegant card and was pleased to see that Granville had indeed misspelled afternoon. Brigid was an exceptionally bright woman, and while James was wise enough not to mention it, in the past he had noted in his wife a certain disregard for the niceties of spelling. He then thought for a moment and said, "I don't recall ever meeting him. An aristocrat and a guardsman; I do hope he is not some strutting little prig."

"You know, I have always meant to ask you why the Guards have such outrageous ranks as 'lieutenant and captain.'"

"Oh, it is a shallow little device instituted to pad the status of the god-like Guardsmen. Officers in the Household Cavalry and the Foot Guards, so they might inflate the status of their regiments and elevate them above the level of mere mortals, hold two ranks: one for the regiment and a higher one for the rest of the army. So when this Granville character presents himself, courtesy will require me to refer to him as captain, though is he a mere lieutenant. Do hand me that copy of the *Army List*, please, love, so that we may look him up."

Brigid smiled broadly at her husband and said, "You realize, I hope, *a grah*, that a month ago it would have taken you ten minutes to say what you just said in a few seconds? God bless dear Kelly and Veilleux." She then eagerly grabbed a slim, green book from the shelf and sat beside her husband, and with a conspiratorial air they flipped through the pages. Soon James said, "Well, Granville is not in the Household... thank God for that, at least. Cavalrymen can be so tiresome, and I have never met a Guards cavalryman who did not consider himself God's own equal."

"Well, let us look at the Foot Regiments," said Brigid, then after a moment of study, "Oh, here he is! The Third Foot Guards!" with a degree of triumph in her voice. She stuck the tip of her tongue out at her husband and said, "I found him first."

James made a playful frown and allowed, "Yes, yes, Mrs. Lockwood, you are the finest reviewer of the *Army List* of my acquaintance." Then running his finger along Granville's place in the list James went on, "As I feared... his seniority dates to just six months ago, but he is still technically my senior. Likely he was Ensign and Lieutenant for just a year or two before buying his way up. Bah... most Guards officers scarcely have the experience to command a squad. But they have the finest enlisted men and NCOs in the army, which is the sole reason they did not rout like a herd of sheep at Waterloo. The question remains, though: why does this fellow wish to call on me?"

Brigid got to her feet and said with determination, "Well, he *is* going to call, sir, so I shall brush your uniform, and you had best shave, unless you intend to intimidate this fellow with your bear-like visage."

James sat at the drawing room window with his sword across his lap. He was uncomfortable. His uniform felt stiff and heavy, the house seemed stuffy, his chest flashed in pain, and above all he had a bad feeling about Granville.

When Granville rode up on a fine black gelding James saw he rode like a civilian, with a rein in each hand. He also saw that Granville was wearing a sword. It was not a social call. James slowly got to his feet and strapped his sword on as well.

Mrs. Cashman showed Lieutenant and Captain Granville into the drawing room, a heavy, pale, lumpy young man of perhaps twenty years. After the requisite introductions, Granville said in a jaded tone, "Begging you pardon, sir, but in Dublin it is widely assumed you are dying. But I believe I see you recovered?"

Brigid scowled and replied, "I trust you are here on army business, Captain Granville, so I believe I shall leave you—"

"It is primarily army business, Mrs. Lockwood, but I believe it concerns you as well. Please remain."

Granville's tone bordered on rudeness; his comment was very nearly an order, in the Lockwoods' own home. From where she stood Brigid could see the door to the kitchen open a crack, and from behind it she heard Mrs. Cashman issue a sniff of derision. Brigid shot Mrs. Cashman a look, and with a gracious nod and a smile she remained with her husband. James, however, was not so charitable. He had quickly concluded that Granville was a soulless functionary, and a man he need not ask to sit.

"I have a sensitive matter to discuss, indeed a court martial may be convened if these matters cannot be resolved today," Granville said flatly. "I trust I may speak freely?"

James did not flinch. He only nodded and said, "Our children are visiting their Aunt. Pray continue, Captain." James had been in the army a very long time, and had developed a subtle way of addressing men he did not respect. He thus managed to say the word 'captain' with something like derision.

Granville, however, had not been exposed to army life long enough to catch James's meaning, but Brigid had, so she placed her hand atop her husband's and lightly squeezed. He felt her hand shaking.

Even on official calls, common practice allowed officers to chat for a few minutes before turning to matters of army business, to share experiences, to report on common acquaintances, or perhaps inquire about past postings. Captain Granville, however, did not do so, only formally saying, "I am charged by General Arbuthnot, Military Secretary to the Lord Lieutenant, to raise two issues. I am to note your responses and immediately convey them back to the Colonel."

"And you shall have one, sir, believe me." James nearly clenched a fist, but he felt Brigid's hand still atop his, her hand still shaking. He glanced over at her and saw she had gone quite pale.

Granville drew a pencil and a small notebook from his pocket and said, "First, I must ask if either you, Lieutenant Lockwood, or you, Mrs. Lockwood, are aware of a plan to defraud the pension system through false claims."

The accusation was so unexpected, so ludicrous, that James and Brigid could react only with open, honest astonishment. James furrowed his brow, shook his head, and said, "A Court Martial? On such foolishness as that? Who would ever think such a thing?"

With a shaking laugh in her voice Brigid said, "Captain Granville, you can see my husband, quite alive, right here before you. There has been no talk of a pension, sir, let alone a fraudulent one. You may assure the Castle of that much, certainly?" She hated the Castle, and her tone carried it.

Grenville went on, "I am allowed to share very little, only that an informant"—when Granville said 'informant' both James and Brigid flinched; Barr, it had to be Barr—"is prepared to offer proof that you, Lieutenant, in company with you, Mrs. Lockwood, are in some manner intent on filing a fraudulent pension claim. A complete denial, then, is your reply?"

James recovered from his astonishment enough to feel his anger returning. "Yes, sir, a complete denial, and I very much resent the accusation. Further, Captain, you may wish to challenge this informant of yours, to produce this 'proof,' as anyone who would say such a thing is certainly mad."

Brusquely, Granville replied, "The matter has been raised, and duly responded to. I shall proceed. Secondly, General Arbuthnot desires that I inquire into the nature of your marriage, as again our informant reports that your marriage in 1798 was performed by a Catholic priest, in violation of Penal Law."

Both the Lockwoods went pale, Brigid trembled, and Granville proceeded in his flat voice, "I require a reply to this second charge, if you please. Is this allegation true?" Getting no response, he pressed, "You must certainly understand that a marriage by a Catholic priest was once a felony, and is still highly penal, unless the parties were previously married by a Protestant Clergyman? It may be proper to observe, that one of the parties having been a Protestant, the other a Protestant or Roman Catholic, the marriage, is not by law valid. What say you?"

The Lockwoods were holding hands, both clearly distraught, but they then looked at each other, and took a degree of comfort. James gave Brigid the smallest of reassuring smiles, turned to Granville, and said, "We have nothing to say on the matter."

"You must realize, sir, that such a response will certainly prompt a full Court Martial. I ask again: were you, Lieutenant and Mrs. Lockwood, married in a ceremony conducted by a

Catholic priest, according to the Romish rites, in direct violation of the law barring such marriages?"

"You have my response, sir."

Granville shrugged, made a brief note in his book, snapped it closed, straightened his coat, and said, "Good day, then." Without looking back he let himself out, mounted, and rode away to the north.

"Begging your pardon, My Lord, but General Arbuthnot is here, and begs a few minutes of your time." Graham typically left the Lord Lieutenant undisturbed during the middle of the day, as Kerr was fond of napping at his desk after luncheon, but the arrival of the Military Secretary was no small matter.

After allowing his master a moment to rouse himself, Graham showed Arbuthnot into the ornate office. Graham disliked most of humanity; but his dislike of Arbuthnot was especially sharp, as the General was small, trim, experienced, and a stickler for form.

Arbuthnot made a practiced salute, and in a formal tone he said, "My Lord, per your instruction of 25 July, court martial proceedings were initiated against Lieutenant Lockwood of the 3rd Veteran battalion, under our command. But since those orders were cut, my Lord, other factors have come to my attention, factors which I deem pertinent to government's case."

"Lockwood?" asked Kerr sleepily.

"Lieutenant James Lockwood, My Lord, who is accused of violating Penal Laws limiting the Papist Rite of Marriage."

"Oh, yes, that fellow. Fraud as well, I think?"

Graham flushed and reluctantly admitted, "Unfortunately we were required to defer the charge of fraud, My Lord, as it seems that Lockwood is not dying, and a pension fraud necessarily requires a death and resultant pension claim."

"This is most irregular, My Lord, most irregular indeed," said Arbuthnot with a sharp edge to his voice. "This Captain Barr, who seems to have been the sole source of these charges, proves upon closer examination to be a wholly unreliable fellow."

Kerr was growing angry, Graham's discomfort was obvious, and Arbuthnot's military voice continued to sharpen with, "And now, My Lord, and now! I am in possession of a letter from Lieutenant Lockwood in which he, in turn, denounces Captain Barr! He claims that Barr has been afflicted with the French Pox since 1798. 1798! As evidence he attaches a letter from a Militia Surgeon named Oades—who was, Lockwood notes, killed by Barr in an affair of honour in 1798, and our records confirm this—which substantiates the diagnosis of syphilis. My God, if Barr has carried the pox for these twenty-odd years, he must be barking mad!"

Kerr indignantly turned to Graham and barked, "Well, Graham, what have you to say for yourself?"

"My Lord, as I was not personally acquainted with Captain Bar, I relied solely upon the strength of his written testimony and his reputation as a King's officer...."

Kerr flipped open the Lockwood file and continued, "First, Graham, you tell me Lockwood is dying, and we can bring his widow to trial with wholly provable charges of fraud and violation of the Penal Laws. An excellent example to set, you said, to knock down a Papist wench who does not know her place, to teach the Papists by her example, and to remind the Anglicans to keep their distance from the bloody Papists. Then, you tell me that Lockwood shall live, but a court martial would be an even grander stage upon which to teach these critical lessons. And now, disaster!"

Arbuthnot took the opportunity to burst out, "Our chief informant and sole witness is evidently a syphilitic madman!

And when I attempt to contact Barr at his wholly disreputable dwellings, I find him gone! By all accounts fled to England, and by those same accounts Barr is mad as a hatter!"

Kerr looked confused, and turning to Arbuthnot he asked, "What is especially mad about hatters, for God's sake, General? My hatter is a perfectly sober fellow."

Arbuthnot looked nonplussed and muttered, "Merely a cant soldiers' expression, My Lord."

Graham was pale and perspiring as Kerr gathered himself and returned to the file. Flipping slowly through its contents Kerr went on, "So, the charges of fraud have been dropped as mere frippery, and, lacking our madman's testimony, the charges of violation of the Penal Laws are best supported by Lockwood's refusal to deny them."

A long pause followed as Kerr pondered his options. It was only when he was angry that Kerr was capable of decision. Snapping the file closed he said crisply, "This government shall not be humiliated. And despite the evident bungling, the intended message remains one valuable to this government, and this society: the Catholics are to be kept in their place. The charge of violation of the Penal Laws shall be pressed. But in doing so, I do not wish to engender the wrath of Horse Guards, Palmerston, the Prime Minister, or, God help us, Parliament. Thus, I shall rely on you two gentlemen to get a quick, decisive, unequivocal, and complete wrath-of-God verdict."

Arbuthnot nodded and said, "I know just the officers for the jury, My Lord."

Graham, looking very much like a man just excused the gallows, said, "And I, My Lord, believe that I may offer up popular opinion on a silver platter. Lieutenant and Mrs. Lockwood shall be widely loathed within a fortnight."

The Dublin Tattler, *26 July 1820*

This correspondent is made privy to highly confidential Sources, Sources which allows the unfortunate news that His Majesty's Army (God protect and Preserve such valiant, honourable men!) contains at least one Bad Apple, indeed one Exceptionally Bad Apple.

We may make so bold as to <u>assure</u> the Devoted Reader that Our Sources are most reliable; the first a Senior Official of His Majesty's Government, and thus unimpeachable in both character and capacity, and the other a most honourable man, a <u>Captain</u> wounded at <u>Waterloo</u>, and thus worthy of all honour this humble correspondent can offer.

The Bad Apple pointed out by our Noble Sources is not worthy of anonymity. He is called James Lockwood, and he fouls the otherwise noble rank of Lieutenant. He has been caught in the act of perpetrating notorious crimes against Government, crimes in which he was in all elements supported and encouraged by his WIFE. That woman, a radical Papist and a suspected member of Secret Rebel Organizations, is yet to be charged, having thus far hidden herself from The Law's ceaseless gaze.

But this James Lockwood has been found out, Dear Reader, and thanks to evidence provided by our Trusted Sources, we are Assured that a COURT MARTIAL is likely, and <u>Justice</u> will at last be served.

It was a cool, rainy afternoon when an orderly dragoon rode slowly up to Fáibhile Cottage to deliver the summons. James had known it would come, of course, but it was just days after his interview with Granville that the dragoon pulled it from his pouch and James saw the bright red seal of Dublin Castle.

The dragoon looked tired and soaked through so James told him, "Go around back to the kitchen, Corporal, and you shall have a bowl of something hot before you head back north."

The dragoon smiled his thanks, but then grew serious and said with a Cornish accent, "Begging your pardon, sir, but I might not be welcome in this house once you read that letter."

Without a smile James said, "Are dragoon orderlies now familiar with the contents of confidential dispatches?"

"Ah, now, sir, those dispatches are in no danger from me, me being as capable of reading as this door post. But now rumors, sir, you know how soldiers love their rumors. So I might be able to tell you the contents of that letter, sir, pretty close, as it were, and as we've both seen our share of what it means to be a soldier, you might allow me the liberty of saying that every real soldier in the Castle knows what's in that letter, sir. I'll add that we soldiers think it's a crime, sir, and I beg your pardon for carrying such a thing to your very home."

James frowned at the letter and said, "It is no fault of yours, soldier. Now go and get something to eat. Oh, you shall also ask Mrs. Cashman for a pint of cider. It is likely to rain on you all the way back to Dublin."

James carried the letter upstairs to read it away from the children, and a few minutes later Brigid silently joined him, ashen and near tears.

He stood by the window, staring at the horizon. Without moving his eyes, he quietly said, "It is as I expected. The court martial is to be convened at the Castle on 14 September. Two weeks from now; they are in a hurry."

"And so my foolishness is finally come to ruin us," Brigid whispered with anguish in her voice. But then with some anger she added, "But in two weeks' time? Can they think you well enough to travel to Dublin so soon?"

"Oh, they explain it away." He read aloud, *"It is recognized that the Defendant is not in the best of Health, and so it is decided to hold the proceedings as soon as they can be arranged, so that the Defendant might travel before the onset of the cold and wet of Autumn.'* It is a ploy, of course, the dogs. Two weeks allows me very little time to garner anything like a defense. I must write to the regiment to ask for letters of support. I know that Colonel Nelson is in Fermanagh on leave, so I should be able to reach at least him in time."

James held the notice with such strength that he nearly crushed it. Reading it again, he tensely said, "The Castle has had sense enough to drop that nonsense about defrauding the pension system. Barr's madness must have given rise to that, and doubtless he lost some credibility over it. But still we cannot avoid this:

<u>The Charge</u>: That you did, in the year 1798, wed Miss Brigid O'Brian, that ceremony conducted by a Papist Priest, and in that no lawful Protestant minister was in attendance, you did knowingly violate a Penal Law prohibiting such marriages."

For just an instant he was angry with Brigid, for having insisted twenty-three years earlier that Father McGlynn perform the service, and he alone, as a sign to Brigid's family that this young Protestant Ensign truly loved their daughter.

James recognized that rising anger; it was his father's voice, an easy way out, a furious insistence on blaming others for his problems. So he allowed the anger to flash for just that instant, and without a word he walked the few steps to Brigid and held her as she wept into his chest.

Chapter Fifteen

Joseph, Richard, and Lucy tearfully left to return to school, and James and Brigid left for Dublin the very next day. It had been decided that Mary and Cissy would remain at home while their parents were away, as Mrs. Cashman had fallen ill and could scarcely leave her bed.

Mary and Cissy cared for Mrs. Cashman with the same tenderness that she had shown the Lockwood children on countless occasions, and one evening as Mrs. Cashman was comfortably sleeping the girls made for themselves a simple dinner.

"The news of the Court Martial is out," said Cissy, smoothing the front of her dress as she sat across from her sister, "and I, for one, have noticed that some of Mama and Papa's friends have grown very quiet, excepting the Butlers, of course. People are so willing, even eager, to believe the worst."

Mary pursed her lips and said, "I saw Elsie Fitter in town this morning and she was very cool, only asking how I was bearing up under the shame of having been born outside marriage. I have expected such nonsense, but still, it burns. It is odd, is it not, how quickly things turn? We seem to be painted in colours invisible to us, yet vivid enough to the rest of the world. Neither fish nor fowl; too English for the Irish, and too Irish for the English.”

“Yes, I have noticed; you need not point out the obvious. Neither need you point out that I no longer receive gentlemen callers. My sole suitor is that loathsome Thomas Flanagan, a hedge poet, staring at me like some stricken cow. You have Guillaume, but I shall certainly die an old maid. A penniless old maid, at that.”

Hesitantly Mary said, “I have not dared ponder it, but I wonder if the Dumons might find father’s court martial—”

Cissy firmly interrupted with, “Mary, Guillaume’s affections for you are immovable, of that I am convinced. Further, Colonel Dumon is an old military man, and he holds father in very high regard; some nonsensical court martial in Dublin will certainly mean nothing to him.” Then in a softer tone she added, “It is as father said: the court martial shall be quickly dealt with, and then you shall travel to France to be wed.”

Mary gave her sister a soft appreciative smile and tentatively asked, “Have you given thought to the Dumons’ invitation, Cissy? Will you come to France with me?”

“Yes, thank you, dear, I have considered it. They are so kind, but my French is terrible, and France is your life, *mo grah*. I believe I shall return to school; there is so much that interests me. I shall work on my French, so that I might one day visit you without shame. And one never knows, I may meet some charming young man some distant day.”

“I was thinking, after Papa settles all this court martial nonsense, that Colonel Simon might make some introductions amongst the yeomanry officers. I am certain he would be interested in helping.”

Cissy rolled her eyes and said, “I wager that is not all that Colonel Simon would be interested in.”

"Oh, you are terrible!" cried Mary with a laugh. She then mischievously added, "You know, we could always invest a shilling with Mr. Toomey...."

"Oh, Mary Lockwood, you wicked little creature!" screamed Cissy in laughter and horror at the mention of the slimy village matchmaker.

Both of the girls were soon laughing with unrestrained glee, like their mother laughed, as Cissy stamped her feet in pure mirth and shrieked, "I might marry an O'Riordan brother!"

"The Dirty O'Riordans! And just imagine, the Lockwoods and the O'Riordans together at St. Brigid's!"

Cissy leapt to her feet with her hands to her cheeks. "The Muirs! At a Catholic chapel! Can you imagine Aunt's face?"

It was some of the first open laughter that the girls had shared since the announcement of their father's court martial. It came as a release and a bond to two young women who were learning that the world was perhaps something to be feared after all.

The next Sunday the three younger Cashman brothers came to visit their mother. No mention was made of the eldest, the fugitive John.

The rough men came to the back door with their caps in their hands, stiffly formal and polite, but less than friendly toward the two elegant sisters. The Lockwoods were foreign to the Cashman men. The Lockwoods were their mother's employers, and while the Cashmans were never obvious they somehow managed to convey the notion that the Lockwoods had not taken proper care of their mother.

They were all three older than the girls, all three married, fathers, serious fisherman, bronzed and hardened by the sea. After the uneasy greetings in the kitchen, Cissy showed the men into their mother's cozy room. The girls then left the Cashmans alone, retreating to self-consciously stitch in the drawing room.

It was an awkward visit. The three brothers were uncertain of their roles; three good souls, but like so many of their gender they were not used to the soft, quiet, floating time that measured the days of the sick. They were not so old or hardened as not to feel the pain boys so sharply feel when they see their mother grown weak and frail. Not knowing how best to deal with it, their nodding smiles and formal good wishes eventually drifted to talk of fishing and the lives of the grandchildren.

Mary and Cissy heard only the distant whisper of voices until there came a tentative knock, and Paul Cashman stepped shyly out of the kitchen.

"Begging your pardon, ladies, but might I beg a word, please?"

It was painful to see such a strong, capable man look so ill at ease and unsure of his manner. The girls were thus uncomfortable as well, though Cissy tried to put Paul at ease by saying in Irish, "I trust, Mr. Cashman, that your visit has raised your mother's spirits? It was she who so looked forward to you coming."

Paul Cashman, tall and thin, relaxed a bit to hear Irish spoken in a gentleman's house, and replied, "You'll know, gentlewoman, that our mother is a strong-willed woman. It is we who are here to ask her to come to live and recover in my own home, with her own family, but she says she is at home here."

"Of course, she must stay here, her own home," replied Mary without reflection.

Cashman looked cross, and said, "As she cannot work, how can she pay her way? My brothers and I cannot pay for her, can we? I mean, Miss, if she cannot work, how can she stay here?"

"Why, because we love her, of course," said Mary softly. "Does that ring so odd to your ears?"

Cashman seemed a practical man, and Cissy deemed it best to address him so. "Mr. Cashman, you and your brothers work long days to bring home boats laden with the good fish. Your wives are busy tending to their homes and children. Pray, allow us to care for your mother here in her own warm room, and you shall come and see her often, and see her loved and cared for as if she were with her own family."

Paul made a quick, thoughtful nod and returned to the kitchen to discuss the matter with his brothers. At length they agreed with their mother's wish to remain with the Lockwoods, where she would contentedly lie in her own bed and listen to the wind spark music amongst the crisp leaves of the beeches.

Nearly a month had passed since their parents had departed for Dublin, and every day one of the Lockwood sisters would visit the Post Office to pester Mr. Hobgood for a letter. As a veteran of the Royal Mail, Hobgood was used to such anxious badgering, and while he was polite he could not make correspondence appear from thin air.

The girls' anxiety and disappointment in not hearing from their parents was exceeded only by their surprise at a letter that eventually did arrive from Dublin. A note from their Aunt Muir announced her intention to visit in two days' time.

Aunt Muir's carriage, gleaming black and pulled by four greys, clattered up to Fáibhile Cottage at precisely the appointed time. When Aunt Muir was handed down by her footmen she was mildly disappointed at the condition of the cottage; she had hoped for a shabby hovel, but the cottage was neat as a pin. Aunt Muir, who had never done an honest day's work in her life, would have had little appreciation for the days of frantic work done by Mary and Cissy, who had pruned, weeded, trimmed, swept, and mopped with a fierce determination that pleased, and perhaps surprised, the bed-ridden Mrs. Cashman. The girls were still sufficiently prideful to have done much of the outside work early in the morning and late in the day, when they thought there would be less chance of being seen doing such work themselves. They would have died rather than be seen in their old shifts by Elizabeth Boyle or that lizard Elsie Fitter, with dirty hands and red faces, reduced to doing work done by the lowest servants at the great houses.

The young Lockwood ladies, once again perfectly, if simply, groomed and elevated to the status of gentlewomen, were sitting anxiously together on the settee when Aunt Muir's coachman knocked harshly with the butt of his whip. The girls briefly held hands, and before answering the door Cissy whispered, "For Mama and Papa." Both the girls made a low conciliatory dip as their Aunt entered. She, in turn, barely acknowledged her nieces as she forged ahead into the drawing room, moving like a seventy-four gun ship of the line, with similar offensive potential.

Aunt Muir spun on her nieces, however, much more quickly than any ship of the line, saying, "I never thought I would see a day when a Lockwood was reduced to answering her own door. This is Ireland, after all."

"Our dear Mrs. Cashman is, sadly, very ill," replied Mary. "Pray, will you sit down, Aunt? And might we bring you some refreshment? After your travels from Dublin you must certainly be—"

"I will not sit, girls, until I am assured that my time and energy expended in such a trying journey have not been wasted. Muir himself said that I was going far beyond the bounds of familial obligation in making such an effort to re-establish a civil relationship with you children. Pray tell me, am I to be treated with the same insulting wilfulness I witnessed in my own home at our last meeting?"

"We do apologize, Aunt, for having taken such a tone with you," said Cissy submissively.

"Very well, then," said Aunt Muir, "we shall have no further nonsense. As to you children: as your parents are in such a state of disgrace— "

"There is no disgrace, please, Aunt, as— "

"Do not interrupt, girl! I thought that we had agreed that you two girls would cease this rude, conceited, prideful prating. Very well. To business, then. Your devoted Uncle Muir has highly placed sources in Dublin Castle, and we are informed that when the verdict comes down next week, your father is to be found guilty, and shall be dismissed the service."

Both girls looked stricken, and Mary quietly said, "Oh, dear God."

Cissy could only whisper, "This might well kill father! The service means everything to him." She reached across and held Mary's hand and they nearly wept.

Their aunt continued with a flash of triumph in her eyes. "Further, it is likely that your mother shall face criminal charges in her flagrant violation of the Penal Laws. I trust you two might appreciate the impact this scandal shall have on the rest of the family, though your Uncle Muir and Uncle John are valiantly working to salvage the Lockwood name. Through great effort and expense they have arranged for the criminal charges to be dropped if your father accepts a lieutenancy with the Company, and that both he and your mother leave for India within the month."

Mary was silent and pale, while Cissy could only wonderingly whisper, "India?"

"In such a situation," continued their Aunt, "leaving Ireland, and a passage, I shall not say flight, to India is the very best they might hope for. Now, as to you children. Your uncles and I must step in to manage everything. Your brothers will remain in Surrey, where we might hope they will learn the manners of English gentlemen, and have this willful Irishness beaten out of them. You two young ladies, if I might be allowed to stretch the term, will return to school until we might find two weak-minded men who might be willing to marry you, though I tell you here and now that your Uncle Muir will allow only the most modest dowry. He will not be taken advantage of by some adventurer. You must marry according to your station, and situation; I will not add, predicament. Two of Muir's clerks, both older, steady men, are being considered for that duty, however poor a prospect that may pose for them. You will obey our decisions in such matters, as with your unbridled country manners Dublin society will be far above you."

Mary and Cissy made no response beyond a quick, shared glance, with which they silently agreed not to mention Guillaume Louis Antoine Dumon. From the kitchen the arthritic, grey-muzzled Sergeant woke long enough to utter a low, impotent growl. The girls had been wise enough to use the family's massive old Bible to block the kitchen door (James would have been amused), thus restricting both Sergeant's ability to join in the discussion and Mrs. Cashman's tendency to eavesdrop, even from her sickbed.

Assuming the girls' silence implied compliance, Aunt Muir continued, "This little house will of course be sold to pay some of the debts I am told your mother incurred." She looked about the quaint, low-ceilinged little room as if she was in the deepest depths of Dublin gaol, and spoke the words "debt" and "mother" with equal and unbridled loathing.

"Please, Aunt," offered Cissy, "the house is leased."

"The house is leased? Like some common labourer's hovel!" cried Aunt Muir as if she had found a rat in her soufflé. "This is worse than I had ever imagined. Your parents must be quite mad. You girls must compile a written account of any debts hanging over the Lockwood name, so such criminal behavior can be erased at once, at once!" As she was a very poor actress, Aunt Muir went on in a slightly different tone of voice, "Further, you will oblige me by signing these documents which our attorney has prepared."

"What documents are those, please, Aunt?" asked Mary with a hint of wariness.

"Do as you are told, please." Aunt Muir laid several documents onto the side table, saying, "Do not trouble yourselves with attempts at the legal terminology. Suffice it to say that your devoted Uncle Muir and I have taken it upon ourselves to assume guardianship over you four children. With your parents removed to India we cannot have the five of you roaming the countryside unsupervised, carrying the Lockwood name into heaven-knows what foolishness. In essence Muir and I shall act as your parents, and with that all the incumbent rights and responsibilities. And such responsibilities!"

While Brigid had never spoken to the girls about her fears regarding the Muirs' intention toward her children, they had inherited enough of her pride and suspicion to have expected such a manoeuvre by their aunt.

"My sister and I are touched by your kindness, Aunt," said Cissy, "but we are convinced that our parents will certainly escape these foolish charges, and in any event our parents shall see to our care."

"Further," said Mary in a prideful tone, "I am twenty years old, Aunt, and perfectly capable of managing our affairs if it comes to our parents being away."

"Twenty. Do you truly feel that qualifies you to care for a family of five? I should think not. I have spoken with both your Uncle Muir and Uncle John, and we are in complete accord: the allowance which so generously but vainly supported this family will not be reinstated. Your father is in disgrace. Your mother, who in other circumstances might otherwise have found work as a barmaid, took advantage of the Lockwood name for many years, and the family will not continue to support her legacy of willfulness and ill-based pride."

If a calm, disinterested party had been in the room, they may have noted that both Lockwood girls lost their temper at the exact same moment.

"A barmaid!" cried Mary. "Why would you think, madam, that you could step into our mother's own house and say such a thing?"

Cissy, who had inherited her father's habit of unconsciously adapting a heavy Irish accent when angry, and she was very angry, said, "We have held our tongues in hopes of preserving our relationship with our father's family, but we can bear this no longer. It will no doubt disappoint you, Aunt, to hear that there are instances in which honest people will deny themselves the advantages of money and status in favour of their own peace. I believe my sister and I now fully appreciate the choices made by our parents throughout their lives. We have nothing more to discuss; I would thank you to leave now, ma'am."

Aunt Muir had thought herself ready for this trial of wills, but in the face of the open fury of the two sisters she found herself quite overmatched. "Very well," she said, taken back-footed for the first time in a very long time, "as you wish. I shall make it a point never to see you again."

She started for the door, then turned back to her nieces with an ugly spite in her voice. "Where shall you turn now, I wonder? Once your father is found guilty every door in Ireland will be closed to you. Every decent door, at any rate. Shall you turn to your mother's people? Your mother. I recall a Yeomanry officer making mention of her; she is suspected of harboring rebels, and having a direct hand in the assault upon Leamaneh, and the attempted murder of my father. You children may now add traitor to the list of your mother's less palatable traits."

Mary was rarely as outspoken as her sister, but her searing anger inspired her. "You are impertinent, madam, an odious liar."

"You will not be so bold, child, when the yeomanry comes to your door asking questions, and they will not be put off by the sharp tongues of undisciplined Irish harpies!"

Cissy quickly stepped closer to her Aunt, close enough to make her Aunt very uncomfortable. In all her life Aunt Muir had never once suffered a blow, but the look on her niece's face made her fear one, and made her fear it very much. Cissy was a typically lovely young woman, but she nonetheless managed to adopt a visage that was very similar to the look her father had wielded on such occasions. "You will please keep in mind, Aunt, that no matter what happens, our name is still Lockwood, whether you care for that or not, and you of all people understand that in Ireland a family name can be ruined by even the hint of scandal."

"I had resolved not to mention this one last source of information," said Aunt Muir with a degree of triumph in her voice, "but as you girls cling to these foolish notions of your mother with such tenacity, I shall share it. I am in possession of a letter from an officer of the 27th, Captain Charles Barr, an old friend of your father and a man of great integrity. He knew your mother before she trapped my honourable, foolish brother into that sham marriage, and he has explained in great detail how your mother sought out an officer to marry her, giving herself to any man with an epaulette, playing the harlot—"

Cissy's hand flew. She slapped her aunt with a force that sent her reeling. Aunt Muir was stunned, her hair and bonnet knocked askew, and there was a sudden animal terror in her eyes. Mary stood frozen, eyes wide in shock. Cissy was not a tall woman, but she stood tall above her Aunt, and in a voice that trembled with anger she said, "You had best go, Aunt, if you are to make Cork town by dark. The roads here can be very dangerous, very dangerous indeed. At night the Whiteboys own these hills and, while you have seen some violence in this house, it is child's play in comparison to what you might find at Ballinascarthy Crossroads at the new moon."

With that, Aunt Muir's resolve crumbled and she retreated in a rapid, graceless hurry, a handprint scarlet on her high cheek.

Tom Mainwaring went straight to the Castle, but found no satisfaction there. He was, in fact, kept waiting for two hours in an anteroom and addressed in a fashion little short of rudeness, once it was learned that he was a friend of Lieutenant Lockwood.

Tom had asked to see an aide to the Military Secretary, but it was only an elderly porter who eventually stepped in to inform Lieutenant Mainwaring that the court martial had been adjourned two days previous. In nonchalant tone the porter flipped through a file and told the handsome, scarred officer that after a lengthy trial, Lieutenant Lockwood had been found guilty, and dismissed the service.

Tom stood unbelieving for a long moment, then loudly demanded to see the Military Secretary, anyone, but he was bureaucratically ignored until a sympathetic young officer pulled him aside and suggested he call on another acquaintance of the Lockwoods, a Dr. Kelly, who had sat beside Mrs. Lockwood throughout the affair, the entire ugly affair. Kelly had been staying at the Hotel Portobello; perhaps he was still in town.

Even with the young officer's mumbled directions, Tom lost his way twice as he hurried to the Portobello through a misting rain. After sending up his card, Tom was shown to Dr. Kelly's rooms, where Tom found Dr. Kelly drunk, drunk even by army standards.

Kelly sat at a desk in his shirtsleeves. He made as grand a bow as was possible from his chair, and with a slurring elegance he said, "Lieutenant Mainwaring, I do beg your pardon for receiving you in such a state, but if I rose to shake your hand I do believe that I might collapse into an ignominious pile. Pray, may I pour you a glass?"

"You may," Tom said with resignation. "James speaks of you often, Doctor. A pleasure, at last." Tom took the proffered glass, sat on the battered settee opposite Kelly, and drank with a purpose.

Kelly noted Tom's mood and said, "You have heard the news, then."

"I have." And the glass was emptied.

"And you are acquainted with this fellow Barr?"

"It has been my displeasure to have known him these twenty years. If I had known his madness would come to this, I would have put my sword through him years ago, and damn the consequences."

Kelly handed the bottle across to Tom, then purposefully shoved his own glass away and muttered, "I have a regrettable weakness for self-pity in such times as these." Then gathering himself, he asked, "You are recently arrived from Gib, I assume?"

"Just this morning. My wife was with me, so I saw her to the Post Office so that she might catch the Mail to her family's house in Belfast. Off she went, by herself, never a word of complaint, only best hopes, prayers, and wishes for the Lockwoods. A wonderful woman, is my wife. Have the Lockwoods returned to Clonakilty?"

"They have not. They are staying at Colonel Nelson's town home; he, at least, has been a great support to them."

Tom nearly jumped to his feet, but Kelly motioned him down. "Ach, do relax, man. They have been refusing callers. And while I am sure they would make an exception in your case, I should caution you. They shall certainly be appreciative of your presence and your support, but sympathy of any ilk seems to be... acutely painful... to them." Kelly unconsciously reached over and took another pull from his glass. "Regrettable," he muttered. Then again rallying, he said, "Before you go, Mainwaring, shall I tell you of the trial?"

"Yes, I suppose I should hear of it before I see them." Tom took a long drink from his glass, exhaled sharply and winced theatrically.

"Vile stuff, is it not?" said Kelly with a grin. "I hadn't expected company, and so turned to a base Irishman's consolation. Vile, but cheap, and it has the desired effect."

Kelly stood, swayed, ran his hands briskly through his hair a number of times, and commenced.

"The trial. As ugly a political job as I've seen." With a flicker of nostalgia in his voice he went on, "I studied for the law, once, before it sickened me and I turned to medicine. Not many people know that, my dear sir. So, my opinions regarding this God damned trial are moderately well informed, and they were in turn confirmed with two old acquaintances, gentlemen of the law with whom I shared a wee drink."

Kelly moved to the window and looked out onto misty Dublin, more in control of himself. "Originally, it seems they planned to prosecute Brigid only after James's death. The pension fraud nonsense seems to have been solely a product of

Barr's invention, but the Castle would likely have pressed it, and in their Ireland she would be by-God guilty. Certainly the penal law charge would have been easy enough to prove, against a distraught widow with limited resource, a Catholic with rumoured ties to rebels. God, what slaughter that would have been."

Tom raised his eyebrows and said, "But then James lived."

Kelly gave a quick, fleeting grin and continued, "Just so. And if I might return to my medical façade, I might mention that he *should* have died. Our operation was well done, but I wonder, sometimes, I wonder if he has God's hand on his shoulder."

Tom smiled, deciding he liked this doctor.

Kelly waved his hand dismissively and said, "But such thoughts do not dwell in the rational mind. I continue. When our friend recovered, to the Castle's great inconvenience, it surprised, nay, astounded many in the law when government continued to press the case. Such a case against a Catholic widow of dubious loyalty is one thing; a vile political exercise, of course, but not one beyond the Castle's normal range of action. But those charges against a wounded hero of Waterloo, an officer of long service and a fine record? Well, now, that is another proposition entirely. The Castle is taking a great chance to make their point: the Catholics are to be put down, and no one, not even a Waterloo veteran from a prominent Ascendency family, dare cross the established order."

Tom poured himself another tall glass, shook his head slowly, and said, "I cannot tell you how tortured I am by this. One of the best officers, one of the best men I know, and to see this done to him. Certainly there must be something I could have done, that I might yet do." He got to his feet, disgust marring his face. "Protestants and Catholics, the rich and the poor, the powerful and the weak. I am sick of the whole bloody damn business. Perhaps I shall proclaim myself a Deist, relocate to some desert island, and free myself from the rest of humanity."

Kelly shrugged, poured himself another glass as well, and mused, "I have considered the same course, but perhaps without the false trappings of faith. Have you ever noticed, my dear Mainwaring, that while women share their souls at the drop of a hat, men typically do so only with a drink in their hand? Such an unfortunate tendency." Holding his glass aloft, he offered up, "*Slainte.*"

Tom waved his glass, tilted his head in understanding, and replied, "Your good health, Doctor."

Kelly proceeded, "And so. The Castle was required to throw a great deal of mud to destroy Lockwood. He had little time to gather support, you know; a few letters, and a few allies. Just a fellow named Butler, their local minister, an imposing fellow, who made a good impression, and your Colonel Nelson, who was enraged by the whole affair, and myself. I must say, though, for just three men we raised long, steady, howls of protest. Lord Musgrave threatened us with contempt more than once, and in truth we were in contempt of the whole bloody affair. Bastards, they are, to do such things."

"Did Barr appear?"

"He did not. Major Verecker—he appeared as the prosecutor, and did a masterful job, absolutely ruthless— explained that Barr was ill, incapacitated by the wounds he suffered in defence of King and Country. But word has it that Barr has fled, out of favour now with the Castle, and in fear of his life for having crossed Lockwood. Rightly so, too, as I have never seen a man in such a silent, wounded, anguished, seething rage, as Lockwood. May God keep me from seeing another."

Chapter Sixteen

Colonel Nelson still kept a house on Fitzwilliam Square, and while he left two servants to care for the place, he typically stayed there only during the season. When he heard of the court martial he placed it completely at the disposal of Lieutenant and Mrs. Lockwood. When the court's shattering verdict was announced, the disappointed old fellow retreated to his Fermanagh estate only after begging the Lockwoods to remain there as long as they had business in town. The house was tall, narrow and moderately fashionable, and while it was far from the most exclusive address in Dublin, it suited their purposes.

The Lockwoods had spent the days after the court martial there, alternately enraged, incredulous, and lost, but as was typical of them they had together developed a plan of action, and were determined to put it in place. They were not by nature vengeful people, but they had been betrayed, and were intent on retribution.

On that particular evening they were sharing a pot of tea in the elegant drawing room, as Brigid stitched and James tensely paced the floor. Brigid eyed him from the top of her hoop until she finally accused him of acting the caged bear, and he forced himself to sit and wait for the arrival of the post.

James crossly flipped through yesterday's papers until finally he heard the front door open, and he sprang from his chair and strode into the foyer to unceremoniously deprive the butler of the mail. The butler, unused to the subalternly ways of Lieutenant Lockwood, made some token resistance, prompting James to angrily mutter, "Oh, for God's sake, never mind the salver, man."

James returned to the drawing room tearing open a letter, and Brigid looked up with an anxious look. James hurriedly scanned the letter, but then looking crestfallen he said, "It is from Colonel Nelson's man in London; no sign of Barr there, none at all, damn it all anyway."

James tossed the letter aside. While Brigid's face reflected the disappointment she also felt, in a hopeful tone she said, "One of our friends shall find him, sure. We must be patient, my love."

Their friends had fanned out in pursuit of Barr, following any hint. While Colonel Nelson's health prevented much travel, he had left a purse of golden guineas to be used to finance the search, as the reputation of the regiment was at risk.

The one point of the plan on which Lieutenant and Mrs. Lockwood disagreed was what to to do if Barr were found. While Brigid hoped for some other outcome, James was determined to go to wherever Barr went to ground, and to kill him.

Barr had no friends or family to whom he could turn for shelter or counsel. Nevertheless, his various frauds had earned him a notable fortune, and he might travel as he pleased. His very lack of any discernable plan made him exceedingly difficult to track.

He was also quite mad. For years an image of James Lockwood had haunted the back of his tortured mind, an image both feared and hated. And now that he had broken his word to Lockwood he believed his life forfeit. He traveled in a surging panic.

He took the mail coach to Sligo, but when a woman there eyed him askance he scrambled aboard the next coach, south to Galway. As the coach moved slowly across the barren bogs of Curragmore, Barr was suddenly convinced that Lockwood was in close pursuit. He screamed at the coachman to halt, to let him out, and so the incredulous driver watched as the wild-eyed madman staggered off into wilderness with his valise over his shoulder.

Barr gave an old woman a guinea to let him sleep in a cave on the shores of Lough Corrib, then in a sudden burst of terror he fled once again, eventually reaching Galway, and blindly booking passage back to Dublin.

Grinning wildly, convinced he had doubled back on Lockwood, Barr stiffly climbed out of the mail coach in Sackville Street, at the foot of the elegant Post Office. But he instantly found himself surrounded by prying eyes, and he fled staggering to the docks. He ran to the Eden Quay; at the Customs House he booked passage on a merchantman carrying barley to London.

He was not clever enough to use a false name.

"Major Dillon, a Mr. Lockwood to see you, sir."

Dillon was the Dublin agent for the East India Company, a chatty former officer of the Company who possessed one leg and heavily scarred features, who winced with nearly every movement. He was tasked with the recruitment of new officers for the Company, an ongoing process, as Europeans died with such inconvenient frequency in India. He knew his trade; he had hopes of this Lockwood. He had studied the papers, and knew the details of the court martial.

To keep his pain within reasonable bounds, Dillon routinely sipped the alcoholic tincture of laudanum throughout the day, and by that afternoon he was feeling especially gregarious. He was disappointed to find Lockwood poor company: stiff, formal, and on edge.

"I shall be frank, my dear Lockwood," said Dillon, "your misfortune may seem quite oppressive to you, but let me assure you, sir, that fortune and opportunity awaits! The Indian heat is abominable, of course, but it serves to keep a man limber, what, limber! This cool damp shall see me in a grave sooner than later. I personally came home a rich man, hail the conquering hero, what, but no woman can bear the sight of me. I suppose someone might marry me yet, but I'll be damned if I'll marry some cast-off whose only interest is my money. I'll die alone, thank you, and leave my fortune to my cat. That'll teach 'em, eh, Lockwood, eh?"

James, who had once had an intimate acquaintance with laudanum and readily recognized the signs in Dillon, only nodded stiffly and said, "I am obliged to you for your opinion, sir."

"Now, Lockwood, the Company is offering you a captain's post, a captaincy, sir! The Company is, in fact, so impressed with your record that it moved to offer a three hundred pound bonus, payable upon your receipt of the post. And of course all your travel expenses will be honoured. This captaincy, I may add, sir, is with the Eighth Regiment, Native Infantry. A most honourable regiment; I served with the Eighth myself, you know, at Assaye. The Second Maratha War; gave your Wellington his first victory. Bloody business, that. Their damned Pindarry cavalry rode me down like a dog and quite mauled me. But I survived, sir, and prospered! Let that be a lesson, to you, young man, a lesson indeed! Turn misfortune on its ear, and thrive!"

James fixed Dillon with a long stare that brought Dillon to an unsteady halt, until James said, "As Mrs. Lockwood shall accompany me to Madras, Major, my misfortune is, sadly, hers as well. You may thus understand that relocation to India is exceptionally difficult for her." He shifted uncomfortably in his chair. "For me as well, if I might mention it. While Mrs. Lockwood is making a brave face of it, I must make every effort to consider her feelings."

After two further interviews with representatives of the Company, James received a draft for three hundred pounds and the elegant document which confirmed his captaincy with John Company. He placed the draft in his billfold, and after returning to Fitzwilliam Square he folded the company commission several times and stowed it in the bottom of his chest.

After two months of inactivity in Dublin, James and Brigid had given up any hope of finding Barr. They received a pointed letter from Colonel Arbuthnot, stating that any further delay in their departure from Ireland would require Arbuthnot to proceed with forwarding the evidence of the Lockwood marriage to the civil authorities for investigation, and likely criminal prosecution of Mrs. Lockwood.

The Revolution of 1688 nearly put an end to the Jesuit presence in England. Nearly, however, is not completely, and a small chapel off Gutter Lane was the parish, perhaps more correctly termed the outpost, of Father Sims McDougal, S.J., as intelligent and secretive a Jesuit as England had ever known. McDougal's congregation numbered less than twenty, but his primary responsibility was recruiting and training new priests for the Society.

McDougal was studying the life of St. Thomas Aquinas, mulling over the disappointing weakness of that gentleman's dying words, when an old soldier came into his chapel. The soldier genuflected in only the most cursory manner, but that was of no great concern to McDougal, as strict adherence to traditional Catholic practice had never been of great import to his order. Before the soldier had said a word, McDougal unconsciously applied his powers of discernment to advantage. The soldier was sixty or so, thin, a tough old creature. The red coat was that of an enlisted man; it was worn, but clean, his person as well. Those were not a soldier's boots. No longer a soldier, but certainly no pauper. He could likely afford a civilian coat, but he chose not to; a sentimentalist? The soldier held his shako in his hand, displaying a nearly perfect ring around his balding pate; a veteran. Missing a thumb as well; lost in battle?

"God be with you, my son," said the priest.

"God and Mary be with you, Father."

McDougal's mind effortlessly spun with more analysis. The soldier was an Irishman; buff facings, and the '27' on the shako plate: an Inniskilling. An Ulster accent with a tone of derision in his tone, but still perhaps betraying a hint of devotion. Not nervous, not uncomfortable. A steady man. Formidable? "Pray, how may I be of service?"

"It is a letter I need to have written, if you please, Father, if I may impose on your goodness, as I have never acquired the skill, and my need is great, so it is."

Intriguing. Much unsaid, using that busy tongue to mask a quick understanding. "Soldier, there must be a dozen scriveners in Cheap Ward. What prompted you to come here, to a simple priest in this modest chapel on the most obscure of back streets?"

The soldier offered the tiniest of conspiratorial smiles. "My work requires, ah now, what is the word the Lieutenant once used... discretion... discretion it is, a grand word, don't you think, Father, elegant as Our Lady's touch."

Sharing a bit; he is a Catholic, he feels his work is important, and he knows very well what discretion means.

"In my travels," continued the redcoat, "and sure it's Paul's own travels that I've seen in these past weeks, I've been finding that when the occasion rises for me to report back to my officer, as it were, that it's God's own priests that are so helpful. And God bless them, Jesuit priests are both helpful and discreet, by both nature and training, as it were, if I may be so bold, no offense intended, Father, as it's the important work of the world that you do here, and I hope that I might be allowed to donate a coin or two to your work with the poor, though the English poor can't hold a candle to the Irish poor, in number or depth of need."

Thus, in McDougal's cell-like chamber, Diarmuid Doolan dictated while the priest, silent but intrigued, acted as his secretary.

"To Lieutenant and Mrs. Lockwood, care of Colonel Nelson, Fitzwilliam Square, Dublin, Ireland." In the echoing silence, the scratching of the priest's quill seemed inordinately loud, but Doolan did not notice, as his tongue was stuck in his cheek as he sought to compose his secret message in genteel terms. "Lieutenant and Missus, *a grah....*"

"*Agra?*" said McDougal in a puzzled voice, as his impressive language skills reached from Greek to Latin and much in between, but did not extend beyond the Pale.

"*A grah*, please, Father, though I haven't a child's notion as to how a Christian might spell it. Perhaps you might write it as 'dear'. She herself speaks the Irish like an angel, unlike Daidi, the creature."

Doolan grinned with such feeling that McDougal decided to like his Irish soldier.

After a considering pause, Doolan went on, "Our quarry is taken. Arrested in London for fraud, criminal trespass, and murderous assault. A joy to see."

"It is a sin to revel in a brother's pain, soldier."

"Truer words were never spoken, Father," said Doolan, not unkindly, "and I intend to discuss it with your Jesus at the first feckin' opportunity." Politely gesturing the priest back to the letter, Doolan went on, "I shall stay here long enough to see him safely put away. My pension is come through, so I am living a king's life. So, you may travel with contentment, with God's blessing, and my own. I shall see Barr put away, and then it is me who shall go home to Ireland, and stray no more. May God bless your travels, and my own. Very fondest, if I may be so bold, regards, Diarmuid Doolan, Private, Six Company, First Battalion, 27th Regiment of Foot, retired, I am."

James opened *The Times* and deliberately turned to page seven, where the police reports detailed the more unseemly side of life in far-off London. He scanned through one murder and several robberies before he came across the piece he was searching for, and with a burst of triumph he said, "Here it is my, dear! It is just as Doolan said!" He then read aloud,

The Times, *Friday, 30 November, 1820*
POLICE
Hatton-Garden,—Yesterday Mr. John Booth, of No. 6, Great Coram-street, Russell-square, who prosecuted Captain Charles Barr, of the 27th Regiment of Foot, on Saturday last at this office, on a charge of attempting to commit a fraud upon him, attended before Mr. BENNETT, with Mr. Roberts, his solicitor, to press charges against the prisoner.

Bayliss, an officer of New Prison, was dispatched to apprehend the captain, and then to proceed with him to that establishment. The captain, however, drew his sword, offering strenuous physical resistance, causing serious injury to Bayliss.

It was fortunate, then, that as Captain Barr made as to flee, a passerby, a discharged private soldier and an <u>Irishman</u>, came to the aid of Bayliss, and bludgeoned Captain Barr to the ground.

The captain was incarcerated upon the magistrate's order, who further ordered that no bail was to be offered, in light of the severity of the wounds suffered by Bayliss, and that the full weight of the law might be applied in the face of such conduct.

"Oh, thank God for Diarmuid Doolan!" cried Brigid.

As she read the article over again and again, James's smile broadened, and having a mischievous notion he went to Colonel Nelson's desk in search of paper, pen and ink. He quickly wrote,

To the Editor of The Times
Sir,

In justice to a regiment not less distinguished for the gentlemanlike conduct of its officers than for tried gallantry in the field, I beg to refer you to the Army List, and to assure you, that the person calling himself Captain Charles Barr, of the 27th Foot, alluded to in your police report of this day, does not hold a captain's, nor any other commission, upon either the full or half-pay list of the 27th Regiment.

It might be suggested that the Captain Barr referred to might be found as holding a commission in the 24th Regiment of Foot.

I am, Sir, your obedient humble servant,
AN OLD ENNISKILLER

He had a look on his face that Brigid had never seen before. She struggled to read his emotions; relief, satisfaction, but disappointment, as well? She knew he was holding something back, thoughts and emotions, both, when he said, "I do believe that my brothers... rather, the officers of the regiment, those gentlemen, would be pleased to hear themselves separated from Barr. If they were here they would certainly deny any connection between themselves and Barr. If the 24th was foolish enough to take Barr in, let them claim him now." He folded and addressed the cover, walked out to the hall, and placed the letter on the salver that held the outgoing post.

James made a last call on Major Dillon, as the final arrangements for their travel had yet to be agreed upon. Dillon flipped through his notes and said, "Yes, Lockwood, I see you have five children. My goodness, man. Well, doubtless this relocation to India will require some decisions regarding your family. The Company will make what allowance it can, within limits, sir, within limits."

"Thank, you, sir. Our eldest daughter, Mary, is to be married in Marseilles. Mrs. Lockwood and I intend to travel with her first to London, where we shall gather our three youngest children, who are in school there. We six shall then travel to Marseilles, see to Mary's wedding, and only then proceed to India. Is that agreeable to the Company?"

"It is, of course, an additional expense to the Company to divert your travel to France, and for such a number of people! But frankly, sir, the Company is so determined to secure your services that I am going to allow this exception to policy." Major Dillon then smiled broadly, offered his hand, and said, "I believe that is our final hurdle, sir, the last jump! I must say how pleased I am to have you in the service of the East India Company, *Captain* Lockwood."

James paused half a beat before shaking Dillon's hand.

Dillon wrote out a few additional notes, finally saying, "I am no great hand with numbers, Captain Lockwood, but I believe that you have mentioned plans for just four of your five children. Shall you leave one behind?"

"Our second daughter, Cissy, well, her name is actually Brigit, sir, will remain in Clonakilty to care for a dear friend of the family who has fallen ill. Mrs. Lockwood and I are most hesitant to do so, but our friend is precious to the entire family, and my daughter is quite... independent. We shall have Cissy join us in India when the opportunity arises."

"A young woman living alone, sir?"

"Oh, believe me, sir, we have been most thorough in securing the safety of her situation. She remains in the family home, and I have engaged a trusted friend to look in on her. There is not a threat in the world to her, none at all."

Chapter Seventeen

James had only two civilian coats, and he did not care for either of them. Brigid had hinted that he still might wear his uniform, but he would not. He was no longer in the service of His Majesty, and had no intention of falsely claiming the honour. He thus wore a bottle green coat as he stood at the great bay window of the Admiral Rodney, overlooking the forest of masts that filled Queenstown harbour.

Brigid settled their bill and joined him at the window, saying, "Mary will be a few moments more."

James frowned and said, "Of course she will. It would be a great shame if the people of Queenstown were not to see Mary Lockwood at her best."

Brigid shot him a look and said, "James...."

He looked so unhappy that Brigid thought of taking his hand, but he had his arms firmly crossed across his chest as he stared out at the shipping.

"How did it ever come to this?" he muttered, half to himself.

"We have endured difficult days before, *a grah.*" In a voice meant to cheer him she added, "We survived those days in Naas, in those tiny rooms in Mrs. Toon's house, and we can certainly survive these. Remember Mary's teething, and her howling like a chorus of banshees?"

In a serious tone he replied, "India, in the service of the Company, will be another matter entirely. Madras in July! The *Company*, for Christ's sake."

"We cannot give up hope. We shall make good use of our time in London."

"We shall likely have just three or four days in England. In that time we need gather the youngsters, and so will have time to make perhaps one call at Horse Guards. Lacking a pardon, we need to be en route to Marseilles by the 23rd or risk arrest. We can have little hope."

Brigid Lockwood had a way of raising her eyebrows and tilting her head that was both comical and a signal that she was deadly serious. With that look she said, "James Lockwood, if you do not cease this *feintrua páistiúil*, this childish self-pity, I may well go to India without you, so that you might remain here and devote every moment to cursing your situation."

He swallowed hard, and without turning to her he said, "I shall go down to the dock and engage a boat to carry us out to the ship."

Brigid watched him as he walked down the broad steps of the Rodney and joined the hustle of the dockyard below. She had never seen him act in such a manner, so irritable, so hopeless. Her husband's air of desperate unhappiness was soon dispelled by the arrival of Mary, who fairly flew down the steps, scattering joy in her wake. She glowed with a blind happiness, a happiness scarcely capable of heeding, let alone understanding, any emotion short of ecstasy. "Mama, I cannot think of anything but Guillaume! Is this all not so very marvelous! I am so excited! I am to be a bride! Just think! Guillaume, and France!"

A very terse James Lockwood engaged boatmen and porters, and eventually herded this family and their baggage to the edge of the sea. James stepped into the boat, his face clenched, and took a seat. Only after glancing up, and seeing Brigid looking at him with an astonished look, did he recover himself, and quickly stood to assist his wife and daughter into the boat.

As they stowed the luggage into the bows the two boatmen shared a look. They pushed off, and as they rowed out into the harbour the stroke oar muttered to his bowman in Irish, "Sure the Saxon is in a rage, and him ignoring his two lovelies, a disgrace it is."

The bowman grinned, and looking out to starboard quietly said, still in Irish, "A pity it would be, if his two lovelies should grow tired of his rages, and opt for the company of two strong, handsome boatmen, don't you think?"

Mary, who sat closer to the two boatmen than her parents, leaned forward and said softly, but with a knowing look, "The two lovelies speak Irish as well as your own mother, and if you do not mind your manners the Saxon may have you swimming back to the dock, and you both bleeding like holy martyrs."

For such an elegant young woman to speak Irish, and a Munster Irish at that, was such a surprise to the boatmen that for the next few strokes they were a disgrace to their profession. They had sculled Queenstown harbour for many years, like their fathers before them, and for them to lose their time and clash oars in such a lubberly fashion brought a derisive cry of "Farmer!" from a nearby boat.

Mary smiled a bit, the oarsmen instantly assumed wooden expressions, and James, who had lost his King's commission but not his ability to intimidate, glared at the oarsmen and growled, "Row dry, there."

The Lockwoods of Clonakilty

The three Lockwoods had wanted to stay on deck as long as possible, as Ireland was beyond dear to them. But as soon as the *Colgate Swan* reached the chop rolling in from the Atlantic, Mary turned rather pale. The *Swan* was an elegantly appointed merchantman, and so carried a nearly naval crew, including two eager midshipmen who offered to show Miss Lockwood to her cabin; one tall and handsome, the other a boy whose voice had not yet broken. After a dismissive glance toward the handsome officer, Mary turned to the boy and said, "I should be very pleased to have Mr. Brewer see me to my cabin."

Brigid put a hand to Mary's face, gave her a mother's smile, and said, "It looks as if it may be a while for you to find your sea legs. We shall trust Mr. Brewer to see you below; I believe I shall stay on deck with your father for a few minutes longer."

A beaming Mr. Brewer escorted Mary below, while Brigid and James stood at the stern rail. Most of the passengers had gone below, though one young officer of a Yeomanry regiment remained, leaning over the windward rail, trying to look inconspicuous. Brigid nodded toward him and quietly said, "That young man was at the Admiral Rodney last night. And he has been steadily watching us since we came aboard."

James did not turn. Keeping his eyes on Ireland he said, "I saw him come aboard; I believe he is the Castle's man. He had no baggage, so he evidently did not expect us to take ship. It is some consolation to know that he shall be wearing the same clothes for the next several days."

Her suspicions confirmed, Brigid looked at the officer with a steady glare, which appeared to make him even more uncomfortable.

James tossed the awkward, slender young man a glance, and in a flat voice he said, "I have a notion to knock him on the head and toss him over the side, the vile little toad."

She took his arm and grinned enthusiastically. "Oh, do allow me to help! We Irish are capable of great violence, you know."

James barked a laugh, smiled down at his beautiful wife, and said, "I do believe you would."

"Of course I would," she murmured as she drew closer. "It is a good wife's duty to assist her husband however she can, up to and including murderous assault."

James's grin grew deeper, and as the wind gusted he put an arm around Brigid and pulled her closer. "You are the best of wives. I have been convinced of that for the past twenty-one years."

"Twenty-two, dear. We have been married for twenty-two years. Your memory, or your arithmetic, is failing you."

In a playful voice he said, "Have you considered, my dear woman, that we might have been married for a year before I concluded that you were the best of wives?"

"Humph, sir," she said as the sea and the ship rolled sharply beneath them, but they held each other and scarcely noticed. Ireland was steadily fading from view. James quietly said, "I am very sorry, my dear. For everything."

"It shall all work out for the best, *mo stor*. In my heart, I am sure of it."

Several minutes passed. "Do you recall when I swore to you that I would return from Waterloo?"

"I do. I believe you said you would return 'though hell should bar the way.' I still hold that letter very dear."

"I shall venture another vow. I shall see you home some day, Brigid O'Brian. I cannot venture an estimate as to when, but we shall one day return home."

They stayed there together at the stern rail, watching with dry eyes as Ireland disappeared into the distant mist.

Only a thin light managed to find its way through the thick London fog and the sooty windows of the War Office. The corridors of that vast building, never particularly cheery, were thus positively morose as two clerks hurried down a narrow back hall, both franticly flipping through a stack of papers.

"I do not know the details," said the first, whose thin, grey, officious countenance made him nearly indistinguishable from the other. "All I know is that Mr. Andrews has called for all the pertinent data on the case, and that as soon as he has assembled the file, Lord Palmerston is most anxious to personally review the files."

"Oh my, Lord Palmerston himself?" said the other with as much emotion as his narrow range of humanity would allow.

"Yes, yes, it seems that he has received some pointed correspondence from a number of officers. Many are Waterloo veterans, and you know what weight that carries, within Horse Guards, and without."

"Those military sorts get all the glory, but who does all the work behind the scenes? Honest, hardworking clerks such as ourselves, that is who. I wager they'll try to blame all this on us, just wait and see."

The clerks' paperwork was soon reverently placed atop the desk of the capable Martin Andrews, Senior Secretary to the Secretary of State at War, Henry Temple, 3rd Viscount Palmerston. Andrews dismissed the anxious clerks, quickly reviewed the assembled documents, and with a satisfied look on his face he carried the files down the ornate public hall to Palmerston's office.

Palmerston was engaged in drafting a speech regarding military budgets for the upcoming year. Oratory was an activity in which he reveled, and he was in a high roar of spirits as Andrews glided in.

"The matter of Lieutenant Lockwood's court martial, my Lord," explained Andrews, holding up the file.

"Yes, excellent!" said Palmerston. "We shall deal with this immediately; we must not have His Majesty's officers doubting the justice of courts martial! And without the guarantee of justice what shall we have, Andrews? Injustice breeds dissension. Dissension, that most contagious of vices, might well spell defeat, collapse, and an ignominious end to empire!" Palmerston's parliamentary persona ebbed a bit as he finally sat down.

Seeing Palmerston recede, Andrews said, "In the wake of Lockwood's trial we have received numerous letters demanding a War Office review of the case. We have letters from every officer of the 27th, and a surprising number of letters from officers of other regiments, some of great influence. Gregory of the 44th, who will stand for Liverpool, and Brooke of the 4th, for God's sake, beg pardon, my Lord, who would not say two words for his own mother, has written a most glowing recollection of the subject's gallantry at Waterloo. Brooke is thought to be considering a switch to the Harries contingent, my Lord."

Palmerston, intrigued, said, "To add to your stack of correspondence, I have received a personal note from Lord Enniskillen, and it would be useful if I could oblige him. Pray give me a summary of the situation."

"Lieutenant James Lockwood," said the unflappable Andrews, glancing at his notes, "served in the First Battalion, 27th Foot; that is an Irish regiment, my Lord, the Inniskillings. Ensigncy with the regiment in1799... lieutenancy November, 1806... Peninsula... Badajoz... Plattsburg... Waterloo, where he was wounded... a chest wound... a lengthy recovery that was evidently most unpleasant. He was court martialed on charges of violation of the Irish Penal Laws, found guilty, and dismissed the service."

"Penal Laws?" said Palmerston in surprise. "I thought the application of such foolishness had been quietly forgotten."

"This prosecution was at the insistence of Dublin Castle, my Lord," said Andrews with an inflection to his voice that recaptured Palmerston's attention. "It appears that when the good lieutenant could no longer serve with his regiment he was honoured with a posting to the 3rd Veteran Battalion." This was met with a blank look on Palmerston's face, so Andrews added, "The 3rd Veteran Battalion is on the Irish Establishment, my Lord."

"Oh, indeed?" said Palmerston, this bit of knowledge fodder for his politically fired mind. "So, this trial and conviction do not reside with us; there is no fault of this office. Rather, it lies with the Home Office, indeed in the lap of Dublin Castle and Lord Kerr himself. This may well give us an opportunity to give them a sharp rap on the knuckles. I would so enjoy finding a method to make that weasel Graham squirm. The Lord Lieutenant of Ireland abuses his power, igniting this firestorm of protest, when hey presto, the War Office rides to the rescue. Christmas, come early."

In the fashion typical of government communication, Lord Palmerston's letter took an interminable time to reach Dublin Castle, but only minutes after Henry Graham read it he hurried it into the Lord Lieutenant's gilded office.

"I beg pardon, my Lord," said Graham, "but we are in receipt of a letter from the War Office, Lord Palmerston himself, that seems quite urgent. Indeed, the tone is very challenging. I have taken the liberty of pulling the file; you may recall the court martial of Lieutenant Lockwood."

Kerr's brow crinkled in thought, as he said, "Is he the fellow who was accused of bestiality...."

"No, my Lord, he is the officer who was so roundly denounced by Captain Barr of Lockwood's own regiment."

"Lockwood, the fellow who wed that papist strumpet? I am tired to death of these whining missives from papist-loving weaklings, crying a review for that fool and his harlot! Whatever would Palmerston want with such people?"

As Kerr read the letter his demeanor passed from incredulity to fuming indignation. "My God! Who is he to speak to me in such a tone? Impertinent little shit! I shall certainly not respond to such a letter. No, you shall reply, Graham, and while you must keep it civil, by God you shall spell out the situation; a damned unnatural, criminal union."

"That is certainly an equitable reaction, my Lord, but I feel it my duty to point out the veritable flood of correspondence in support of the Lockwoods, some from very influential officers. Lieutenant Colonel Archibald, a hero of Waterloo... Colonels Pritchard, Nelson and McLean of the 27th...."

"Pritchard!" cried Kerr in alarm. "His estates in Fermanagh border my son's holdings; a valuable neighbor. My, my. Damn it all, anyway. All right then, we must explain ourselves. Draft something, Graham. You will explain the damned odd nature of the marriage. But take your time, man, take your time. We do not wish to give the appearance of hopping every time that popinjay snaps his fingers."

"Of course, My Lord."

"And for God's sake, get Lockwood and his tart out of Ireland. The decent elements of his family agreed to hustle them off to India, and it must be done immediately. Once these two are gone this foolishness shall all be quickly forgotten."

Viscount Palmerston was a politician of great experience and of unlimited potential. He enjoyed his life as a fashionable, powerful, urbane gentleman of means. He was a Tory, albeit a

Tory with some liberal leanings, but above all he was a realist. He knew that men of passionate conviction rarely lasted long in government; adaptability and compromise were the keywords of the successful Cabinet member.

Palmerston was in his office at nearly midnight the night before a motion for Catholic Emancipation was to be debated on the floor. As Secretary at War, his input into such a topic was not critical, yet still he was a member of government and a rising star, and his opinion carried great weight. He was very tired, and had allowed himself more than his usual two glasses of French brandy. He was in something of a quandary, as Catholic Emancipation was becoming an increasingly visible, divisive issue, and both supporters and opponents were growing more vocal and passionate. Palmerston had some sympathies on the issue, and, though he had yet to declare himself, he suspected that perhaps the time was coming. His desk was covered by stacks of correspondence on the subject, but he kept coming back to a letter from Dublin Castle that Andrews had quietly dropped on his desk.

> *Dublin Castle, 1ˢᵗ February 1821*
> *Sir,*
>
> *I have received and laid before the Lord Lieutenant your letter of the 27ᵗʰ ultimo, with the Marriage Certificates produced to clarify the condition of the marriage of Lieutenant and Mrs. James Lockwood.*
>
> *And I am in answer, directed by His Excellency to state, for the information of the Secretary at War, that the Certificates in question (herewith returned) appear, on inquiry to be authentic, but that Lieutenant Lockwood is a Protestant, and Mrs. Lockwood a Roman Catholic.*

It may be proper to observe, that one of the parties having been a Protestant, the other a Protestant or Roman Catholic, the marriage, as now certified, is not by law valid- A marriage of persons so circumstanced by a Roman Catholic Priest, was once a felony, and is still highly penal, unless the parties were previously married by a Protestant Clergyman.

It is thus not the Lord Lieutenant's intention to reinstate Lieutenant Lockwood into any position within the Irish establishment, particularly not to a post with His Majesty's forces, when one considers their sworn duty to <u>enforce</u> rather than <u>violate</u> the law.

I have the honour to be, Sir,
Your most obedient,
Humble Servant,Henry Graham

Palmerston had been deeply involved in British politics most of his adult life. He reveled in the negotiation, oratory, and conflict. But on that night he stared out the windows of his splendid offices, drinking more than he ought, disgusted with both the business of government and humanity in general.

There were times that Mrs. Cashman's breathing was so shallow that Cissy was afraid that she had passed. That morning Cissy's beauty was faded by sleepless nights as she leaned over to listen to the whispering breath, then as she straightened the blankets she said, *"Atomriug indium niurt tréun...."*

She was startled to hear Mrs. Cashman whisper, finishing the prayer, waking from a distant dream. *"... togairm Trindóit, faístin Oendatad, i nDúlemon dáil."* Mrs. Cashman looked old, old beyond years.

"Did you know, Nana Kay," said Cissy softly, "that before the boys left for school they helped me work out the English? 'I bind to myself today, through the strong virtue of love, the strong name of the Trinity, by invocation of the same, the three in one, one in three.'"

Mrs. Cashman managed a flicker of a smile and whispered, "Dear Richard, and his verses, and Joseph and his laughter. How I miss them."

They were silent again for long minutes until Mrs. Cashman motioned Cissy closer and softly, slowly, said, "*A cuisle*, there is much you need to know. Your parents try to protect you. But you must know. There is a letter hidden under the flour barrel. Read, *a cuisle*. Read. You must know the devil."

Mrs. Cashman then slept again, long hours until Paul Cashman came to sit by his mother's side, and Cissy went in search of the letter. It took some effort to tilt the flour barrel back far enough, but she did find the letter. She quickly stuffed it into her pocket, wrapped a shawl around her shoulders, and walked purposefully into a misty afternoon, up into the hills above her home. She found a sheltered spot among the hedges, and leaning against a tree she pulled the letter from her pocket. She saw it was from Captain Barr, the Barr of whom John Cashman had warned her. Impatient to know how the mention of the man's name could spark such terror in Mrs. Cashman, she opened it.

Cissy was aghast. The letter was beyond suggestive, beyond obscene. It was written by a man who was obviously out of his mind, a mind that switched with frightening rapidity: harsh threats, protestations of piteous love, offensive intimacy, unbelievably foul hatred. Barr explained in some detail how he had denounced the Lockwoods to the Castle, and how he had written to James's family to destroy what little sympathy they might have had for them. With shock and terror in her eyes

Cissy slowly slid down the tree trunk, finally sitting in the wet grass as the letter closed with the madman saying that Brigid Lockwood's only chance for salvation was to abandon her husband and children and offer herself to him, body and soul.

The room was quiet, but she was never alone. The raging fever was relentless, though mercifully Mrs. Cashman slept for hours without count. She was awake for just brief periods of time, hazy, dream-like time, drifting, while Cissy sat by her bedside, silent, thinking, as the hours slipped away unnoticed.

At one point Mrs. Cashman was awake and lucid, and she looked up to see Cissy sitting beside her. Cissy saw Mrs. Cashman's left hand balled into a fist and softly asked, "Nana Kay, does your hand trouble you? It is clenched so tightly."

Mrs. Cashman's voice was coherent but paper thin, and to hear her made Cissy catch their breath. "I am grown so thin, I am afraid that I shall lose my husband's ring. It is just a little thing from a tinker's cart, but I would not lose it for the world, you know."

Softly, "Of course, *a stor*. It is a lovely ring. Here, now, let me wrap some ribbon around the band, and it shall fit like new again."

Cissy started to draw a length of ribbon from the pocket of her frock, but when she saw it was black she quickly stuffed it back. Instead, she found a length of bright green silk, and with great care the lovely young Irish woman, strong and agonized, wrapped the ribbon around the band and returned it to Mrs. Cashman's finger. Cissy raised Mrs. Cashman's hand so that she could see the flash of gold and green, a rare sunny day lighting the room, making the colors vivid beyond memory. God had allotted Catherine Agnes Cecelia O'Leary Cashman nearly a million smiles with which to color her life, and it was then that she chose to use her last, contented.

Her sons came, and their wives, and the children, all comforting and strong. Then Father McGlynn came to Fáibhile Cottage for the first time. His politics aside, he was serious about his duties as a priest, and so offered Extreme Unction to Catherine Cashman, giving her great peace of mind as she began to slip away.

Mrs. Cashman died that afternoon, her passing earnestly mourned by a thousand and one good souls, all of whom, in Church or Chapel or field, would come to beg God that she should be welcomed home. It was one of her granddaughters who ran into the fields to whisper to the bees and cows, asking that they might help guide her to heaven, but in this case at least their aid was not needed, as her path was straight and bright and pure.

Apologies were offered to Mr. Lockwood, but while his application for pardon was to be given every consideration, at the time of his call upon Horse Guards no such pardon was yet to be offered.

The next day, the Lockwood family went aboard the *Belle Dames*, bound for Marseilles. There, Mary would be married, and then five Lockwoods would make for Madeira, whence passage aboard an Indiaman would be arranged, with the mysteries of India beyond.

Chapter Eighteen

In recognition of his past service to the Crown, Captain Barr was not to be remanded to the Surrey House treadmill, but was instead sent to Borough Compter, a small prison on Tooley Street which was typically reserved for London's finer debtors and gentlemen of a felonious nature. Upon his arrival Barr was greeted by one Israel Brownlow, the chief gaoler, who gave Barr an appraising look, then with a polite bow said, "Welcome to Borough Compter, Captain, welcome indeed. It is my privilege to ensure that gentlemen of quality... gentlemen of means, at any rate... are not overly inconvenienced during their stay here. I trust, sir, that you may be interested in one of our more commodious accommodations?"

Barr had been treated with deliberate discourtesy through much of his trial and confinement at New Prison. Two of the gaolers were former soldiers, and they took every opportunity to laugh, to remind Barr of how the mighty had fallen, of how he would lose his precious commission, now, wouldn't he, and as they kicked him into a filthy cell they howled over how the world had turned upside down. But through it all Barr had retained his purse and the considerable funds he had accumulated during the larcenies he had perpetrated over the preceding months.

And now at Borough Compter, he was being addressed as a gentlemen and a man of superior ability. Barr mustered the portion of his mind that still functioned near reality, managed a dull nod, and muttered, "Your best, please, master gaoler."

Brownlow led Barr to the narrow stone stairs that led to the upper floor, though he had to do so slowly, as Barr's every step was made in an odd, disjointed, manner. As they climbed the stairs Brownlow said in a confidential tone, "I need not expose you, sir, to the lower chambers. Down there we are quite packed, cheek by jowl, sir, with gentlemen who are up to their eyes in debt, and not tuppence to their names. No, no, sir, you need not be exposed to such squalor. You, sir, shall be privy to whatever we can humbly offer in the way of comforts. It is our duty, our pleasure, indeed, to mollify whatever misfortune has brought you to us, sir, until your honourable return to society."

Barr heard little of Brownlow's chatter until he grasped at the word that sparked his soul. Brownlow was startled when Barr bitterly snapped, "My honour! My honour is sacred!"

A large room stood at the top of the stairs, from which narrow hallways led back to the more or less desirable chambers. A number of men were gathered there, assembling for their afternoon walk on the streets below. Brownlow introduced Barr to his other clients: six debtors, two rapists, three embezzlers, two extortionists, and one dapper pederast. Those felons, however, soon found Barr's snarling countenance so off-putting that they backed away at the first opportunity.

Brownlow then made a point of formally introducing Barr to one short, fat man in clothes which might have been stylish if they had not been so horribly dirty. "Captain Barr, pray allow me the honour of introducing the Honourable Mr. Thaddeus Soames. Mr. Soames, Captain Charles Barr, of His Majesty's 24th Regiment of Foot."

Soames was obviously thrilled with the introduction, crying, "At last! The Lord has graced my penurious purgatory with the presence of a true gentleman! An officer in the service of our blessed Sovereign! A man who places honour before all else! God be praised!"

Brownlow was interrupted from the bottom of the stairs, as one of the turnkeys called up to him, "Beg pardon, sir, but Gripper Oakes has stabbed the new dandy, them scrapping over a place to sleep."

Soames burst out, "Oh, Mister Brownlow, pray tend to your business in yon dungeon, and allow me the honour of showing our esteemed friend the available quarters. It shall give me an opportunity to explain the various fees, gratuities, perquisites, and emoluments."

Brownlow paused, looking expectant, until Barr handed him a guinea, and with a smile the gaoler retreated. Brownlow joined the turnkey at the bottom of the stairs, and as they passed into the dim passages that led to the squalid debtor's chambers he told him, "As mad as Soames, this new soldier, but we must keep to our usual practice. Fleece 'em slow, like; no outrages. We shall milk that cow for months. Christ, but these are happy days."

Barr was nearly silent, but his eyes flashed with life as Soames showed him a vacant chamber. The fat little man chattered steadily, "A barrister named Williams had these apartments, though regrettably he died a month or so ago. He was sentenced for debt but he was, like me, wise enough to keep sufficient gold at hand to ensure a comfortable abode, a gentleman's confinement."

The apartment was small and bare, but two rooms, one with a window, were luxury indeed compared to what Barr had recently seen. Soames rattled on, "Williams was a fine companion, until he decided that his chances of heaven were superior to his chances of escaping the weight of his debt, and so he opted to exercise that option."

Soames pointed overhead and went on, "That is the very rafter upon which Mr. Williams chose to end his life. He very nearly failed himself at the last moment, you know, growing tremulous, so I helped preserve his honour by giving the chair a solid kick, and then holding his feet down, so that his honour remained unblemished 'til the end."

Soames was working to maintain a nonchalant tone, but Barr could hear the glee in his tone. Barr, who did not trouble himself over his chances at heaven (that issue having been decided some years before), studied Soames's face for a long moment. Barr found a mirror in Soames's eyes, a mad gleam, and for the first time in weeks Captain Charles Barr smiled.

The next morning, as the privileged prisoners strolled Tooley Street, Soames sought out Barr, and as he took his arm he quietly told him, "I believe that you, my dear Captain, will agree with me in holding that honour requires a gentleman to act, and act boldly, if oppressed."

Barr grunted his agreement, so Soames threw a look over his shoulder and hurriedly said, "Through the discreet application of my sadly dwindling gold, and the use of bible-based tactics of persuasion, I have wholly corrupted one of the turnkeys, a Sojourner Smee, a Methodist and therefore a heretic. As such, he is a man beyond God's grace, a mound of clay to be shaped and used in any manner honourable men choose appropriate."

From a doorway, an aging whore beckoned to them. Though they were both quite mad, the two men differed in build, loquacity, and their responses to the whore's invitation. Soames muttered *"Quicunque vult,"* and spit at the woman's feet. Barr, while he continued to walk with the fat little man, eyed her and subtly, achingly, rubbed his crotch.

Oblivious to Barr's cravings, Soames went on, "It seems that Smee has a brother in America... Virginia, if memory serves... America is where Smee belongs, a land of traitors and heretics. Smee is desirous of joining his brother, and while he has been steadily hording the shillings he steals and extorts from the denizens of the lower chambers, he has informed me that one hundred pounds, in gold, *in auro*, mind you, would buy our freedom. If you, my dear Barr, might be persuaded to produce said one hundred pounds, we shall soon be as free as honourable Englishmen deserve."

Smee set the fire a week later, just after three on a Sunday morning. It was sparked in a damp storage room, a cramped, ignored space in the main wing where the straw for prisoners' mattresses was stored. Beyond extinguishing the lives of innumerable rats, the fire generated massive amounts of smoke. That smoke in turn incited panic amongst both inmates and staff, and in the smoke-filled darkness and screaming panic the prisoners of both the upper and lower chambers were freed from their cells and herded to the central yard. It was understandable, then, that two prisoners, released into dark, smoke-filled corridors, might somehow manage to escape their jailor and find their way to an unguarded wicket, a side door unaccountably left unlocked.

Captain Barr strode into the enveloping darkness, Thaddeus Soames padding along in his wake. Barr suddenly felt strong, triumphant. A month in prison had lightened his purse, but had left him with a renewed sense of purpose. He was a military man; he would need to regain strength, reconnoiter, and lay in his plans. But he would soon go to Clonakilty, and the Lockwoods, all of them, would pay.

An hour of furtive darting through dark streets and alleys brought Barr and Soames to a fashionable home in Belgravia. Soames hammered on the front door for several long minutes before a sleepy footman opened the door, and in a surprised but respectful tone said, "Welcome home, Mister Soames."

The nut that was Thaddeus Soames had not rolled far from the oak that was his wide-eyed father. That gentleman, who had spent his evening speaking to his late wife, was in no way surprised to see his son return home in the middle of the night with a sullen infantry captain in tow. The house staff, who had believed that a conviction for murderous assault had removed the erratic Master Thaddeus from their lives from some years, shook their heads and resignedly saw to Thaddeus and his viciously short-tempered guest.

The next morning the Soames family business agent was summoned to the house. While that rational gentleman was shocked to see Thaddeus returned home, he decided that assisting a fugitive from the King's justice was a better career option than risking the living he made from the Soames fortune.

That night the agent's carriage carried two heavily cloaked men down to the quay, where they were hustled aboard a chartered schooner. That schooner set sail with the dawn tide, bound, at the ranting order of Mister Soames's guest, for Ireland. Soames told Barr of a distant family holding, where they might hide in complete safety until they reestablished their situation.

Soames was mad, but he was clever, and he had a purse full of family gold. Once they reached Galway he purchased two saddle horses, thus making them hard to trace. He also had a poor sense of direction, and so a long rambling, but again, difficult to follow path took them south, deep into Clare, to the crumbling tower of Ballynagowen.

It was a great square tower that stood alone along a narrow valley. Built by the last Irish King of Munster, the upper floors of the tower were in ruins, but the ground floor was intact. It was there that the two exhausted fugitives went to ground. A spiral stone staircase led up to ancient stone rooms and the crumbling parapet, where Charles Barr communed with the devil in the steady moonlight, his screams and ranting frightening even the unhinged Soames.

"She has died here, and she shall be mourned here; it is the way of things." Cissy Lockwood insisted that tradition would be held to. Mrs. Cashman's wake would begin immediately, in the home where the death occurred. But after so many sleepless nights at the bedside Cissy was hollow-eyed and exhausted. Moyra Cashman, Catherine's kindly sister, who had arrived from the wilds of Kerry in time to bid her sister farewell, gathered up Cissy and gently helped her upstairs to her bed, and the mourners gathered.

Cissy woke into the trackless hours of darkest night. Fáibhile Cottage echoed with the *caoineadh*, the keen, the ancient rite of weeping women, wailing for hours, their shrieks echoing across the hills. The family had brought a *bean chaointe* to the house, an ancient woman whose keen was her living, known throughout Cork for her heart-rending shrieks.

Cissy did not change her clothes; she wore her frayed old shift, her hair was tangled and unkempt, and her face was worn with exhaustion and grief. She went down the steps of her home as if in a dream, the house dark, dark, her feet knowing the way, drawn by the aching wails of grieving women.

She stepped into her kitchen and into the flickering lights of a dozen candles, placed around the body. Cissy had known every inch of the kitchen since she was a girl, but now the room was strange to her, the wailing both frightening and comforting.

Draped in white linen, Mrs. Cashman's body lay atop the great old table, the same work table which had been the center of her work day for years. The flickering candlelight played across twenty or more people. The women were drawn up around Catherine while the men stood smoking and drinking in the dim corners. The rolling song of the keen softened and slowed as Cissy entered; some faces turned up to watch her, some ignored her, some deliberately turned away. Cissy did not care, she cared only for the kind woman who now lay still.

Tears rolled down her face as she walked to Catherine's side, and Cissy softly kissed the quiet face. She saw that the Cashmans had laid out pipes, tobacco, and snuff as tradition required, so she went to her cupboard, drew out a bag of salt, and poured it out onto the table, a sign of welcome to all who had come to mourn. A murmur of approval rose from the men, and sighs of sharing and of sorrow rose from the women as Cissy went to sit amongst them, their arms reaching out to welcome her. Her hands went first to her face as she began to sob, then flew down to her sides in fists as she wailed in grief, a heart-wrenching cry that sailed beside and beyond the keening of the *bean chaointe,* and she was with them, of them, as the Irish mourned their loss.

The Shannon Arms was the sole public house of repute in Clonakilty. Low shebeens near the quay or on the fringes of town served poteen and cider to the common folk, but the Arms reserved the right of serving the more prosperous people of the town. The Arms' standing was reinforced once a year, on Saint Patrick's day itself, when Lord Bannon would come to the Arms to stand his round and share a drink with men whose names he would never know.

In the town's complex code of manhood, for a man to stand his round there marked his place amongst his fellows. But when times were hard, and those were difficult days, many a man had to choose, sometimes unwisely, between standing his round and caring for his family.

The end of the wars against America and Napoleon had brought hard times to Irish farmers, and English trade laws kept it that way. Maurice O'Leary, one of a rare handful of Catholic farmers who held his own land, now had few buyers for his milk, butter, and cheese. But on that crowded Saturday evening O'Leary stepped into the Arms with a determined air, nodded to Liam O'Flynn behind the bar, and circled one finger in the air. Most men there could afford only one pint, and by slowly sipping a fellow might make that pint last a long hour with their friends. To have a man, let alone a good man who had long before won the respect of them all, buy them a second was a most welcome surprise.

Following the low cheer that followed the announcement of his round, O'Leary roared to the sea of expectant faces, "I have ill news, and I shall not bear it alone, or dry-throated."

Liam O'Flynn knew his business, and thus it was some time before he could properly pull so many pints of Irish stout. Thus everyone sat dry-throated until they all had their pints in hand, whereupon O'Leary raised his mug and solemnly called "*Sláinte agus táinte!*" The room erupted in long pulls and echoed calls for health and wealth, but then came voices calling for O'Leary to share his news.

O'Leary waved down the crowd, and with his voice breaking he loudly said, "I shall tell you now that Catherine Cashman, the good woman, is passed, and never again shall we see her kind smile, or hear her sweet voice."

Muted discussions broke out amongst the scattered tables, and Catherine would likely have been pleased by the kindnesses, tears, and pained smiles that dotted the room. They were hardened men, but there was more than one display of unaffected sorrow, some tearing eyes, some flashes of remorse at once not having treated her kindly, of not having called upon her sick bed, of remembrance, perhaps, of the girl she once was, pretty, sparkling, and laughing.

O'Leary went on, "And with those pints in your hands, boys, I am also come to ask a favour! I want all here to know that when I called upon Catherine Cashman, she herself begged me, on her deathbed, mind, that all men of good heart are to watch over Cissy Lockwood, as her family has left for India itself, but like the good young woman she is, Cissy stayed here in Clonakilty to tend Catherine in her last days."

One disgruntled old voice called, "But remember, O'Leary, how Lockwood murdered our men at Leamaneh! The Proddie bastard, in his red coat!"

There were several Protestant men in the house, and there might have been some bad feelings, or worse, but O'Leary strongly called, "That's enough of that shite, Colm Gavin! Her father is a Lockwood, sure, but did he not treat the people of this town fair and decent, no matter their church? And is her mother not an O'Brian, who brought her children to Saint Brigid's every Sunday, and yet had friends amongst the Protestants as well?"

O'Leary had noticed, but did not mention, that Cissy had not been attending Mass these past several months. Instead, he turned the men back to their drinks with, "No matter what you might think of Cissy's father and his father, remember there is Irish blood in Cissy Lockwood, dear Brigid O'Brian's own, and we are to remember that, and help that child along as we can, as good neighbors. Now drink up, ye devils, and God bless you and yours."

Late into the second night the Cashman family mourned. Catherine Cashman's prized jade elephant, the gift of the wandering John, was found in her room and placed in her hand so that it might be buried with her, a talisman.

On a stool by the front door Liam O'Flynn piped *goltraí*, the mourning music that opened the souls of the grieving. At the back of the house the Cashman men gathered with their bottles, and it was there that John Cashman, who would hide no more, stepped out of the midnight darkness, back into his brothers' lives as if by magic. The wake was long and bitter and joyous, but after hours of tears and talk the brothers' conversation in the predawn darkness grew sharp and heated.

"I say it again," said John, "it was her dying wish, and I shall carry it out."

"Ah, don't be daft," said Paul. "Mamaí was delirious with the fever. She said a lot of nonsense in her dreams."

"Nonsense!" cried John, "which of Kevin Cashman's sons dares call his mother's words nonsense!"

They were all near blows, drunk and crying.

"It is I who said it!" cried Paul, "Her son that stayed by her side all these years, after you picked up the gun, leaving her with a heart broken with the grief!"

Paul half lunged, half staggered toward John, but David and Stephen held him back, held him up, while John pointed a finger and said, "Aye, and sure it was me who was the only man in the house who had the stones to fight for the people!"

"For the people, is it now? You bring war to our homes, death and terror! You and your damned rebel friends! And now you say you must hunt down this damned fellow Barr, an English officer, no less, just because a woman mad with fever said so!"

"It's a great wave building, Paul, and Whiteboys are everywhere, doing the people's work. And now I've been given a mission to bring peace to our Ma's soul, her own dying words, I tell ya! Father McGlynn himself heard them, and told them to me with his own lips! From a priest, mind you, so you can fucking stick it in your arse, Paul, and I shall do what needs done!"

Chapter Nineteen

Fáibhile Cottage was empty of mourners, and Cissy sat alone. She ran a hand across the top of the old writing desk, ink-stained and scratched, the same old desk at which her parents had once sat. She missed her family, tearfully, if she gave them much thought, but she took some comfort in the house and the solidity of the memories it held. She eyed two letters that lay on the desk. The first had come two days before, from a Mr. Brownlow in London.

Miss Lockwood,

Your father, Lt. James Lockwood, upon his recent visit to London, visited this prison, and made a generous provision to ensure that a notification would be sent to both he and you, Miss, if there came any change in the status of Captain Charles Barr, who had been remanded to the custody of the prison in which I serve as Chief Gaoler.

I am grieved, Miss, to inform you that Captain Barr has escaped this prison and that despite desperate searches he has not yet been re-apprehended.

The Lockwoods of Clonakilty

In fulfillment of the agreement with Lt. Lockwood I
am also writing to him at the headquarters of the East
India Company in Madras. If I have any further news I
shall write again.

With all due regards and apologies,
Israel Brownlow
Borough Compter Prison

That morning's post brought the second letter, and with it came terror. Cissy's anger flared and quickly did away with something so contemptible as fear. Now resolution and intelligence marked her face as she re-opened the letter, brief and unsigned.

I will come for you.

She studied the water-marked paper, the aggressive, razor-thin style of the script, and she tried to picture the hand that wrote it. She knew it was Barr, of course. She had never seen his face, and so he remained only a dark figure in her mind, shapeless, but very real.

She was alone in the house. She assumed Barr knew that as well.

Cissy, sitting at her desk, was determined to stay at home. She was not without resource, or allies. One word to the Cashmans would bring a dozen strong men to her aid, of that she was sure. And Mr. O'Leary was just up the road, and her Aunt Anne was just across town, though Cissy was unsure of the rest of the O'Brians, her mother's family, as they seldom spoke. She could certainly turn to the Mainwarings in Belfast, and in Clonakilty there was Reverend Butler, or indeed Colonel Simon, and the possibility of his yeoman cavalry. Cissy briefly grinned at the notion of a skulking Charles Barr suddenly confronted by a troop of sabre-wielding horsemen. Dr. Kelly, she knew, was traveling again. Though he had always been a friend to her father, he seemed a difficult man, and she would hesitate to speak with him.

Then she thought of John Cashman, one of the few people on earth who might understand the threat posed by Charles Barr. But Cashman was just as much a shadow as Barr.

And, still, a single letter bearing a single line of text did not warrant a hysterical visit to anyone. In an emergency, the people of Clonakilty would do the right thing, but they were people who did not love her as they might. They were not her family.

She could make for Cobh and sail to India; she had the Company-paid passage available to her at any time. Mrs. Cashman had passed, and there was no reason for Cissy to remain in Ireland. But she enjoyed being on her own; she readily admitted it to herself. She would not allow some creeping fool to take that from her.

Cissy devised a plan, and she set about it. She wrote three letters to her parents, addressed to Marseilles, Madeira, and Madras. Doubtless the letters to Marseilles and Madeira would be too late to catch them, and the letter to Madras might be six months in reaching them. Still, she had to try.

She then dressed rather plainly, and after tucking her everyday bonnet into place she called Sergeant. Patting his massive head, she took some comfort in reflecting that he weighed more than she did. But he was old now, grey around the muzzle, and while still fiercely loyal he was not the alert house guard he once was.

Cissy was careful to lock the door behind her, and with the big old dog beside her, strode up into the hills above town, toward Liam McCarthy's farm. As she walked she kept her head up and her eyes moving. She had left her father's pistol in the desk drawer, but in her bag was a razor-sharp knife.

"Your Sergeant has been at my Daisy again, Miss, and it's no mistake. So here I stand, knee-deep in pups. But they are good, stout pups. I shall keep one or two, likely." He did not tell her that the smaller, weaker pups would end their lives tied in a sack in the farm's well. Death was common on the farm, but McCarthy did not feel the need to share that with the elegant Miss Lockwood.

A stall in McCarthy's small, ramshackle barn had been closed in, where Daisy McCarthy lay in a tumble of straw, being steadily trampled by eight romping puppies. There was little doubt the short haired, coal-black puppies were Sergeant's, particularly as Sergeant stood at the stall's door with his ears up, his tail wagging, staring at Daisy. Daisy only occasionally returned his stare, and then only with an accusatory glint in her eye.

McCarthy self-consciously rubbed some of the dirt from his hands and went on, "I danced with your mother once, when we were young, you know, at McKesson's Crossroads, with the great fires roaring. She was kind to me, as beautiful as she was, and me a plain old sod. So, in her honour, you shall take your pick of the litter, Miss, and God bless you, and her."

Cissy smiled and said, "You are most kind, Mr. McCarthy. They are all so darling, but which do you think would be a good companion to Sergeant, and a good dog to help watch the house?"

McCarthy studied the pups with an expression on his face that showed that he was thinking deeply, until finally pointing out one pup, saying, "That big fellow, there, I think, Miss. A gentle soul, normal, but if he gets crossed he's a good 'un, sure. Yes, he's your boy."

McCarthy reached down and pulled the pup out of the stall. The pup was ecstatic, Daisy looked relieved, Sergeant looked jealous, and when McCarthy placed the puppy in her arms Cissy nuzzled it with delight. Sergeant looked up at her and gave out a heart-felt yelp of concern, so Cissy frowned at him and said, "Oh, Sergeant Lockwood, you great jealous cow. I shall name him Corporal, so your status remains intact, sir."

"A bother!" cried Colonel Simon. "It is no bother at all, Miss Lockwood, I assure you. Why, it is so damnably, eh, I beg your pardon, Miss, it is so very dull most days around here that I should be most pleased to teach you to ride."

Cissy had dressed nicely, but very modestly, to call on Colonel Simon. She deliberately said, "You are most kind, Colonel, most kind indeed. I did so hesitate to ask, but you might understand it is time I made an effort to join society, as it were. I have ridden a bit, but it would be wonderful to become an accomplished rider, and I do hope you might help me. Both my parents always speak of you with the greatest regard, and I believe my mother thinks of you as a second father."

Simon nodded and said, "Yes, a wonderful woman, your mother, I have always felt most eh... paternal, yes, paternal, towards her. My man M'Vicar taught your brothers to ride, you know, a couple of years ago, what? And now you shall have your turn! I have a gentle little mare, a lady's hunter, in my stable that would suit you admirably, and there are two or three side saddles from my sister's time in the house. We shall have such fun."

It took a moment for Simon to rise, but he eventually led Cissy toward the back of the house and its view of the extensive stables and fenced runs. "A week or two with us, Miss Lockwood, and we shall have you prepared for the fall hunts!"

"Oh, hunting! Perhaps I ought to learn to shoot as well? That would be great fun, don't you think, Colonel?"

Simon looked at her in some surprise, and with a smile he said, "Well, you need not learn to shoot for a fox hunt, Miss, but as you are so keen, perhaps I might show you a light shotgun for grouse season, or a light rifle for small game?"

"Oh! A rifle! And my father left a rifled pistol in the house, a lovely thing which I have always found fascinating. This is all so exciting, Colonel. I do hope, though, that my interest in shooting is not improper, sir?"

"Improper? Oh, God's my life, no, Miss. You are from a military family, after all! Rare, perhaps, but I know of several women who shoot amazing well. I knew a Mrs. Fortescue once, a stout Northumberland woman who could shoot with the best of 'em. Capital woman, that. Yes, Miss, if you have an interest, I shall soon render you a threat to anything that flies, walks, or crawls."

What little remained of Charles Barr's sanity was now devoted to avenging his honour. He would erase his humiliation, his catastrophic shame. And he now had an ally, a man unknown to the Lockwoods, who could reconnoiter for him, and aid him in his honourable quest.

Through brooding hours of hiding in the crumbling tower, Barr dreamt of eliminating the Lockwoods, every damned one of them, and so force society to forgive his earlier transgression. He had lain with a whore, and was marked with the disease of shame. But only Lockwood and O'Brian knew. They *knew*. So they had to die. He would expunge his record. Society would forgive Charles Barr, and when he was once again in grace he could reestablish his reputation, his precious, golden reputation.

In the meantime he would wipe the world clean of those who knew of his shame.

Cissy was not afraid of horses, but neither had she any extensive experience with them. She had ridden the Butlers' ancient pony on several occasions, but she had never before taken a true lesson. For her first appointment with Colonel Simon and Corporal M'Vicar she wore a bottle-green riding habit that belonged to her mother, topped by a dashing little hat and its black ostrich feather.

"I was toying with the idea of you trying Hala, my Arab mare," said Simon as he escorted Cissy toward the stable. "Hala is a beauty, but she can be very willful at times, and sometimes...." Simon nearly called Hala "quite a howling bitch" but he caught himself in time, and instead muttered to an old man's mumbling conclusion.

In the stable Cissy was glad to pass Hala's stall, as she kicked the wall with a flashing hoof when she was ignored. Cissy instead met Abby, a light-weight hunter who snickered with delight at the introduction. She and Cissy Lockwood soon grew to love one another.

Cissy's love for Corporal M'Vicar, however, was slow in coming. As Simon was fond of his afternoon nap, he soon left most of Cissy's training to M'Vicar. He was grimly approving of Cissy's handling of Abby at the walk, but when she elevated to a trot M'Vicar opened a volley of commands that quickly rattled her.

"You must sit the trot properly, Miss, properly! You have too much bounce! Ah, will you not establish a seat, girl! Taut reins, trooper! Stay in contact with your mount! Sit forward, will you, and grip low!" Cissy was puzzled as to how she might grip Abby low with only one stirrup, but she did her best to respond to the corporal's staccato commands, and in just a few days she had made impressive improvement. She was stiff and sore every day, but she was quietly proud of herself, and growing confident.

Cissy came to riding naturally, but shooting frightened her, and it required several lessons before she learned to bear the sharp crack of the rifle. She quickly learned to wear her oldest coat when she went shooting, no consideration given to fashion, as it took great effort to rid her riding habit of the smell of powder smoke.

Here, too, she was a determined student, and while she never got on well with the rifle, she was soon competent with pistols, and from her first introduction to a light Thomas Bird double-barreled shotgun, she was a prodigy. While Simon mentioned that her determination to load and fire as quickly as possible (she insisted that M'Vicar time her) was admirable, and that loading was a dirty business best left to the hunt masters, Cissy pushed herself hard until she could fire both barrels, one after the other, hitting six inch targets at twenty yards, then reload, fire, and hit again, all in less than a minute.

The grizzled old corporal was pleased to instruct such a willing recruit, and with a knowing look he soon set aside the birdshot, instead giving Cissy buckshot and a professional's suggestions on how she might load more quickly. As he timed her he urged her on, and eventually taught her to load with her eyes closed, telling her, "Even the best of souls might have an enemy, Miss, and if that enemy turns harsh, like, then buckshot is a sure cure. Good Lord, Miss, buckshot will keep all the hounds of hell at bay, when delivered proper."

Chapter Twenty

Colonel Simon had suggested to Cissy that she stay close to him. After the first hour of following the pack across the hills near Caherconway, however, his energy waned, while Cissy was so intent on the chase that she eventually left the Colonel behind, cantering Abby across the fields alongside even the most experienced riders.

Cissy was prudent enough to decline the jumps, instead turning Abby toward the gates, however inconveniently they were placed for close pursuit. She soon fell behind the dogs and lead riders, let alone the fox, and at one point she came to a complete halt while she and a group of other riders waited for a grumbling young farm labourer to open a gate. As the stamping horses caught their breath a young woman in a powder blue coat sitting atop a pretty little chestnut introduced herself as Lizzie Fitzgerald, and she and Cissy were soon chatting like old friends. Lizzie introduced Cissy to her father, and her numerous friends, some of whom were young men who were most pleased to make Miss Lockwood's acquaintance.

The Fitzgeralds were part of a large party which had come down from Dublin, as Mr. Bennington (a heavy, older gentleman who smiled and bowed from atop a steaming black gelding) had recently purchased Brook Park Hall near Dunmanway for the shooting. Lizzie did so hope that Miss Lockwood would join them for dinner on Friday, and Cissy was so comfortable with Lizzie and her party that she accepted without hesitation, quite overcoming the caution that often hampered her ability to make new friends. Lizzy's friends were pleased to hear that Miss Lockwood would be joining them, and Mr. Bennington promised to send his phaeton down to carry her to Brook Park.

Cissy and Lizzie were in close conversation, their horses at a walk, when the fox, who had been hunted before and who was a wise old hand, cut to the south toward the ditches and woods that bordered the north edge of the Arigideen. When the hounds discovered the fox's trick, they turned and went pounding across a field just to the right of the relaxed party. Both the young ladies turned their mounts in pursuit with such dash and beauty as to cause several of the young men in their trail to fall madly in love with them, young men being vulnerable to such moments of spontaneous rapture. The rest of their party, old, young, skilled riders and not, joined in the thundering pursuit with considerable laughter, bellowing, and general gaiety.

To no one's surprise, and honestly to no one's regret, the fox gave them the slip. The hounds, panting and puzzled, were recalled, and the various groups of weary and mud-spattered riders shared farewells, plans for future hunts and dinners, and went their separate ways.

There was no sign of Colonel Simon, so two hopeful young gallants offered to escort Miss Lockwood back to the Colonel's stables. Cissy was much more familiar with the narrow twisting lanes north of Clonakilty than either of those two eager gentlemen, but she accepted their offer with a demure, if somewhat forced, acquiescence.

She found them pleasant enough, moderately handsome, not overly bright, but kind, and good company. They had ridden a mile or so, and one of the gentlemen was sharing a humourous anecdote of life in Dublin, when they turned up a narrow, muddy lane. They came upon a man coming down the lane in a red coat, a battered shako on his head, and a worn pack on his back. Both the gentlemen were astonished to see Miss Lockwood rein in, stare at the soldier, then throw herself from the saddle to embrace the battered old fellow.

Diarmuid Doolan had come calling.

For an instant after she recognized him, she was shocked at how he had aged; he had become an old man. She shook that thought away and said, "Mr. King, Mr. Edwards, pray allow me to introduce Private Diarmuid Doolan, late of Six Company, First Battalion, 27th Regiment of Foot."

Both Mr. King and Mr. Edwards were gentlemen of some experience, yet neither was in the habit of being introduced to vagrant old redcoats along muddy lanes. But they were both determined to stay in Miss Lockwood's good graces, so they each gave the old soldier a nod of acknowledgement and a polite, "Your servant, sir."

Doolan waited a beat, giving them each an appraising look before knuckling his forehead and offering a reserved, "Your servant, your honours."

Cissy was beaming, and both her suitors were enthralled by the beauty of her delighted face. It was, then, a bit of a disappointment to be summarily dismissed with, "Gentlemen, I do hope you will not mind, but I should like to walk Private Doolan into town. I wonder if I might ask if one of you would be so kind as to lead Abby back to Colonel Simon's stables, with my best thanks and regards?"

Mr. King took Abby's reins, eagerly saying he would be most pleased to oblige Miss Lockwood. Mr. Edwards made a polite farewell, looking displeased to be outdone by Mr. King, and as he turned his mount away he gave Diarmuid Doolan a last jealous, wondering look.

It had been some years since a woman had been so pleased to see Diarmuid Doolan, and many years indeed since one so achingly lovely had given him so such much as a glance. He was startled to see how she had blossomed; her girlhood had quite departed, and from the shadows of her youth quite a remarkable young woman had appeared.

They walked down the lane together, both unconsciously taking a soldier's path, walking a straight line, with no prancing attempts to dodge the mud. As they chatted—she was amazingly well, had come to love riding; he had been to Donegal to see that his family was still safely and honourably in the ground, and he had sold off the scrap of land they owned; she missed her family, and very much wished to speak to him, after they had him settled, about a matter that troubled her—Doolan took her measure.

Her dark hair and perfect complexion were her mother's, sure. A spot of mud on her cheek, thrown up by the horses of the hunt, was enchanting. Her flashing blue eyes were her father's gift to her, full of a laughing, sparking intelligence.

But herself, the essence of her being, was of God's making, or her own. She struck him as elegant, bold, and confidently, unconsciously, beautiful. At one point she turned toward him, laughing, and a glimpse of her face triggered a memory from his boyhood. He remembered a term from a poem his grandfather would recite, *gile na gile*, brightening brightness, and only now did he know their meaning. His worn old heart leapt to be in her company.

Her first concern was finding him a decent place to stay. She suggested the Bandon Arms, but he scoffed at the notion, (doubtless the Arms would have as well) and he told Cissy of a wee shebeen he had heard of, down near the quay, a decent enough place where a man might get a sup, a pipe, a tot, and a bed for a pittance.

Doolan walked Cissy home, being granted a cherished kiss on the cheek for his trouble. He then found his shebeen with the practiced air of a tough man who had seen and done a great deal, a man old enough not to give tuppence for much of anything. Almost anything, at any rate.

It was unusual for a house as small as Faibhile Cottage to have an oven capable of baking bread, as most families opted to buy their bread from the baker in town. As Cissy was alone in the house there really was no need for her to fire the ovens as Mrs. Cashman had taught her, or to knead the dough on the great old table where the Lockwood children had spent so many hours, the great honoured table. But every Thursday Cissy would do so, Mrs. Cashman's spirit at her shoulder, warm and happy, and she would bake until her arms ached and Fáibhile Cottage was hot with the oven's heat, and heavy with the exquisite smell of newly baked bread.

The day after Doolan's arrival in Clonakilty was Cissy's baking day, and Doolan dutifully volunteered to assist. The private had no experience with the fine art of baking, so Cissy made him responsible for the fire, teasing, wondering in lilting Irish, "if he might still be capable of building a hot fire with God's own peat, two years in the drying, after him gone to the far corners of the world like a wild goose?"

Doolan, whose polite tone with Cissy had not lasted two minutes past his arrival, scoffed and replied, "A wild goose, am I, now? Goodness, girl, could I not build a cook fire with two rocks and a handful of wet sand?"

"You couldn't."

"I could. And haven't I, tending to your father, God bless him?"

Cissy was quiet for a moment as she busied herself with scooping flour from the small barrel that sat in the corner. She did not look up as she quietly said, "He loves you, you know."

"I do," Doolan replied, and he then spent a long while staring into the fire, softly toying with the memories reserved to old men.

He had debated whether or not to tell her of the letter from her father that had reached him through the regimental agent, and read to him by Father Doherty in Ballybofey. He decided not to; she need not know that her father believed she might need minding, as she clearly required no one's help to live her life. This business with Barr, however, that was another matter.

They each tended to their work until Doolan looked over at the mountain of flour that Cissy had piled on the table. "Will you bake for an army, Cissy Lockwood?"

Cissy grinned as she mixed her first batch of dough and said, "Two loaves for me, and three for you, Diarmuid. And the balance of, say, twelve or so, shall go to the Sisters of Charity for their work."

They spent the whole day together, pleased with one another's company. The only contrary words they spoke were when Cissy cut the tops of her good Irish soda bread with what she called the sign of the cross, though Doolan insisted that those traditional cuts were intended to let the Devil out of the baking bread, an explanation he had heard from his own mother in Donegal many years before. Cissy took umbrage to the notion that Lucifer was lurking in her bread, and in no uncertain terms she told Doolan that he might stuff his superstitious notions.

Doolan surrendered the point, convinced Cissy Lockwood was her father's daughter.

Cissy was accustomed to a morning walk, even on rainy days. But now she kept the door locked, and contented herself with an old novel until the postman, the very familiar postman, brought a letter from Lieutenant Mainwaring in Belfast.

My Dear Miss Lockwood,

I write to inform you, Miss, that I have purchased a captaincy in my regiment, and rather than remaining in Ireland on leave as previously planned, I take ship in the morning to join my company in Gibraltar. I also regret to add that Mrs. Mainwaring will join me in Gibraltar; a great comfort to me, but she had so hoped to have the pleasure of your visit.

Please understand, Miss Lockwood, our hesitation to be away from Ireland, but like your father, Mrs. Mainwaring and I are content in knowing that ~~Captain~~ *Barr will remain imprisoned for some years yet.*

But so that I might keep you fully apprised of the situation, I shall share something which your parents hold quite secret, and used to control Barr. I doubt that your parents have informed you of this, but I am personally certain that you need to know with whom we deal.

Charles Barr has been afflicted by syphilis for some many years. Any man would be shamed by such an affliction, but Barr is so thoroughly humiliated, so unmanned, by the stigma that any threat to reveal that fact might be used to control him.

That, at least, was the method employed by your parents, Miss Lockwood. At this point Barr may be so far gone into his madness that even threat of exposure, humiliation, and dishonour may no longer deter him.

As your parents are removed to India, you must promise, Miss, that you shall alert me if you receive any threat from Barr, and I shall return to Ireland immediately. I owe that much, and much more, to your parents, who remain our dearest friends. The distances between us are trivial in comparison to the bonds we share.

I remain, Miss Lockwood,
your most devoted servant,
Thomas Mainwaring
Captain, 27th Regiment of Foot

P.S. Our things are packed, we are nearly out the door, and an express from Colonel Nelson is come, telling me not to proceed straight to Gib, but rather to first go to London and give testimony regarding your father's case at Horse Guards. Your father's friends continue to work—this may be the best of news. I must fly.

T.M.

Cissy sat and stared at the letter, digesting its contents. The Mainwarings obviously had no knowledge of Barr's escape, and now they were gone, off her list of possible allies, of possible refuges. But Diarmuid Doolan was at hand, and she would try to keep him so. She would need to tell him everything, and soon.

She was unfamiliar with the intricacies of military law, and she was puzzled and angry over how a court martial review could take so very long, months after her family had been forced from their home.

Lastly, she considered the revelation of Barr's syphilis. As a young woman in rural Ireland she had little knowledge of the specifics of such a malady, but she was very aware of the social stigmas. She busied herself with her usual dinner of bread, cheese, and apples, the whole time her mind churning on how she might employ that knowledge.

The next morning Doolan came up to Fáibhile from his shebeen looking pleased with himself. He did not smell of whiskey, and Cissy could not get anything more out of him beyond the mention of a new friend in town. She had heard from her father of Doolan's ability to take up with even quite respectable women, and she wondered who might be the object of his attentions.

Together they carried baskets of bread down McCurtain's Hill and then to the western edge of town, where the sisters kept their house. There were only ten nuns in the house, though their impact on the poor and sick was far beyond their numbers. The nuns were an independent lot, and did not much care for any interference from Father McGlynn at St. Brigid's. That fact alone pleased Cissy, and she did all she could to support them.

At the home Doolan carried the bread back to the extensive pantries, and Cissy rolled her eyes as he shamelessly flirted with the older nuns, those brides of Christ evidently delighted with the attentions of a man of a more corporeal nature. One of the younger sisters, whom Cissy knew as Sister Margaret, drew Cissy aside and quietly said, "I have a message for you from my uncle. He says, 'Sergeant, Elizabeth Bennet, and *mo cuisle*'."

Cissy did her best not to look startled, but failed. Sister Margaret put her hand on Cissy's arm and said, "Pray, do not be alarmed, Miss Lockwood. I am a daughter of the clan Cashman.

My Uncle John Cashman asks if he might come see you tonight at your own house, as the moon rises."

Cissy was concerned she might need to invent some excuse to see Doolan away from Fáibhile Cottage that evening, but he told her that he had an appointment for supper with his new friend. She nearly cautioned him not to get overly involved with the tarts that haunted the quay, but she recalled with whom she was speaking, and contented herself with bidding him good evening.

Cissy was not a nocturnal creature, and had to guess as to the time of the moonrise. She was correct in thinking it was about ten that night, and she prepared tea and sandwiches for her visitor. She wondered briefly if he would prefer wine, or perhaps whiskey, but thought better of it and put the kettle on the hob.

It was just after ten when there came a gentle knock at the kitchen door. Cissy was startled for the second time that day when in the darkness of her back stoop stood both Diarmuid Doolan and John Cashman. Doolan grinned, tossed at thumb at Cashman, and said, "My new friend."

Cissy scowled at Doolan, as she once again displayed her dislike of being taken by surprise. She recovered enough to politely welcome John Cashman back to Fáibhile Cottage.

Still, she poured the tea with a hint of annoyance as she said, "And so, am I to assume you two gentlemen are in league?"

"In league, Miss Lockwood?" mused Cashman. "Sure, that sounds a mite underhanded. A Crown Attorney might even claim it to be conspiratorial in nature. No, I think the good Private and I are...ah, now, Diarmuid *a grah*, how might a Christian phrase it?"

Doolan offered, "Mates. We're mates, now, Miss, and there is no shame, or criminal intent, inherent in such a relationship, as it were."

John nodded, and with a grin said to Doolan, "Ah, 'inherent', is it, Diarmuid? It is always a pleasure to hear a man of your parts wax philosophical."

"And you, brother."

Cissy plunked two mugs of tea down in front of them, and put an end to their lilting antics with, "Thank you, gentlemen, I shall not be mocked in my own kitchen."

The two rough men traded a look, and Doolan gave Cashman a wave to proceed. He grew serious and said, "Right you are, Miss, as we should not linger here, as pleasant as it is, so as not to compromise you. You should know that I am once again in the employ of the priest's organization. I may not much care for them, but our goals are much the same, and there are few markets for a man of my talents."

They were all three sitting at the kitchen table, sipping their tea. Cissy had the curtains drawn and just a few candles in the room, and once again her kitchen took on a strange air, now very secret, very tense, and not a little dangerous.

Cashman went on, "Now that I am counted amongst the priest's men I hear things, such as the arrival of our mutual friend Diarmuid, and so I sought him out."

Doolan grinned and said, "And sure didn't we nearly cut one another's throats, each being of a suspicious nature, until we determined we had common cause, like."

In a challenging tone Cissy asked, "And what cause is that, please, gentlemen?"

Both Doolan and Cashman sat up straight, raised their eyebrows, and in a voice meant to explain the perfectly obvious Doolan said, "Why, to see Charles Barr in the ground, of course."

Some aspects of the Whiteboys' organization were laughably amateur and ineffective, but there were times when even John Cashman was impressed. A handful of the most trusted Whiteboys in the south of Ireland had been asked to keep an eye out for a tall, thin, bent madman, likely dressed as a redcoat captain. Not a week passed before word came back of such a man in Macroom, just twenty-five miles from Clonakilty. Their madman was acting the part, drawing the attention to himself in a manner not compatible to discreet movement. He was traveling in company with another Englishman, whose bizarre rantings also drew attention.

Whisper-quiet steps glided up the back stairs of the Irish Kings in Macroom. The two men who had taken the lone room at the top of the stairs had left strict instructions with the house not to be disturbed upon any excuse, but the house was away, and the maid who ought to have ensured their privacy had quietly been called away. In fact, Mr. O'Rourke himself had spoken to her, had given her a crown and told her to take a pint or two with her friend Maggie at the Rover down the street. Everyone in the parish quietly obeyed Mr. O'Rourke, the local, very secretive, chief of the Macroom Whiteboys.

A quiet knock at the chamber door, but there was no answer. The door was locked, but John Cashman was not to be denied. He quickly slipped the lock and burst in, a knife in his hand. The dim room was filthy, scattered with papers and possessions... and it was empty. He had missed them by just minutes; a cigar still burned where it had been hurriedly abandoned.

Barr and Soames were gone. Cashman hissed a curse, then quickly flipped through the papers. He was stunned, horrified, to find a sketch of Fáibhile Cottage, and a map of the surrounding paths and lanes. He tossed the papers aside and hurried back to the stairs in a rage.

Cashman rushed down the stairs, but the house had returned, heard the noises from above and pointed him out, crying, "Thief! Thief!"

Doolan had been keeping watch at the bar, and was preparing to knock the house on the head. It was bad luck that a large party of yeoman and their officer was just then coming in the pub door.

Four days later Cissy was again delivering bread to the Little Sisters when Sister Margaret pulled her aside. Margaret was nearly frantic as she whispered, "My Uncle is taken. Taken! He and your Private Doolan! Both thrown into the dark hole of Cork gaol itself!" The nun made an effort to gather herself, and after looking over her shoulder she went on, "As a holy sister I was allowed to call on him, and Uncle gave me this for you." Margaret urgently pressed a dirty scrap of paper into Cissy's hand, then hurried back to her work, clearly frightened.

Barr is coming. Flee.

Chapter Twenty-One

A few blocks down from Lizzie Fitzgerald's Dublin townhouse, three members dined in an upstairs room of the Kildare Street Club, an extravagant edifice devoted to aristocracy, claret, and whist. The men, all three excessively devoted to their comforts, had garnered a table at one of the great bay windows overlooking St. Stephen's Green, where they drank their champagne in enormous quantities and studied the steady flow of humanity that passed beneath them.

"There goes that Clabo fellow. A Scot, isn't he?" said the first.

"I quite loathe Scots," answered the second, who was in a foul humour after his soufflé had proved a crashing failure.

"Oh, here come Beard and Melhorn. Decent company, if they have a glass or two in them," said the third.

"I suppose, I suppose. Ah, yonder comes Kathleen Lee. I had hopes of her once, but she is fond of keeping her knees together, and is she now quite taken with that emancipation nonsense."

"What a pity. Such a lovely creature, such potential, and yet she opts to devote what little sense she possesses to puzzle over issues that are well beyond her."

More people passed their window, none worthy of comment, until the least drunk of the men looked up the street and said, "Ah, now here's a beauty for you, gentlemen!"

"What, the fat one in the pink coat?"

"No, there, the small one in the blue coat. I was introduced to her last night at Hill's. A Miss Lockwood, come up from Munster, staying with the Fitzgeralds."

The other two gentlemen leaned forward and raised their eyebrows in admiration. The youngest one asked, "Staying with the Fitzgeralds, you say? I may invent some excuse to call on them this evening. Perhaps this Miss Lockwood is less devoted to her virtue than Miss Lee."

"Stand thee warned, sir, this young lady is a renowned hell-cat. Catholic as a cardinal, lives alone in her own house in the wilds of Munster, and rides and shoots with the best of 'em. I hear Carmichael made a run at her when she first arrived in town, and he was promptly tumbled from the house with his tail between his legs, yelping like a whippet."

"Ah, so that is the famous Lockwood girl," said the third after pulling his face from his tankard. "Recall, gentlemen, I still hold my estate in Cork, so in my travels I have heard tell of your hell-cat. She has no fortune to speak of, though her father is a certified hero, a veteran of Waterloo, and now off to seek his fortune with John Company. I know little of her mother, other than she is of a renowned beauty as well."

The three men watched Cissy move past the club, as the third continued, "Miss Lockwood and her branch of the family are estranged from the Malahide Lockwoods and Muirs. Some scandal there, as I recall, but the details escape me."

As Cissy turned right onto Grafton Street the youngest whistled softly, then muttered, "By God, if there was ever a scandal involving her, I should care to be part of it."

Cissy was ostensibly on her way to meet Lizzy at the Theatre Royal on Hawkins Street, but a block short of the theater she slipped slyly into the maze of book sellers' booths bordering Trinity College. The rendezvous was for sundown, as her contact had no watch, and had no desire to wear one, despite an offer from Cissy to buy him one. Nonetheless, her contact was very prompt, for as Cissy leafed through a copy of Siborne's *History of the Campaign of 1815* a heavily cloaked figure with a ridiculous broad-brimmed hat pulled low over his eyes slipped into the booth, feigning interest in Saint Thomas Aquinas' *Summa Theologica*. Cissy worked her way over to the shadowy figure, and without looking directly at him, said, "Diarmuid Doolan, your reading would look much more convincing if you held that book the other way round."

Quickly flipping the book around, the flustered Doolan replied, "Ah, Cissy *a grah*, it's a joy to see you again. I do not believe that Barr has followed me here, but it is best we are cautious, sure. And so here I am in Dublin itself, free of that foul gaol, though I reek of it yet."

"Thank God. But what of John Cashman?"

"The magistrate who turned me loose, the wise fellow, said that John was to be held over for the Assizes. They would charge him with housebreaking, but as nothing was stolen, and no one saw him in the room, with the blessing he should be free in a few weeks. Please God, no one will recognize him and denounce him, or he will be in... well, Cissy, he shall be in great trouble, and that's the way of it."

Cissy crossed herself and said, "May God protect him, and keep his secret. Now, Diarmuid, have you been to Fáibhile Cottage? Has there been any sign of Barr?"

"Your Aunt has been tending to the dogs, and says she has seen no strangers, other than a barrister who has come by once or twice. He says he has some papers for you to sign, about the portion of your father's salary to be consigned to you."

"Well, then, since you and John should soon be scouring all Cork, I shall certainly go home next week when the Fitzgeralds go south. Will you travel with me, Diarmuid, *a grah*?"

"I will not. Cashman gave me a good handful of coins—the priest has been generous of late, it seems—so that I might take up the hunt again. I think it would best serve if I was to make my own way back, and look into a few dark corners on the way. I shall meet you at Fáibhile Cottage itself. Until then, I beg you to stay near your friends, *a grah*, while I go hunting. No matter where Barr goes, it will be Diarmuid Doolan in the shadows, making his life a screaming misery."

Cissy studied Doolan for a moment, then said, "Diarmuid, it is not fair that I ask you to spend all your days looking for Barr. After all your years with my father, you have earned some time to do as you please. Is there not somewhere that you would care to go? Someone you would wish to see?"

Doolan, who still had his nose in Saint Thomas's genius, said, "Sure and it's good of you to offer, but as I've said before, I've seen enough of this world, and I have no one, though I do wish that I had been given a chance to see your parents, your brothers and sisters, God bless them, before they sailed off to the edge of the world."

"When you are ready to settle yourself, Diarmuid, I shall see you cared for, as only a true friend might."

"That's grand in you, *a stor*, but both you and I know why we have taken on this work. You carry your Irish blood well, as you hold a grudge near as well as I do, and it's Satan's own grudge I hold against Barr, the black thief."

On a cool morning in Saint-Maximin-la-Sainte-Baume, the wedding of Guillaume Louis Antoine Dumon and Mary

Catherine Lockwood took place in the nave of the Sainte Marie Madeline Basilica.

Mary brought her wedding dress from Ireland, its lace the envy of every woman in attendance. A beautiful dress, then, but even at that it was scarcely worthy of the stunningly beautiful, joyously happy bride who wore it, standing at the side of her handsome young groom.

James was an Anglican, and while he found the ritual of the Mass excessive, he did not find it ridiculous. The music he found intoxicating, soaring and echoing across the ancient sun-streaked spaces that arched overhead.

It was a grand affair, far above anything the Lockwoods had ever expected, as the Dumons had arranged every detail, and every comfort for their guests. James had first known Jean Dumon as a captain in the rag-tag Royalist army that had remained with the exiled King Louis XVIII in Belgium during the Hundred Days. While he knew Dumon was now a colonel and a man of some property, he was surprised to learn that Dumon was a prominent member of the Var département aristocracy, and obviously a gentleman of considerable estate.

In their home above the vineyards of Saint-Maximin-la-Sainte-Baume, Colonel and Madame Dumon were kind, generous hosts. The Lockwoods were instantly comfortable in the elegant rooms of the Château Var-Ollières, and it was while sipping a glass of the excellent wine of the region that a letter reached James from Ensign Digby, the Waterloo veteran.

Dear Lieutenant Lockwood,

We have heard, sir, that you will be some time in France for your daughter's wedding (pray give her our very best regards, sir) and so I address this letter to you there, in hope it finds you there in the very best of health.

Things here in Gib are in such an uproar, sir! ~~Lieutenant~~ Captain Mainwaring has forwarded us a transcript of your court martial, and goodness, sir! The outrage in the mess would do your heart good, sir. We officers have voted to forward a petition to Horse Guards, and I have been voted the battalion scribe! I shall write such a petition as they have never seen!

Captain Mainwaring says, too, that he has written to all of our brother battalions; the 4th and 40th stood with us at Waterloo, they shall certainly stand with us now! This is all so thrilling, sir; we are determined that justice be served!

Your most ardent admirer and devoted servant,
John Digby, Ensign 1/27th Foot

On a walk through the manicured gardens, James shared the letter with Brigid, and she was instantly energized. "This must certainly mean the pardon will come! It is only a matter of time!"

James shook his head, uncertain. "Perhaps. But Horse Guards is unpredictable. The pardon might come tomorrow, a year from now, or it may never come at all. I have signed an agreement with the Company, and in all conscience I cannot lie about waiting for a hypothetical pardon. My honour will not allow it."

Brigid would not be denied. "But what fools we would be, to spend months in traveling to India, only to find a pardon had followed us all that way? A year of our lives wasted, traveling there and back? Surely we can hold out hope?"

He let out a deep breath, folded the letter back into his coat pocket, and muttered, "What to do? What to do?"

After weeks in France and tearful farewells, the Lockwoods took ship at Marseilles, and upon their arrival at Madeira found bundles of letters awaiting them. Officers from across the army were writing to voice their support, and more importantly, were writing to Horse Guards to express their violent opposition to the verdict of the Lockwood court martial. Even the enlisted men of the 1/27th had submitted a petition, a rare step for rankers of any regiment, men who had to be very careful not to cross their officers. But now those men of the Inniskilling Regiment spoke out, respectfully requesting that Lieutenant Lockwood be returned to them.

And so, the Lockwoods did not sail upon the first Indiaman that might have borne them to Madras, or upon the next, or the next.

James and Brigid took an apartment at an inexpensive inn that sat high above Funchal harbour, and considered their chances. They opted to gamble, recklessly rolling fate's dice. And so, James, Brigid, and the three youngest Lockwoods remained anxiously at Madeira, living as simply as possible and scanning the horizon for any ship that might bear news.

While they were aware of, indeed shared, their parents' anxiety, the younger Lockwoods, long accustomed to the cool dampness of life in Ireland, reveled in the sunny warmth of Madeira.

James and Brigid had been very protective, very involved, parents with their elder children, but had grown rather more relaxed with the younger three. That inherent freedom, coupled with the fact that their parents were distracted, loosed Joseph, Richard, and Lucy upon the town, lean, sunburned, and, when removed from the parents' tense anxiety, prone to gleeful happiness. The innkeeper's children, Fernão and Faustino, who had quickly befriended the young Lockwoods in that complete, whole-hearted manner exclusive to the young, introduced them to the joys of island life.

Faustino, for example, kept a small pet capuchin, a creature of endless fascination to the Lockwood children. Sadly the monkey had a tendency to grow snappish when tired, and allowed only Lucy to hold it while it napped. Joseph, Richard, and Lucy were enchanted, too, with their introduction to sugar cane, and on one unfortunate but memorable evening, to a surreptitious skin of young Madeira wine.

The high point of their adventures, however, came one sparkling day when Fernão and Faustino coaxed their Irish friends into a long march up the *Monte* that dominated Funchal town, promising them a great treat once they reached the peak. The Lockwoods had thought themselves rewarded with the magnificent view of the city, the bay, and the shimmering sea beyond. They were delighted, however, when Faustino borrowed his uncle's toboggan, essentially a wicker basket on skids. With a lack of caution which would have horrified their mother, the three Lockwoods bundled into the open basket, the Imbo boys behind, ostensibly steering, and the toboggan rocketed down the mountainside in a dusty bone-rattling daredevil ride down the road to Funchal.

James and Brigid typically spent their mornings in the dappled shade of the patio of their inn, sipping coffee while they discussed their options in an endless frustrating loop. One clear, hot morning, Joseph, Richard, Fernão and Faustino came racing up from the quay to report amazing news, followed by Lucy, that outraged young lady shrilly calling, "You promised that I should tell them, you *quatro imbecils! Trapaceiros! Filhos de burros!*"

Tom and Julia Mainwaring had arrived from London. Tom was taking a risk with his reputation in not immediately reporting to Gibraltar and his new company, but the Mainwarings had thrown their lot in with the Lockwoods. And there the four friends waited, trying to enjoy the sun and the wine. There was no guarantee that any news would come, or that the news would be good. They had only hope.

The packet from Portsmouth arrived two weeks later, bearing the government mail pouch. Tom, who had attended Government House every afternoon, finally returned to their simple lodgings with a copper-plate letter from Horse Guards.

He laid it before his closest friend with a formal bow, and James stared at the cover with eyes that misted over.

Julia Mainwaring, frantic for resolution, burst out, "James, James, will you not open it, for God's sake?"

Brigid was dry-eyed, but her voice broke with near hysteria as she said, "Do you not see, Julia, *a grah*, that the letter, the dear, dear, letter, is addressed to *Lieutenant* James Lockwood, not *Mister*, that foul title?"

James broke the seal with steady hands; he recalled Waterloo, where he had noted his steady hands, and he was again vaguely pleased, pleased even above his soaring happiness and relief.

Still, James was speechless, only smiling in a cracked, trembling manner, until the impatient Tom took the letter from his hands and slowly said, "A pardon, by God, a pardon!"

He reached over to grab the back of James's collar, and slowly shook his silent, stoic friend as he read on, "Due to perceived irregularities in the Court Martial proceedings, the Prince regent has deigned that the Lieutenant is to be pardoned, and granted restitution of rank, seniority, and privilege, into the 3rd Royal Veteran Battalion. Secondly, due to the improved state of the Lieutenant's health, if he so pleases, he is to be returned, without purchase, to the Lieutenancy currently vacant in the First Battalion, 27th Regiment of Foot!"

James gathered himself and said, "I shall have to tender my resignation to the Company. After all they have done for us, I do not wish to do this shabbily. And I need to reimburse them for the expenses they have incurred on my behalf." He then gave Tom a crooked grin and said, "Brother, I may need borrow the fare home."

Brigid laughed brightly and said, "Oh, let us not spoil the day with thoughts of money, *a grah!*" She then went trembling to her husband and held him for a long silent, minute before she broke from his side to run up the stairs, happily calling, "Children, children! Gather your things, *mo chlann ionúin!* Oh, I must write to Cissy and Mrs. Cashman and tell them the great news! We are going home! Home!"

Chapter Twenty-Two

"Private Doolan, you will please recall that we agreed to use our best manners, no matter how humble the dinner."

"Faith, am I not using my best manners?"

"And certainly the King's service required you to comb your hair before coming to table?"

"Ah, Miss, it is the Colour Sergeant of the world you are become, sure."

Barely a moment more passed before Cissy was prompted to cry, "Oh, Diarmuid Doolan, will you not get your sleeve out of the butter? You can wash your own shirts if you are going to be such a sloven."

"I thought that 'sloven' meant something else?"

"It most certainly does not, sir."

The Fitzgeralds had escorted Cissy back to Fáibhile Cottage just that morning, though Doolan had been home for several days, scouting the neighborhood. He had received only one note from John Cashman. There had been no sign of Barr.

The morning post arrived. Cissy lived for letters from her family, and the postman brought a long letter from Mary, her first as a married woman, bursting with joy. Antoine's proposal to Mary had carried an offer for Cissy to come to France as well, and that day's letter again carried the invitation: to come live with the newlyweds in their home above the sunny vineyards. It all sounded impossibly romantic to Cissy, and though she flirted with the notion of a life in France she was determined to tend to other business, business yet unresolved. She enjoyed the life of an independent woman, enjoyed it more than she could ever have imagined.

The postman also delivered a copy of the Cork *Mercury*. Cissy, who in the past had never been a student of world affairs, had conceived the notion that a serious woman studied the newspapers in depth. Self-consciously seated in her father's chair, she was startled to see her father's name in a letter to the editor written by Captain Mainwaring. The letter was quite blunt in accusing Captain Barr of the 24th Foot of "cowardly, infamous, and wholly unjustified attacks" upon the honour of Lieutenant James Lockwood.

Cissy read the letter to Doolan, prompting the old soldier to slowly shake his head and say, "Dear old Mainwaring, never one to pull a punch. But that kind of talk will bring Barr to a round boil, sure." Doolan thought for a moment, raised an eyebrow, and added, "Shall I move into Mrs. Cashman's old room, now, Cissy Lockwood, *a grah*? Barr is capable of the devil's own work, and now, thanks to these newspapers, his tail will be afire."

Cissy pursed her lips and said, "You know very well, Private Doolan, that I am capable of minding my own affairs." Softening a bit, she went on, "But I do confess you add a degree of cheer to the house. And you might save the cost of your shebeen." Then with a mischievous grin she went on, "I am already the talk of the neighborhood; won't they cluck when they hear of a man living under my roof?"

Doolan scoffed and said, "No one will cluck within earshot of me, the *cearca aois*, and me as old as your grandfather.

Today I shall get to work on that front garden, with its weeds and brambles. And the roof needs tending before winter blows in, and I might—"

Cissy leapt to her feet and cried, "Oh, I am late for my ride with Colonel Simon!"

Doolan started to rise, saying, "I shall walk with you, *mo grah*—"

Cissy waved him back down, saying, "You shall not, Diarmuid. Yesterday you and Corporal M'Vicar nearly came to blows."

"He is an arrogant ass of a cavalryman, he is, and needs to be shown the flaws of his opinions."

"The corporal has been very kind to me. Please, it is only a mile or so; I very much doubt that Charles Barr is lurking in the baker's shop, waiting to pounce."

"All right then, if you are so set in your mind. I may just stroll down to see the dear sisters. As Cashman is once again prowling Cork I'm hoping he may have left a message with Sister Margaret."

Cissy's walk to the stables was indeed routine, though she got a sharp reaction from the Colonel when she showed him the letter in the Cork *Mercury*.

"The same letter has been published in several other papers as well! I have never seen the like. For an officer to be so roundly condemned in public! This is a rare one indeed. Barr... Barr... no, I do not recall having met the fellow, I shall not call him gentleman, and all indications are that I should never care to. He must be a... well, Miss, quite a bad fellow... to merit such a beating; I wonder what evil he has been up to."

Cissy was quiet, thinking, as the Colonel went on, "This Barr will have no choice: he must defend himself, and answer this challenge immediately. He must face your father, or Lieutenant Mainwaring, and perhaps every other officer of the

Inniskillings, and face them like a man, or be scorned by all society and be branded a coward, a man completely without honour."

The Colonel's energy waned, and he wearily said, "I confess, though, my dear, that I do not feel terribly well today. Would you care to take Abby out alone? Or should you prefer to have M'Vicar ride with you?"

"Oh, pray do not trouble the Corporal, sir. Thank you, I shall gladly take Abby out by myself; she is such a joy."

Cissy would ride alone, but with a pistol in her bag, and her eyes alert every foot of the way. She enjoyed her time alone, and riding gave her opportunity to explore. She went as far as the seaward side of Inchydoney, smiling to think of her brothers' calling it 'Itchy Donkey'.

She then turned Abby to the west, toward Garranagoleen, where her mother's people had worked the land for endless generations. She was in high spirits, wary but confident. She felt sure that even if Charles Barr should appear on winged Pegasus she would still out-ride him.

She rode back toward town on the Western Road, where the Sisters of Mercy kept their home. As she drew closer she saw several of the sisters some running to the road. Cissy urged Abby into a canter, then when she saw a redcoat lying in the road she spurred her to a gallop.

It was Diarmuid Doolan laying in the road, stunned, his head bleeding, as the sisters tended him. Cissy, trying to contain her panic, tried to rein in, but for the first time Abby behaved badly. The mare, unhinged by the running people and the smell of blood, threw her head and danced sideways until Cissy yanked her head back around and gave her a swift kick. The scolded Abby returned to her senses; Cissy leapt from the saddle and ran to Doolan.

The sisters helped him to sit up. He looked very old, but very angry. As Cissy knelt by him in the road he said, "Oh, no tears for me, Miss, it is nothing at all. But Barr is near, *a grah*, all too near. I was stepping up to this house when I saw him, riding by as proud as Pilate. Jesus, Mary, and Joseph, how surprised he looked, seeing me after all these years. I tried to stop him, didn't I, but he rode me down, the dog." Doolan sniffed, dusted the front of his battered coat, and added, "I do not know what it is about me, that gives every scoundrel with a horse such an urge to knock me down."

The sisters helped Doolan to his feet, making a fuss over him that he made no efforts to resist. Cissy found Sister Margaret giving her a significant look, and once again the nun slipped her a note from John Cashman.

Doolan,

Barr is at Bandon Barracks, hiding under a false name, as a volunteer officer to the Muskerry Legion Cavalry. The regiment was called up and sent here to help hunt the priest's Defenders. Clever in Barr—I cannot reach him when he is surrounded by a hundred troopers. Tell our friend to <u>*Beware.*</u> *Burn this.*

Even surrounded as she was by the holy sisters, Cissy Lockwood stamped her foot in rage and cried, "That bastard! Enough of this!" Grasping Doolan's arm, she tensely asked him, "What did Barr look like? How is he dressed? Diarmuid, please!"

Doolan frowned, then nodded in resignation. In a tone of loathing, he said, "He is riding a dappled grey. He is tall. Thin. Pale—dead pale. His hair is black, tied back in a white ribbon. A blue cavalry uniform, but no line regiment; some pack of amateurs."

Cissy kissed his cheek, nodded her thanks to the sisters, and quickly mounted the prancing Abby. Bandon was twelve miles away.

The barracks were newly built, a three story structure that backed onto Bandon's Chapel Street. The gate was open, though a red-coated sentry stood beside it, looking bored. When Cissy turned Abby through the gate he turned to speak to her, but she boldly passed him by and rode into the central yard. She had not expected that the barracks yard would be such a hub of activity; several carriages and saddle horses were being tended by twenty or more troopers.

A corporal stepped up to Cissy, but before he could speak Cissy curtly said, "Your commanding officer, please, Corporal."

"General McCutcheon is here on an inspection tour, Miss, and the gentlemen have just sat down to their dinner, but if you'd care to wait—"

Cissy slid from the saddle, tossed the reins to the startled soldier, and said, "I won't be a moment, corporal," with such ease and authority that he took the reins and watched her stride toward the elegant doorway labeled Officers' Mess.

A sentry stood at the door, this one more intent on his duty, but when he stepped in front of Cissy she stuck a finger in his face and threatened to see him get a dozen for disrespect, and another dozen for buttoning his tunic like a French whoremaster.

The sentry, pummeled into compliance, slid aside, and Cissy opened the door. She strode into the mess, only to find forty and more men sitting down to dinner. The officers of the Bandon Barracks were entertaining; officers of a dozen yeomanry and militia regiments, red, blue, and green coats, filled the room. A large table crossed the head of the room, where several gold-braided officers sat. A dozen smaller tables, each filled with elegantly dressed officers, lined the walls to either side.

The men near the door noticed her first; as their heads turned so eventually did every head in the room turn to see this lovely young woman march into their mess. Some of them laughed, some scowled, some called out to her, though the general at the head table jumped to his feet and called out, "What the deuce! Who is this person? This is an officers' mess, Miss, and your presence here is improper, most improper!"

She was taken aback; she had thought that she would know Barr in an instant, but they were all so similar in the uniforms and their garrison grooming. She frantically searched the faces, running Doolan's description through her mind as the man at the front continued to rail at her.

"Withdraw, Miss, or I shall have you forcibly removed! Damn it all! Sentry, call the Sergeant of the guard!"

She nearly turned to go, was nearly defeated by the mass of uniforms and the harsh bellowing voices. But then she noticed a man sitting alone at a table at the back of the room. Every officer in the room was sitting with other men at his table, but that one man was alone, ignored, in a blue coat. Pale as the moon, gaunt, long dark hair, he sat staring from under hooded eyes. He eventually turned his head and she saw the white ribbon at his neck.

"You, sir! You!" she screamed, pointing him out, suddenly certain, *certain.*

Laughing, one of the men at the head table looked at the man with the white ribbon in his hair and yelled drunkenly, "A spurned conquest, Lieutenant Loveless? I stand impressed!"

The general roughly pounded his tankard on the table and yelled, "Silence in the mess! Silence, there! You, Miss, are behaving like a woman of the street, and I shall not have it! You shall be silent, and you shall leave this room! This instant, young lady!"

With her certainty, her rage and resolution returned, and she clenched her fists at her sides and called, "I shall not be silent, and I shall no longer bear the conduct of that man!"

"Lieutenant Loveless is a volunteer, and a member of this mess! His conduct, his honour, is not in question here! You will cease this unfounded attack and withdraw, Miss! Immediately!"

A ringing silence followed, Cissy breathing hard in the center of the room.

"I shall not withdraw, sir, I shall not!" Staring silence. She turned to Barr. "Lieutenant Loveless, are you? How droll," she said, undaunted. "Gentlemen, you may be surprised to learn that this man's name is actually Charles Barr! Deny it, sir, if you can!"

Barr was silent, glaring at Cissy with a seething hatred.

"*Captain* Charles Barr, gentlemen, who served with my father, Lieutenant James Lockwood, in the Inniskilling Regiment. And while my father fought like a lion at Waterloo, falling wounded as the battle was won, where was Captain Barr? In the rear, rifling the baggage of his fellow officers, then stealing a horse to gallop back to Brussels!"

A roar of surprise, consternation, some voices supporting Lieutenant Loveless, others calling for his explanation, but still Barr sat silent, seething. Several of the officers called out that they were acquainted with Lieutenant Lockwood, and two Clonakilty men who recognized Cissy called out for Loveless to explain himself.

Still, Barr was silent, until Cissy called out, "He does not deny it! It is the truth, gentlemen! Barr faced court martial and was dismissed His Majesty's service, disgraced, a pariah, an outcast, and he now sits amongst you, the most dishonourable of men! Tortured by syphilis! The French pox, branded—"

Barr, brittle and insane, would not bear that. He was on his feet in an instant, whipping his sword from its scabbard and lunging toward Cissy. Mayhem erupted. Some officers recoiled, a few quicker men leapt up, reaching out to stop Barr, while Cissy frantically worked to pull the pistol from her bag.

Barr was so quick. The point of his blade sliced a deep groove up Cissy's forearm as she freed the pistol and pulled the trigger. The pistol went off in his face. In an instant Cissy rolled to the floor screaming, clutching her arm, while Barr clutched his face and staggered from the hall. His face was a mask of burned flesh and blood as he blindly slashed at anyone who tried to stop him.

He reeled into the yard, where he pulled himself into the saddle of the first mount he came to. None of the men there moved to stop him; he was an officer, and they would not risk laying hands on an officer. Barr viciously spurred the horse, and as he galloped through the gate away he was screaming that he would kill her, would kill them all, they would all regret the day they crossed him.

Several officers came to Cissy's aid. Handkerchiefs bought her wound, and she was helped to the barracks hospital. As her fury abated, Cissy found her hands visibly shaking, and she scarcely had the strength to walk.

The regimental surgeon proved a kind man, who tended both her arm and her spirit. "Eighteen stitches, Miss Lockwood, and while I am justifiably proud of my handiwork you shall nonetheless have a discernible scar to remind you of today's theatrics."

Since the barracks was unaccustomed to the care of young women, General McCutcheon dispatched his wife to assist with

Miss Lockwood's care. Sadly that lady proved odiously vain, and instantly jealous of a woman who was so young, so lovely, and now so admired by every man in the barracks. Fortunately, a lively young woman named Meredith, who was attached in a rather unofficial capacity to one of the young lieutenants of the Youghall Yeomanry, proved very helpful. She loaned Cissy some fresh clothes, as Cissy's riding habit was rather more slashed and bloody than fashion typically allowed.

The surgeon had a chatty, almost feminine, air about him as he casually said, "General McCutcheon may not approve of your methods, but he is, in his own way, grateful that you exposed this Barr character. Barr is obviously and completely off his head. As a mere surgeon I am unsure as to how these things work, but I would think that once they catch him he will be a resident of Kilmainham gaol for an extended period."

"Once they catch him? Surely he cannot have escaped!" Cissy said in anguished surprise. Dismay, anger, and tears competed for control of her face as she said, "I saw several officers ride after Barr, and they were just a moment behind him!"

"I do not know the details, Miss. The regiment, the whole of the military establishment, will be shocked and humiliated by this, and believe me, they shall find this fellow. A murderous assault upon a young woman in the middle of a regimental dinner? I have never seen the like."

When Miss Lockwood was sufficiently recovered to receive visitors, General McCutcheon called to tender his respects. "Will you spend the night here, Miss? We shall find some suitable quarters, and a good night's sleep will set you up amazing."

"Thank you, sir, but I believe that I shall return home. I must see to the health of a friend, my father's old soldier servant, who was attacked by Captain Barr near my home."

"If you so insist, ma'am, then you shall at least have a suitable escort." Calling over his shoulder, he said, "Major Luebbert! You will please muster a sergeant's guard and see Miss Lockwood home. You will then establish a picket near her home, and see that she is not disturbed by Lieutenant Lov— Barr—whatever that lunatic cares to call himself. Full dress, if you please. This young lady merits what honours we may bestow."

While Cissy was being tended to, Abby had been pampered by the men of the regiment as only cavalrymen can pamper a horse. With her arm in a sling, Cissy Lockwood rode home that evening in the company of a dozen stylish troopers.

They rode slowly toward Clonakilty, Cissy trying to collect herself. She soon found Major Luebbert an interesting man. Born in Hanover, he was a retired officer of The King's German Legion who had fought at Waterloo, and knew of the Inniskillings' stand there. He had married the widow of a fallen British officer, and had retired with his wife to Ireland.

Cissy found his German accent fascinating, and he was not shy about sharing his opinions on Ireland. "Ach, Miss Lockwood, such a beautiful country! Such glorious rain, *mein Gott*, how I love rain! But this island of yours has far too many madmen. Catholics, Protestants, rich and poor, common man and aristocrat, one cannot swing a dog by the tail without striking a zealot of some colour. I shall stand for no such nonsense in my troop! Duty, respect, and adherence to law. I am a humanist, Miss, a modern man. No religion taints my opinion of any man, and my troop shall adhere to my policies."

As they entered Clonakilty, the riders drew a great deal of attention, especially as it was one of their own who rode with the cavalrymen. If she had been completely honest with herself Cissy would have been forced to admit she reveled in it.

Up ahead, Cissy saw Father McGlynn standing at the door of St. Brigid's. He stood glaring at the Crown forces, as was his custom. When he caught sight of Cissy Lockwood, however, he staggered and turned remarkably pale.

She shook her head, her opinion of him confirmed. He was deathly afraid, and she sniffed in derision. Doubtless he feared she would denounce him in some vindictive rant. Instead she steadily rode past St. Brigid's, giving him only a cursory nod. She would play the game her mother played with such skill: to sit amongst the Irish and English, and yet not betray either. She had cards to play, now. She grinned a bit at the notion of Cissy Lockwood as a force to be reckoned with.

When Cissy and her escort rode up to Fáibhile Cottage, they found Diarmuid Doolan in the front garden. His head was bandaged, but that did not damper his raging anxiety.

She had not dismounted before he let forth a long string of shrill Irish. "Where on earth have you been, girl, and me frantic with worry for you? And your arm in a sling! Have you taken a fall?" Then suspiciously eying her escorts, "And who, may I ask, is this lot of dandies? Have they been fresh, *a grah*? Your father is far away, so if need be I shall fight every one of these impertinent horse-riding sons of Saxon devils."

Major Luebbert helped her to dismount with a level of courtesy that satisfied even Doolan's lofty standards. At the door, Cissy turned and made a one-handed curtsy to the men of the escort, a gesture that made them love her. As Doolan took her inside they gave her a rousing cheer which brought a blush to her cheeks, though Doolan glared, muttering, "Oh, they're awfully good at seeing young ladies home, but in a real fight? They gallop about and do shite... have I ever seen a dead cavalryman? No, Miss, I have not...."

The Lockwoods of Clonakilty

Cissy enjoyed her new-found ferocity. She sat at her parents' old desk and wrote to her Aunt with a bold, aggressive hand.

Madam,

You will please realize the difficulty I face in corresponding with you, but in light of certain information recently shared with me I feel it necessary to address you.

I understand from friends in Dublin (are you surprised, Madam, that I have fashionable friends in town?) that you have been speaking of my parents, my siblings, and myself in a most derogatory manner. No lady should be forced to remind another lady that to speak ill of one's family members is a most odious practice, and a habit which clearly marks the speaker as a base and common person.

You shall certainly deny it, but I am informed by persons in position to know, madam, that you have been especially slanderous of my mother, my sisters, and myself, on numerous occasions, and have gone so far as to deliberately paint us, when in the company of persons of influence, as lacking traits which would mark us as ladies of quality. It might in other circumstances be humourous to muse upon one woman slandering those whom she might otherwise hold dear, when it is she who paints herself the villain by indulging in such reprehensible behavior.

In short: when you speak ill of us, Aunt, we hear of it, and I trust you are not so foolish as to believe that we are incapable of striking back.

Cissy stopped for a moment to sharpen her pen. She knew that she and her family had very little ability to cause the Muirs even the slightest discomfort, but she thought it prudent to at least make an attempt to give her Aunt pause.

"You shall understand if I insult Aunt, will you not, my dear ones?" Sergeant and Corporal, both lying half-asleep at her feet, thumped their tails in agreement. "Very well, then." Cissy grinned as she returned to her letter. "Aunt shall certainly be horrified at your disapproval. Though I suggest you consider a long bath before your next appearance at Dublin Castle. I understand the Lord Lieutenant is most particular."

Lastly, madam, I understand that you have been corresponding with a Captain Charles Barr. I wonder if you have included him amongst the guests of your various soirées and entertainments? It would be humourous to see you doing so.

Evidently, Aunt, you do not realize (or is it simply that you do not care?) that Captain Barr was court-martialed and dismissed the service following his theft of two horses and, far worse, stealing from the trunks of his fellow officers at Waterloo? Your own brother, my dear father, was openly robbed by this man, and yet you allow him to advise you, and perhaps you have him in your house?

Will you be surprised, I wonder, to hear that this man has hidden himself in the ranks of the Muskerry Legion Cavalry, under a false name, and is currently a fugitive from charges of fraud and assault? You are certainly the worst judge of character, Aunt, to have placed faith in the word of such a man.

You will understand my open astonishment, Aunt, when I hear of your evident devotion to a man aggrieved by, what is the genteel term? The French pox? Yes, the French pox, that ignoble and vile disease of the corrupt.

I can only trust, Aunt, that you shall be honestly surprised at the notion of the captain's malady, and that your concern with his health will not be of an especially personal, frightening, nature.

Perhaps I shall write to Uncle and amuse myself with informing him of the nature of your choice of companion. I have so little income to spare, but I am content in knowing that paper, ink, and postage remain within my budget.

I close, relieved in the knowledge that I am happy and content, while you, Madam, despite your riches, are not.

Brigit Anne Lockwood

Chapter Twenty-Three

Francisco Imbo was the postmaster at Funchal. He was a small, trim man with a carefully manicured beard, and he was an iterant busybody. He knew far more than anyone else on Madeira about who was on the island, and what they were up to. That trait rendered him a difficult man to love, but it did make him an efficient postmaster.

On a sunbaked morning, the *Lord Mornington* Indiaman anchored in the narrow harbour, and one of her midshipmen was dispatched to carry the mail pouch up the steep slope to the Post Office. There Imbo flipped through the contents of the pouch, none of the correspondence being of much interest until he found one letter addressed in an elegant feminine hand.

Imbo called for the gaunt office boy, and handing him the letter he said, "You shall carry this to Lieutenant James Lockwood. At this time of day you shall certainly find him at Joselito's, taking coffee with his wife and friends. My God, what women. That wife of his! A goddess! Now, repeat the name: Lieutenant James Lockwood."

The boy spoke only Portuguese, so his pronunciation rang more of Coimbra than Cork, but Imbo patted him on the cheek and said, "Close enough. The letter is marked urgent, and as good stewards of our profession we shall see it delivered immediately. As you are an illiterate little beast, I shall explain that the letter is from a Miss Lockwood, of Clonakilty, Ireland. Do you know Ireland, boy?"

"Is that near Jerusalem, please, sir?"

Imbo rolled his eyes, gently thumped the boy on the head, and said, "Fool of a boy. It is an island far in the stormy north, ruled by heretics, and while the common people call themselves Catholics, they see God in trees and rocks and the sun. One step above mud-eating pagans. Still, duty requires us to do what we can to help them. Run, now. Lieutenant Lockwood has had good news lately, and if this letter holds more, he shall certainly reward you with a shining coin."

The letter from Cissy burned in his pocket as James kept the deck of *The Dove of Tralee* for hours at a time. His presence was a burden to the ship's officers, as the soldier urged them to wring every inch of progress from the lumbering merchantman. A day out of Funchal the wind dropped, and James suggested to the captain, "Certainly, sir, you might consider spreading your stuns'ls? And your bosun mentioned having skysails aboard. I have been aboard many a ship very much like this, where the captain spread his stuns'ls in a wind much stronger than this. Certainly boldness might be called for, sir? Timidity cast aside, and a stout soul's audacity rewarded?"

The captain checked his first reply and instead only locked his jaws in frustration, as Lieutenant Lockwood had made his life a misery for every mile since they had raised their anchor, indeed since the Lockwoods had come aboard.

"I appreciate your advice, sir," the captain said with a notable tension in his voice. "I equally appreciate the urgency of your need to return to Ireland and see to your daughter. But certainly, sir, you have noted our fished mainmast? I entreat you, Lieutenant; did I not show you our rotten knees? This is a merchant vessel, sir, not a dashing Royal Navy frigate. Do you not see our pumps throwing water in even these moderate seas? In all honesty, sir, am I not doing all in my power to see you home as quickly as possible?"

Lieutenant Lockwood was unmoved. "There is not a minute to lose, sir. For God's sake, make haste." Charles Barr was loose, and run mad. James would remain relentless until he was home, and Cissy safe.

Dr. Kelly was soon expected to return to town from yet another conference in France, but until then his practice was once again being tended by the young Dr. Hickman. It was that young man who was called to Fáibhile Cottage two days after Cissy's return home, after she had confessed to Doolan that her arm had grown deeply painful.

Doolan showed Hickman up to Cissy's room, where she was growing hot and feverish. When Hickman slowly peeled back the bandages from Cissy's arm, Doolan's fears were confirmed: the wound had grown red and inflamed. Doolan had seen many wounds in his day. He knew the signs of infection, and he knew how little doctors could do to fight it.

He could not bear to stay there, to know what he knew, afraid his face would betray him. He hurried out with a vague excuse about a young woman's privacy, though when Hickman came downstairs he found Doolan standing at the bottom of the steps with a bottle in his hand.

Hickman was intimidated by Doolan's glaring ferocity, so he reverted to a gentleman's status with a gruff, "Have you taken to drink, soldier?"

"I have not, Doctor. But you will tell me now, how that young woman will recover from the poison in her arm?"

"The infection is recent; I have hopes of saving the arm."

"Hopes, gentleman?" snarled Doolan. "You had best muster more than hopes, Doctor." He brushed past the young doctor and started up the steps, then turned, pointed a finger, and went on, "That girl means all the world to me. She shall lose nothing, *nothing*, unless you care to lose it yourself!"

Seven years before, Doolan had tended Lieutenant Lockwood at Waterloo, and he now tended Cissy Lockwood in the same manner. He washed the wound with whiskey, profligate with his Donegal *uisce beatha*, the water of life, faithful in its healing power, willing it to work. He then held Cissy's hand, muttering prayers, the plaintive ancient tongue like a song. "*A Naomh Mhuire, a Mháthair Dia, guigh orainn na peacaigh....*"

Cissy joined him in the familiar prayer, and when they finished she softly said, "Even if I grow very ill, I shall not take laudanum, Diarmuid. I shall not."

"Is it your father that you are thinking of, *mo mhile stor*, my thousand treasures?"

"No laudanum, Diarmuid," she said fiercely, a break in her voice. "No laudanum. Promise me, Diarmuid. You must promise me."

Cissy had long hours to think. Doolan or Hickman sat with her a great deal, but her mind was always active, and she ceaselessly considered her situation.

She was strong, but not immune to fear: she was especially afraid of losing her arm. As a girl she had often been frightened by the sight of a gnarled old woman in town, an old woman who had only one arm, the stuff of nightmares to the sensitive young Cissy Lockwood.

Doctor Hickman administered his medicines, Private Doolan changed the dressing and washed the wound with Irish whiskey, and Cissy Lockwood silently willed her body to heal itself.

She steadily improved.

The Dove of Tralee hove to in the Cobh of Cork. Even before the anchor dropped, her jolly boat dropped from the davits and was frantically rowed toward shore. Lockwood had given every oarsman a guinea.

Five months earlier the Lockwoods had left Cork and the *Admiral Rodney* for Marseilles, and now James Lockwood, huge and relentless, was returned, calling for a horse.

With his pistols in the saddle and his sword at his side he spurred the horse toward Clonakilty and Cissy.

Cissy was dozing in her bed, her arm in a sling. Doolan, his head still bandaged, sat at her side, Colonel Simon's shotgun across his lap. He reached across and held the back of his hand to her forehead; the fever was quite gone. His battered face was not much given to smiling, but as no one was watching he allowed himself a satisfied grin.

But Cissy was soon awakened by the sound of a horse galloping up Scartagh Lane. That was unusual, as a rider would have to push his horse very hard indeed to gallop up the hill. She sat up and grabbed the pistol that lay on her bedside table. Following the incident at Bandon Barracks, the colonel had stocked Fáibhile Cottage with all manner of arms. The yeomen still patrolled the roads, but that was no guarantee that Barr could not slip past and appear at their door.

Doolan was on his feet in an instant, quickly saying, "I shall see to it, *a stor*." He then rumbled down the steps, hobbled down the hall, threw open the front door, and leveled the shotgun, both hammers back.

In the misting rain the rider vaulted from the saddle, threw back his cloak, and strode into the garden.

It was trial, sure, but Doolan clung to his ways, only twisting his mouth, lowering the shotgun, knuckling his forehead, and muttering, "Evenin', sir."

Lieutenant Lockwood also played his part, growling, "Make your report, Private."

"Captain Barr has been about, sir. Gave me a sharp knock, escaped, pursued by your Miss Cissy. She found him up at Bandon Barracks, wounded the captain, but got a sabre cut on her arm. Every hand in the country is now turned out in search of the captain, but no sign yet, sir, if you please."

With a mix of shock and grief, James lost some of his bearing and cried out, "Cissy! A sabre cut?"

He started to push past Doolan, but the old soldier took his arm. "Go easy, now, sir. She's a rare one, is your Cissy. She's in her bed, now. The cut was a bad one, sure, but didn't that Doctor Hickman see her through the worst, and didn't I kick his arse a few times to make sure he did so. She has a load to tell you, sir, but you can be right proud—"

From upstairs, they heard Cissy call out, "Father! Father! Is that you? Father!"

James bolted past Doolan, taking the stairs three at a time, calling Cissy's name, and Private Diarmuid Doolan, for the first time in his long hard life, sat down and wept with joy.

The life of a fisherman makes few men rich, but many men content. After a life of conflict and roaming, John Cashman was determined to find that contentment in a simple house by the sea. The priest and his friends had done nothing to aid him while he was in gaol, and John had escaped the noose by the narrowest of margins. He turned to the sea.

Contentment with his livelihood was followed by contentment with his life. He began calling on a beautiful widow, and found himself thinking of becoming the father of her three young children.

In the early days of his new life, his old life sometimes came calling, shadowy men late at night who were summarily turned away. The priest himself came once. When John brusquely turned him out, the priest threatened exposure and the end of the perfect life by the sea. But when the priest returned to his rectory in Clonakilty he found a dead rabbit pinned to his headboard with a razor-sharp knife, and he quickly and completely dropped any further dealings with John Cashman.

While he would have nothing to do with Whiteboys and rebels, John still had some trusted former comrades who would share the latest over a jar. They shared bits of news, news from all across Ireland, the gossip of men who still idly dreamt of independence. One of those bits of information prompted John to pick up a pen. He wrote a pensive note to a man he should have hated, the act a fulfillment of a promise to someone he loved. His own mother had asked him to do what he could for the Lockwood children, and he would do so.

A cold, wet, Irish winter set in. The Lockwoods had been together in Clonakilty for a month, trying to reestablish their lives but largely failing.

Charles Barr dominated their every thought, their every breath. No one could leave the house without an escorted by James or Doolan, bristling with arms. Both Sergeant and Corporal adopted the family's anxiety, barking and growling at anyone approaching the house; when Mr. O'Leary came by to deliver a gift of his good Munster cheese it required all four Lockwood children to keep the dogs from tearing him to pieces.

But still no one had any notion as to where Charles Barr might be hiding; newspapers all across Ireland carried his description, the military and yeomanry patrolled the roads. He had disappeared completely.

Finally, an afternoon came that found Fáibhile Cottage in a mad rush of activity. James put on his uniform coat and was acting the officer: "Cissy, pray run upstairs and throw a few clothes in my haversack. I shall carry my cloak on the saddle. Lucy, please run outside and tell Uncle Tom and Dr. Kelly that I shall join them in two minutes. John, run and fetch my sword. Richard, my pistols." He then turned back to Brigid and continued with her. "Barr has broken his word by denouncing us to the Castle, and has made an attempt against the life of our daughter. Our *daughter*. He has removed himself from any considerations of honour, and I shall act accordingly. I shall find him, call him out, and put an end to him."

James's face was locked, but still Brigid tried to reason with him. "I wonder, should you really fight him? Perhaps it would best serve if you found him and had him arrested? After this affair with Cissy and the yeoman he will certainly be imprisoned for many years, long enough for—"

"He escaped prison once already; I shall place no more faith in Government's notions of justice. You of all people should agree with that, dear. Now, I must go."

Brigid nodded, but would not yet release him. She bowed her head, thinking, then looking up she said, "Very well. But Barr is unwell. What shall you do if you find him infirm or dying?"

Without flinching James said, "If I must, I shall slaughter him in his bed. This will be the end of him."

Three horses waited outside Fáibhile Cottage. Tom was saying goodbye to Julia. Dr. Kelly, just a day back from France, mounted, and looked impatient to be off. When James and

Brigid stepped out of their home, Tom gave Julia a reassuring smile and mounted as well.

James paused to embrace Julia and kissed her cheek. "With the blessing, I shall have your husband back to you in a fortnight." Then with quick, reassuring goodbyes to his children, an especially long embrace for Cissy, a hearty kiss from Brigid, and with something like joy behind his rigid exterior, he mounted, and without looking back they rode off to the north.

A crumpled note was tucked into James's breast pocket.

If you yet seek Barr, you shall find him in a crumbling old pile of stone called Ballynagowen in the County Clare, not far from your Leamaneh. And you may want to hurry, Lockwood, as he and his new friend are of a mobile nature.

Chapter Twenty-Four

Thirty wet miles to Cork town; once there, the three men switched from their horses to the mail coach that departed daily for Galway.

The mail coach contained only one passenger, a young midshipman bound for his parents' home after years at sea. Having attended a lengthy farewell dinner the night before, the midshipman fell asleep as soon as he settled in the coach. He woke with a start, however, when the coach door opened and he found two infantry officers and a rather shabby civilian looking up at him. The larger of the two officers, who did not look as if he had a shred of humour remaining to him, growled, "Sailor, it is such a lovely day. I believe you might enjoy outsides."

The midshipman glanced up at the misty Irish sky, but as he was intimately familiar with the arbitrary application of authority, he promptly said, "Yes, sir, thank you, sir." The midshipman then climbed up on the coach roof as Lieutenant Lockwood, Captain Mainwaring, and Doctor Kelly climbed inside.

As he took his seat, Kelly said, "You know, this coach will seat four very comfortably. I have seen six inside more than once."

James quietly said, "We need to talk, and we need room for our swords." They were all three wearing their swords; even as a civilian Kelly wore his with unreserved ease. The driver lost no time in getting the coach moving. Tom and Kelly unbuckled their swords and stacked them in the corner. James, however, drew his blade, pulled a whetstone from his pocket, and deliberately began to sharpen the edge. He had developed the habit of doing so at every opportunity.

Kelly mused, "Assuming we do find your Captain Barr, James, I think it unlikely that he would agree to swords. After twenty years of syphilis, he is likely to indicate a marked debility, and likely a pronounced mania, even delusion. If anything, you may wish to direct this compulsive behavior to your pistols."

James did not look up, but only muttered, "If he should choose rusty butter knives, I will oblige him."

There was a long, awkward silence until Tom cheerfully offered, "We constitute an ideal trio for an affair of honour, do we not? A duelist, his second, and his surgeon. All we lack is the target of our duelist's attentions."

James made a brief, fierce, nod of his head and looking directly to his friends he said, "I am ashamed of myself for not having put an end to Charles Barr years ago. By not following that path, I have put my family at risk. I intend to correct that error: I shall kill him, or he shall kill me. I thank you both for you joining me, and seeing this done according to form."

Dr. Kelly, who was uncomfortable with this humorless James Lockwood, one so intent on killing, made an attempt to reach him. "I, for one, trust that my talents will not be called for. I have tended to the battered Lockwood corpus upon so many occasions that I confess a lack of any desire to do so again."

James said nothing, and Tom filled the gap with, "Very well, then, Doctor, we shall mark your professional presence in our merry band as merely a matter of form."

James did not look up from his work as he grimly said, "With the blessing, you will soon be tending only to Charles Barr, Doctor."

Tom winked at the rumpled surgeon and added, "And if you do so, Kelly, you need not apply your skills with any particular devotion."

Three days later, Captain Thomas Mainwaring rode up to the derelict Ballynagowen tower in an immaculate dress uniform. The ancient door was barely on its hinges, though when he pounded his fist on the old oak a little man promptly opened it. When Tom asked for Captain Barr, Soames self-consciously buried his shock at being discovered, and adopted a demeanor he hoped was that of a man used to such proceedings. He proudly introduced himself as Captain Barr's most loyal friend and companion.

Captain Mainwaring then formally tendered a challenge from Lieutenant James Lockwood, asking Mr. Soames to forward it to Captain Barr's attention.

Soames had never been out, but for years he had carefully studied a copy of the *Code Duello*, which assured the potential duelist that it had been "adopted at the Clonmel Summer Assizes in 1777 for the government of duelists by the gentlemen of County Tipperary, County Galway, County Mayo, County Sligo and County Roscommon, and prescribed for general adoption throughout Ireland." He accepted the challenge on behalf of Captain Barr in a formal, if somewhat scripted, fashion, and added that he would proudly act as the honourable Captain Barr's second for dawn the next day.

Despite his show of confidence with this gruff, uncultured Mainwaring fellow, Thaddeus Soames was not terribly sure how his dear Barr would take the news of their discovery, and of Lockwood's shocking presence. He was especially doubtful of how his friend might take the news of a duel the very next morning.

Truth be told, he had not seen or spoken to Charles for some days, as the poor fellow had been unwell, and locked himself in an icy chamber on the top floor, just below the crumbling parapet. Twice a day Thaddeus would climb the cunning circular staircase to lay food and wine at the door, but would beat a hasty retreat at the sounds of the screams and ranting curses that echoed though the upper rooms.

Thaddeus sat at the low fire of the dank ground floor room, pondering, when he was startled by the sounds of footsteps coming downstairs. He was amazed and delighted, though a bit frightened, by the sight of Charles Barr in his uniform, his sword at his side, emaciated, unsteady, but lucid.

Barr stared at him, slowly raised his eyebrows, and croaked, "That was Mainwaring?"

Unsteadily, "Why, yes, brother."

"And, so Lockwood is come?'

"Um, well, it seems so. He... they... wish to meet...."

Barr's head tilted to one side, and in a hopeful, nearly pure voice, he said, "My redemption, then? At last, my time is come?"

With aching delight, Soames replied, "Yes, dear brother. Your reclamation is at hand. You shall act as God's hand, and wipe the world clean of such filth as this Lockwood, and then we shall once again walk the earth as virtuous men, purified in the honourable deaths of God's enemies."

Barr nodded in agreement, jerking, sudden movements, until he said, "I must eat, and drink, and rest, to ready myself."

Soames jumped to prepare their dinner. Barr slowly sat, drew his sword and held it up for Soames to see. "A trick I learned from the guerrillas in Spain. I dip my blade in shit. I shall roll my pistol balls in shit as well. Poisoned wounds."

Soames nodded in bewildered fascination, and Barr went on in a vile half-whisper. "Shit in Lockwoods veins. So... fine. And then... sweet Christ, how Brigid O'Brian shall scream beneath me. And her slut daughter, too. Oh, the tearing, biting, cutting, pounding, and only then, pure redemption."

Thaddeus Soames felt himself aroused, deeply aroused. He wanted to help, oh how he would serve and aid his friend! He paid no attention to the last dying flash of his rational mind, the tiny voice that cried out that he was in the presence of a monster.

In Clonakilty, Brigid Lockwood prayed at St. Brigid's for hours. Though the younger children were not informed the nature of their father's mission, the boys quickly guessed, and escorting Lucy to town they often joined their mother.

Cissy walked with her mother into town, but confused her by gently refusing to step inside the church. She instead spent those hours walking about the church yard in the winter air, until the Sisters of Mercy found her there. They were no friends of Father McGlynn, knowing much of how he ran his parish. They summarily gathered up Cissy and escorted her, despite that young lady's polite protests, into the church like a herd of matriarchal elephants, Cissy a closely guarded calf in their midst.

Father McGlynn kept his distance.

Dawn, and a heavy frost lay on the field where the five men gathered. The lonely tower of Ballynagowen was a dark ghost in the foggy valley below.

There was no mistaking their purpose. There was no veneer of pretense, no notion of making an appearance for honour's sake. Each of the two principals was determined to kill the other.

Lockwood was intimidating. Tall and grim, he successfully masked any shortness of breath, any lingering trace of his chronic weakness. He was entitled to wear his uniform again, and wore his best with a private pride. Live or die, he would do so in his red coat, his lieutenant's epaulette, and the buff facings of the Inniskilling Regiment.

Barr was bent, razor thin, his face ghastly pale on one side, burned and scarred on the other. His dark eyes glittered, distant and menacing, like black water at the bottom of a well. He had given up the charade of the Yeoman Cavalry; he too, wore his red infantry coat, but with the green facings of the 24th Foot.

The seconds met on the middle of the ground to arrange the proceedings. Soames opened by saying, "If I may, please, Captain Mainwaring, explain how these things are done. This will be no pell-mell military affair. The *Code Duello* is quite clear as to how gentlemen are to conduct themselves. I quote: 'In a pistol duel, the parties would be placed back to back with loaded weapons in hand and walk a set number of paces, turn to face the opponent, and shoot. Typically, the graver the insult, the fewer the paces agreed upon. Alternatively, a pre-agreed length of ground would be measured out by the seconds and marked, often with swords stuck in the ground, which are referred to as points.' We shall use a dropped kerchief as the signal to fire. I trust, sir, you have no objection to points and, say, twenty paces?"

Tom agreed, then held his temper throughout the rest of Soames's meandering speech, until Soames made as if to dismiss him. Tom then hissed, "We are not finished, Mr.

Soames. You must make sure of your man. He *must not* fire until the handkerchief reaches the ground."

"You insult my friend, sir!" cried Soames, instantly scarlet. "His honour, our honour, is beyond reproach! You are impudent, and a fool!"

"Watch your tongue, sir."

"I will show you what I am made of, sir! For honour!" With that Soames reached up and struck Tom Mainwaring across the face.

Tom scarcely reacted, only staring at the panting, wild-eyed Soames. From their end of the field, James and Kelly stared in amazement, while from his end of the field Barr suddenly came to life, wildly screaming, "Huzzah! Huzzah! Huzzah!"

With shrill triumph Soames called out, "Rule Twenty-five! 'Where seconds disagree, and resolve to exchange shots themselves, it must be at the same time and at right angles with their principals!' My God, what glory, this, what a thrilling display of honour!"

Tom stalked back to his friends, his face a mask. Both James and Kelly understood what had to happen. Kelly loaded a second pistol, and James quietly said, "Oh, Tom, I never knew it would come to this. I am so sorry."

"It seems that Soames is as mad as Barr, which is no small insult."

Across the field, Soames consulted with Barr. Soames then trotted a few steps back towards the three friends and called, "I shall have to run down to my chest to fetch the other pistol! I shan't be a moment!"

Three sniffs of derision was their only response, Tom adding a muttered, "Civilians...."

Soames then trotted away down the steep hill. He soon slipped and fell in the icy grass, earning a sigh of exasperation from James, before the fat little fellow disappeared into the cold fog below.

Barr stood rigid and still, his hands at his sides, staring from under hooded eyes, studying James with a reptilian glare.

His pistol was in his hand.

Stepping close to James, scarcely moving his lips, Tom said, "Do not turn your back on him. He cannot be trusted. Will you take your pistol?"

James shook his head and quietly said, "Do not concern yourself. Let us leave the pistols in their box for now. I believe that Barr shall play the gentleman until the end." James folded his arms, threw Barr a glance, and added, "For years, this madness has been about honour; his notions of honour, at any pace. Now, it is about mine as well."

James walked a few paces off to one side, occasionally eying Barr, then striding back to Tom and Kelly he asked with some impatience in his voice, "If any man alive can define honour, I shall give him a hundred guineas and my undying regard."

Tom shrugged and said, "Define honour? I could not do so; perhaps some Oxford Don might attempt it, though I doubt he could do so in less than a thousand pages, writ small."

Kelly sneezed and said, "Still, gentlemen, defined or not, it is honour that has brought us all here. And it is honour which now requires you two fellows to place your lives at risk, while attempting to end the lives of those two lunatics yonder. Defined or no, we dance to honour's tune."

More long minutes ticked away as the three friends stood together, impatient, looking across the field to see the breathless Soames return, then awkwardly load his pistol. Tom tried to break the tension by idly saying, "Did you know, when Julia's father heard of my intentions toward his daughter, he had only two questions regarding me. His two qualifications were, 'Of what family is he?' and 'Did he ever blaze?'"

Kelly pulled on a pair of very unmilitary woolen mittens and asked, "Did he ask about your willingness to go out in hopes that you were a fighting man, or in hopes that you were not?"

"Julia asked him that very question, and you know, while not a bloody man himself—Julia did not know of her father going out in all his life—he surprised her in saying that he wanted a son-in-law who would fight if provoked, which I took very well in him."

They were silent again for a few moments, and James thought of how his perception of time had altered at Badajoz, and again at Waterloo. So too, now, did that strange trick of time play out in the field above Ballynagowen. Time expanded and compressed. Some moments dragged out, so that he could note every detail, was able to ponder his fear and determination, but other moments flashed by so quickly as to scarcely leave even a trace of memory. He noted with startling clarity the beauty of the frost on the grass, and how his breath, however weak, clouded in the still cold air.

Soames and Barr stepped forward, ready at last. As the seconds were now combatants, Kelly was the only man left to act as intermediary. With deadly earnestness he paced out the ground. He collected the duelists' swords, and marked each man's place with his blade, the point in the ground. As Soames wore no sword his place was marked by Kelly's blade, and soon four upright swords marked a cross in the frosty grass.

"Gentlemen, as I assume there will be no discussion of apologies, you will please now stand to your points." James stood beside his sword, and wondered what would happen to it if he died in the next minute; he loved that old sword. He loved so many things. He took some solace in thinking that Tom, or if the worst happened, Kelly, would see to things. James would not allow his mind to wander any further; his was a soldier's mind, and he consciously closed it to anything but the moment.

A few yards to James's left stood the now-quaking Soames; a few yards to James's right Tom stood, rock steady. They each took a duelist's pose: turned ninety degrees to their enemy, a slender target, but still so terribly vulnerable.

And across from James stood Charles Barr, a snarl on his face. For a long, languid second, James marveled at how Barr had decayed, how truly horrible he looked.

All four pistols were cocked, pointed to the ground. Kelly stepped off to one side, then in a firm voice he said, "Gentlemen, due to the unusual, but still wholly prescribed, nature of this duel, I shall give the four of you the signal to discharge"—he was an old hand, and did not risk saying the word 'fire' in such a charged atmosphere—"your weapons, by tossing my handkerchief onto the ground that lies between you. When it strikes the ground, you may discharge at your earliest convenience."

Kelly found a suitable stone, and tied it into his handkerchief. "Ready yourselves, gentlemen." The pistols raised; only Soames quivered. Kelly waited a few seconds, then lobbed the weighted handkerchief in a high arc. To James it seemed the handkerchief's flight took an eternity.

The handkerchief struck the ground. All four pistols sparked and fired at the nearly the same instant. The four balls passed within inches of each other above Kelly's bouncing handkerchief, all four whistling with deadly intent toward their target, eagerly seeking flesh.

James felt a whisper of air flash past his cheek, an angel's kiss, but nothing more. The roar of the shots faded, and he was surprised to find himself unhurt. In the still air the smoke of the four pistols stood dense, and for an eternity he could see nothing of the other duelists. The sharp, acrid smell of powder smoke was familiar, and almost comforting. A gentle waft from the sea slowly pushed the smoke aside, clearing his view from left to right.

Soames lay motionless on the ground.

More smoke drifted off, and James saw Barr, still on his feet. But Barr was reeling, his hands to his throat. He then thrust out his arms, threw back his head, and mouthing some silent curse to the sky he fell backwards into the waiting frost, an arch of spraying blood marking his passage.

Then James saw Tom lying in the grass, holding himself up with one arm. James ran to him, calling his name, and Tom waved his hand as if it were nothing, but then he rolled onto his back, vainly trying to bark out a laugh.

James knelt over him, saw the blood soaking into his coat, and grasping his hand he said with anguish in his voice, "Ah, Tom, I am so sorry, brother."

Tom dismissed the apology with a quick wave of his fingers, and in a breaking voice he said, "There could never be any offense between us, brother."

Tom took his breaths in heaving, wincing, gasps, as James gently opened the bloody coat and shirt. Kelly sprinted over, lugging his ponderous bag.

Kelly began his work, and James found time resuming its normal pace. He had killed men before, and seen many others die; after such a spray of blood, he was certain that Barr was dead. He tried to focus on Tom, but he still found his own feelings running amok; a sense of relief, certainly, but also a rising, overwhelming joy, of knowing that Barr was finished, and that he himself was still alive, *alive*. But he caught himself, ashamed of his selfishness.

A long ugly wound scored across Tom's chest. Kelly quickly examined it and said, "Not to worry. Bloody, painful, but there is no puncture of the chest cavity."

Tom gasped a laugh and said, "Why, yes, Doctor, it is bloody painful."

James could not help but grin, though Kelly frowned and said, "Bloody *and* painful, please, Captain Mainwaring. I take my profession seriously; I do wish you gentleman would be less flippant. Now, be a good fellow, lie still, and bleed quietly. I shall give you a quick bandaging for now, and when we get back to our cozy little public house I shall wrap you properly. My *cingulum pectoris* is the stuff of legend."

"I hardly think that will be called for, Doctor," Tom said from his back, trying very hard not to laugh. "Mrs. Mainwaring and I are quite happy together."

James laughed long and loud, tension flowing from him in waves, and even Kelly grinned as he said, "Only uneducated minds think of Latin solely in terms of the erotic, gentlemen. Your affection for Mrs. Mainwaring shall not be challenged by my *cingulum pectoris*. In my studies on the Continent, I have become acquainted with that method, that most modern method, of dressing a chest wound. It shall serve to speed your healing, and while it will lessen your pain that is the merest coincidence. A moderate period of pain, delivered at regular intervals, might well dissuade you mad duelists from this endless defense of honour, not to mention this irrational glee. Now sit up, please, so that I might get a few turns around you. Slowly, now, Tom."

They helped him to sit up, pulling his bloody coat and shirt off, and Tom winced as the pain sharpened. Still, he only looked down, sniffed, and muttered, "Soames has ruined my new coat, the dog."

They grew quiet and serious, James still clasping Tom's hand as Kelly wound the linen around his chest. After throwing a look across the field James told Tom, "You did for Soames, at any rate."

"I did no such thing. I threw my shot into the fog. Soames is a harmless little fool; whatever his state, I had no hand in it." With a mix of pride and regret in his voice, a tone that James found puzzling, he added, "I have yet to kill a man."

Kelly finished with Tom, then lurched to his feet and jogged over to Soames. He briefly checked him, then strode over to Barr, gave him just a glance, then returned to James and Tom. "Not a scratch on Soames. He fainted dead away, and all that is required to put him to rights is a new pair of breeches."

James only nodded, and left it for Tom to ask, "What of Barr?"

"A radical resection of the carotid; quite an effective shot, James. Despite appearances, I am still a man of moderate faith, and so stand convinced that Captain Charles Barr is now experiencing all the fires of hell."

Chapter Twenty-Five

Soames blinked back to consciousness, but even then it took him some time to recall what brought him to be lying half-frozen in an open field. The clatter of an approaching chaise prompted him to sit up, and he passively watched as Lockwood and Kelly helped Mainwaring into the carriage. Soames watched as the coachman snapped his team to life, and the chaise rolled away down the narrow lane. The details of the duel suddenly came back to him, and he frantically checked himself for wounds. He was puzzled to find himself whole.

"Doubtless one of those scoundrels struck me down from behind. That is certainly it."

Then, after some further examination, "Oh, dear, I have shat myself."

Stiff from the cold, he achingly got to his feet, and saw Barr lying in the grass. "My dear Barr!" he cried as he shuffled toward the body, his arms reaching out to his only friend in the world. "Dead! Fallen upon the field of honour!" As he was a great reader of romantic novels, he thought it proper to then dramatically shake his fist at the sky and call, "As God as my witness, I shall see you avenged! The name Lockwood shall be struck from the face of the earth!"

Soon enough, however, Soames recalled the realities of his situation. He was a fugitive from the King's justice, he was wet and cold, and while dueling was typically accepted in Ireland he might find it awkward to explain the dead man lying at his feet. He grew very afraid. A wild look grew in his eyes as he wondered, "What if the peasants heard the shots, and have summoned the magistrate? What if Lockwood and his cronies determine that I must be silenced, and return to finish me off?"

Soames had no desire to ever again stare into the wrong end of a pistol, and he had an equal dread of a return to prison. He decided to resume his flight, alone now, as Barr lay in the frost, ivory and scarlet turning to blue and black.

He bent to kiss Barr's forehead, and shed the only tear to be shed over that particular corpse. He then hurried back to Ballynagowen, changed his clothes, threw his few possessions together, saddled his horse, and spurred away, as awkward a horseman as ever mounted.

He stopped at the first labourer's cottage he came across, where he found a frail old man milking a cow. Not deigning to dismount, Soames pointed toward Ballynagowen, and said, "There is a noble gentleman lying dead in yon field. If you give me your solemn word, man, that you will bear his body away in honour and see him properly buried in an Anglican graveyard, you may have whatever money you may find amongst his possessions, and you may keep his horse, in compensation. What say you, man?"

The old man's name was Seamus MacBride, while his cow was called Ciara. MacBride had only a little more English than Ciara, but he was long accustomed to deferring to English-speaking men on horseback. Thus after a long, considering pause, he nodded respectfully and offered a soft, "Dia agus Mhaire duit." God and Mary be with you.

Soames took that as an affirmative, and so he awkwardly turned his horse and, madly spurring the beast, rode away.

McBride had heard tales of the odd ways the Saxons fought one another, and everyone in the township had heard the pistol shots at dawn from up at Gortpeacach, the sinner's field. Curious, McBride gathered his uncle, his brother, and his two sons, and went to investigate. They soon came across the body, but the instant they saw the corpse's red coat they fled in panic.

They let Barr lie for a full two days before they convinced themselves that no one was coming for him, red coat or no, and so late that night they crept back to Gortpeacach. They were frightened, but they were poor, and, despite the fact that the ravens had been at the body in their typically hideous manner, the McBride men looted the corpse. In the moonlight the putrid body was pale as milk, but the McBrides were country men and thus familiar with death. They were pleased with their booty; while they had little use for the watch and snuff case, they were delighted with the eleven pounds, three shillings, and fourpence they found in the pockets. They found one knife in the dead man's coat, and another in his boot. Barr's sword was still standing upright where Kelly had placed it, so it was taken, along with the sword belt and scabbard, to be hidden in the rafters of their home in anticipation of the French coming again.

They then dragged the body to the back of the field, where they hurriedly threw some sod over it. And there Captain Charles Barr remained, alone and forgotten, barring the occasional attention of rooting hogs.

My dearest Brigid,

A quick note from sunny Galway, where we three wanderers have gone to ground for a few days. As I am the most considerate of husbands, I write to keep you from worrying.

My business has been tended to, and we no longer need worry about the particular issue that had been troubling us. I am quite well, though Tom managed to get scraped up a bit; we shall explain when we get home. But do tell Julia not to concern herself, as Kelly says all shall be set to rights in no time at all.

I have been thinking of Cissy a great deal, and while I find myself horrified by the thought of her facing Barr alone, I am so desperately proud of her. Pray do tell her so.

Things are looking up, are they not? With this business tended to, I feel very much like my old self, free of the burden that we both have dragged about so long. The three of us here are making quite merry; such good friends.

I so much look forward to seeing you again. Pray give the children my dearest love, and know how very dear you are to me, Brigid Marie O'Brian Lockwood. Such a lovely name.

Always,
James

The Soames family owned property all across Great Britain, though Thaddeus was concerned with just one townhouse in Dublin, one that was standing vacant due to a fire that had ruined the ground floor. He made his way there, again doing his best to leave a difficult trail, and holed up in the upper floors. He then set to work. He would take up his late friend's noble quest, and destroy James Lockwood. But he would destroy him slowly, painfully.

Soames spent long hours pondering how best to harm Lockwood. He was mad, but Soames loved his father; with a flash of insight he decided the most painful blow he could strike would be to kill Lockwood's father, then the rest of his family, one at a time, and so teach him the meaning of anguish.

The next morning Soames scurried out to purchase a copy of *The Peerage*, and back at the old house he closely studied it, soon grinning with satisfaction.

And so, two days later Soames was dressed in a new suit of clothes and had hired a fashionable barouche to drive him out to Malahide. Soames had the driver pass Lockwood House numerous times before he could muster the courage to order him to turn up the gravel drive.

Soames's best London manners earned him an entrance, and he soon found himself shown into the ornate library of Lockwood House and introduced to old man Lockwood.

To Lockwood Senior, the fat little man airily said, "I beg pardon for calling unannounced, sir, but as I was dashing through Malahide on my way up my holdings in Fermanagh I simply could not deny myself the honour of paying my respects, sir, as I am a great friend of your son."

"Oh, he is just upstairs. I shall have Collins call him."

Soames went completely pale and nearly bolted for the door, but he shakily said, "I had been led to believe, sir, that James had returned to Clonakilty—"

The old man frowned and said, "You must be more definitive in your claims of acquaintance, sir. My eldest son, John, lives here with his wife, his most reputable wife. Young James lives with that pack of people down in Cork."

Soames looked relieved, then with growing realization he said, "Oh, so it is not just Lieutenant Lockwood's father in this house, but his brother and sister in-law as well? Oh, how perfect!"

Soames openly giggled until the old man eyed him with disdain and muttered, "Collect yourself, sir."

Soames swallowed his glee, then looking about the ornate room he asked, "You keep no dogs, sir?"

"Certainly not, sir. Filthy curs, shitting in every corner, thrusting themselves most improperly against one's leg... no, sir, not in my house, as long as I draw breath. But what would bring you to ask such a question, sir? "

Soames made no response, only badgering the old man with further random questions until old Lockwood, who was not accustomed to being questioned in his own home, cut him off and had the footman see the fellow out. The old man returned to his chair with a grumbling, "What a God damned fool. Doubtless a Papist as well, which makes him doubly qualified to be a friend of James."

Soames made his second visit to Lockwood House late that night. He waited from the depths of the park's massive oaks, watching the last of the lights to go down, and for silence and complete moonless darkness to cover his approach. He moved awkwardly, as he struggled to carry two large cans of wood alcohol. He had a pistol tucked into his belt, and as he was no soldier he carried the pistol at full cock, at an angle that would emasculate him at the slightest provocation.

He had no experience in burglary, but he found a door to the kitchens that had a broken lock, and so slipped into the house with ease. The kitchens were dark, so he stumbled and bumped around for several minutes until he found the stairs up to the main hallway, where a lantern dimly burned. Grinning and skipping, Soames poured the alcohol all around the main floor and at the base of the grand staircase, splashing it up on the walls and dousing himself in the process.

Soames was a fortunate burglar, but his luck did not extend to arson. In the library he had thoughtlessly poured a large amount of alcohol in front a fireplace that still glowed. It took a few minutes, but the fumes wafted up to the embers, and with an enormous *whoosh* a wall of flame blew across the library and up the main hall. Soames had just a second to contemplate his error as the fire roared toward him, then swallowed him whole.

The fire was massive, and complete; Lockwood House was quickly and irrevocably reduced to a lifeless brick shell, all within it reduced to ash.

James, Tom, and Kelly had reserved a cozy private room off the main tap room at the Shannon Arms to celebrate the end of Charles Barr, and lingered there longer than they had first planned. They shared several bottles of wine with a triumphant air, though after the fourth bottle Dr. Kelly found it necessary to pull his hat over his eyes and go to sleep.

Tom said, "I was just thinking... I have now been shot twice, but I have never shot anyone. That seems, somehow, unfair."

With a knowing air, James said, "Hmm, I have been shot twice as well, and on top of that, stabbed and slashed several times."

"I thought you had been shot only once?"

"Waterloo. And Leamaneh."

"Leamaneh was only a scratch."

"Yes, but it really hurt."

"Do you truly believe my wounds are not as painful as your own?"

James waved a hand and said, "Well, you never complained about them hurting."

"That, brother, is because I am a stoic of the first order."

"Really? An order of stoics? You amaze me. Do you have meetings, wear sashes, hold secret rituals, those types of things?"

Tom burped deeply and said, "My sacred vows prevent me from divulging any details." But waving a finger from the prone position he had assumed on a bench, he loudly added, "But stand thee warned! We are numerous, and we are... well... stoic!"

They had believed that Kelly was sound asleep, but he corrected that impression by barking out a roaring laugh.

As the rejuvenated Kelly ran a hand across his face, James asked, "Have you ever been shot, dear Kelly, preserver of lives and boon companion?"

"I have not." Then after a moment's consideration he added, "But I did have my heart broken once. Well, twice, truth be told. Same woman, twice. Ghastly creature."

James grinned contentedly and said, "I have never had my heart broken." He glanced out the window and saw Brigid walking quickly toward the Arms. "And witness, please, gentlemen, the graceful arrival of the woman of my dreams—" He came to a sudden halt when she came into the room, her face ashen, holding a letter out to him.

"Oh, my dear James," she said, "a dispatch rider has come from Dublin...." She handed him the letter with a shaking hand.

He read it through twice, his face growing as tortured as Brigid's. In a wondering, anguished voice he said, "My father, my brother, and his wife, are all dead; Lockwood House is burned to the ground. My God, my God. Many of the servants perished as well; Mrs. Hawkins, Jones, several others. It is hard to tell, it seems; the fire was massive."

The party that had been so merry was shocked into motionless silence, all eyes on James as he blinked back tears and went on, "They think it was a flue fire. Mrs. Tweeddale got out through the kitchens, and said she heard the fire roaring, like only a flue fire can roar. All that old paneling and those brittle paintings would have burned like mad. Jesus, they are all gone."

Brigid went to her husband and held him, his face torn with grief and disbelief.

James was grim and stone-faced, a black mourning band on the arm of his best uniform coat. He had cause to be grim. He had seen to the funerals, the wrenching, grievous funerals, from his father down to Melissa Ashton, the junior house maid.

A cold Dublin rain soaked him as he returned to their hotel. They had taken a room on the second story, and he found himself gasping for breath at the last flight of stairs. He paused in the hall to recover, then proceeded to their room, where he gave Brigid a soft kiss on the cheek and pulled a rolled-up copy of the *Gentleman's Magazine and Historical Chronicle* from his pocket. He quietly said, "The obituary is out. Quite lengthy; it is as good as one could hope for, I suppose. Now that he is gone, I am surprised at the number of people who feel free to confess how they despised my father. I knew there was ill feeling, of course, but not this degree of loathing. Still, a number of people have expressed regrets and regards for John and Elizabeth, which is of some comfort."

Brigid put a supportive hand on his arm, but did not know what to say. He went on, "I am the sole heir, and will be made master of the Lockwood estates, such as they are. Our money woes resolved, and I cannot tell you how awful that makes me feel."

She stayed with him for a moment, then stepped to the side board to pour a glass of whiskey. Handing it to him, she said, "You were a good brother to both John and Elizabeth, and a far better son than your father deserved. Grieve for your loss, *mo stor*, but please, do not grieve what you have gained." She kissed him softly, then took the magazine to the window to read.

Gentleman's Magazine and Historical Chronicle, *December 1821*

Obituary; with Anecdotes of remarkable Persons

At Peckham Rye, Aged 16, Mary-Anne, only child of Mr. Joseph West, of Shoreditch

After many years' illness, aged 67, the widow of the late William Bussard, esq. of Manchester, most justly beloved.

SCOTLAND—In Argyll square , Edinburgh, Alex Christison, esq. late Professor of Humanity in the University of Edinburgh.

IRELAND—At Malahide, John Lockwood, former Captain, 43rd Foot, in a fire at Lockwood House. Also, his son John Lockwood, and daughter-in-law Elizabeth. The fire was so sudden and of such magnitude that it was initially feared to have been the handiwork of REBELS, as the Lockwood family had of late been the subject of a large and coordinated attack at Leamaneh in the County Clare. But as no men of such description had been reported in the neighborhood, a flue fire is suspected. Lockwood senior is survived by his wife, who remains hospitalized in Dublin due to lingering ill health.

Brigid set the magazine aside, and with grief in her voice she said, "Poor, dear Elizabeth, to never have had a baby." She wiped her tears away; then her strength rose, and she asked, "I will ask now for an honour your father always denied me. Will you take me to meet your mother, James?"

His face softened, and with a nod of resolution, he said, "Yes, my dear, it is time."

At Fáibhile Cottage, Doolan had not lost the habit of sitting beside Cissy at every opportunity, the rumbled old man and the lovely young woman. He frowned at her, and said, "What is that you are drinking, *mo cuisle*?"

"Doctor Hickman said that a little rum in my tea would help ease the pain in my arm."

"A sound suggestion, sure, but is your wound not nearly healed? Did I not this morning change the dressing myself, and your arm as strong and healthy as a Donegal summer?"

Cissy took a deliberate sip of her tea and said, "It still troubles me."

They sat together in the drawing room for several silent moments, the old soldier and the young woman, content in one another's company, but with words hanging between them that had yet to be spoken.

While looking into the low fire, Doolan quietly said, "Are you unhappy, *mo stor*?"

She pondered the question for a moment, finally saying, "I would be a selfish person, Diarmuid, to be unhappy, would I not? My family is returned, safe and happy. My sister is married, and as happy as I could ever wish for her. And my father has seen to Charles Barr; he shall never again haunt this family."

A thoughtful moment passed before Cissy went on, "Still, I do feel... unsettled. I need some time, I think, to come to terms with all that has happened. And whatever shall I do with myself now, make of myself? I would never marry simply for a lack of anything better to do; I shall lead apes in hell first. But then, after all this, how could I ever return to school?"

A corner of Doolan's face briefly grinned, and he said, "You would have some grand tales to tell the fine ladies at Malahide, sure. Riding? Shooting? Deadly combat in an Officers' Mess? You'd be the center of attention for months on end." Then the grin faded, and he went on, "But you're thinking, you could not again be satisfied with life in that world?"

She gave him an equally quick grin, then turning away, looking into her tea, she said, "To think of spending my days stitching and conjugating French verbs seems ridiculous." She then looked up, adding in a stronger tone, "But worse than that —I would be lacking *purpose.*"

Doolan nodded and said, "I learned a bit of Spanish when I was there, you know. One of their sayings stuck in a wee corner of my head. They say, *'Que no haya novedad,'* which means 'May no new thing arise.' But I shall not say that to you, Brigit Anne Lockwood. I shall instead wish for you, that some new thing shall arise, and give you purpose again, and perhaps contentment."

James dreaded the visit to Bloomfield Hospital where the Society of Friends cared for his mother, his blank, uncomprehending mother. He would not call it an asylum for the insane. The attendants were kind but efficient, and the small room was bare but tidy. Brigid sat holding his mother's hand for hours, silent, somehow sharing. That night James and Brigid wept together, vowing to bring the children to see her, to try to reach her.

James spent the following days with Mr. Bettany, the family man of business in his over-heated office. James was growing tired of the seemingly endless papers to read and sign. At the first of their appointments he had become the new master of the Lockwood estate, but since then he had been handed endless accounts to review.

"One last signature, if you please, Lieutenant Lockwood, and I believe our business will be complete." Bettany handed across a formal-looking document, and as he did so he said in a forced tone, "As our business concludes, sir, I wish to raise an issue that I find painful to address. You may know, Lieutenant Lockwood, that your father and I differed on some details on how the estate was to be managed. I would, however, be honoured if you would allow me to continue to do so, under your direction."

James nodded, "Yes, Mr. Bettany, my father and I differed on several matters as well. I would be pleased to have you continue to manage the estate, though I hope my direction will tend to be less—harsh—than my father's."

With a bow from his chair, Bettany said, "I thank you for your continued faith in me, sir. Now, this final document, drawn up at your direction, is the power of attorney. I am herewith directed that once you return to your regiment, Mrs. Brigid Lockwood is to be your voice on any matters requiring immediate decision."

"That is correct, Mr. Bettany," he said, as he signed with a flourish.

Bettany straightened the stack of documents on his desk, stood, and extended his hand, "Our business is complete. I congratulate you, sir." James stood and shook his hand, looking relieved, and Bettany continued, "I have taken the liberty, sir, of anticipating your need for some ready money." Reaching into a strong box, Bettany handed James a roll of bills. "I trust three hundred pounds is sufficient, sir?"

When James found Brigid at the Trinity College booksellers' booths she was just sending a porter to their hotel with a box full of books. As she took James's arm, she said, "I have had a most successful morning."

"That is a prodigious pile of reading, Mrs. Lockwood. I trust you have not become frivolous in your spending?"

Cheerfully, she replied, "I have not, sir. I purchased every one of those books as used, at quite remarkable prices, thank you very much. Novels and histories; the children shall be pleased. Pray, now, is all your business seen to?"

It was a clear, sharp day in late winter. The cold air and the low winter sun lit her face in a most remarkable manner, a manner not wasted on several appreciative passers-by, but especially appreciated by her husband, who marveled once again that such a woman would consent to be his wife.

He smiled, a broad, untroubled smile, the first in some time, and said, "It is indeed seen to. We are now, certainly not wealthy, but comfortable." As they walked together, relaxed and happy, they came across a jeweler's shop, and he casually mentioned, "I have long thought of getting a diamond to augment your wedding band."

"Oh, *mo stor*, how sweet of you to think so," she said, hugging his arm. But she extended the fingers of her left hand and said, "But I think not, thank you. I am very pleased with my ring as it is."

With a playful frown he said, "It is difficult to spoil you, Mrs. Lockwood."

"I do not wish to put on airs, *a grah*. I believe we agreed that we shall go on living as we have, even if we need no longer fret over quite every penny." Then with sudden delight she went on, "Oh, but we must go by Doyle's! It is not far to Fishamble Street, and I wager your new coats are finished by now. That shall certainly raise your spirits! And then we must go to Barnet and Parkes to look for epaulettes! What fun!"

James, who unsuccessfully tried to hide a smile, said, "Very well, my dear. As you wish. It may have been bad luck to order the coats before Horse Guards finalized the paperwork, but when I spoke to the regimental agent yesterday he said it was as good as done. Still, I am not yet jaded with our new fortune; I cringe at the thought of spending nine hundred fifty pounds, plus the agent's percentage, the hound, all for the honour of serving His Majesty as a captain."

She gave him one of the open, dazzling, laughing smiles that had touched his heart from the first day he met her, and said, "Damn the expense, sir! Tonight I shall be sleeping beside a *captain* of the Inniskilling Regiment. A captain!"

The End

In 2006 Mark Bois fulfilled a long-time ambition and returned to school to earn a Master's degree in history. His Irish ancestry and a fascination with military history prompted him to write his thesis on the Inniskilling Regiment and their bloody stand atop the ridge at Waterloo.

Amongst the dusty rosters and letters in the British National Archives, and then in the artifacts and records of the Inniskilling Regimental Museum, he found what he needed to write his thesis. He also discovered the fascinating personal stories that inspired *The Lockwoods of Clonakilty.*

As a happily married man and the father of five, Bois finds it interesting to tell the stories of families. He thinks it especially important to share the stories not just of soldiers, but also of those who wait for them to come home; the burdens they bear alone, and together.

The Chosen Man

by

J. G. Harlond

From the bulb of a rare flower bloom ambition and scandal

Rome, 1635: As Flanders braces for another long year of war, a Spanish count presents the Vatican with a means of disrupting the Dutch rebels' booming economy. His plan is brilliant. They just need the right man to implement it.

They choose Ludovico da Portovenere, a charismatic spice and silk merchant. Intrigued by the Vatican's proposal—and hungry for profit—Ludo sets off for Amsterdam to sow greed and venture capitalism for a disastrous harvest, hampered by a timid English priest sent from Rome, accompanied by a quick-witted young admirer he will use as a spy, and bothered by the memory of the beautiful young lady he refused to take with him.

Set in a world of international politics and domestic intrigue, *The Chosen Man* spins an engrossing tale about the Dutch financial scandal known as tulip mania—and how decisions made in high places can have terrible repercussions on innocent lives.

PENMORE PRESS
www.penmorepress.com

Assassins of Alamut
By
James Boschert

An Epic Novel of Persia and Palestine in the Time of the Crusades

The Assassins of Alamut is a riveting tale, painted on the vast canvas of life in Palestine and Persia during the 12th century.

On one hand, it's a tale of the crusades—as told from the Islamic side—where Shi'a and Sunni are as intent on killing Ismaili Muslims as crusaders. In self-defense, the Ismailis develop an elite band of highly trained killers called Hashshashin whose missions are launched from their mountain fortress of Alamut.

But it's also the story of a French boy, Talon, captured and forced into the alien world of the assassins. Forbidden love for a princess is intertwined with sinister plots and self-sacrifice, as the hero and his two companions discover treachery and then attempt to evade the ruthless assassins of Alamut who are sent to hunt them down.

It's a sweeping saga that takes you over vast snow-covered mountains, through the frozen wastes of the winter plateau, and into the fabulous cites of Hamadan, Isfahan, and the Kingdom of Jerusalem.

"A brilliant first novel, worthy of Bernard Cornwell at his best."—Tom Grundner

PENMORE PRESS
www.penmorepress.com

Rocamora

Donald Michael Platt

No man is closer to a woman than her confessor, not her father, not her brother, not her husband.

-Spanish saying

Vicente de Rocamora, the epitome of a young renaissance man in 17th century Spain, questions the goals of the Inquisition and the brutal means used by King Philip IV and the Roman Church to achieve them. Spain vows to eliminate the heretical influences attributed to Jews, Moors, and others who would taint the limpieza de sangre, purity of Spanish blood. At the insistence of his family, the handsome and charismatic Vicente enters the Dominican Order and is soon thrust into the scheming political hierarchy that rules Spain. As confessor to the king's sister, the Infanta Doña María, and assistant to Philip's chief minister, Olivares, Vicente ascends through the ranks and before long finds himself poised to attain not only the ambitious dreams of the Rocamora family but also—named Spain's Inquisitor General

PENMORE PRESS
www.penmorepress.com

WILDFIRE IN THE DESERT

BY

BRUNO JAMBOR

Action Adventure, Crime, Mystery,
Southwest History

Highly entertaining, well researched
and original:

A Navy veteran returns home to his ancestral land to escape the pace of modern life. His nephew begs him to hide the drugs he is transporting to escape his pursuers.

An astronomer trying to find a replacement for his estranged wife finds solace in his work with the stars.

Police and the drug cartel try to recover the missing shipment, regardless of consequences, ready to sacrifice any opponent.

The antagonists crisscross the desert of Southern Arizona in a chess game where the loser will be eliminated.

Unexpected help comes from a famous missionary who blazed new paths through the same desert three centuries ago.

The climactic resolution will captivate readers of this thriller with deep spiritual undertones.

PENMORE PRESS
www.penmorepress.com

Knight Assassin

The second book of Talon

by

James Boschert

A joyous homecoming turns into a nightmare as Talon must do the one thing that he didn't want to - become an assassin again.

Talon, a young Frank, returns to France to be reunited with the family that lost him to the Assassins of Alamut when he was just a boy. But when he arrives, he finds a sinister threat hanging like a pall over the joyous reunion. A ruthless man is challenging his father's inheritance, aided by powerful churchmen who stand to profit by his father's fall. When Talon's young brother is taken hostage, Talon has no recourse but to take the fight to his enemies.

All is not warfare, however; Talon's uncle Philip, a Templar knight, brings him to the court of Carcassonne, where Queen Eleanor has introduced ideals of romance and chivalry. There Talon is pressed into the service of a lion-hearted prince of Britain named Richard.

Knight assassin is a story of treachery, greed, love and heroism set in the Middle Ages.

PENMORE PRESS
www.penmorepress.com

Penmore Press

Challenging, Intriguing, Adventurous, Historical and Imaginative

www.penmorepress.com